THE

FATEWREAKER

The Fatewreaker

Book 3 of the Bookminder series

M. K. Wiseman

Xchyler Publishing,

an imprint of Hamilton Springs Press, LLC

Scott Tarbet, Editor-in-chief

1st Edition: June 8, 2021

Cover Illustration Egle Zioma

Interior design created with Vellum

Edited by MeriLyn Oblad

Published in the United States of America

Xchyler Publishing

THE

FATEWREAKER

TOURS DE MERLE IN THE SOUTH OF
FRANCE,
LATE SEPTEMBER 1660:

Nagarath, youngest magus to ever apprentice under Archmage Cromen, lay upon his back on the floor of his novice's workroom at Tours de Merle. He lay thinking, his thick black robes bunched under him as a cushion and books forgotten at his elbow —indication enough of his emotional state for anyone who knew him but halfway. On his workbench, another book sat open alongside the scattered remains of several botched spells.

Earlier in the day, he had been elated. Now he was merely annoyed. Annoyed and frustrated. His magick would not obey him; his mind refused to settle. His latest skirmish with Anisthe, fellow pupil under the archmage and six years his senior, had ended in victory.

That victory had quickly turned hollow. Nagarath might have won back Amsalla's praise and fickle regard through his sound thrashing of the older boy in an unsanctioned duel, but he would have to win again tomorrow. And the next day. And every day thereafter.

Was that all that magick was? Was that wizarding? If so, he was already tired of it. Tired after two years of schooling in the south of France. Tired of not seeing his family and his home. Tired of having sham friendships built upon little more than the strength of his Art and faith in his own judgment. Amsalla and Anisthe certainly did not care for Nagarath himself.

Or perhaps they did, and this cutting competitiveness was a mere side effect of their situation. Master Cromen wanted his pupils to best each other. That was how young mages bettered themselves.

And there was something to it. After all, Amsalla DeBouverelle's vanity had been well earned. Her talent and intelligence, in turn, spurred Nagarath's magick on to greater things. She encouraged him merely by being brilliant and by driving Nagarath's fear that he could lose her approval.

So too with Anisthe, if for somewhat different reasons. The six-year difference in age and four-year gap in schooling between Nagarath and Cromen's eldest apprentice meant a semi-permanent disparity in their levels of experience. Or so it felt, outside of the occasional flash of brilliance which would then incur both Anisthe's annoyance and Amsalla's praise.

Brilliance such as had earned him his victory today. Nagarath smiled to himself, trying to rekindle the pride he had felt. A clever bit of work, that. And a lesson: know your enemy and you half-know how to beat them. Victory was merely the product of anticipation, preparation, and quick thinking. Simple formulae. A spell.

As Nagarath had arrogantly said, he looked forward

to the next. Victory at a price. In the saying—in the doing —of foolish things. Goaded in large part, again, by Amsalla.

For Nagarath did not want the next duel. He wanted the study leading to it, certainly. But . . . to earn that, to keep his place within Anisthe and Amsalla's game, he had to be exactly the sort of things those two respected. He must employ their weapons; brandish magick as they would, say words they would use. And at cost to himself.

Really, he had made a fool of himself, too. His challenge to Anisthe was thoughtless and, if anything, showed Nagarath's own limitations of knowledge in the Art. And though part of his resulting moodiness had been rooted in a quick, sharp fear, no less than eight books had confirmed for Nagarath that his misstep would prove to be nothing other than embarrassing. He would be safe in his cowardice. Neither Anisthe nor Amsalla could inform on him to Cromen without also having to disclose the circumstances in which the challenge had been made. He recalled his boastful words: *'Change the Laws of Magick.'*

Nice work, fool.

The question now was, of course, how that would factor into his next skirmish with Anisthe, the other wizard being nothing if not predictable. Wincing, thinking of the confrontation which must come, Nagarath reached up, his fingers brushing the cover of a grimoire which he distractedly inched towards him.

The feminine clearing of a throat arrested his movements. Nagarath looked up to find Amsalla standing in the doorway to his mage's study. She waited, ensuring she had his full attention before saying, "I thought you would be interested in hearing that Anisthe went down to Lac de Boue a little while ago."

A thrill went through Nagarath at her words. He beat it down with a scowl, responsibility shouldering in.

"You're a better mage, Amsalla, than to be his messenger." Nagarath pulled the book in front of his face, effective dismissal. A smile tugged at the corners of his mouth, a smidge of self-satisfied pride masked by his pretense at reading. "Tell him he can fire spells at trees for all I care. I am busy."

Amsalla did not move. Sighing, Nagarath put his book aside and sat up.

"You really are busy." She flicked her eyes over his workbench. "If unsuccessful. Have you figured out why, yet?"

"I—" He grimaced. Confessing his state of mind, his state of heart, to her was something Nagarath might have done two years ago. But now?

But now he could feel what it was Amsalla was getting at. Something nibbling at the edges of Nagarath's aura, some tension in the air. It was then that he realized that Amsalla's lingering in his doorway carried not mere insolence to match his own, but an undercurrent of fear.

She inched forward, hesitant. "He's only trying what you told him to do, you know."

"It's a feint," Nagarath scoffed and tried his hand at a lecture. "What Anisthe is attempting—if he were to attempt it—is impossible, Amsalla. That was the whole point of my bringing it up to him. The Laws cannot be circumvented."

"You don't think he can do it?" Amsalla's poise had returned. Her usual defense. The undercurrent of fear remained, however. It charged the air alongside the loosed magicks.

It sounded an answering fear—another thrill—within Nagarath, and he gained his feet, reaching for his robes. "Did you not tell the archmage before coming to me?"

"What? And risk Cromen's wrath? Besides. You never know—Anisthe might succeed."

With that, Nagarath brushed past her, foregoing such niceties as taking leave. While he knew that rankled, his aim was not to insult her—though he welcomed the unintended insult it provided, for it better showed his annoyance. No, his fury. Didn't Amsalla realize she should have stopped Anisthe? Or perhaps it really was another game between them, and the wizard had no real intent of carrying out his threat. That would be more like Anisthe. Nagarath had already said as much. Or very nearly.

Anisthe wanted to fight. And Amsalla stood in between, ready to gather the spoils yet again.

So be it! Nagarath's temper rose to meet the danger.

Nagarath entered the main hall, reaching out with his aura, testing the air, and staggering from the impact of the magick already called by his rival. Another tremor threatened to unnerve him completely. What in the world was Anisthe attempting?

Circumvent the Laws. A magus couldn't do that. Not without endangering— Nagarath sucked in a breath. "—not without endangering everything that magick touches."

Everything that magick touches.

Tell Cromen.

No time. And besides, Anisthe's actions were Nagarath's fault. He had goaded him, challenged him to do the impossible when he refused to duel a second time.

When Nagarath had chosen petty insult over hard action.

When the archmage finds out about this, I'll be in as much trouble as Anisthe. My punishment will be the same as his.

There was no time to waste. Master Cromen had to feel what was going on. His spells upon the castle would be reacting, alerting him. Nagarath was no tattle. And again: time.

"Tra'shuk," Nagarath muttered his half-hearted attempt, already knowing that the spell to transport him to Mud Lake would likely fail. Anisthe's freed power sucked at any and all magicks even a mile from where he worked his Art. Yes, there was likely no need to tell the archmage a thing at that point.

The warm night air welcomed Nagarath as he left Cromen's castle. Sticky and heavy, the oppressive atmosphere was odd in that district and odder still for late September. The perfect weather for such sorcery, Anisthe could wring the air for its humid vitality. Yet it still would not be enough. Not for what he was attempting.

Hence the lake.

Hastening his steps, Nagarath noted a weakening of limbs, a lessening of his spell-enhanced senses. His novice's robes dragged heavily as all his personal enchantments fell away.

"A stripping of vanity," Nagarath voiced the bitter remark aloud. He deserved such.

Silently, Nagarath cursed the fact that his rival's actions robbed every mage in the vicinity of their workings. For it allowed Anisthe the privacy he needed, the safety of non-interference in his dangerous task. Nagarath ran, his lungs burning and his limbs screaming for relief.

"I am no book-clutching, gangly-limbed weakling!" he cried, returning one of Anisthe's latest insults to the darkened skies. The stars winked back at him, a quiet conspiracy.

He ran on, sprinting past houses and trees, fence posts and lonely horse barns. The woods called. As did the lake beyond. The knifing, wild sliver of fear continued to grow within him. And through it all, Nagarath wondered, "Where is Master Cromen?"

Suddenly, it was not merely magick which Anisthe's spell drained from the world around him. The air itself seemed to warp and bend. Nagarath found he had to expend effort to slow his rush towards the lake's edge and the young wizard who stood chest-deep in its seething waters.

A whirlpool of frothing and foaming darkness had formed. The nearby trees groaned in anguish under the sudden and gusting wind. Anisthe stood at the center of all, his arms outstretched and head thrown back.

"Anisthe!" Nagarath's warning cry was lost to the gale.

"Anisthe, stop!" He ran forward, no longer fighting the tide. Nagarath felt icy fingers of tears rake across his cheeks. Helplessness and culpability. Resentment, too.

The current of Power immediately swept him into its grasp. Gangly-limbed weakling, indeed. Nagarath would be snapped like a twig, bent and broken and rendered incantate, if the rush of magick were not soon stemmed. He and Anisthe both.

He swam forward into danger. He must stop Anisthe. He must.

Anisthe had to have known Nagarath's challenge to be in jest. No mage could break the Laws. Certainly no sixteen-year-old novice.

And yet, Amsalla had seemed impressed. Which had been Nagarath's point. She had certainly not moved to stop Anisthe's foolhardy sorcery, had been inclined to make a joke of it.

She'll die, too. Nagarath swam in the lightning-bright mists of Anisthe's magick. Gravity no longer held sway. He could not reach his friend. It mattered not.

"For I haven't any time."

For there was no time. Anisthe's spell had shattered all. Every clock was broken. The invisible essences which made the air breathable had ceased their movement. The world had died.

Or soon would, once Anisthe's hex reached outward past the pond, past Cromen's home, past Paris and London and Madrid and Vienna until it had touched all, slain all.

No.

Nagarath would not stand for it. He would let the magick take him from this earth before he let that happen. Lightning, magick's pure fire, tore across the skies. The concussive boom of thunder followed fast. Bright sparkles swam in his vision. He blinked them away, muttering a spell to hasten his recovery.

My fault. My challenge and my foolhardy words have led to this. And therefore, his was not an altogether meaningless sacrifice.

But Nagarath hadn't thought that Anisthe would do it!

No. You hadn't thought he had the power or knowledge to begin.

Anisthe's arrogance was unmatched by anyone's save for Nagarath's own.

I did this. I did this, and I will stop it. But how?

Passages from books, snatches of spells, flitted through Nagarath's brain. None gave answer. This was beyond books. There was no answer writ down. He needed to act.

The stuff of the world had been fractured. Magick bled through the cracks. An unsealable storm rained down from injured skies. Power hemorrhaged from torn trees and murdered seas. Wrapped in his magick, caught at the center of his own sorcery, Anisthe screamed.

There. An answer. One that would probably get Nagarath killed. Not that it much mattered.

Reaching out—with his Art, with his frail human hands—Nagarath tried to pull Anisthe from his spell.

"No!" Anisthe turned blazing eyes onto his rival. The powers in the air changed, gaining new pitch and tone. In response, Nagarath opened the heart of his magick and bent his will against the loosed magicks, against Anisthe. In doing so, color and light, sound and consciousness faded from him.

No matter. His spell would continue without him until his magick was used up. Until one or the other of them had won. Their spells became a battle of wills. Arrogance and animosity. Enough to hold the world together until . . .

The pressure burst. The skies grew clear and silent. The magick, the pain—all stopped, receding under Cromen's awesome sorcery. For, having been freed, Nagarath could now see the archmage standing at the edge of the water, a warm reddish glow in his outstretched hands.

Oh, thank the powers above . . . Wearily, Nagarath moved to wade back towards the shore. Again, his consciousness wavered—consequence of his overextending of himself through his magick. The dark waters rose up to meet him, and he closed his eyes, utterly spent.

❧

Nagarath came to on the edge of the lake. He and Anisthe both lay half-in, half-out of the water. He had no memory of how they had made it to shore. Rising, he turned Anisthe onto his back and tried to drag him further from the water's edge

"Help!" Nagarath looked around. They were alone.

Where was the archmage? Swaying, Nagarath considered. *Had I dreamed it all? No—impossible.*

Still. He could not be sure.

A bobbing magelight rushed forward from the edge of the woods. Even with his magick inclinations dulled by exhaustion, Nagarath recognized the power signature. Amsalla.

Relieved, he cried out again, "Help."

He stumbled, falling to his knees onto the muddy shoreline alongside Anisthe.

"What happened?" The spark of Amsalla's healing spell danced over them. Anisthe regained his color and stirred.

Nagarath's limbs stopped their quaking, but words were beyond him, and he merely bowed his head. To recount that horror, to own that guilt—

"Why you back-stabbing, undermining, magick-stealing, jealous-of-my-power ruiner!" Anisthe launched himself at Nagarath. Luckily the older wizard had not yet recovered anything akin to strength, and Nagarath scrambled out of the reach of Anisthe's ineffectual blows.

Eyes wild, his chest heaving, Anisthe's rage sharpened, even as Amsalla gently held him back from Nagarath. Anisthe's whisper cut like a knife as he said, "He stopped me. He interrupted my casting and by so doing, endangered not only me but every one of us."

"Your spell was out of control. You had made an anomaly, Anisthe. Your error—"

"It would have worked!"

"You would have died! And taken all of us with you. Yes, we were all in danger. That much I will agree on. But at your hand. Not by mine. The Laws cannot be changed, Anisthe."

"I wasn't working to merely change them." Rising, Anisthe shook off Amsalla's gentle restraint and started forward, his fists raised. "I—!"

He paused, and then seeming to change his mind, Anisthe let his hands drop. "I don't need any of you. I know myself now. I know what I am capable of. What I can offer and how I can do better than here and now. I— I don't need you."

With that, Anisthe turned and ran, disappearing into the darkened woods.

Nagarath tried to follow. He instead stumbled and landed hard on knees and wrists. He looked to Amsalla. "Go after him."

She met his gaze, hesitant, and then nodding, Amsalla fled into the woods in pursuit of Anisthe. Nagarath watched her magelight waver and fade.

At length Nagarath turned over onto his back and stared up into the stars. Amazing to think they still blazed away, whirling in the nighttime sky far above. He closed his eyes, looking inward to see to the answering sparks within his einatus, to see what of his aura had survived the testing of wills. The magick was there. Weak. But it might yet recover.

A sound. Some small moaning, shifting noise broke the oppressing stillness. Nagarath opened his eyes and saw, further away in the darkness at the water's edge, a lump of something. A body.

"Master Cromen!"

Summoning strength, feeling half-dead with any effort and burning the smallest bit of his magick, his own life's spark, to do so, Nagarath crawled to the archmage's side. He wondered if he had power enough to help the elder wizard without killing himself in the process.

Without warning, regret seized Nagarath with a force almost physical. Regret and magick, both. Reminiscent of Anisthe's broken spell and yet somehow contained, concentrated, he realized the sensation emanated from a dull reddish rock lying at Cromen's side.

Instinct warned Nagarath away from it. His fingers twitched their repulsion.

But the archmage's need had Nagarath reaching forward to grasp the captured magick. Making contact with the stone, everything within him wanted to run away screaming. He held firm even though, with the magick's touch upon his einatus, Nagarath could have gone anywhere, done anything for himself in that moment. He blinked back tears and concentrated on the archmage. There seemed to be little for him to do, however.

Master Cromen had kept Anisthe's error from cascading out of control. But whatever he had done to rein in the broken spell had damaged the heart of his magick. The archmage was not incantate. Of this Nagarath could be mostly certain. The old wizard hummed with power. But it felt scattered. The aura refracted like light through a prism and so could not be bent back into proper use. Equally, it seemed to Nagarath that the magick bled from his teacher, a slow leak which could take any number of days or months. But it would kill the man in the end. In mending the crack in the world, in fixing the loosed power into the form of this cinnabar stone, Archmage Cromen had rent his einatus asunder.

"I'm sorry." Nagarath bowed his head and surrendered the stone. With the act, he felt his own well of magick fall back to dangerous fragility. His teacher's eyes fluttered open, and the mage drew a ragged breath.

"Tra'shuk."

A moment later they were, the two of them, back in the archmage's home. Nagarath wasn't even certain that his teacher had spoken aloud. He certainly had not felt the sorcery. He found himself mesmerized anew by the warm reddish glow of the newly-made stone. Cromen seemed to note the look and quickly hid the talisman beneath the folds of his cloak. His voice like blank parchment, the archmage whispered, "Whose spell, Nagarath?"

Whose spell? A quaver of guilt rose in Nagarath's chest. Surely Master Cromen's sensitivity to magick was not so far gone that he must ask such a question. Anisthe's signature was all over his attempted subverting of the Laws.

"It was Anisthe's spell. I tried to stop him, Master." Bleakly, Nagarath met the archmage's hard gaze. Honesty followed accusation. "But he only tried it because I had challenged him to try the impossible."

"And your aura bears the scars of your entanglement with your fellow magus." The archmage rose heavily to his feet. Nagarath followed suit, swaying when, a moment later, he looked inside the heart of his magick and found that it had changed. A young wizard's magick signature was not fixed until the age of twenty and so, with time, grew to reflect his master's.

Apprenticeship in the Art provided with it a semblance of heredity. Now? Threads of darkness darted amongst the light which Nagarath had come to know and love.

"His will be just as tainted. Or worse." Cromen stamped across the room on leaden legs, catching himself upon the doorway and stopping to draw more unsteady breaths. "Come. This way."

"But Anisthe, he—"

"He is gone!" In whirling on Nagarath, the archmage proved he had more strength than expected.

It both heartened and terrified Nagarath to see it. Cowed, he pressed, "He will be back, though. Archmage, he will come back. And Amsalla. I told her to—"

"Leave her, Nagarath. She is not your concern." Again, the wizard would not allow Nagarath to fully voice his fears. Perhaps it was easier for both of them to bear if he did not.

Cromen softened and beckoned his one remaining apprentice forth. "You will have my books and what wisdom I can yet impart. You are correct in that Anisthe will be back. Maybe not today. Maybe not a year from now. But he will want to finish what he started and what you prevented him from finishing."

Nagarath's head shot up.

The archmage turned away, but not before Nagarath saw the small flash of pride cross Cromen's face. "Yes, it was you who stopped him. Clumsily. And at danger to yourself."

They walked in silence until they had reached the archmage's own workroom. There Cromen withdrew the stone from one of the hidden spaces in his cloak. He said, "And I finished it, saving the magick so that it did not burn both of you in its wrath."

Nagarath smiled to think of the archmage humanizing magick so much as to give it emotions and will. He asked, "That stone. It is the power which I fought?"

"What remains of it. Yes. What I could capture and save from doing further mischief and ruin. You kept Anisthe from going further into a space that would have made the magick unstoppable. While I crystalized it, and to my own peril." Cromen made a show of browsing amongst his books before turning to his lone apprentice. "I will die for my efforts, of course. As you will have already surmised through your own discernment on the shore of Lac de Boue."

No.

Nagarath realized he must have spoken aloud as, a moment later, Master Cromen chuckled. "I am old, lad. Too old to have been taking on students, perhaps. Which is why I allowed you to begin at an earlier age than either Amsalla or Anisthe.

"Time. Besides magick, she is our greatest enemy, and mine was coming to be well up, with or without your friend's mistake."

Nagarath squirmed. Until that night he would never have considered magick an enemy. But from then on he would have a hard time seeing the Art as anything else. Perhaps he should quit it. Let his Gift die unused within him.

Again, Cromen seemed to be reading his mind. The archmage crooked a finger and, placing the cinnabar stone upon the large table whereupon he worked his spells, he waited for Nagarath to approach. "With my books here, you have a chance of hiding from him while still working your Art."

"I will not run from magick nor from Anisthe, Arch-mage." Nagarath shook his head. "I goaded him. I fought with him. I have as much made him the wizard he has decided to be as he himself has."

"And if you are charged to protect this stone and its power from the likes of him?"

Nagarath took an involuntary step backwards at the words. His mouth was dry as he said, "Then I would do what I must, Archmage. But I should like to finish what I started, finish what I began when I decided that Anisthe was worth saving, and save anyone who would suffer because of my error in judgment."

In the way Cromen looked at him, Nagarath knew he had passed the final test the archmage would give.

CHAPTER ONE

Running amidst the dark labyrinth of hedges which wove through the gardens of the Palace of Versailles, Nagarath felt the shift in the air. The bubble of Anisthe's shielding spell gave one half-hearted shimmer, then faded.

Liara, hurrying alongside, pitched forward. Nagarath caught her arm. Not stopping, he gave her a quick, raking assessment. His apprentice looked ill. And not merely from shock or expenditure of power. Her very aura seemed to pulse around her. Unchecked, it flared strong; it flickered weakly.

Nagarath's heart clenched as he again thought of Anisthe. Liara's progenaurae, the wizard upon whose life hers depended. Anisthe, disgraced war mage of Vrsar, who had wanted Khariton's Mirror, had wanted the soul of Kerri'tarre himself, to serve his own ends. Anisthe, the man who they had to leave in the hands of their enemy.

Enemy. Was Amsalla really an enemy?

No. Anisthe. Anisthe was the enemy. Had always been.

But then he had saved them.

"Or tricked us." This time, Nagarath sounded his worries aloud.

"He'll be fine, Nagarath," Liara said, though from the tone of her exhalation, she ought to have saved her breath.

Nagarath had no choice but to conserve his. He slowed his steps and listened intently for any signs of pursuit. The silence of the night pressed upon him and his companion, though his pulse still pounded in his ears. It was his turn to sway unsteadily. The truth of his own deteriorating condition reflected back to him in the hard sparkle of Liara's eyes, the quickness with which she threw a steadying hand of her own. She had her wand out and ready.

"We can't—" Nagarath gasped. He pressed a hand to his side. As if such a feeble gesture might stem the blood, keep the searing agony of the gunshot wound from over-taking his thoughts. "No magick. Else the spellpiercers might see. We have to go on; try to get more distance."

"Anisthe's healing didn't take."

Nagarath managed a wry smile. "As I said, his studies were not of the same—"

"You had the same teacher, Nagarath!" Liara bent to inspect the wound. Her hair fell over her face, a dark waterfall which she impatiently tucked back behind her ear. "You all did."

Did Nagarath imagine the accusation in that last, or was it merely the pain coalescing into peevishness? At any rate, Liara's touch was gentle while she inspected the point on his side where the bullet had entered.

Nagarath pulled back. "He did what he could, Liara. The rest can hold until we're away to—"

"Hsst." Liara held up a hand for silence. She whispered, "Someone's near."

Never before had Nagarath missed Anisthe's magick. But as hushed voices and cautious footsteps approached along the other side of the hedge, he wished the war mage had not given himself up for their sake and doubly wished his own state was such that he might take on any number of assailants. Still, if he and Liara were about to be discovered by their pursuers, it would not matter that he kept from doing magick to hide from the spellpiercing talents of the king's men. Tightening his grip on the walking stick with its cinnabar stone, Nagarath wondered: had he strength enough to simply whisk them off to safer lands? The staff had ample magick, but in his weakened state, he could well trap them between this place and the next. He could fall to the power of the stone itself.

The caution was enough to keep him from attempting anything rash.

The booted feet moved past.

At Nagarath's side, Liara crooked a finger, whispering when he bent close, "Where would you suggest we head?" Her eyes glanced meaningfully to Nagarath's walking stick.

Out of the question! Nagarath wanted to shout his objections at his apprentice but knew better. She was skilled. She had the art and the will. But she had never been to the British Isles, much less Little Larkhill. And in the previous case of witching them across the sea, Liara had been very lucky, the situation had been extraordinarily desperate, and she had spent far too long bending the ears of the sailors who had meant to take them to Sardinia in the end. He whispered back, "England."

Liara blanched.

Good. There would be no trying something reckless. They would simply have to wait out the guard's inspection of the palace grounds and hope that Anisthe's gesture held meaning with Amsalla. In other words: no change, merely patience.

Of which Liara, of course, possessed very little.

In fact, Nagarath could practically hear her thinking, mentally rehearsing the necessary spellwork.

No. He shook his head at her.

"The one will not suffice. She wants all three."

"You check that way. I'll look over here."

Gruff voices drifted through the thick leaves. Liara's face turned white with anxiety, and Nagarath felt his own hair stand on end. The guards had come back 'round the other side. He and Liara had nowhere to run. Blast the king's labyrinth!

This time Nagarath nodded when Liara raised her wand in caution. He shifted his grip on his walking stick, and new worries rose to torment him. It occurred to him that he had not made any attempt to use the artifact since transforming it from its form as a staff weeks before.

As if in answer, the cinnabar stone sparked crimson fire in the night, and the familiar bite of its power snagged at Nagarath's mind. He felt, more than saw,

Liara grab hold of his arm as three men in the trappings of the king's guard rounded the corner of the nearest hedge. Distantly, he wondered what it might look like, as the magick took hold and the nighttime labyrinth disappeared in a wave of sparkles.

The spell faltered, and the Versailles gardens swam back into focus around the two mages.

"Spellpiercers!" Liara went on the attack, throwing hexes at the advancing enemy. Flame and fury, she still had care enough to not catch the surrounding leafy canopy in her spellwork.

Without hesitation, the leading man struck, dodging Liara's onslaught and reaching out with a bare hand to grasp the cinnabar walking stick. Still glowing in Nagarath's hands, the arcane item let out a blinding flash, splitting the night in two with its power. With the spellpiercer's touch, the walking stick became a staff once more. The man himself lay screaming upon the ground, clutching his wrist to his side, his eyes rolling in his head.

Action and thought aligned. Nagarath swung his staff at the remaining attackers. The act gained him and Liara separation from the enemy, as well as the opportunity to draw a breath. His apprentice furthered their position with a well-timed curse. Both spellpiercers fell unconscious upon the gravel path.

"Look out!" Liara's warning came a second too late.

A hand on Nagarath's shoulder set him to silently screaming in agony. Sound followed belatedly, as though it were itself stunned. In the heart of his aura sprang a pain that far surpassed having been shot earlier in the evening. At a spellpiercer's sole touch, he was being extinguished, drowned in the darkness of aborted magicks.

Liara's answering shout mingled with Nagarath's own. The harsh discordance made his heart grow suddenly chill. Magick lit the night anew as his apprentice's hands poured pure magefire. Nagarath's attacker broke off the connection with a gurgling moan and slumped to the ground.

Without pause, Liara whirled around and, grabbing Nagarath's wrist, shouted, "Tra'shuk!"

That time, the spell worked as it ought. The king's dark labyrinthine garden faded into the brightness of . . . where was it exactly that Liara had taken them?

$\sim$

"Liara." Nagarath turned a dizzy circle in the polished entryway of the Jeffers' Parisian home. Squirming under Nagarath's stern gaze, Liara tried to drag the mage into a room less exposed than where she had deposited them. "I'm sorry. The magick wasn't easy. We needed to get somewhere fast. Somewhere I had a connection."

"Good God!" Julien Jeffers' shocked pronouncement wafted from the landing above. For a moment, it appeared his legs might betray him into a tumble down the curved stairway. He mastered himself an instant later, descending to meet them with what dignity he could summon. From the way he greeted his two guests upon reaching the main level of his home, one might almost believe the gentleman of court was used to having wizards materialize in his foyer.

Hands shaking, Liara lessened her grip on Nagarath's sleeve and instead pointed her wand at the mage's friend. Swallowing the tightness in her throat, she tried to sound menacing. "Don't call anyone. Or else."

Whatever "else" she might mean, even Liara did not know. She hadn't thought much past the threat. Still, she kept her wand trained on the man as she looked to Nagarath. Her voice tight, she said, "I think it's up to your magick, Nagarath."

Nagarath moved to intercede, then stopped short, aware that their very presence imperiled his friend. He shifted to call the power within his mage's staff, pausing to lock his gaze to M. Jeffers.

"JJ. I'm sorry."

The apology came tinged in the blood-red glow of the cinnabar stone stirring to life.

"I won't tell anyone. I swear it, Nath," Julien sputtered, holding his hands out in front of him, a desperate plea and promise.

"I know you won't." Sighing, Nagarath closed his eyes and, to Liara's complete and utter shock, waved a spell at the helpless courtier. Julien's eyes rolling back into his head was the last thing Liara saw as Nagarath's magick whisked them from the gentleman's home.

They did not land in England. At least, Liara was pretty sure they hadn't.

The quiet whisper of French met Liara's ears as nighttime again coalesced around them. The tang of coastal air tickled her nose an instant later, confirmed by the familiar creak and soft bustle of a late-evening harbor. The skeletons of ships rose to her left while, at her right, the wizard Nagarath stumbled and fell to the cobblestones.

Angered and alarmed—*How could he have used magick against JJ like that?*—Liara tried to help her friend back to his feet. She quivered as her fingers met the hot wetness of blood. Nagarath's gunshot wound had reopened. The mage's staff slipped from his weak grasp and clattered loudly to the pavement, effectively providing Liara with a second invalid as it feebly glimmered and sparked its distress.

"JJ . . . Spent—" Nagarath gasped. "I couldn't— If they thought him complicit . . . fine in the end."

Steeling herself, Liara did not waste any words as she struggled to hide both mage and belongings from the sight of passersby. Unlike Paris with its magnificent system of street lights, this coastal town—wherever-that-might-be—was dark. Dangerously dark. She was out of breath and out of strength by the time she managed to conceal them both within a nearby alleyway. Sitting heavily against the close-pressing wall, Nagarath let out a low groan. The wizard's eyes fluttered, then shut.

"Nagarath. Nagarath! Do you know where you've whisked us to?" Liara's whisper rang harsh in her ears as she gently tapped Nagarath's face. Yet it was not enough to rouse the mage. Which terrified her.

Liara shuddered, remembering Sophie and what her spellpiercer abilities had done to Liara's own Art at a mere touch. Though milder and but temporary, the sensation had been all too similar to zielsor, the forceful theft of one's magick by another.

The tumble of thought set Liara to reliving her own last minutes within her rooms at the king's palace. The summons from Father Adessi; Sophie's body; the confrontation with Domagoj, Anisthe's half-human, half-fey servant that had ended in the man's death; Liara's struggle to keep her einatus, her mage's soul, from being torn from her . . . and blood. Blood on her hands.

Undone at last, Liara could not keep the sob from rising in her chest, helplessness clouding her vision. Was there nowhere safe for them to go? Perhaps . . . perhaps, after everything she had done, the fates had decided she did not deserve such. But—

"But Nagarath does." Arguing with herself, Liara wiped clear the tears with the back of her hand. She called her Art into her fingertips. Nagarath was always on her that healing via magick was best done by the patient themselves. But if Anisthe could attempt it, so might she.

Under her touch, Nagarath stirred. Jerking back, afraid she had hurt him, Liara darted her eyes to his face and read approval and apology. Still he did not speak, and she found the silence unnerving. More unnerving, the way his eyes followed her movements, as though the man was removed from the situation itself and merely spectating with distant interest. Shock, most likely.

For all that the wound still bled, Anisthe really had done a halfway decent job of things, considering the damage. The rifle-ball had blasted a wide and destructive path. Anisthe's intervention had likely saved Nagarath's life. At present, Liara's best—and only—course of action was to stem the bleeding and quiet the pain.

A hand brushed Liara's temple, and she looked

sharply to the wizard's face. A spark of power leapt between Nagarath and herself. And with it came the knowledge Liara lacked. *West by northwest; eight leagues hence. Dover or Folkestone; either would suffice.* The picture having been thrown into her mind by Nagarath's magick, Liara nodded and reached for the mage's staff.

Sending up a quick prayer to the fates, to luck, to God Himself, Liara let the cinnabar stone lead the way with its light. A wordless spell but for the pounding of the stone's voice within her head and heart:

Ha-y'k shel ha Olam shinah . . .

Perhaps the stone spoke truth. The powers of the world might well change.

CHAPTER TWO

Stars winked overhead in a black sky. A fresh breeze chilled Liara's face and gave whispering chase through grass and brush. The waning moon did its best to illuminate what it might as it made its westward descent into the nearby grove of trees. And all was silent save for the dull roar of crashing waves and the untimely chiming of a lonely church bell somewhere in the distance. A prayer answered.

Liara turned to get a better idea of where she had whisked them. Gravel shifted and slipped beneath her feet. The resulting echoing ping and rattle of rocks informed her that the sea was much closer than initially gauged, and she tensed, feeling the pull of the empty space directly next to her.

Nagarath's hand tightened around Liara's. His solid reassurance kept her from tumbling over the cliffside after the loosened bits of stone. "I've got you."

He pulled her back to him before Liara could much

process how close she had been to the edge. It was only after a quick look back that she began to tremble. A half a step closer and they both would have gone over.

Familiar arms folded around her, soothing. Nagarath murmured, softer this time, "I've got you. Thought you'd try flying, magpie?"

Still shaken, Liara scrambled to get further from the precipice. Simply knowing it was there, not even a handful of feet away. She hadn't realized she had grown into a fear of heights. Or perhaps it was the dark doing it. Or how frayed her emotional state after using so much of her Art to get them there to—

"Dover." Nagarath loosed his hold on her and turned back towards the sea. Liara could see him leaning outward—just slightly. But it was more than enough to make her stomach flip uncomfortably. She reached out a hand to call him back. Eyes straining to see down into the dark, her mage gave a low whistle of appreciation. "I would say that was a rather close call, actually. Well done in getting us here."

Liara said nothing. Merely stood with her hand held out and waited, her heart doing frantic leaps within her chest. *What's wrong with me?*

Even with the fluttering of her anxiety, she felt dulled. Not herself.

And then her knees went soft on her, and Liara found herself in a controlled fall to the ground. Seeking purchase with her hands, she managed to sit without too much loss of grace. The mage noticed and quickly came to her aid. She assured him, "I'm fine, Nagarath."

There it was. The wizard's name felt wrong in her throat. Even her tongue felt foreign, as though controlled by someone else. It was like looking through the wrong end of a telescope. Liara felt stretched, thinned out and compacted at the same time.

And then a subtle shift and everything became real and right again. The throbbing of Liara's recently sprained ankle came rushing back at her. The prickly grass. The lemony smell of the sea. She turned to note that the wizard had simply claimed a place on the ground beside her, having taken her at her word. Hands behind his head, he lay staring up into the night sky. It was his turn to be removed, his expression unreadable. Unusually so.

The fitful breeze again fanned Liara's growing unease. She did not like not knowing what her mage was thinking. She couldn't remember a time when she hadn't at least an idea of what was going on behind those gray eyes of his. He looked so far from her. Somewhere behind a locked door that even she did not dare circumvent. A wall she did not know how to breach.

Well, someone was going to have to take charge. Dover, the mage had said. Liara couldn't see any evidence of civilization nearby. She had, of course, heard it in the haunting toll of the late-night bell, itself an unusual occurrence at such an hour. If the walk was unmanageable, she would simply have to make their current location habitable for the night. A tall order, considering they hadn't much of anything with them. Wands and Nagarath's staff. Cloaks—and whatever implements of magick which might have been carried within their cleverly concealed pouches. Not a book, not a keepsake. Certainly nothing to indicate the station to which they had recently pretended outside of the clothes on their backs. And those had been through much in the course of the long evening. Hopefully Nagarath had money. Or at least the means to conjure such.

Liara moved to rise, sucking in a breath.

Someone was coming. Dark on dark, she could see the vague outline of a man bobbing in cadence with his hurried footfalls as he crossed the field towards the two fugitive wizards.

Her alarm drew Nagarath's attention at last. Glancing backward, the wizard unfolded his arms and rolled to his side so that he might better see the stranger's approach. That his hands strayed towards the abandoned cinnabar staff eased Liara's heart. She could feel her friend thinking much the same as her. There was no call for a man to be out on his own at such a strange hour of the night. To be wandering about so was a dangerous thing . . . unless the man himself were the danger.

Though the moon had slid past most usefulness, in the dim light Liara could see the glint of white teeth as the man picked up his pace and jogged the remaining steps toward them. Grinning as someone who had lost all wit, the stranger waved his arms and shouted at them in a language Liara barely comprehended.

Nagarath jolted to his feet, and for a moment, Liara was fearful he would hex the newcomer same as he had JJ. Instead, he hastened to Liara's side, giving a gentle touch to her elbow as the man garbled madly on. The sounds coalesced into words as Nagarath's spell took hold of her.

"Tell me, masters. Tell me how it is that you did that. You're wizards, are you not? Real and true wizards."

They were discovered!

Oh, hex him, Nagarath. Breath tight with fear, Liara shrank into the mage, losing some of the stranger's words in her distress. But the meaning was clear. The wild gesticulating continued. He had seen them materialize on the cliff's edge. A miracle! Magick!

Oddly, the man seemed more excited than alarmed. It was not how folks generally reacted to magick. Perhaps the Art had a different reputation in England?

Nonsense. Liara shifted her stance to unearth her wand from its hiding place amongst the folds of her cloak.

"I am sorry, but you are much mistaken, friend," Nagarath interjected at long last. Never taking his eyes from the stranger, he waved his arm towards the coast-line. "I, too, have thought there magick in this stretch. I have found it but a trick of the eyes. Something in the way the light comes off the sea when the moon is entering her wane. I am very sorry, but we are not wizards nor in the least bit magick."

Not to be put off, the man turned to Liara to make his appeal. "Please, lady. If I am the first to prove to the king that the Art survives, he'll put in a good word for me. I'll be granted power of my own. I'll—"

"Have you a coin or crust for us, master?" Nagarath inserted himself none too smoothly into the one-sided conversation. Hair mussed, his cloak askew, he thrust a dirty hand toward their accoster. "We haven't a place to stay, you see."

A half-step of retreat. "Back. Back, I say." The stranger, the unknown danger, had deftly been placed on the defense. Liara followed the man's gaze and noted the flash of metal in Nagarath's other hand. A small knife of some sorts.

Amésos. Guilt wracked Liara, thinking of her own knife—the wizard's last resort—and the use to which it had been put but recently. She stepped back and quietly called to mind what spells she might employ.

But their assailant was a coward. He turned and ran.

Looking back to Nagarath, Liara watched as he tried to un-dishevel himself.

Putting away the knife, he smiled grimly. "Now that was a bit of a surprise."

"Do you suppose he'll talk?"

The wizard shook his head. He closed his eyes and raised a hand, murmuring the quiet words of a spell. Swaying, he opened his eyes and, seeing how she still waited for answer, turned from Liara, saying, "No. No, he most certainly will not."

Liara knew better than to ask what he had done. A quick, searching gaze provided the answer in the guilty slump of the mage's shoulders, the haggard way in which he swept his fingers across his brow. And the brusque manner with which he directed her, "If you please, I should like that we camp here for the night. Have you the strength?"

Without a word, Liara did as asked. Setting out the warding spells, she made her wide circle around the wizard as he sat down upon the grass. Crossing his long legs and resting his chin on interlaced fingers, he again wore his unreadable expression. Halfway between excitement and moroseness, Nagarath's mood was so unsettled as to be catching.

The witching came easy. Strangely so. At least, so it seemed after the tumult and terror of their misadventures in Versailles . . . and every moment after. A perpetual unease, it fluttered somewhere behind Liara's eyes. But then, any number of things could be the cause.

The shattering of the king's mirrors; their encounter with Julien Jeffers; Anisthe's words to her. Liara put a hand to her cheek, feeling the blushed burn of her confusion and recalling the war mage's intensity. His touch upon her face had not been sweet or even all that gentle. A strange fervor had gripped him, had guided his whispered words to her. A charge. *'Find the book. Don't come back.'*

The latter? Granted. They were not going back for him. Liara would see to that. Nagarath had been shot. He again used magick from his staff in a manner all too free, she and Nagarath both. They had stopped Khariton's return—or, more accurately, a rifle-ball from the king's own had done so. They had made it out of France alive, and that was enough. As far as Liara was concerned, the business of keeping her safe had become altogether too dangerous.

As for Anisthe's other plea . . . Liara's heart clenched as it did whenever she thought of books, her mind inevitably straying to a broken library, destruction wrought by her own hand. The surge of guilt buried any consideration that she might ask Nagarath if he had an idea of what her progenaurae had meant by the words.

"Liara."

Liara froze at the tone of Nagarath's voice. A whole world lay within his use of her name, and she did not turn around. Perhaps if she chose not to have heard him, he would not try again?

Her heart pounded in her chest. Liara did not want to have this conversation. They had escaped France. And barely at that. Whatever he wanted to talk about? It was behind them.

Or maybe it wasn't an apology. The hammering of her fears escalated, grew louder. Mayhap he intended an explanation, a justification at last for his actions at Versailles. She herself had not acted above reproach. In many ways, Liara had been looking for a fight the moment she had found herself within Anisthe's reach. Yes, a scolding from Nagarath, some patient and patronizing elucidation would be more like her mage. A lecture.

One she could not endure. Not without him possibly knowing then the source of her distress and guessing at the truth of her feelings. He could never know the whole of why his words on the night of the king's fete had wounded her so, of why she had, for so many days thereafter, avoided him.

I need Sophie. The thought caught her unaware and refreshed Liara's grief over the loss of her lady's-maid-turned-confidante. Now Liara found she could not turn to Nagarath lest he see her sorrow. Instead, she retreated deeper into the gloom. Ostensibly to finish her warding of their camp.

Deep breaths helped Liara to master her rioting emotions and stem her tears. She returned to the mage to find him waiting. Him and the conversation she most certainly did not wish to have.

"Liara." Nagarath's eyes locked to hers.

That time, his angst had Liara weighing his pain against her own.

In the balance of her concerns against his? He was worth more.

Smiling in what she hoped was a reassuring manner —likely it was brittle and broken—Liara came and sat by his side. She would save him the humiliation of an apology when she was culpable as well and so spoke first. "I eagerly met him. I did, and you were right to judge it so. Anisthe, he . . . I hate him. I absolutely hate him. But sixteen—seventeen—years of wanting to know him? I still had to know more. Even after Vrsar."

"You needed to confront that pain."

"Yes. Where he could not, dare not, hurt me." Liara took a deep breath before continuing, "I never considered how it would hurt you. And I am sorry. So sorry."

There. She'd taken his words and made it an apology of her own. Safe reparations. She certainly had more than enough tallied to her account.

Still Nagarath tried, "Even so, I acted cruelly. Unforgivably so. In an effort to protect myself, for I . . ."

The pleading look in her eyes, the fearful begging that he not say more, must have stopped him. Nagarath trailed off and relief took hold of Liara's heart. Relief and misery. She pressed, "I forgive you. If you are able to have ever forgiven me—and I know I have been guilty of so, so much. I forgive you, Nagarath. Of course I do. And that . . . that is how things stand between us. How they've stood between us before I even heard of Sophie's— Heard that she—"

Nagarath's arms surrounded her so that she need not say more. And this time, Liara made no effort to hide her tears. Through it all, Nagarath said not a word, was simply there for her. He made no move to discourage the pouring out of her grief, voiced no further interruption.

At length her eyes dried of their own accord. Settling in beside the mage and wrapping herself in her cloak, Liara checked the warding spells one more time and waited in silence for the light to return.

～

Nagarath could not remember waking. Same as he could not recall having fallen asleep in the first place. Though the light in the sky was but newly birthed, a morning chorus of birdsong filled the air. It was a wonder that Liara could sleep through it.

At Nagarath's side, the young woman's shoulders rose and fell at even intervals. Face relaxed in sleep, her mouth hung open slightly. Every so often, her eyelids twitched. The mage dare not move, though he longed to sit up and watch the sun emerge from the dark and uneasy sea. For some time in the night, Liara's hand had met his own. She clasped it now, wholly unconscious of the trusting act.

Though they had grown close once more—forgetting past betrayals, forgiving indiscretions and lapses of judgment—the gesture was so unlike Liara that Nagarath could only marvel at it. Normally she was reserved, closed off and unavailable to him in any way other than as companion and colleague.

Which was as it should be.

Carefully, Nagarath extricated himself from Liara's unconscious touch. With the separation, small as it was, his breath hitched in his chest. It was as much about saving face for her as for himself. He couldn't lose her.

Eleven years his junior. Daughter of his enemy. No, in no way could Nagarath ever let on how deeply he had come to regard the woman at his side. Had Liara not saved him with a look, he might well have confessed all the night before. Such had been his intention.

Eyes to the horizon, Nagarath waited in stony silence for the sun to make its appearance.

How could he have let it happen? Liara was his apprentice. She had been placed under his protection by Dvigrad's priest. And there was Krešimir to think of. Had Dvigrad not fallen, had Liara not herself been exiled from the town . . . She had made no secret of her feelings for Limska Draga's woodsman. The man was nearer her age, too, if potentially less steady in his regard for her.

The shining arrow of the sun's first rays broke over the horizon and pierced Nagarath's heart. Temporarily blinded by the orange blaze, he let the new day wash over him and followed the path of his wandering mind. His last thought on Krešimir was as uncharitable as it was inaccurate.

Liara's Krešimir, who had escaped Dvigrad's destruction and who Nagarath had finally met in Messina during their pursuit of Anisthe. Then the young man had misguidedly tried to kill Nagarath, having been taken in by Anisthe's lies, much as Liara once had. Shortly after, Nagarath had been forced to spellbind the young man, sending him away as a hapless messenger in case all went wrong in their quest for Khariton's Mirror.

To England, no less.

"To England, at long last." Bowing his head, Nagarath again lost himself to the emotions stirred by their arrival the night before. It wasn't coming home. Not really.

A distant ringing peal signaled judgment, and though this time the bells were being rung at a more reasonable hour, Liara startled at Nagarath's side. Noting the mage sitting up, she emitted a yawning sigh and moved to rise. " 'M sorry. I was more tired than I realized."

"The spells did their work. We are safe." Nagarath's eyes roved the horizon. "I slept as well. Thank you, Liara."

Her gaze followed his, settling on the distant fortification now visible in the daylight. He tried to gauge the distance into town. It was walkable. But only if his wound from the day before could be addressed first.

The night on the ground had done neither of them any good, and Nagarath stretched his stiff joints with no small amount of self-conscious reluctance. Liara watched his every move, solicitous but also clearly guilt-ridden.

"I should have witched us straight to an inn," she said.

Nagarath took the hidden apology and turned it aside. "Money we ought not be wasting, what with our not knowing the state of things in these parts. You saw as I did how that wayfarer reacted to our magick."

If Liara agreed with his position, it was hard for him to tell. She simply pursed her lips and moved to gather their few scattered belongings. Nagarath turned from her to busy himself with the wound in his side.

Finger prodding the torn and bloodied shirt and waistcoat, Nagarath briefly attempted to work around the material. Finally giving up, he simply reached for his staff and, summoning his own power, tugged at the magick within. The ache subsided, and his unconscious tension dispelled.

Nagarath turned his eyes upward to find Liara standing over him, judgment on her face. She offered him a hand. With her aid, he arose, and together they set off for the distant fortifications of Dover. Hunger driving their brisk pace, they soon found themselves on the outskirts of civilization and were therefore left with little opportunity to further discuss their situation. Sustenance and scrying. Only after satisfying such priorities would Nagarath inform Liara of his plan.

Practical and no-nonsense, the town fanned out below the hilltop fortification and along the water's edge. Cheerful folk called greetings to one another. Raucous seagulls wheeled overhead in the bright summer-blue sky. To Nagarath's ears, it all sounded much the same.

Rusty with disuse in spite of his brief exchange the night before, English made halting return to Nagarath's mind, but he stoutly refused to employ for himself the spell he had passed on to Liara. His native tongue—well, more accurately, the language of his forebears—wove through the air, jovial and rounded, sharp and colorful. It lightened the heart, sparking in him memories he had long forgotten. He had had a home once. A true home and not one he had carved for himself out of necessity and sadness.

Or at least that's the lie Nagarath allowed himself to believe as he and Liara strode straight into the center of the town, seeking rest, shelter, and safety. Relieved, for no suspicion preceded them, only the glances of the innocently curious, Nagarath let his own inquisitiveness have a bit of rein. His eyes grazed shop windows and street corners. What he found forced his feet to a halt.

Magick. And much of it.

Or at least of a flavor the Artless would find interesting.

Nagarath heard Liara's shocked inhalation and felt her move minutely closer.

Wooden signs advertised exotic and fantastical wares. Open doors beckoned passersby with promises—and odors—both enticing and repulsive. Potions. Spell components. Artifacts and arcane rarities. At least three different bookstores jostled for attention on the small thoroughfare in which Nagarath and Liara had paused.

"Magick all the rage." Nagarath narrowed his eyes. "How modern of them."

"So what do we do?" Liara looked up at him.

"Not sure." Nagarath did a quick turn in place, thinking fast. "This is either incredibly helpful or incredibly suspect."

"Books, not breakfast," Liara gave her smile even as she grumbled the complaint. She shouldered her pack, turning back to Nagarath. "Come on, then. I know you'll need to look into it all before we so much as blink. But know this: I'm not carrying everything you feel you need to purchase."

"No need, magpie. No need," he muttered under his breath.

CHAPTER THREE

Not wizards. Nor were they in the least magick.

And yet, there they were, two hooded and cloaked figures—one carrying a large, ornate staff—walking towards a store which claimed to carry spell books. How subtle. Why had they even bothered to lie to that man outside town if they were going to wander about looking so plainly like, well, like wizards?

Liara glanced to Nagarath and found that her silent sorcery clashed with his.

"Sorry."

"No. It was a good idea." A smile flitted across the mage's face. Liara could feel him cease his casting. "And you're right. You are better positioned at present for such protections."

Liara nodded, noting the care with which Nagarath had hidden the evidence of his injury. A wizard's cloak did have its upsides, copious amounts of material none least. He stood stiff and unmoving. His eyes were on one of the shops.

"They don't even know what they've got, I would bet." Nagarath had adopted his maddening, faraway look.

Liara snorted at the endless attraction books held for the wizard even in such a time.

Narrowly escaping death. One of their party wounded. As it was, the cinnabar staff had only barely gotten them to safety. Swallowing the sudden tightness in her throat at the thought, Liara concluded that, perhaps, what she had sensed from the artifact was simply the side effect of panic and exhaustion. And, besides, she had no one with whom she could voice her concerns, Nagarath having ducked into the store without her. She hurried to follow.

For a moment, Liara's breath failed her. Familiarity— painful familiarity—stung her eyes. She found that she was glad for Nagarath's distraction. Dark, cramped, and rife with the odors of disuse and disarray, the shop felt much like the library in Parentino had before Liara's having put it to rights. Books had become shelving for other arcana. The visitor had to step around bundled herbs lying in untidy piles, and their mingled smells made Liara's nose wrinkle. Those had the Power, true. True also their potency had likely been compromised, not merely from the jumbling together. Liara spotted the tracks of small animals marking the dust of the floor, and she hurried to catch her wizard up.

Nagarath already had his craggy nose buried in a book. Liara smiled fondly and turned away. A moment of peace. Her worries could wait. And besides, her training as the wizard's librarian had spoken up. Nagarath was right: the sellers likely had no idea what they had. There might well be something truly special concealed amongst the chaos. She crossed into the next room, curious.

If the front room was merely chaotic, the next overwhelmed the senses. Liara would have backed out of the doorway had another gentleman at her back not blocked her retreat. Far easier to fall to the current of foot traffic than test her tongue on Nagarath's enchantment of translation. She trained her eyes downward, instinctively sorting sham from serious.

Some of the titles were quite convincing fakery, she had to admit. Small wonder the store had such bustling clientele. Art-less replicas of Baresch's manuscript lay open on display, tantalizing the unwary with its mysteries. Liara watched as two women argued none too softly in the corner of the room, each having put a hand upon the same volume at much the same time. Bemused, she put out an invisible charm to see what all the fuss was about.

For there were auras present amongst the books. Just not proper ones. Rather, the flavors of magick that peppered the air were muted, pale shadows of the real thing. Liara assumed the shop owner to be but a clever hobbyist to the Art. Someone with a bit of the power but no true academic. She wondered if Nagarath was disappointed.

Turning, Liara felt a brush of real magick touch her aura. She turned back, curious. Not all was fakery, then. In fact, her palms itched as she moved out of the way of the arguing women as they passed by, intent on taking up their dilemma with the shopkeeper.

Alone at last, Liara bent to see which codex had

called her einatus. A discovery? Pulse quickening, she reached for the leather-bound text—

Nagarath's hand on her shoulder called Liara back out of the book. She blinked, flushing embarrassed under the mage's stony frown. Her mouth felt dry and people were staring. Why? Nagarath steered her from the back room of the shop before she could find that answer. Liara moved to put the book down on a tottering pile as she passed. Nagarath's hand swooped to scoop it up. He glanced to the shopkeeper.

"We'll take this." Nagarath tossed a coin, thrusting Liara still forward towards the door. She could feel the hard press of the book into her shoulder blades, and she quailed under the affront.

What in the world, Nagarath? She slowed so that she might catch his eye.

"Out. Quickly," Nagarath muttered, not allowing her to turn 'round. Curious gazes stared them from town. But for all the wizard's disquieting urgency, no one followed.

At length Nagarath slowed. Bringing his hand back to her shoulder, he turned Liara to face him. Liara was shocked to see the fear in his eyes. And she recoiled as she felt, at last, the icy-water trickle of his Art against her own.

"Sorry." His face fell, and he turned his attention on the book in his hand. "How do you feel?"

"Fine. What's this about, Nagarath?" Liara failed to keep the insolence from her voice. She cringed as Nagarath roughly shoved the book into his pack to the tune of crumpling pages.

Regarding her again, he passed a hand over his lips.

Deep concern. Possibly too deep for words, considering his lack of explanation. Taking in a slow breath, he blinked away the fear in his eyes and tried to summon one of his carefree smiles.

Liara wouldn't allow him to put her off. Hazy memories had surfaced underneath the mage's anxiety. She'd done something or said something while under the thrall of the book Nagarath had put in his pack.

Liara kept her eyes on the now-hidden codex. A book Nagarath had paid far too much for, if her judgment of the coin was sound. "What did I do?"

He looked at her. Hard. "We'll find out, magpie. But in the meantime, I'd rather we not attract undo attention, what with everyone so mad about magick. And so, I apologize, but I would rather we press onward to the next town. We can walk or—" He eyed his staff.

"We'll walk." Liara's whisper scratched at her throat. When Nagarath didn't move, she again looked to the book concealed within his bag, wishing she could remember what she had said or done while in the shop.

Seeming to make up his mind at last, Nagarath glanced back along the path. He dropped his pack, asking, "You'll be fine here for a moment if I go scrounge us some breakfast?"

His fingers strayed to the collar of his shirt, unearthing a silvery chain.

Liara felt the magick at her own throat sparkle in answer. It felt good to have the pendants returned to their place. *Even if I cannot tell what my mage is thinking and haven't any idea what my own magick is doing.*

She buried her complaint and nodded. She would be

fine waiting alone for a few minutes. Even so, her exhalation caught in her throat when Nagarath whisked himself away on a word of power.

Sit yourself down, Liara, and be patient. He'll be back. She scolded herself for her neediness and found a seat on a nearby stone wall, affecting an obscurity spell even though there was nobody near on the path and she could see, more or less, clear to the village below. Her stomach gave a rumble—petulant agreement with Nagarath's decision to go find food for their hike. It distracted her enough that she found it hard for her to settle on calling the soul of her Art. But even with her unspoken fears, even with the strangeness of the morning thus far, she could sense nothing wrong with her magick. The problem was in her mind.

~

Nagarath shrugged off the lingering effects of his spell and strode towards the edge of town. That nobody rushed forward to harass or bother him, that few people paid him little heed at all outside of common courtesy, reassured him that he had likely overreacted to Liara's fit inside the bookshop.

Already he had felt a fool under his apprentice's surprised apprehension. And, yet, Liara's bewilderment alarmed him all the more. He had found her, book in hand, eyes unfocused, spouting some sort of nonsensical incantation. And with a small audience of artless folks, no less.

Still, he ought not have alarmed her so, that was certain.

"Especially if . . ."

Nagarath stopped himself. He would not say it aloud. Even by himself. Even if it was little more than untried theory.

An unnamed threat he could deny.

And deny it he would!

The brush of his magick against Liara's own, however, had whispered doubt into his soul. Nagarath had been forced to lie to her. To lie to her in the same way he had always lied to her. Telling half-truths and no-truths so as to protect his magpie.

Only this time there was another from whom he strove to hide the truth.

In his mind's eye, Nagarath again saw the crystalline fireworks of Liara's destructive act in the king's Hall. Shattered mirrors sparked in the light of the setting sun, their broken glass littering the polished floor and shaking both him and Anisthe from their melee. They had barely scrambled to their feet as the guards' first volley found purchase. Even under the shock of being shot, Nagarath's immediate fear had been for Liara, standing an easy target and caught in the act of her vandalism. He had distantly noted Anisthe's discomfiting heroics while he himself had screamed his warning. In his agony, even stumbling and panicked and pained, Nagarath had seen Liara pause. He had seen his cinnabar staff slip within her grasp as she looked into the mirror and opened her mouth to speak. Liara! Her name had made his throat raw.

Smash it! Kill the mirror and kill the archmage. Kill

Kerri'tarre. He honestly thought his unspoken plea had succeeded. Or perhaps that was mere hope feeding its seductive lies to Nagarath's heart. For he did not wish to face any other truth. Even having come to England. Even having come within Merlin's ken.

He would need his books, he would. Nagarath would need his books and his brain and his magick and every bit of wile, if Liara had taken Khariton's einatus into her magick. And even then? There was likely little he could do. Save reason with the ancient archmage. Bargain and beg.

Deceive.

Oh gods. To deceive Khariton would be to deceive Liara. Nagarath found the realization sickening.

But first . . . first he had to be sure.

Nagarath quickened his steps, following his nose to the nearest bakery. His worries pursued him through the basic niceties surrounding the transaction. They chased him from Dover. They infected his next bit of spellwork, adding shame atop his already deep guilt when he reached into the power of the cinnabar stone.

But he successfully affected invisibility. The hum of the pure power from the staff brushed against his own inconsequential magicks, and Nagarath paused to take a slow centering breath before approaching the spot where Liara awaited his return. If his enchantment failed, it would look as innocent as though he had employed the ever-common "Tra'shuk." But he wanted to observe her when she thought herself unobserved.

Liara had sat herself on the low tumbledown of rock used to mark the path's edges. Head bent to the book in her lap, she casually turned a page and ran her fingers over the dense text and detailed drawings. Nagarath wished he could lean in and read over her shoulder. But he did not dare. Not with the tenuous hold he had on his spell. There would be time enough to see what he had purchased with his guinea.

Nagarath's conscience panged him again. Not at the cost, no. Though that had been exorbitant considering how that shop likely had nothing approaching even a twentieth of that value. Rather, his rush to leave the store —and desire to blame Liara's fit upon anything save what he feared most—had led him to act in a way that could have drawn more suspicion in the end.

Nagarath lost his hold upon the current of the cinnabar stone's magick. The spell ended abruptly, revealing him to his apprentice in the space of an eye blink.

Liara jumped, then scowled. "Subtlety is never your forte, is it? Did you magick our fare out of the shop, or did you at least deign to walk there like a normal person?"

"Expediency is prudent in our case today, Liara." Nagarath cocked an eyebrow, a touch of good-humored chastisement of his own. At Liara's exasperated shake of her head, he held out his hand, an offer to exchange bread for book.

"Not a fair trade, but I'm hungry, so I'll let it slide," Liara quipped, lifting the codex so that Nagarath could better see what had so engrossed her attention.

He sidled close, trying to gauge the work's purpose based on the abbreviated sample of one open page. A block of dense Hebrew; three pentacles. Nagarath squinted, noting the inscription ringing one.

"This is the Fifth Pentacle of the Sun and meant to aid one in instantaneous travel," Liara said, noting Nagarath's interest. "Though I prefer the simple elegance of our 'return' spell. This book is the *Mafteah Shelomoh,* Nagarath. Or a very good copy. Its magick called to mine in the shop."

"The Key of Solomon." Nagarath whistled. "I suppose it stands to reason that La Voisin's effects could have made it as far as a Dover shop within a half a year of her death. The store's lack of obvious magick apart from this book probably kept it all the safer. I wonder . . ."

Nagarath felt a gentle tug on his sleeve.

"Come on, Nagarath. There are other shops with other books." Liara's look was arch. "Did you not say yourself that 'Expediency is prudence'?"

"That I did, magpie." The knot in Nagarath's chest lessened, and he laughed in spite of himself. There was his Liara. Perhaps . . . perhaps he was wrong. Again. It would be nice if he were.

Together they made for the next town and rest for their travel-weary selves.

CHAPTER FOUR

Nagarath's face grew ashen during the walk to the next township.

Twice they stopped along the path for the wizard to catch his breath. At each juncture, Nagarath refused treatment of his injury, muttering that he would get to it himself once they were safe indoors. Liara thought him a great idiot for it. She kept her scolding to herself, however, as the mage continually looked back along the road as if in anticipation of pursuit.

Prickly anxiety kept their pace brisk. With the morning air bright and bedewed, the dirt road open and easeful, Dover fell behind and a nameless little town soon could be sighted down a long, gently sloping hillside.

They gained a room at the inn without incident, Liara working her cautionary hexes the whole time. Cramped if comfortable, the quarters were lacking in some of the niceties to which they had become accustomed when traveling of late. Granted, they had been doing so under significantly more genteel footing. Nagarath seated himself before the washstand and immediately lost himself to his spell work.

Oh, no you don't. Liara didn't care one whit if she interrupted his scrying. Reaching forward, she splashed the water in the bowl to get his attention. She considered the danger of her act, her rudeness, didn't much matter. He hadn't been doing it properly anyhow.

Blinking, Nagarath focused on her. That he did not admonish Liara was proof enough to her of how his condition had deteriorated. Reading her look, he reached for his mage's staff and then, wincing, let his hand drop.

"For goodness' sake, Nagarath!" Her breath caught on the mage's name as Liara murmured her frustrations. She pointed to the bed, a non-negotiable request. Wordlessly, he complied.

Liara waited, unsure if by lying down and shutting his eyes, he was inviting her assistance or no. At length Nagarath turned to look at her. He smiled and said, "I haven't the strength, magpie. Not this injury. Not without the stave's help, and I would ask that you leave that be. I can tell you how to perform the necessary spells. Or perhaps . . . Solomon might be the easier solution than my trying to think and to explain. You'll find the book in my pack."

His words sent a bolt through Liara, a brief paralysis prompting shivery guilt. *'Find the book.'* Angrily, she shook off the recollection. During her momentary hesitation Nagarath's eyes had fixed upon the cinnabar stave.

"I can do it, Nagarath. I can. If you teach me." Liara sat herself by her mage's side, determined. Desperate, really. For this time—even after everything they had been through—this time she could have lost him. And while she was gazing stupidly into some magicked mirror.

"Do you remember Magus Dubrau's *Guérison Complète*, magpie?"

Liara gulped, and her mind raced through all the books she had worked on within Parentino's wrecked library. She did not remember, no. Embarrassed, she shook her head.

Grunting, Nagarath furrowed his brow while he considered until, impatient to the last, Liara reached forward and simply grabbed his hand. "Strength is what you need, yes? I've more of that than knowledge."

Nagarath's eyes widened and his fingers twitched. Liara half-suspected an instinct to pull away. The realization nearly drew her concentration off her spellwork—the magick little more than a throwing of her aura outward towards Nagarath.

But it worked. Liara could tell it in the color which returned to her wizard's cheeks and the lessening of the pained tension in his fingers. She, in fact, found her attentions fixed on said fingers as Nagarath gave her hand a gentle squeeze and then did not let go.

"Liara, we— I should have said this before now—" Nagarath paused and seemed to hunt about for the words. It appeared to Liara that he changed tack, for he smiled sadly and then said, "I realize that I have never said that I had forgiven you. For the events in Parentino, I mean. I suppose that, at some point along the way, I believed that you knew."

Liara waited, thinking that perhaps he would say more. Instead, Nagarath turned from her and directed his gaze out the window. Seeing nothing that would draw his attention thus, Liara focused on his face, crisply outlined by the afternoon sun. The mage's pale gray eyes sparkled with unknowable emotion; his brow furrowed in argument with his sensitive mouth. She twitched with the desire to comfort him, to draw her thumb along his temple and cheek. Just to touch him at all.

Liara turned away. She focused on the washing basin and asked, "Have you water enough to scry?"

"As I am working imperfect magicks today, Liara, yes."

She could almost hear the smile in his words, but the warmth came colored by a strange distance which had already rebuilt itself between them. Rising, she let go his hand and waited while he returned to the table with its makeshift scrying bowl.

❧

Sitting back down at the window-side table, Nagarath debated the wisdom of scrying. He certainly felt stronger. And he could feel Liara's eyes upon him. To not, at the very least, look into Anisthe's situation would cause suspicion and likely provoke a flood of questions.

Besides, he was worried about Liara's progenaurae. Nagarath had already resolved not to use the cinnabar stave in her presence so as to keep Khariton's eye off it for as long as possible. But if Liara's ties to Anisthe per the Laws Creatio were the problem rather than . . .

No, Nagarath. You know full well what your magick

sensed in her after the incident in the bookshop, you second-guessing, faint-hoped fool. There. Now he was angry with himself.

Good. Better that than at Liara, or Amsalla, or even Anisthe, none of whose actions Nagarath could control or help. At present all he might do was scry and think.

Two things you are rather good at, magus. Be glad of that.

The water in the bowl had long gone still under Nagarath's worried waiting. He made the appropriate sign and settled his chin onto his interlaced fingers. The picture formed almost immediately. Anisthe paced the perimeter of a circular stone-walled room. The former war mage did not appear the worse for wear.

"And where are we today, old friend?"

Anisthe had appeared to give himself up to Amsalla in order to give Liara and Nagarath time to escape. A ruse? Madamoiselle DeBouverelle would have more answers, perhaps. Sighing—carefully, so as not to disturb the quiet water into which he gazed—Nagarath separated his hands and flicked a wrist. The scene shifted, growing blank and gray.

"Oh, come on, then," he growled, making the gesture again. The water shimmered but no scene materialized. Amsalla DeBouverelle appeared to have taken precautions against scrying. Annoyed, Nagarath shoved back from the table, and the water sloshed in its bowl. "Demons take the woman."

He eyed Liara and explained, "Apologies. Amsalla is blocking my attempts at scrying."

Liara nodded wordlessly.

Nagarath pinched the bridge of his nose. His thinking came out as fretting rather than anything productive. He could look in on Anisthe but not Amsalla. Were the two of them working together, or were they not? Where was the room which Anisthe paced with such vigor? Was Amsalla nearby? And did he and Liara dare go back? Was it a trap?

Nagarath's conclusion remained the same: he must get Liara somewhere safe. But then nowhere was safe so long as Amsalla could simply slay Anisthe so as to force Khariton's magick into a dupe with whom she had already tried to reason.

But that only works if Amsalla can see what Liara and I are about. And only if she is willing to cross such a line. Nagarath reminded himself that Amsalla had forwarded a tearful plea to him and nothing more. Take away her jealousy of Liara and her actions had been that of an old friend who found herself in a spot of trouble.

An old friend famous for her conniving nature. Do remember that the mirror was at Versailles through her direct interference. Nagarath reached for his mage's staff. Two could play at DeBouverelle's game, if game it was.

He stopped short. *No. No using the cinnabar stave.*

Nagarath gazed into the scrying bowl once more. Whispering sharp words of the Green Language, he winced when the spell took hold. Surely Liara had noticed? He looked to see that his apprentice had merely taken up a spot upon the bed and lay staring vacantly at the ceiling, arms crossed behind her head.

The water had grown still. He made the sign. A brief wavering image threatened to coalesce and then . . . a deep gray nothing. Leaning back, Nagarath breathed a sigh of relief. They were now as invisible to scrying as Amsalla was to him. Provided one used the traditional methods, of course. Luckily Miss DeBouverelle had shown him a rather unconventional method months and miles back, giving Nagarath a good chance of blocking that as well. The memory of that night by the fire rose in his mind, swift and wicked—a heart's revenge. Amsalla's jealousy was well-founded considering how close he had allowed her to get, only to push her away.

Nagarath had since come to terms with what it was he wanted, however. And so Liara's safety was paramount. No matter the cost. Sure, the spell which concealed their movements would have to be renewed, causing a constant small drain upon Nagarath's personal magick. Small price for the relative safety of keeping Amsalla from seeing their movements while they tried to figure out hers.

As for Anisthe, it was a far trickier business keeping him from spying upon them if Nagarath wanted to still be able to see him. But then, the danger to Liara did not lie at Anisthe's hand. Not this time. As Anisthe had once asked of them: what benefit to him if he died?

Forcing his mind from the bleak thought, Nagarath considered the other puzzle, that of Dover and the book-shop and the words of that stranger the night before. How was it magick had such a different reputation here in England? What had come to stir people so? Was he to take it as a sign? Or a mere distraction? Or some chal-lenge to Khariton and therefore another thing to keep Liara's interest off of? It had him wondering if, perhaps, his message to Merlin had been received. Against all odds and every bit of worry Nagarath had leveled upon his luckless messenger, there was a chance that the only mage capable of standing up to Khariton was alive and well after a thousand years under his own terrible curse.

"Now you are giving in to false hopes, Nagarath."

"Sorry. Did you say something?"

Nagarath grimaced. "Apologies, magpie. I was just thinking aloud. It is nothing."

Yes, lying to Liara was not a habit easily revisited. Even if it was not only for her good, but for the potential safety of everyone her magick might touch.

2 0 0 MILES WEST OF DOVER OR
FOLKSTONE:

"Hold up there, lad. You haven't yet told me when you'll next be by with the latest of the wizard's prophecies."

Krešimir hunched in alarm and then turned around to confront the man who printed and posted Merlin's missives in that particular town. Carefully, oh so carefully, he let his hand drift away from where he had reached for his wand—borrowed power only to be used in the most dire of needs. Or if Krešimir managed to locate the two wayward mages who the prophecies were meant to rouse.

Liara.

And Nagarath.

Each from faraway Istria. Like Krešimir himself.

Krešimir fought a frown and cast his eyes to his now-empty hands. It did not much matter what lie he gave the man. He would not be returning to the area. Nor would he be remembered with any particular clarity. He hoped. Again Krešimir's hand itched for the concealed wand.

Such weakness.

He forced his thoughts back onto Liara. New resolve gripped Krešimir, and he answered, "Next new moon. Same as before, Bafford. Same as all summer."

"I'll be seeing you, then."

This time Krešimir could not outstrip his guilt and so had to turn away. He waved over his shoulder and sauntered off as nonchalantly as he could manage. With each step away from civilization, such as it was in this tiny hamlet, he moved further from Liara and towards Merlin's prison.

"A true mess you've made of things, Krešimir." He left the path and set out across a gently sloping meadow. A small grove of trees in the near distance would provide easy cover for the trick that would send him back to the archmage's home.

"Or is it even my mess?" he corrected his peevish scolding.

He had offered to help from the first. Well, he had from the moment Dvigrad's priest had come forward with something for Krešimir to do. But he had wanted, of his own volition, to do something to help Liara's plight.

"It was Father Phenlick's error first," he grumbled. Said error had compounded, saving Krešimir's life, incidentally. Even so, the small fact of Liara's circumstance had grown itself into—

"It grew into a problem for me!"

He admitted it at last. His muddled morality. In order to help Liara, Krešimir had, at every turn, stepped closer to that burning desire for the very thing he ought not— could not—have. Magick. Power.

Which was, perhaps, why it all had gone wrong on him. Tricked by Anisthe in Vrsar and set to tear Liara from the mage protecting her; that terrific storm at sea; Krešimir's having finally had Liara back in his arms one moment and the very next almost losing her entirely.

And then being ensorcelled, thrown to Merlin in his cage at the edge of faerie. This last still stung. The affront of it. How dare he! How dare Nagarath, he who considered himself so important to Liara's safety and well-being, and yet somehow managed so poorly.

Nagarath, who had managed so terribly at keeping Dvigrad safe from that other wizard.

Krešimir surprised himself with his easy anger. He had become so used to heartache and the conviction it honed within him. In some respects, he should thank Nagarath for sending him to Merlin. The archmage was still spellbound from the curse laid upon him centuries before, but he had such power that, if freed, he could reverse the fates of everyone in doomed Dvigrad. Only one like Merlin could undo what had been done. And in exchange, all Krešimir had to do was post Merlin's prophecies far and wide, signposts to draw Nagarath and Liara near.

Already Krešimir had vowed: this time he would make the offer he once considered but had foolishly left unsaid. This time it would be him or the wizard. Which left the borrowed wand a heavy temptation for Krešimir. If he could have magick, too, when next he saw Liara . . .

No. Her choice would be magick or a real life in the real world.

"But have I not learned that magick is real?" Krešimir

let his ire rise again. Of sorcery's strength he had ample proof.

To that end, he had now reached the distant stand of trees. Taking out the wand, he regarded it, feeling an odd drop in his stomach. He felt silly every time he used it, in fact. A stick of whittled wood. How many had he tooled for himself and Liara and the other children of their town over the years. Had it felt foolish then? No. Children so rarely feel foolish. He smiled fondly, sadly. Dvigrad's memory would keep him from the temptation of magick. And he would turn Liara from it. Eventually. Once they had their home to return to.

Sucking in a breath, he enacted the spell and was returned to the foot of a lonely low-rising hill in the middle of a lonely field. A lonely hut squatted at the top of said hill, and a lonely ribbon of smoke rose out of the chimney. Krešimir approached, trying to see—as usual— if he could feel the barrier, the stopping point for Merlin. But not a barrier to Merlin's messenger-elect. Strange. Spooky.

Yes, there would be no magick for Krešimir, thank you very much.

Entering the little house, he announced, "I'm back."

As if it could be anyone else. Krešimir looked around. As though Merlin could be anywhere else.

"Yes, lad. Welcome back. Fine weather. Any troubles? None at all. Good, good." Merlin stamped out from behind a tall, twisted bookshelf full of curiosities. That he had immediately adopted both sides of the conversation brought a smile to Krešimir's face. A thousand years of living alone left quite a mark upon one's habits, or so the archmage was fond of saying.

"You tell any of them anything?"

"The printers? No." Krešimir shook his head. "They'll have their disappointment in a few weeks when I do not return with your next series of statements."

Merlin nodded and stamped across the room to settle in the hearthside chair. Lighting his pipe, he took several long drags before blowing the smoke out in one hearty exhalation. The resulting cloud hung heavy in the air. The ancient mage drew a quick pattern with his wand, and the smoke seemed to twist itself into the shape of a woman for a brief moment. And then the image was gone, the scrying spell broken.

"And Liara and Nagarath are similarly unavailable to my scrying," Merlin harrumphed. He put aside his pipe and stroked his long beard. "Amsalla was the first, you understand. Then Anisthe who, I suspect, was moved to less comfortable accommodations in *La Bastille*. With a bit of time, I've no doubt I could come up with something that looks past the magick-cancelling iron of doors and locks. But the effort would only be worthwhile were I to glean anything worth knowing from him."

"Then what are we to do, Archmage?"

Merlin set his piercing gaze upon Krešimir and again reached for his pipe. "We find our patience and stay our course. I've a fairly reasonable notion of Nagarath's intended path. You shall move ahead of him and Liara to draw their attention upon me, as we had previously planned. Then again, with Amsalla now invisible to scrying— No. No, you're right, of course. She serves me.

Else she would not have first sent word that, in addition to Liara's having taken Khariton's einatus into her magick, Nagarath carries with him that stone. A thing which could help your friend should my magick prove insufficient."

To this Krešimir had nothing to say. Well, he did. But he could not voice it. This Amsalla DeBouverelle was Merlin's other contact with the outside world, one whom he had pointedly admitted to not trusting fully. And she, like Anisthe, had a past with Nagarath.

Everything comes back to that wizard. Krešimir clenched his teeth to the inner complaint. For, in spite of everything, in spite of having been ensorcelled by the mage and jealous of the man's connections with his Liara . . . On a beach in Sardinia, Krešimir had come to realize that there was simply something trustworthy in Nagarath of Parentino. Which meant, to Krešimir at least, that Amsalla DeBouverelle was unworthy of any sort of regard or reliance.

CHAPTER FIVE

Rest came fleeting and thick with tension. Both Liara and Nagarath said little during their quick march through the countryside, the wizard's newly healed wound and repeated scrying of Anisthe driving their pace. Amsalla, he claimed, he still could not see. On that issue, Liara gave Nagarath the trust he had earned, for she could not stomach the idea of scrying that woman for herself.

Tiny hamlets sprang up in their path with comforting regularity, towns whose names Liara did not note but the mage seemed to recognize. To her, it mattered little what the place was called so long as nobody looked sideways at them and at the end of the day she could lapse into blissful unconsciousness on a real bed. Nagarath made sure that both happened.

But the reprieve from scrutiny did not last long. Whispers of magick carried through on the wind itself, it seemed. Unavoidable and therefore all the more tantalizing, gossips claimed information on magick both real and fantastic; more storefronts positioned themselves as having the secrets to the universe—or at least the means to gain such—within their shelves. Newspaper sheets proclaimed loud and long the latest from Merlin. Prophecies.

Surely this last was a hoax? At one point, Liara tried to get her hands on one such news sheet only to have Nagarath correct her with a glance. Blushing, for she knew better than to fall to the glamor of rumor and simple superstition, Liara put herself into Nagarath's capable hands.

And so they went. Neither of them mentioned the incident at Dover. Both of them spent a fair bit of time examining La Voisin's book. In doing so, Liara found some measure of relief. She recalled how her aura had tingled, calling her attention to the nearby magicks. Perhaps the strange fit she had experienced truly was related, somehow, to the book. After all, it had taken her weeks to adjust to Nagarath's collection in Parentino.

'*Find the book. Do not come back.*' Books, books, always books. Anisthe's words haunted Liara still. To be honest, Liara was fairly sick of books.

Nagarath, of course, was far from done with them, considering it a moral imperative that they check every shop now that they had stumbled so fortunately upon a codex as powerful as the *Mafteah Shelomoh*. He, too, seemed to have found solace in the theory that Liara's strange fit of magick in Dover had been something so benign as a collision of her signature with that of the book's. Nothing strange had happened since—not that she was going to tell Nagarath, anyhow.

The periodic blunting of her senses persisted. Yet, with each occurrence, Liara found that if she thought directly at the problem, it seemed to dissipate. Thus able to hide from Nagarath this private worry, she considered Anisthe's situation anew. Perhaps what was happening to her had something to do with his having surrendered to Amsalla? Was he safe? Well? And with Nagarath apparently able to see little more than where her progenaurae's jailers had him locked away, how was Liara to satisfy herself on this point? How was she to know if Anisthe had truly meant to be on their side?

Am I ready to face that answer?

Far easier to follow Nagarath's lead as he browsed first one shop of magick wares, then another. The aimless quest was a welcome distraction.

In Liara's estimation, it wasn't exactly as perfunctory an approach as the mage claimed. Ten minutes wandering the third such shop in the third such town and the wizard already had six hefty codices and two scrolls balanced within his lanky arms and had pressed Liara into carrying four more besides. Still he looked on. And so she suffered through the mage's endless exclamations of interest, disgust, and chagrin while he explored yet another dusty store of arcane wares.

A painless enough burden for, under the generous application of reference materials, Nagarath positively glowed. Liara found the whole thing heartening. If pointedly, publicly odd. She had caught Nagarath smelling the books at one point, eyes closed in a sort of rapture. It had become so that she wouldn't be the least bit surprised if he tried next to taste a codex.

Trailing him half a shelf back, Liara waited for the moment that he'd simply shove another book into her waiting arms. She had to admit, that particular shop in that particular town seemed to have a better idea than most of what real magick entailed. Less flash and glamor. More practical hexes and histories.

"So, are you considering moving to England?" Liara teased as her mage compared two books, peering from one open page to another.

"Would you miss your home, Liara?" Nagarath casually inquired, startling her with one of his penetrating glances. She hadn't really thought he was paying attention.

"Being with you is home now."

Liara blinked. Her words surprised even her.

Oh, they felt true enough. She just, well, the admission sounded stupid coming out of her mouth. Pulling down a title at random, she pretended to read. A handy distraction. *Maybe that's why Nagarath buries his nose in books so often; it's easier to avoid saying foolish things.*

And then a hand tugged at the books she had shifted to hold under her free arm. Instinct had her gripping tighter and throwing a glare until she saw it was Nagarath himself who had made the claim. Lost within the pages of her clumsy retreat, she hadn't noted the wizard's negotiations with the shop owner. Attuning, Liara found that the two haggled over the delivery of Nagarath's purchases.

Delivery? That would imply staying put in a place for more than a few hours, Nagarath. Liara raised an eyebrow in accompaniment to the thought. She and Nagarath were out of the shop before she could voice her complaint. Not that she would have so blatantly exposed whatever game the mage was playing at. Smiling to herself, Liara followed the wizard from the shop.

A book could provide a handy distraction, sure enough. But the blade could cut both ways. Her chosen diversion had equally served in disarming Liara in her vigil against herself. Squinting in the midday sunshine that punctuated their short walk back to the inn, she felt as though she might again disappear into the sort of trance which had struck her in Dover. She could sense that same strange thickness in her mouth and at the back of her eyes. Though this might well be blamed on continued embarrassment over her impulsive statement.

Trailing the mage as Nagarath lost himself in one of the scrolls he'd deemed too sensitive to be left behind, Liara similarly lost herself to her thoughts. She barely noted the greetings from fellow travelers that hailed them upon reentering the inn, hardly felt the stairs beneath her feet as she fixed her gaze on the hem of Nagarath's swirling robes. In moments they'd be alone, and she would feel with full force the import of her hasty words.

'Being with you is home now.' The sentiment was not so much stupid as, well . . . too honest. How dare she put the man in such a position with her thoughtlessness. Liara's magickal education had become a hodge-podge of misfires and false starts, but the relationship of master and apprentice would one day reach its natural end. Nagarath could then continue his life, unbeholden to Liara's safety and concerns, and she could pursue her own dreams at long last.

But Liara's dreams had changed. The thought of separating from her mage? The very idea tore through Liara's heart like lightning and left her gasping. The door to their room shut behind them, trapping Liara with her memories of Versailles and the sleepless night which had followed the king's grand party. But this time jealousy, rather than misery, gripped Liara. It hardened into hatred in the space of a breath.

The shadow in the back of her eyes shifted. Magick bubbled out of her, and she flailed about in the bright blur of her panic, drowning in the Art. The fit subsided as quickly as it had come. But it was too late. Her curse had already been loosed. And at Nagarath's unprotected back.

The mage whirled around, drew his wand, and cried the words of his own counter-magicks, all in one smooth motion.

Once. Twice. Thrice. The blows from Nagarath's spellwork left Liara gasping for breath. Still, hands firmly clenched at her sides, biting her lip, she weathered the onslaught. A solitary tear snuck down her cheek, and her opponent withdrew his magick an instant later. Nagarath looked to the wand in his hand, his face crumpling. "Liara, I—"

"It's fine." Liara's voice came out a whisper.

It was not fine. But she'd die sooner than tell the mage that.

He knew, anyhow. Knew and had his arms wrapped around Liara before she could shy away. The gesture freed more of her tears.

She sobbed into the wizard's robes, "I'm sorry."

"It is I who ought to be sorry," Nagarath's voice came muffled to Liara's ears, and she merely shook her head in response, afraid that if she removed herself from where she hid, more rogue magick might follow the first. "I was too quick to act."

"I don't know why I—" Liara sniffled. "I mean, it's like I couldn't stop it. I didn't even intend to use any magick at all."

"Thank the gods we were out of sight this time. Did it feel like the first time in Dover?"

Liara shook her head and stepped back from the mage, clarifying, "I don't know. I didn't even remember the book shop incident. This felt . . . fuzzy. Like someone had stopped my tongue with cotton and veiled my eyes. But that's nonsense. Unless, somehow, my magick has—?"

"Liara. Please drain yourself of the Art," Nagarath's command travelled down the point of his outstretched wand, wounding Liara with its cool detachment.

Bowing her head, Liara fished out her own wand—a wand previously Nagarath's, and Master Cromen's before him—gifted in another time, under very different circumstances. She had warned him, had known that she would go wrong someday. Nagarath, being the man and mage he was, had thought her caution over her handedness something they could simply get around.

Liara hated being right. She held the wand out to him, looking away.

"I am not taking your wand from you, Liara," Nagarath's words rose over her despondence. "I am asking you to disarm yourself for the time being. Bleed out the magick and leave yourself bereft. I want to try something."

"You're not . . . ?" Liara risked looking into the mage's fiery impatience.

Seeing her falter, he softened. "Not dis-apprenticing you, no. Never. Merely requesting a certain set of circumstances under which I might be able to better root out the problem in your einatus."

"Better I should be without it, then." Liara thrust her wand at Nagarath. Surrender.

"Stop that. Do you trust me?" Angrily, Nagarath snatched the wand from her outstretched fingers and flung it away. It clattered across the floor, background noise to the intensity of emotion in the wizard's repeated plea, "Do you trust me?"

Liara nodded in spite of her misgivings. It really was that simple. As simple as the act of bleeding out her power.

She closed her eyes and reached into her magick with the most harmless, useless spell she knew. Her sparkling aura dancing in her mind, she looked to Dvigrad. And not Dvigrad as it was, but Dvigrad as it had once been. Father Phenlick enjoying a meal. Đerkan Babić waving a nervous smile in her direction and then pretending otherwise a moment later. Krešimir. So much of Krešimir. And such memories as sparked a blush to heat Liara's cheeks and brought a coloring of guilt to her jealousy of Amsalla from moments before.

A part of her considered it a curious choice of expenditure when Liara might have, instead, with all her strength done so much with her Art in that moment. To peer into the past, to cross time with her mind was folly and had no real purpose. Costing so much to do so, wizards rarely bothered with such sorcery. Her knowledge of the spell was only incidental, coming from her early attempts at making a catalogue book for Nagarath's Parentino library. But it served to empty her of her magick. And with no real danger to others.

Liara opened her eyes and found that Nagarath had laid his hands upon her shoulders. She could feel the trembling of his normally sure and sensitive fingers. His eyes, too, shone their apprehension—just a bit brighter, a tiny glint of fear and desperation. Fear for her, not of her.

"Magick is woven. Its countless threads connect all things. The rocks and trees. The mountains. The flesh of man. The air we breathe." Nagarath closed his eyes. His fingers twitched, and Liara could feel the warmth of his aura as it met hers. "Your magick has undergone a change, Liara. Though what it means I cannot say. But it is a dramatic shift and one you cannot control at present. There is a snag in the cloth. Whether through your connection to Anisthe—gods keep him safe—or an artifact that I . . . that I might have led you across, I do not know."

His hands moved from her shoulders, Nagarath's fingers brushing Liara's temples. The gesture, the soft warmth of the wizard's magick, recalled another memory. Liara's first incursion into the mage's workroom in Parentino; her voiced fears, even then, that she had such darkness to her Art. Her friend had assured her that day.

And now?

The spell ended, and the mage dropped his hands. Though he tried to hide it from her in the careful blanking of his face, Liara could tell that Nagarath hadn't found the answers he'd sought.

"Your einatus is sound and unchanged," he said. "I had hoped that—"

He stopped and shook his head, trying again, "I had hoped I might find and soothe the snarl that plagues your control and wrecks your intents."

"The only thing wrong with me is me."

Nagarath turned from Liara, not rising to comment on her bitter observation.

Liara's thoughts swirled in a dizzying dance. *The only thing wrong with me is me.* She still felt like herself, all right. Confused. Angry. Powerful. And Nagarath . . . well, he was Nagarath. Clutching at his hair as he tried to puzzle out a new course of action, he ignored Liara while he disappeared into his well-meant academia. "Trantson's *Theory of Sortilegus*? No. Suthe? No. No, too dangerous. Think, you stupid mage. Think."

Feeling dizzy, Liara moved to sit upon the bed. Again she felt the fire of his magick burning through her. Not the sorcery he had attempted on her just now, no. It was the other she recalled. Tears pricked Liara's eyes. She had attacked him. Nagarath had retaliated. Without hesitation.

He hadn't hurt her. His pulling back on the bite of the spellwork had been as swift as his having hexed a quick defense. But it could have gone so very badly.

And why? Why could she no longer control her Art?

Motion in the corner of her eye distracted Liara from her thoughts. Nagarath. With her wand in his hand. She shied away, mumbling that, for all his good intentions, his judgment might not be the most—

He did not wait for her to finish. Liara's wand was placed back into her possession, and Nagarath's fingers gently closed over hers. "Now to the matter of personal safety—both yours and mine. You are my apprentice still and therefore have much to learn. Repeat after me: *kiih'ed einatae.*"

"I don't have any magick left right n—"

"*Kiih'ed einatae,*" Nagarath's soft thunder rolled over Liara's excuse.

She whispered the spell and felt nothing.

Nagarath stepped back, his brow dark and furrowed. "Well said. Remember that one. I would ask that you bind your magick thus when you next feel strong enough."

Liara considered the words of the hex, its implied meaning. *Kiih'ed.* Denial; denial put upon a mage's soul. Phrased thus, it would only work upon the caster. A safe enough curse. Still, Liara's hands trembled, and she hurriedly secreted her wand.

There was no hiding from Nagarath's quick eyes.

Liara licked her dry lips, daring, "That spell is one of dark magick, yes?"

"It is. Yes."

CHAPTER SIX

"Kiih'ed einatae."

Nagarath heard Liara whisper the words as he sat down to scry. His face burned with the shame of even knowing such a spell. Closing himself off to the guilt, he made the sign which would allow him sight into Anisthe's situation.

The water beneath his outstretched hands cleared and then clouded. Shooting a nervous glance to Liara, Nagarath repeated the spell. The results were much the same, though this time he believed that he saw a glimmer of Anisthe lying upon a makeshift pallet or bench in some dark space.

Nagarath sucked in a breath, lest his temper best him and give away to Liara his failure. His self-disgust redoubled. She was relying on him. Same as she had in Limska Draga. And here he was deceiving her, a thing he had promised never to do to her again.

But if he were right about Khariton? Then he could not risk telling Liara all. And not merely for her own safety. Instinctively, Nagarath reached out and drew the cinnabar stave closer to him.

And if I am wrong about what happened with the ancient archmage's mirror? If Anisthe was wrong . . . ? Then Nagarath would simply have to own to the error. His asking Liara to hex her magick closed to her was temporary. Nasty business, yes. But reversible.

"Kiih'ed einatae."

Nagarath winced under Liara's whispering the words again. He risked a look at her. Sitting with her legs tucked beneath her, his apprentice had her face pressed close to La Voisin's copy of *Mafteah Shelomoh.* While he watched, Liara tucked a stray hair back behind her ear, an unconscious gesture of concentration so familiar to Nagarath that it near broke his heart to see it.

Turning back to the bowl, he considered Anisthe's fevered words to Liara. *'Find the book. Do not come back.'* She had since tried to engage Nagarath in conversation about what the war mage might have meant. For Nagarath, the real question was whom the charge had been for.

The answer? Would prove whose side it was that Anisthe truly served.

He serves himself. Always has. For, if Nagarath was right in his suspicions of which book and why, if Anisthe still believed in the legend of Merlin and Kerri'tarre's spell book . . . Then the war mage yet pursued his deluded ambitions from long ago, and Nagarath would learn as much—or more—from watching the movements of his old enemy as he would by guessing at that man's motives.

Staring at the blank water of the scrying bowl, thinking of the Rishon Kesem and the rumors which swirled around the ancient codex—and how Merlin's name kept cropping up in their path now that they had fled to England—Nagarath was tempted to look to his own Aura. Just to compare for himself anew what he had seen in Liara's. Anisthe's magickal signature looked nothing as it once had, though the Laws which tied his life to Liara's held for at least one year more.

But nothing would be learned from such stalling and waste of spellwork. Nagarath knew his own magick and his past. And he certainly knew his apprentice's. There simply was nothing for him to see on that count. His only evidence of Khariton's presence within her einatus were her actions and Anisthe's.

A pairing he most certainly did not wish to think on any longer. For to do so seemed to take Liara further from Nagarath, further from any hopes he might have for her. He thanked the powers he had not voiced his feelings to her yet. To place that on her atop what she was facing within her own magick would be unfair of him.

Silence is, as always, my ally.

And guilt his companion. Nagarath added to it now as, instead of attempting to scry either of the wizards left behind in France, he looked in on Father Adessi. He needed eyes at court—eyes on Amsalla if he could—and for some reason, Nagarath felt that Rodolfo would be the more forgiving of his options. Not that the priest would know of the incursion, of course.

The scene emerged easily. Sound, as usual, followed a step behind. No matter. Nagarath could piece it together.

Interlacing his fingers and setting his chin to rest on them, he concentrated on reining his breath so as not to disturb the wavering image.

He did not have long to wait. The most incredible luck brought his scrying to the edge of Amsalla's defensive spells. Father Adessi now stood at the edge of a gray blankness, chattering away with thin air—or so it looked to Nagarath's scrying, at least.

"*. . . Then you must follow her so that what happened to Monsieur Sauvageau does not also happen to Monsieur Poulin.*"

The spell broke apart under Nagarath's shock and anger. What had Amsalla done to his friends?

"Rather, what have I done?"

It was as much Nagarath's fault as anything else if something terrible had befallen they who had helped Liara and himself pass at court. Julien Jeffers had not been mentioned. Perhaps the curse he had laid upon him in his home had held, and the courtier had forgotten the encounter. Then again, Matty and Tally did not know of Nagarath's Art.

What was Amsalla's game, then?

But first things first.

Nagarath hardly had the steadiness of mind to send his scrying upon Talaffe. As it was, the image was slow to come. Monsieur Sauvageau was in his home and looking no worse for whatever DeBouverelle had reportedly done to him. Nagarath's sigh of relief stirred the water and so he had to wait further to check in on Matty.

M. Poulin, however, had more to tell than Tally had. He, too, was in his home. Nagarath witnessed his angry argument with another gentleman—well, as angry as their sort ever became. Biting sarcasm and thinly veiled accusations flew about the room like autumn leaves, thick and colorful. Watching the men complain, Nagarath felt a pang on Tally's behalf. It was the very sort of discussion in which Sauvageau loved to participate.

Within moments Nagarath had assured himself that his friends were safe. They were only politically at peril. Word was that this was compliments of the king's teller of tales, Miss DeBouverelle. Teller of tales, indeed. More like lying harpie. Nagarath let the spell die and leaned back in his chair to stare up at the ceiling.

Amsalla DeBouverelle. A woman whose loyalties might change more frequently than even Anisthe's. A perfect creature of the politics of court. To say nothing of magick. She had almost trusted him in the terrible moments following the murder of Liara's companion, Sophie. Well, panic had almost shocked Amsalla into candor, more like.

Nagarath tried to recall her words. Amsalla had been afraid. Mortally so. Of who, she had not said. With her ambitions being what they were, that of using Khariton to undermine every monarch who opposed magick, she could have gained any number of powerful enemies. Provided, of course, that she had confided to anyone outside of himself. Himself and Anisthe. Anisthe, who had had his own illustrious connections, once upon a time. Anisthe, who had surrendered to Amsalla and effectively made hostage so as to potentially put Kerri'tarre's magick back within DeBouverelle's reach.

"Kiih'ed einatae."

Oh, Nagarath. What a mess, what a horrid mess you've made.

Loathe as he was to let Liara out of his sight at present, he might need to find an excuse to work his next scrying session alone. Nagarath couldn't rely upon his apprentice being distracted by a book the whole time. *She's not you, you know.*

The thought brought a smile to his lips. A smile and some steadying of mind. Patience, Nagarath reminded himself. His options at present were limited. Which made for an easy task list.

Scrying and thinking. He was rather good at both.

BASTILLE SAINT-ANTOINE:

Anisthe could hear his visitor's approach long before they made entrance. Shuffled from the topmost room of the Trésor tower and thrust into the dank and foul-smelling dungeons of the Bastille Saint-Antoine a day prior, he had been given no trial, no explanation for his imprisonment and change of quarters.

He could only guess that they were trying to intimidate him. That or someone had finally decided that the iron bars of his sleeping pallet and two doors with their multiple bolts and locks might be enough to prevent the king's wizardly guest from utilizing his powers. Powers Anisthe had yet to demonstrate, instead proclaiming his incantate state loudly both in Amsalla's presence and all the moments thereafter.

Shifting on the rough planks of his bed, Anisthe decided to make it as uncomfortable for the individual rattling the locks of the outer door as she had hoped to make him. Perhaps he ought to feign sleep, make Madame DeBouverelle wait all the longer in the stinking, stale air. Let her stand in the mud and filth until he had roused himself for the anticipated tête-à-tête. What harm could she do him? His safety was paramount to Liara's survival. With his aurenaurae having accepted Khariton's soul into her own before the mirror had shattered, Amsalla had every reason to bow to his whims. Perhaps Anisthe would demand better accommodations.

Or not.

"Ge' up, you." The gruff voice at Anisthe's back, its mechanism as worn and protesting as the dungeon locks themselves, was most certainly not belonging to elegant Amsalla DeBouverelle. "Council chamber."

Rising smoothly, Anisthe cocked an eyebrow. An interview? How lovely. Would he be allowed to make himself presentable first? His unvoiced sarcasm, coupled with the slowness of his movements, earned Anisthe a blow across the back of his knees from the guard's staff.

"There's more to that if you make me wait any longer here, see?"

Anisthe merely smiled and lifted his manacled wrists to show how well aware he was that he was at the mercy of the king's pleasure.

Committed as he had been to showing an unruffled aspect to his captors, Anisthe could not help but breathe deep once they had gained the stairs. Oh gods, how fresh the air! Closing his eyes, he let his heart rejoice in the reprieve, certain that it showed on his face and caring little. Mage or not, he was human, and it was time he was treated as such.

Crossing the yard, Anisthe tried not to think how precious little time he might have before he was returned to the putrid graveyard beneath his feet. Perhaps Amsalla could be swayed. Perhaps he could feign illness, something grave enough that she would then have to demand he be moved in order to protect her precious Kerri'tarre.

A chill struck, causing Anisthe to stumble on the steps leading back into the building. What if it were the other way around? What if he were imprisoned in spite of Amsalla's best efforts? Suddenly, the iron on his wrists was doubly heavy, the time of his lessened imprisonment fleeting.

Amsalla DeBouverelle sat within the chamber, a handkerchief pressed to her delicate face. Magick sparkled invisibly in the corners of the room. Domagoj's. The relief brought to Anisthe by the sweet air of the courtyard expanded at the thought of his servant hidden nearby.

Anisthe did not bother to make apology for his state of dress and hygiene, instead seating himself after the guard had left and the wizard indicated, with a quiet nod, that he take the other available chair.

"We've had a terrible three days, each of us," Amsalla offered, with a lift of her eyebrows.

Doubtful. Anisthe bit back the retort and merely waited for Amsalla to say her piece. He certainly was not going to be the one to start the conversation. And besides, he was too curious how it was she would go about what she needed to say; what her plans were and how he fit into them. It seemed she was far too busy considering the state of her prisoner—always the shallow woman. He did not need her sympathy. Not on suffering for which she, herself, was responsible.

"I'm sorry, Anisthe." Lowering her gaze and keeping her voice a near whisper, Amsalla appeared to actually mean the words. In spite of himself, Anisthe leaned forward. The wizard continued, "They're wondering why I saved you."

"Mage. Isn't that reason enough?" Anisthe waved a casual hand, his manacles fighting the gesture and dulling the motion with a heavy clink. It was Amsalla's turn to squirm. He embellished his point, "Does the king want me as part of his collection? Perhaps make me his pet. So far, you appear to be the only one who believes me when I say that I haven't the Art."

"Liara is host for Kerri'tarre's soul. As you said." Amsalla ignored his complaint and closed the space between them, an aid to her whispered words.

The effect was that of a lover, and for all that Anisthe believed himself closed off from the woman's tricks, he felt something shift inside his chest. Old memories. Old feelings. He stamped them down, annoyed.

"Of course she is. I would have been dead had you discovered otherwise. I am not so stupid as to give so base a lie, and so, again, what is it you want of me?" He rose to his feet, growling his demands.

Three days. Three days imprisoned and without a word from the witch about his servant. Anisthe could feel the oriaurant's aura through the magick protecting their conversation. Abiding caution saved him from the mistake of signaling his servant with an unmasking of his own matching signature.

What game was Amsalla playing at? She needed Anisthe for his connection to his daughter-in-magick,

Liara's life tied to his by the Laws of Magick. Surety against Nagarath doing something foolish like trying to defeat Khariton on his own. But Amsalla didn't need Anisthe rotting in a hole, necessarily. The poor treatment smacked of ulterior intents. That or she was testing him. Seeing if he were as utterly bereft of magick as he claimed.

"Where is Domagoj?"

"The oriaurant?" Amsalla's silky voice feigned surprise. "He did not make it, I am sorry to say."

Anisthe had figured himself unshakable by anything Amsalla could say to him. This had him sinking to his knees, however. Trembling, he challenged the claim, "Liar."

"Search for his aura, then— Oh, that's right. You're still just an Artless fool. Incantate. A magickless mage." Amsalla rose, towering over him as she toyed with her victim further.

Anisthe remained huddled where he had fallen. If she hadn't a hint of his powers, and stolen the oriaurant's for herself, then he had more advantages left to him than merely the insurance of his tie to Liara.

Domagoj dead. Hard to call such an advantage.

Anisthe drew a shaky hand across his brow. His rage, that he could safely let show to Amsalla. Amsalla who could have easily saved his man. Who would have had every reason to, considering an oriaurant's strange magick and its ability to render him immune to the effects of the spellpiercers—folk who could nullify magick with a touch.

He had never considered the possibility of Amsalla

simply stealing it. Zielsor. Highest of all magickal crimes. He hadn't thought her capable of such. Truly Kerri'tarre had left his mark on her soul.

"Don't worry," Amsalla continued her taunt. "You'll have magick soon enough. Nagarath refused my offer, and so, unless I leave Khariton joined to Liara, I'll need a new host for the praecantator's einatus."

Anisthe snorted. "I do not believe you have either influence or the opportunity to make that call. You think he will choose to leave Liara and come to an incantate? Kerri'tarre loves power."

"He will if she is dying. But don't worry, my dear. I would see that he brings her back for you." Amsalla's answer came tight. Cold. And the chill infected Anisthe's heart to hear it. The mage was mad if she believed that. But looking at her face, he saw that she was serious. And scared. Scared that she might yet lose. But then why bring him here? Why involve any of them at all? Nagarath. Anisthe. Hers was a risky arrangement.

Unless she had plans within plans, as had always been her wont.

Anisthe pushed further. Huddling, grateful he had given into his fit of pique, he pretended to further weakness. The cough that he affected caught hold of him, becoming real enough that he soon gasped for breath. Wet and rasping, it was as though claws raked at his lungs. Stars burst in Anisthe's vision, and he clutched his manacled arms to his chest. "And if I die here and Liara isn't near enough to Nagarath for Kerri'tarre to find a new host?"

"You're not dying." Amsalla's scorn carried an edge of fear.

"Not the right moment for you? Or is Nagarath smart enough to block your ability to scry him and his apprentice?"

"I'm on your side, Anisthe. You must merely have patience."

"Patience," Anisthe spat. "While Domagoj dies in your arms and on your promise that you'd save him? Patience while I rot in a hole in the ground? A day ago I was in the tower! I was not sitting ankle deep in filth and locked behind five inches of iron. It was you who sent me to the Hall of Mirrors, if I may remind you. And I tried to stop Liara and Nagarath."

"Yes, that was your end of the bargain for Domagoj's life, if I recall. 'Save him, Amsalla. He's all the magick I have left!' It seems that we both were unable to hold up our end of things. Domagoj was a dead man no matter my efforts. What's your excuse?" Amsalla sidled close, looking him over. "You don't trust me. You don't. Which is it? Your regard for Liara? For Nagarath? That's rich."

"I care for me. My life as well as hers. And you know same as I that Nagarath would not easily suffer Liara dying."

Anisthe didn't even flinch under Amsalla's hard-handed slap. Cheek stinging, he smiled, happy at having hurt the mage at her own game.

Backing away, Amsalla regained her scornful poise. "You surrendered to me. Don't think I don't know that this comes with all sorts of hidden strings attached. Go rot in your hole, you artless failure. I, too, can afford all the patience in the world. Your aurenaurae has a weakness alongside her apparent strengths. She's angry. Broken. Khariton has a number of avenues open to his gaining control over such a compromised soul. And failing that? It is only a matter of time before Kerri'tarre's magick strengthens so as to subdue Liara's own. I'll have Nagarath's soul one way or another. And the cinnabar stone that goes with it."

Anisthe could not hide his shock from her. The cinnabar stone? It was real and Nagarath had it?

He searched Amsalla's face for the lie. *Impossible.*

All these years and the manifestation of Anisthe's failure under Cromen had been in the hands of his enemy the whole time?

Amsalla smiled. She glided to the door, pausing with her hand upon the handle, "Have all the facts, dear, before you make your presumptions about what Liara can and cannot do for me."

Anisthe's tortured imprisonment resumed with the opening of the door.

But the cinnabar stone. And in Liara's reach. And after Anisthe had sent her for the archmages' book. He, too, could afford to be patient. Even in the slime and stench and darkness of the king's prison. For he knew that, in the case of his aurenaurae, Amsalla was very much wrong. Impertinent, impatient, unyielding: Liara's weaknesses were her strengths.

CHAPTER SEVEN

Liara waited until the mage had dozed off before making her escape. Not that she had any particular aim in mind by leaving. Nor did she intend to go far. But she simply must get out of their stuffy little room. Something was stirring in her blood, deep within the heart of her magick. A something that demanded fresh air and exercise. Who was she to deny such restless release?

Fingering the silver charm at her neck, Liara considered the foolhardiness of leaving Nagarath on his own. Though the gunshot wound was nearly healed, her mage still required a frightening amount of rest.

Nagarath had managed a bit of scrying before he had practically nodded off in the room's wash basin. The master was as spent as his apprentice. And without his having hexed off his magick as she had. Anxious, Liara had kept watch and considered whether she should not try a bit of spellwork herself. Just to be sure. After all, Nagarath hadn't been able to determine either of Anisthe or Amsalla's actions and whereabouts, and what use was her power if all she was to do with her magick was wall herself off from it?

In the end, Liara slipped out of the inn with a whispered, "Tra'shuk."

Nagarath slept. How much trouble could he get into? As for herself, the itch in Liara's mind persisted, and some part of her, some instinct, told her that she had best satisfy herself on that point somewhere far out of the reach of the cinnabar stone.

The village in which they'd chosen to stay was little more than a handful of scattered homes, a public house, a blacksmith's, and the inn in which she and Nagarath had paid for a room. Its quaintness reminded Liara of Dvigrad. But its inhabitants? Well, they were as mad for magick as anywhere else she and Nagarath had been.

No bookshop with arcane wares graced the roadside. The townsfolk likely hadn't the wherewithal to pull one together of any size worth having. But ears were bent to tongues wagging about sorcery. Here and there a child dashed about waving what could only be a pretend wand, babbling words of make-believe hexes. And one of Merlin's prophetic posts in the local news sheet had been nailed to a post in what Liara guessed was the center of the township.

She was not the only curious onlooker to stand near and read the public missive.

"Oh, if I but had magick. Lot of things I'd be changing in my life."

"What, would you want first wealth or a face worth having?" A rowdy chuckle ran 'round a group of young men who stood idly by, each marking their fruitless hopes to one another.

Liara smirked. If only they knew a wizard stood not ten feet off.

"What a load of nonsense," from somewhere behind Liara's back, an age-graveled voice appraised the archmage's words. Her face grew hot in the half a breath it took her to turn around. The sentence, as well as the tone of she who gave it, sounded altogether too much like something Liara could have heard from the mouth of Old Woman Babić. Arms folded across her bosom, the stout critic even looked like Zarije. Frowning. Judgmental.

Angry and strangely homesick, Liara locked eyes with the woman. Her fingers twitched and her vision clouded. The strange, unsettled sensation in the back of her mind gained momentum and found voice. *'Liara. Liara, what is it you want?'*

For a moment, she was back in Versailles, in the Hall of Mirrors. Kerri'tarre was showing her wonders and horrors. A thousand years of magick. Endless ages of persecution and retaliation. A war without end.

Flames, bright and blinding, left Liara gasping for breath. Wizards were burnt alive, tortured, hated beyond all sense of reason merely for possessing the Art. Liara saw them all, learned their names. Master Triiak. Yuen, Warlock of Summersby. Jivic, Malagon, and Wren of the North. Adalgisa Engel, who had once owned the wand that Liara now possessed.

Tears poured from Liara's eyes, mourning the senseless loss. But she could not look away from that which Kerri'tarre showed her. Generations of wizard-kind, slain before their knowledge could be passed on. And people, like the woman here in this village, spitting on their shattered bones.

'Come, fair one, you have deaths to avenge, have you not?' Khariton pressed home his point. Liara had saved the archmage. Her hands were his, her knowledge, too. Her magick—he would use it to save the world.

The bones in Liara's vision became a funeral pyre for innocents slain by the very magick they decried. An entire township, tucked away deep within the Limska Draga valley—gone in the flash of a cruel curse.

Misunderstandings, all. The bias and hatred? It went both ways, surely. Not all wizards were good, but it was the unbalance, the jealousy of the unknown and the arrogance of those with the Power, which kept each side pitted against the other.

They were fighting ignorance, she and Khariton.

It was the same fight that Nagarath had chosen through his love of books. In saving Kerri'tarre, Liara had chosen right. She had. She knew it by looking into the face of the Zarijes of the world.

A droning filled Liara's ears.

"Bad a-rr'. Bureme kiid gie endur. Saaumun u lah."

Khariton's words and Khariton's spell, given in Liara's voice and through her magick.

The fires of Liara's vision quenched; the screams subsided. A bright magelight pierced the darkness of her mind as those standing in the street were imbued with the Art, a gift from Kerri'tarre. The archmage would begin his restoration of magick's reputation here and now.

"Order from chaos. Magick at its rightful place in the

world. Respected, beloved, and revered. This was your plan."

Liara could feel Khariton smile, hear his words to her reverberate within her einatus. *Yes, Liara. This was the truth that Merlin and I both served before he chose to bow to the wills of our enemies. In choosing peace, he chose surrender.*

No more mages. All gone. All gone, save for a handful who have forgotten. Magick writ down in books that no one reads and sealed away in myth and legend until those with the Art are too weak and too outnumbered to fight back. But you, Liara. You see. You have chosen to fight. You have chosen to rise up and give magick back to the world. See what we can do together.

The street around her snapped back into focus, and Liara saw that the woman who reminded her so much of Zarije had lifted a shaking finger to point at her. "You're nonsense. A falsehood spreading lies and evil."

Go on, then. Show her. The voice in Liara's heart urged her into raising her own hand. Turning, she regarded the others who had stood reading Merlin's words. Three men, they had a curious expression upon their faces, some combination of excited hope and disbelief.

Khariton nodded and whispered, "That one."

Quick as a curse, the three newly-made wizards leapt upon the unbeliever. They did not need a proper education to kill with their Art. Magefire was dangerous in the hands of even the greenest novice. The enemy cut down, Kerri'tarre's new followers turned to Liara for further guidance.

"Not like this." Choking on tears as she eyed the body on the ground, Liara backed away from the scene. "Khariton. Archmage! Not like this!"

In her horror and under her having surrendered control to the praecantator, Liara had spoken in the language of her youth. Nagarath's helpful spell of translation, of course, only worked on her and only so long as she actually used it. The men who waited on Liara did not understand her words for what they were. Likely they thought it magick.

One of them knelt while the other two looked uneasily about to see if their actions had been noted. They had.

Angry shouts erupted from down the lane.

The war begins here. In the open.

"No!" Her hands thrust in front of her, Liara tried to call her magick. But, in spite of it having been her voice and her power which Kerri'tarre had used, she did not know the hex nor even the language he had employed and so could not work up a counter-curse to undo the archmage's spell. She watched, helplessly, as two more artless fell.

A war, Kerri'tarre had called it. Steeling herself, Liara drew upon the knowledge with which Nagarath had bestowed on her all those months prior in Parentino's library. *"Atsmi'i iarash 'khut he'enich ata rg'l gal'iean!"*

Loothemere. Accidental war mage, indeed.

Two of Kerri'tarre's wizards she managed to immobilize. The third escaped.

And now Liara herself was proving to be a person of

interest from the others in the street. Turning, she ran, crying out a hasty and heartfelt, "Tra'shuk!" as she did so.

She arrived back in their room at the inn, shaking all over and listening for the first signs of pursuit. Nagarath lay just as Liara had left him, lightly snoring and with his arm flung carelessly over the mage's staff at his side. It was a small blessing they hadn't unpacked—that they hadn't anything to unpack.

Closing her eyes, Liara prayed there was no one on the path just outside of Dover. Grasping the cinnabar stave, she whisked both her and Nagarath to the relative safety of complete anonymity. The inn disappeared, replaced by a quiet countryside road with a low embankment of stone marking one edge. It was not far from where she had waited for the wizard to return with provisions not scant days prior.

Nagarath jolted into wakefulness. Squinting at the sudden daylight, he locked eyes with his apprentice. "Liara!"

"It's okay. I did it. I moved us," she hurried to reassure him. She tried to let go her hold on the cinnabar staff and found her hands would not easily obey her. Sucking in a breath, she managed to quell her rioting einatus. Kerri'tarre's words—his actions and his magick—receded from her mind like the fading of a nightmare. She continued, "There was a disturbance in that town which made it unsafe for us if they were to discover that we were wizards."

Frowning at the news, Nagarath grunted and made to rise. "Fickle are the ways of men. Stands to reason that the only haven for magick would be inconstant in its passions."

Liara offered the mage her arm, wincing as Nagarath looked about their surroundings in surprise. "Why, Liara, we're back to Dover. Or just about."

He shielded his eyes and looked down upon the town. His stern face seemed to wrestle with his desire to ask Liara for more details and his trust that she would tell him of it in her own time and in her own way.

There. Liara could read her wizard again. Her magick was her own. Her mind, her hands: fully under her control.

Even so, Kerri'tarre's ringing laugh pursued Liara as she followed Nagarath's long strides back towards civilization and away from magick. Both their cloaks had been folded away as best they could manage, though the wizard still openly carried his staff of power. There was not much he could do about that. As for Liara, herself, she had done her best to bleed out the last of her power lest she give the praecantator another chance at using her magick.

'As Fairest, I demand and take. Unto my Soul, your Spirit flies.'

However could she tell Nagarath what had happened? Had Liara a chance of stopping Kerri'tarre herself?

Her only solace: Amsalla had wanted to use Nagarath for the freeing of Khariton. If nothing else, Liara's mistake had saved her mage, saved his magick, from the praecantator's control. Now she simply had to be clever, determined, and steadfast.

Whatever was she going to do?

CHAPTER EIGHT

Liara would not let Nagarath use the cinnabar staff. Yes, she had used it herself to move them from the inn. Yes, she knew it to have been a foolish action in light of finding that Khariton's magick lived within her own. She seemed to be accumulating an entire catalogue of errors in that one afternoon.

But no more. They would find an inn and settle for the night. And when the time came for supper, Liara would claim a headache or some sort of ailment that would keep her apart from her wizard long enough for her to figure out what to do next.

This hasty plan occupied much of Liara's thoughts as they traipsed over field and rolling hillside. Far better to fixate upon that than thoughts of curses, praecantators, and magick mirrors. On no less than six occasions, she opened her mouth to confess, to beg assistance from Nagarath, only to change her mind. He never appeared to notice, lost as he was in his own faltering footsteps.

That was another thing about having to walk onward

to yet another village and seek yet another room and bed. Both Liara and Nagarath hadn't the energy to spare for spellwork. Each had been all but thoroughly drained of the Art. Which left Khariton no easy puppet for his ambitions and no power of Liara's for him to annex. She was safe, if temporarily.

At length they espied a village nestled further down the coastline. Folkestone. Nagarath knew the place. Homely woodsmoke urged their lagging feet onward to the inn and bade stomachs growl. Still, Liara had her plan. Already her growing anxiety was making her pretend headache all the more real.

And besides, the very idea of her error with regards to Khariton made Liara's stomach twist. There was no way she could entertain the thought of supper. Weak and thoroughly out of sorts, she weathered Nagarath's quiet concerns after her health as he secured them a room and saw them safely away from curious eyes.

"Perhaps without every man, woman, and child seeming obsessed with the idea of sorcery here, I may finally work some magick in peace." Nagarath leaned heavily upon his mage's staff and peered into the pale porcelain of the room's wash basin. Side-eying Liara, he waited for response.

She said nothing and hugged her knees to her chest, curling up on the bed as tightly as she could.

"I do not like not knowing what happened to Anisthe. Not one bit. Not with your life still tied to your progenaurae's for two years—"

"Less than. And I know the Laws, Nagarath," Liara snapped.

"And I know Amsalla—!" He bit off his anger before it could best him completely. "I can only hope her regard for me, her respect for what I would do to her if she harmed Anisthe to imperil you . . ."

"It's just a headache; that's all, Nagarath. I'm tired, and my head hurts. You know, like normal people have." Liara shrank from the thundercloud which darkened her friend's face. Funny that Anisthe was no longer the wizard she most hated in all the world. She was most certainly not in the mood to even think about Amsalla.

"Will you be all right, then, if I go down to dine alone?"

Yes, you fool wizard, yes! Liara wanted to shout her frustrations at him. Instead she said, "I can always pester you with magick if I'm not."

In answer, Nagarath slid his fingers along the silver chain which lay half-hid within his shirt collar. Liara felt the pendant about her own neck tingle in answer, and her eyes stung with tears for it. Her mage. He was always so close to her and yet so immeasurably far away.

"Okay, then." Nagarath moved to lay the cinnabar staff against the wall.

"No. Take it with you. Please," Liara whispered. The pressure at the back of her eyes increased. The greedy archmage was stirring. Khariton reached out from the heart of Liara's magick, and her fingers itched. Nagarath needed to leave. Now.

Turning away from him, she held her breath. Liara heard the quiet opening and shutting of the door. The time had come for her to confront the horror of her foolish actions in Versailles.

Rising, she made for the bowl of water that—for wizards at least—would allow for scrying. Such was not her aim, however. Holding back her hair, she sat and peered down into the water, imagining it a mirror. Her wavering reflection stared back up at her.

"Kerri'tarre?" Liara whispered the name. She waited in silence, her heart hammering in her chest.

Power that within Thee lies,

With my Command: Awake!

As Fairest, I demand and take . . .

Unto my Soul, your Spirit flies.

How had she known the words to call Khariton from the mirror? Some long forgotten book in Nagarath's library in Parentino? If so, why had the knowledge not come to her sooner, when they were in a race with Anisthe to find the archmage's prison? That would have been helpful.

The image in the water changed, becoming the words to a whispered curse and the resulting imbuing of magick upon three artless farmers. Liara watched the memory, watched as she, herself, directed the men to hex, to kill.

This is not my magick. This is not my magick. This is not my magick! Liara relived her fear and her having employed Loothemere's counter-curse in an attempt to undo Khariton's actions through her hands. She had stopped two. Could she, with scrying, find the third?

And was it zielsor if she took his magick from him? If so, then Liara's actions against the others made her already guilty of magick's highest crime. So be it. It was a sentence she would rather bear than that of a forced alliance with Kerri'tarre.

The image in the water cleared and became a face once more. Liara found that she looked into the shadowy visage of Khariton. He smiled. Shrieking, she leapt backwards, almost overturning the bowl. With shaking hands, she felt her face, felt her own tears on her own cheeks.

An illusion and nothing more. Liara steadied her nerves and again looked into the water.

Khariton waited for her.

Did you not call me, my dear?

She nodded, obliquely thankful that the archmage did not seem to require the use of speech. Strangled by terror and guilt, Liara's throat was too tight for words.

And you understand, then, the bargain you made when you took my einatus into your own Art.

"No." Outrage saved her. It gave her back the strength the archmage had stolen through his intimidation.

Khariton's smile grew into a wrathful snarl. *I did not think you understood my terms. Not with you so eager to stop me from making your magick useful. That will not be tolerated, my dear.*

"Don't call me that."

Yes, I suppose you would rather I follow tradition and call you the fairest of them all? The archmage had regained his solicitous tone, as though he honestly thought he could bring her back around.

Well. Khariton required the use of Liara's magick and person. His einatus lived within her own and so knew how things stood with her, the traitorous, trickster wizard. He knew she could fight. And would fight.

No, no, Liara. We share a common will now. A united purpose. You cannot make such a promise only halfway.

"I—" Liara gulped, her guilt renewed. "I did not do this. I did not ask for this. I did not— I did not do this."

And yet . . . she had. She hadn't wanted the archmage to die, certainly. After every warning, every caution, standing amongst the king's shattered mirrors, Liara had known she was saving Kerri'tarre with her words. She thought that everyone had been mistaken and that she was helping. She meant for it to do some good. For the prae-cantator had shown her such a story, such a sad circum-stance. A thousand years of death and persecution.

Even now, Khariton knew how to speak to her mage's soul. He knew which parts of her heart yet hurt from magick's incursion into Liara's life—through Anisthe, through Nagarath . . . through the king's spellpiercers, and the doge's soldiers.

Yet you stopped me; thwarted my actions.

"I saved you," Liara corrected hotly. Khariton knew much about her. But he did not understand her. Not enough to control her, anyhow. Her anger could work both ways, and often had in her eighteen years of life. She continued, "I saved you, yes. But I did not agree to serve you, to use me and my magick as you see fit. Your fight —your war—it isn't mine."

Your fight—your war, Liara, will be with me, then. And I wish you luck. I do. You, a half-educated magelet, against my patience. One night you'll close your eyes, you'll let your guard down, and I'll be there. One day you'll be alone and then—

"I'm never alone!" Liara shoved the scrying dish from her and grasped her pendant.

Nagarath was at her side in an instant.

"What? What is it?"

Without hesitation, Liara flung herself into his arms and sobbed.

"Liara, what has happened?"

"I killed Domagoj, Anisthe's oriaurant."

That hadn't been how she'd meant to begin. Shifting, Liara tried to disentangle herself from the impulsive embrace.

"When? How? Why?"

"In Versailles. When you left with Amsalla after Sophie was . . . after Sophie was found," Liara's confession ended in a whisper. "I think he was waiting in her room for me. He was there when I went back for my wand."

When she had gone back alone.

I'm never alone.

Stunned by her words, Nagarath simply let Liara go, and she stood to face him, crossing her arms so as to gain the safety of the forced distance. The look on her wizard's face—she had never seen such a look. No, she had. Once before. In Vrsar. The night he had set his magick against Anisthe's in a bid to save her.

Liara took a step backwards, then another. She steadied herself and looked into the heart of her Art. She'd burned off the power with her use of the pendant. Kerri'tarre was banished. For the moment.

Taking a deep breath, she continued, "Domagoj's magick gave me the knowledge to free Khariton when we went to find the mirror. The archmage spoke to me from his prison while you and Anisthe were fighting. He convinced— No, it was me. My actions. I allowed him to convince me that history was wrong. And so I made the bargain. I freed his soul and saved him in the moments before the guardsman's bullet shattered the mirror."

Her horrid confession complete, Liara waited for Nagarath to react. She watched as his eyes lost their focus, and his jaw twitched with poorly controlled fury. Still he said nothing.

"I'm sorry." Liara's was a poor but heartfelt apology. She was sorry, indeed. Sorry and scared and certain that, at long last, she had found the end of her mage's regard through her terrible mistake.

"Did Anisthe's servant try to take your magick from you?"

Liara blinked, startled into frank surprise. She hesitated.

"Did that half-fey, blue-eyed bastard try to take your magick from you?"

The shame that Liara had felt burned bright under the flame of Nagarath's wrath. Shrinking into herself, she nodded. In doing so, the horrible moment became real again. The world around her turned a hot, dizzying white. Through the haze of her agony she saw Nagarath start to his feet. Shaking her head, she waved him off. "Don't. Don't try to say that it's okay or that my actions were justified or that you should have been there. Because all of that is true, I agree. But in the end, Domagoj's attempted theft of my magick and my reclaiming of it gave me the very words that freed Kerri'tarre. And that is on me for having been so easily fooled in spite of all."

"I know." Nagarath sat on the end of the bed, defeated, the fire gone out of him. "I know, magpie."

"You did? About Kerri'tarre, I mean?"

Closing his eyes, Nagarath nodded his assent. "I suspected. Dover all but confirmed it for me, but I hoped that I was wrong. I ought to have known from the moments after the mirror's shattering—when you managed some rather unusual magicks to aid in our escape. What I did not know was whether or not you knew. And at the time, I myself was rather distracted by my attempts to not merely bleed to death from my injury."

His eyes darted to hers. "You are not to blame for this, Liara."

"Oh, but I—"

"No. You are not." He waited until her gaze was fully upon him before continuing. "The words to free Kerri'-tarre, they were not a normal spell, were they? More like an invocation? Probably involving something which resembled an offer but not so obviously as to cue the mage who made the spell?"

Liara nodded.

"There." Nagarath smiled sadly. "Not your fault. It was a trap. Any wizard who freed Khariton would have had his einatus thrust upon them. The bargain was in the spell, not in the heart that made the magick. Without a source of magick in which to hide himself—without a living mage—Kerri'tarre would simply disappear into thin air and trouble us no more. He designed his escape to help himself, giving thought to no one else.

"You were tricked. Plain and simple. All of us were. That is what he does. Remember the legends of the mirror, the pride and ambition and wilfulness it created in those who have gazed upon it. Look at Amsalla and . . ." Here Nagarath stopped, blushing. He substituted, "Look at Anisthe and me."

"But that's not fair!"

"It is old magick. The kind which wizards used before the Laws. And it was rarely fair."

"Before the . . . ?" The thought was too ludicrous to contemplate. The Laws were magick, so far as Liara understood.

Heartened by Nagarath's return to himself, his intelligent, thoughtful self, Liara came and sat by his side. The memory of his blazing hatred for Domagoj still echoed in her chest. It settled there to tremble alongside her own pain. She ventured, "I think Anisthe might have known. About Khariton and my magick."

At that, Nagarath's jaw again twitched with anger. He said, "Yes. That would explain his feeling utterly safe within Amsalla's hands, since she clearly wanted Kerri'-tarre to be alive and well, particularly in light of her having told me that Merlin has it in for her."

"So Merlin—?"

"Is unfindable, Liara. More so even than Khariton's Mirror. And therefore it is up to us and what wits we can gather to try to find a way out of this mess." He paused and, eyeing her, hastily hid away his anguish. "We will solve this, my— We will solve this, Liara."

K rešimir stayed outside the archmage's home when next he returned from distributing Merlin's prophecies. Sitting himself in the shade and settling his back against the wall near the door, he kept his eyes on the distant tree line. He did not expect pursuit, but he would have welcomed it, for he had grown to crave action.

The likelihood of anything like that occurring, however, was slim. According to Merlin, no more than a handful of people had ever stumbled upon his prison during the thousand years in which he had been trapped. He himself was not certain as to what kept folks from discovering him. It had to be something in the magick, of course.

Even so, the archmage had found ways around the limitations imposed by his curse. His semi-regular contact with Amsalla was one example. Krešimir another, though that particular exception had been forced upon him.

It seemed that, if Merlin intended specific contact with a wizard, he could maintain one or two outside contacts at a time. He had, apparently, been friends with the mage whom Anisthe, Amsalla, and Nagarath studied under. To Krešimir's mind, that wasn't particularly a compliment—either to Merlin's taste in association or Nagarath's. In fact the whole question of this Amsalla DeBouverelle bothered him. From what Merlin had said of her, she was disloyal, dishonest, and borderline reprehensible. Surely the archmage could have found a more suitable person to be his ears, eyes, and hands within the wider world.

To that end, Amsalla now made a point of contacting the archmage with greater regularity. Her reports were full of excuses, sniveling explanations of why she continued to remain invisible to scrying, and complaints against just about everyone who had crossed her path. She had ensconced herself within the court of King Louis XIV and was finding her upward mobility checked by some priest from Venice. Anisthe she was having held on charges of witchcraft and vandalism—reportedly in a bid to ensure that nothing untoward happened to him and, therefore, Liara.

Krešimir was at least glad to note that Merlin did not quite take stock in the woman's words. He had continued to post his prophecies far and wide in hopes that Nagarath would realize that his message had been received and that the archmage awaited them should he and Liara attempt to reach him via the same sorcery by which he had sent Dvigrad's woodsman.

The horrid sensation that he was doing nothing grew

daily for Krešimir. What he would really have liked would have been to fly to France on the wings of magick and confront Amsalla personally. Force her at wand point to return to Merlin and seek out Nagarath and Liara without delay. Time, as the archmage had said, was no longer on their side with regards to Khariton. Even at the doorway to faerie, even hid away from the world as they were in this lonely hawthorn hut, the presence of Kerri'-tarre could be felt.

The prophecies which Krešimir posted were now met with questions and a curious partiality. Archmage Khariton had devoted followers, not having set one foot on English soil himself, without having cast even one spell. Merlin, too, claimed to have sensed a similar shift in loyalties in regions more far-flung. The Republic of Venice, only recently a center of anti-magick sentiments, now demonstrated a different sort of preoccupation with the Art. Even France, site of so much trouble for Magus DeBouverelle, fairly hummed with the ancient wizard's name.

And so the prophecies were cast far and wide. Merlin? He fought for magick's continued self-sovereignty. Whereas Krešimir fought for Liara, as he always had.

And somewhere at the middle of it all: Nagarath.

Krešimir closed his eyes against the consideration that, in the end, Liara might choose mage over man. His heart clenched. But, just as he might go to Amsalla and force her to give Merlin more than empty words and promises, he could not make Liara love him.

What Krešimir had left was to believe. He had to

believe that his regard for her, his steadfast love would win in the end.

"O, deep sea,
    all my joys.
    The flower of my youth
    floats on you to me.

"In my grief
    I can't bear,
    I'll ask after you
    from the sailors I see.

"Because, you're my rose
    planted in the heart.
    Blessed is that hero
    who are you destined for.

"You are destined for me—"

Hope faltered. Krešimir choked on the line and found he could not continue with the last verse. If he could restore Dvigrad, would it matter to Liara? She had not loved those people, that town. Nor had they demonstrated any particular fondness for her. But it was home.

"I would give you anything, you know. Anything you ask of me." Rising, Krešimir left his vow to the breeze and the sunshine and turned to enter Merlin's home.

CHAPTER NINE

Nagarath could not—dare not—sleep. Rather, he lay in bed staring up at the ceiling and pretending, for Liara's sake, that he slept. Their fifth inn in as many nights, they were probably halfway to Little Larkhill.

Little Larkhill. A haven of rest and safety . . . and books. They could not get there fast enough, so far as Nagarath was concerned. But using the cinnabar stone for transport was out of the question.

He hadn't the strength to safely use it anyhow. Not unless Nagarath dare lessen his vigilance against Liara. For all that she pretended, for his sake, that her fits of forced sorcery had subsided, he could tell Khariton's shadow clouded her magick. A growing storm, Nagarath had to admit, at last, that the archmage's eventual triumph had never been a question of "if" but of "when."

Nagarath hoped to control the "where" of it.

Oh, if only they had not found themselves so far from the Limska Draga valley and Parentino.

And if only he could sleep. He well knew that he would soon be useless if he were not allowed to rest.

But two nights ago Nagarath had awoken to find Liara attempting to leave the room, her eyes wide and blank and seeming to glow with a silver light of their own. With a throat gone dry from fear, he had bid his apprentice return to bed and silently thanked the powers above for the small miracle of ill-oiled door hinges and creaky floor boards. For the rest of the night, he had sat up, setting his staff into the crook of his arm and propping his cheek against it in an effort to stay awake.

So, really, he had suffered no more than three sleepless nights. His was a small complaint.

Closing his eyes for a moment, he breathed deep, trying to gauge the hour. Morning would dawn soon. With it, Nagarath would rise and feign calm, assuring his little magpie that all was well and watch impassively as she rendered herself into a near-incantate state under the curse he had taught her. Temporary disarmament. Borrowed time.

For still, in his mind's eye, Nagarath imagined he could see the face of Archmage Kerri'tarre.

Khariton. Poison in Liara's soul.

Shadowy hands reached out from a mirror of inky blackness. Hateful laughter bubbled up out of the glassy surface. That smile, it promised ruin. Defeat. Heartache. Eyes blazing like molten silver, the praecantator's smile cracked wide, and he hissed his challenge. *I know your secrets, magus.*

Looking to Liara, to where she slept in the other bed, Nagarath pursued inner calm.

His magpie was fine. He could not—could not!—see it any other way. He watched his apprentice's peaceful face, lost amongst the dark forest of her loosed hair, twitch in response to a dream. And then those dark branches seemed to close over her. He watched for a moment longer, unbelieving and uncomprehending, until Liara gave vent to a muffled scream. Struggling, her arms flailed uselessly.

Leaping up, Nagarath ran to her aid. His fingers found not hair, but knotty wood that seemed to grow and writhe. Calling his magick, he attempted a spell. The words stuck in his throat. Liara screamed again, chilling his heart. This time, his hands gained leverage against the pressing peril, and Nagarath simply applied his strength. The branches parted—

—And came for him, instead. Tendrils of hair wrapped themselves around Nagarath's wrists, and yet he did not let go, seeking Liara's face amongst the shadowy tangle.

The branch in his hand pulled away. Setting his jaw, he held tight in the tug of war.

He awoke.

In the close-pressing darkness, Nagarath could see that a shadowed figure stood over his bed. Liara. He could both feel and see her magickal signature. It sparkled and snapped around her, uncontainable. Her hands: they gripped the cinnabar staff. Her eyes: empty and gleaming with an eerie silvery light.

Gripping tight, instinct saving him where foresight failed, Nagarath tried to fight his apprentice without having to affect any spells. There was no telling how his magick would come up against hers or how she herself might react. Holding steady in the silent contest, praying the fit would pass swiftly—*before I'm forced to do anything drastic*—he felt Liara's grip go slack through the wood of the stave.

Liara slumped to the floor, and Nagarath hurried to her side.

"I did it again. Didn't I?"

Nagarath could hear the tears in Liara's question, and he lied. He had to. To protect her. To help her fight the evil that strove to quell her spirit and use her against herself. To protect his own hopes. Each word amésos to his heart. A mage's last resort, indeed. "No, Liara. You were merely sleepwalking."

"But I—" Liara's gaze flicked over the scene. The cinnabar staff abandoned on the bed. The blankets and sheets half pulled to the floor in Nagarath's haste to see to her. His own tense fears that, try as he may, he knew he could not hide completely.

"Do you trust me?" Nagarath's voice cracked.

"Sleepwalking." Liara did not believe him, that much was obvious. But she took his silent warning and plea without argument. "Thank you. For . . . waking me."

Nagarath nodded silently, knowing he could not trust another lie to pass from his lips unchallenged. He watched, unmoving, as Liara rose and returned dutifully to her bed, whispering anew the hex that bound her mage's soul. A moment later, he winced under the weight of her gentle plea, "Sleep, Nagarath."

He would. He would sleep when he had solved the problem of Kerri'tarre warring for his apprentice's magick. Nagarath would rest when he saw Liara safe at last. And until then? He would protect her. Even if it killed him.

~

Liara knew that Nagarath lied to her. Yet, somehow, the realization did not spark in her the disgust it once might have. In many ways, it seemed a kindness. A kindness on the same order as teaching her a way to curse herself free of magick. Antithetical integrity. But why?

The thought accompanied furtive tears as Liara turned over in her bed and waited for sleep to come.

You did not get my prize, Liara.

The whispered words came swiftly to her mind. Turning in place, Liara saw that she stood once more in the home of the king of France. The Hall of Mirrors was complete. Daylight streamed through the long bank of windows along her right-hand side, bathing the room in an eerie warm glow. A dream light. Casting her eyes over the archways with their multitude of mirrors, Liara sought a glimpse of the speaker whose voice she recognized all too easily. Kerri'tarre.

I am everywhere. I am in your mind and soul. In glancing into the mirror you will see naught but yourself, Liara.

She looked in any event. Fragmented Liaras reflected back at her, more true to how she felt than a single, pure image might have.

We had a bargain. The praecantator's voice shivered

out from the heart of Liara's magick. The face in the mirror frowned, testing the lie. Her own desperate denial reflected back at her, and Khariton chuckled. The sneaky, sliding sound echoed in the long room. *You extended the offer with your magick and then pulled away. Unfair, magpie. The bargain was made. You freed me from my prison, fairest.*

"What do you want?" Her challenge came out wavery and thin and not at all as she had imagined.

Besides my war on the artless and a reckoning with my oldest friend and enemy? Besides the cinnabar stone and the magick it proclaims?

Liara clutched her chest. She could feel Kerri'tarre smile. The cinnabar stone. An impossible request, and he knew it. He pressed. *Come. Walk with me, child.*

Her feet moved of their own volition, and Liara slowly proceeded down the long, sunlit corridor. Images shimmered within each mirrored alcove. The heart of her magick knew it as scrying but on a scale such as she had never imagined possible. King and courts, the seat of the doge's power in Venice, soldiers' barracks, and torture chambers—all flickered into brilliance within their individual panes of silvered glass. And here and there, a spark of the Art and of a signature matching, she believed, Khariton's own.

And then a return to the Hall of Mirrors as Liara had last seen it. Broken and dark, marred by rifle-balls and shattered ruin. Kerri'tarre spoke: *The pieces may be swept up and hid from men's eyes. But the power is loosed. Each shard, each piece. If you were to reassemble them, you would see as I see. The greater picture of my—our —ambition.*

"Revenge."

If you would like to give it so base a label, certainly. But it is more than that. It is an accounting of past and present wrongs.

"And if I do not want this?"

You are an aurenaurae, else I would not be saying 'pretty please.' What is it you want, Liara?

That same question Khariton had posed to her while she had stood before his unshattered mirror. And what did she want? Truly.

Your choice now becomes whether or not you finish what you have begun—and for that I will give you anything you desire. Or, you can be swallowed up. As I said, the mirror has been broken. Your einatus is already mine. So which will it be?

Angry shouts and the sharp reports of rifles being fired echoed in the opulent room. But this time the memory did not play out as before. As in the way of dreams, everything came topsy-turvy and in the wrong order. The mirror was broken before the guards' firing upon Liara and her companions. In her hands, Nagarath's cinnabar walking stick had returned to its form as a long, twisted stave. And Anisthe knelt swiftly at Liara's side, grasping her chin and whispering harsh words, "Find the book. Do not come back."

"Liara!"

Turning, Liara watched this time as one of the guards' bullets found its mark. Blood spread across Nagarath's chest, and he stumbled. Panicked, Liara reached out with her magick—with Kerri'tarre's magick—to heal her mage.

You see how easily I can make you mine, fairest? Turning, Liara saw Kerri'tarre standing behind her. In his hands he held the cinnabar stave. And a book.

'Find the book.'

Heart pounding, Liara sat upright in bed. The last of her nightmare fled with the dying spark of her magick, leaving her alone and cold in the pre-dawn half-light of the inn's room. Khariton. Biding his time in the heart of her magick. She imagined she could hear the ghost of the archmage's laughter and the fading whisper of his words.

'Look at him, Liara. Look at Nagarath.

'In magick, you can never have friends. Only rivals. It all comes down to power. It always has. Look to the Laws if you do not believe me. Look to the Laws . . .'

She looked over to where Nagarath lay upon the other bed, taking comfort in the steady rise and fall of his chest. A part of her could feel the smooth wood of the cinnabar staff in her hands, the tense resistance by the mage to give it up. Sleepwalking. Bah. Nagarath likely knew how unsolvable Liara's problem was and still comforted, still promised, and still cared. At hazard to himself.

But then, Liara considered Kerri'tarre's position. He obviously had not counted upon the strength of an aure-naurae. Add to that Nagarath's wit and extraordinary knowledge.

'What is it you want?'

A new tear tracked its way down Liara's cheek, and she angrily brushed it away.

The sleeper across the room shifted. Liara promptly

became aware of two tired gray eyes staring directly into hers.

"Good morning, Liara."

"Good morning, Nagarath."

The wizard sat upright in bed. He never took his eyes from her, and Liara found herself fighting a shiver.

'What is it you want, Liara?' The echo of Kerri'tarre's question and her heart's answer to such. Liara felt her cheeks heat in a blush, and she shrank under the covers. Her embarrassment prompted Nagarath's own, and he looked away. While he changed, she busied herself with blocking off her magick. More whispered curses in the dark.

And in that darkness, Anisthe's fervent words to her: *'Find the book.'* They rose again in her mind, a shield against Kerri'tarre's threat. And with it, a realization. Anisthe had not asked her to find the book, so much as he had demanded she find The Book.

'It is old magick, Liara. The kind which wizards used before the Laws. And it was rarely fair.'

'Before the Laws?'

A distant memory sounded. Something from some time back in Parentino's great library; some mention of a book in which the Laws of Magick were writ. Could such a thing truly exist? And if so, should that not be something kept far from Khariton's hands? Perhaps in Nagarath's wide scholarship he would have an answer. Liara vowed to ask him before the day progressed too far.

The incident in the nighttime did not come up while the two of them readied themselves for the road. A part of Liara had the audacity to hope it as much a dream as had been her conversation with Kerri'tarre. But then, Nagarath would settle a sympathetic and wary look upon her when he thought she didn't notice and wreck such bright possibilities.

It was midmorning before Liara found both opportunity and courage to ask her question. By then they had secured a coach to the next inn. Nagarath seemed too spent to walk, and she welcomed the peace and comfort that riding would afford.

Unfortunately, Liara found her way blocked by a newspaper. Her mage was reading again. Even the nonsense. Even eight inches from Liara's nose in a stuffy close-pressing carriage. With little else to do, she craned her neck and read over his shoulder as best she could, taking illicit comfort in the closeness it afforded.

"They're a hoax."

Nagarath made no reply save to smooth the paper and frown ever so slightly.

Liara tried again. "You said yourself that they're not real, Nagarath. I mean, sure they're in the newspapers and all, but they aren't genuine. Are they?"

"They are not prophecy, no," he spoke at last, still not turning to face her. "But I believe Merlin's hand is in them."

"Someone using Merlin's name."

"No, Merlin himself. Well, after a fashion." Nagarath sighed. He turned heavy eyes on her as he said, "The archmage fell afoul of Vivien's magick in the year 545. Yes, some legends say 'entombed beneath the hawthorn' or in a cave or some such. I suppose that's one way of terming such an imprisonment."

"Imprisonment!"

"Vivien's spell was irreversible and of a kind long forgotten. Ascribed to the fairies nowadays for how impossible such acts are by today's standards of magick, the sorcery was Merlin's, and the secrets of such were lost with him."

Fire danced at the back of Liara's eyes, and she shoved it down. *Not here.*

"I dreamt of a book last night. The Rishon Kesem." Liara hadn't meant to blurt it out, but there it was, a question not phrased as a question, lying on the floor of the carriage between them.

"It's a—"

"I know what you mean, Liara." Still he did not look at her. He didn't seem angry. Upset, perhaps. Or lost in the past, more like. Her last theory was confirmed when he continued, "Another of Anisthe's obsessions. One clouded by myth and legend but encouraged by . . . others. A book penned by Kerri'tarre and Merlin in the time before they became estranged and each met their separate fates at the hand of magick. With its spells, one might be able to accomplish what Anisthe had long desired: circumvention or outright change to the Laws of Magick."

Now Nagarath did grow angry. When his eyes met Liara's, she found herself shrinking back from the blaze of emotion in his gaze. "You do realize that, in seeking this . . . answer . . . of his, Anisthe nearly killed us all."

Quailing under Nagarath's wrathful mistrust, Liara decided she could well be playing into Kerri'tarre's hands by asking further.

'Find the book. Do not come back.' Anisthe's words. The words of an enemy.

"Besides, the Rishon Kesem is long lost. Lost along with Merlin some time after Kerri'tarre's imprisonment in the mirror. Anisthe, like any other reasonably learned wizard, would know this. Which either makes him a liar —again—or means that he has discovered that I . . ."

In the heavy silence that followed, Liara feared she had pushed too far.

"Liara. Is your magick locked away at present?"

Nagarath's sudden question made Liara jump. She whispered the words to the curse and then nodded.

He crooked a finger and leaned close. Sucking in a breath, he dared, "The cinnabar stone. It— It has an imperfection. Remind me to show it to you at our next lodging."

"And only when Khariton is unable to use my magick or my eyes and ears."

"Precisely. For if he knew . . ." Nagarath stopped and again grew pensive. "On second thought, forget that I ever mentioned it."

Liara cocked an eyebrow and waited, implacable in all the ways she knew would spark a lecture from the man.

Crossing his arms, Nagarath settled his back against the bench. He smiled and said, "Ah, my magpie apprentice. If you must know. Master Cromen was tricksy. More so than you would ever imagine. You have felt the power of the cinnabar stone, suffered its rough intrusion upon your own Art. A force. Raw and nigh unfathomable magick.

"That is but a fraction of its worth. And you are but peering at its true nature through a keyhole. The archmage understood the risks of openly carrying about such a treasure and so found a way to limit its power and quiet its voice, lest someone like Anisthe learn of it and come looking. As it is, the stone begs for use. The magick cries out to any and all wizards who dare listen."

"A keyhole." Liara believed she had caught on to the aim of her mage's words. "Implying, therefore, a key."

"Correct. If you were to examine the face of the stone, you would find that it bears a rather telling crevice. A sliver of stone which has been pointedly removed for safekeeping. And thus divided . . ." He waved a hand.

Liara could not help herself. She had, after all, worked hard to memorize the Laws a long time ago in a place rather far away. She dutifully recited, "Law The Second of Magicked Artifacts: Damage to either the physical or magickal condition of a Magicked Artifact will affect the outcome of Magicks performed through said Artifact."

"Correct. And so the other piece of the stone—your so-called key, Liara—is hidden. In a book, actually."

"And hence your concerns over Anisthe's words to me." Liara hung her head. "I hadn't meant to force your confidence. But, Nagarath! How could a stone be a key hidden in a book?"

She had her answer soon as the words had left her mouth. Liara exclaimed, "It's a spell."

Nagarath's bright-eyed silence was confirmation enough.

"But it still doesn't tell me . . . Cinnabar stone.

Cinnabar . . . Vermilion! Cromen used the missing fragment to make a vermilion ink, yes? The spell is written in that ink and therefore locks away the power of the stone while still allowing it to be made whole, should the need arise."

The wizard confirmed the truth of it with a nod of his head.

"As I said, the archmage knew that there was little chance of hiding the stone for long unless its power were drawn off on occasion. With his death, the logical place for it to go was to myself, who had vowed to both keep an eye on and stop Anisthe if necessary. Neither Master Cromen nor I had anticipated that, by the time of his passing, we would have so completely lost track of our confederate. But then, with my long interest in the scholarly, the keyspell's security was practically assured."

"Nothing in a book is safe around you, Nagarath. I've seen your—" With a shriek, Liara's eyes met the mage's. Her hands flew to her mouth. "I destroyed your library. Oh, Nagarath, I destroyed the key!"

"Oh, come, Liara. You think I would be so daft as to work at cross-purposes to Cromen's foresight?" Nagarath let out one of his sharp, startling laughs. "Clever as my teacher was, you have not seen all of my tricks yet. The book is as secure as I can render it. You have not ruined all, magpie. Not near."

'Not ruined all.' The discordant jumble of Liara's guilt and fear threatened to overtake her anew. For she had ruined all. Allied with Anisthe. Destroyed Parentino. Apurpose and with a heart bent towards murder. And though she had grown beyond that, finding hard truths

about herself in the process, Liara wondered if, perhaps, her magick would always wend its way back to the darkness from which it had sprung. For even though Nagarath claimed that her horrid arrangement with Khariton was not completely her fault, the fact remained: it had happened, and they must face what was to come from it. Liara fully believed Nagarath ought not have the burden of guarding himself—guarding the stone, with its awesome power—from the likes of her. Oh, if only he hadn't told her!

CHAPTER TEN

Liara walked a path of silence. Silence and pent up tears. Terror. Unspoken horror over what she had unwittingly brought upon herself.

But was that even really true?

Her freeing Kerri'tarre was no trap, no trickery. It had only been weakness on Liara's part. Khariton had promised Liara her revenge, had promised power. He had promised Liara her heart's every desire. And in exchange? She had given all.

And so the tears she withheld were not out of pity for herself but remorse. Regret that she was not a stronger wizard. A bitter and all too vivid realization that she was not a better person.

She understood also, at long last, Nagarath's lies to her in Limska Draga. It was a lesson she'd only half-learnt at the king's court. How deception did not necessarily work in service to conceal one's own misdeeds but, rather, acted as a shield in the service of caring. A lie, shelter set by an individual's regard for another. Protection. Protection he offered her even now after she had proven to be so terribly undeserving of it.

Protection that gave rise to new guilts. Again, Liara's understanding of her mage was furthered. Her actions and inactions—his too—were yet guided by fear.

Liara had learned that to be a wizard was to be afraid.

Yet her mage said nothing. And, in the aftermath of the incident in the nighttime, they enjoyed several quiet days. Things had, in some ways, ceased to feel as though Liara and Nagarath were on the run and more like they had merely decided to embark on a pleasant journey together.

That is, if one ignored the drawn look that had begun to haunt Nagarath's eyes. And their overall exhaustion and simple annoyance over the fake sorcery filling the land. And Liara's continued routine of separating herself from her Art upon waking each morning. This after running from Kerri'tarre in her dreams all the night through.

The fact of the matter was that Liara was growing tired. Tired of fighting herself and tired of their adventure. Which left Nagarath the task of keeping both their spirits up, something he was oddly suited for, now that it had come to it.

For once in Liara's life, it felt good to be petted and protected. For through it, she could be close to Nagarath without falling solely to the guilt of her passions. And with it, she could feel his regard for her all the more.

Nagarath. Her impatient, worried wizard.

Like her, Nagarth would not say aloud what was

wrong with Liara's magick, opting to keep his concerns well to himself and saving up all his smiles for her.

As for all that . . .

Liara could drown herself in Nagarath's devotion. For if the initiating affection came from outside her ken, she felt safe indulging in her own fondness. Secretly. It remained the one bright spot in the darkness through which she stumbled and made such thoughts all the more enticing.

Letting his actions guide her fancies, Liara lived for Nagarath's solicitous touch on the elbow, the mage's gentle bending down to peer into her eyes, the brush of his magick against her own emptied and aching soul. She had almost gotten used to hurting. Almost. Nagarath's regard for her almost filled the spot where her magick had been. Almost.

And only almost because she could not meet it. Not actually. She did not dare. She had lost herself to magick. Could she lose herself to her mage? She wanted to. Desperately. But . . . fear. Fear of a flavor she would rather endure than her terror of what Kerri'tarre could do if he were to gain full control of her magick.

But fear is fear, and it stopped her short. It kept Liara from saying the words that would most certainly ruin their companionship, their friendship, and lead them down a path Nagarath could not walk with her.

She'd seen what sort of woman Nagarath dallied with. She knew the type that attracted him. Liara was, what? His silly little magpie, his ward—offspring of his lifelong enemy—and not . . . not worthy of his attentions on that level. In some ways, her old ambitions of sorcery and revenge, of renown as a powerful wizard were less lofty than the reach of Nagarath's love.

And yet, there was something deep and real and—and, therefore, dangerous—an undercurrent of passion that surely went both ways. Or was Liara merely turning wishes into hopes?

She was falling for him. Had long since. And there was no stopping it. Just hiding it. And she didn't want to. Wasn't sure she even had the strength. Not without her magick.

Liar and coward. You're just afraid of yourself, of rejection, of feeling the way you felt when you turned the corner in Versailles and saw two people—

Shuddering, Liara stopped the thought. She couldn't go to that memory.

So she forced her mind there. Forced herself to look. *Look at it! That is why you don't indulge in such thoughts, girl. What are you to him? A companion. A burden.*

It was getting to be that Liara might say the words so easily as look at him. *I love you, Nagarath.* The sentiment threatened to bubble out of her as easily had her magick. And as destructively. It would wound her, it would wound him, were the feelings not the same on Nagarath's end.

And how dare she hope? After everything.

And yet the signs were there, were they not? Could not Liara trust her eyes, her ears? Certainly she could not rely upon her traitorous heart. It had a mind of its own. It wanted to beat close by Nagarath's, making its own sweet music. It wanted to curl up next to the mage and simply be.

She was in deep trouble—deep danger. Far more than she had ever been with Krešimir. That had been a safe love. She could depend on it to either work out or not. Cleanly. Without shattering her in the process. Which begged the question: had it even been love? She had certainly thought it such. Her and her love-thirsty heart and soul.

And what of how she felt for Nagarath? Was it love or something else? Love should not feel like pain. It shouldn't ache. This deep and powerful longing. She pined for him when he was but an arm's length away. She wept inwardly when he spoke even a word to her, just for the sweetness of his voice.

How could love feel that way?

And through such angst, the persistent shadow of Khariton. Yes, far easier to lose herself to the agony of unrequited love than to the darkness that lived in the back of her mind and whispered nightmares into her soul as she slept. Kerri'tarre's memories could outrun her, even in dreams. She often could remember them upon waking. A book, burning with unfathomable power. Wizards being tested, tortured, and executed. A wall of glass that kept her captive, silencing her tongue and stopping her ears while yet allowing her to see the world on the other side. Harsh incantations in a language Liara did not understand but knew in her heart to be magick.

A stone, blood red and poison to the touch, calling to her einatus.

This last haunted her more than the rest. It made her

vigilant. Careful. And very much afraid that she might hurt he who tortured her with his well-meant kindness. Her Nagarath.

"Liara?"

She stopped without so much as looking up at the wizard. She did not dare. Liara swayed on her feet, newly recalling her exhaustion. Nagarath, he too had to be so tired of walking, walking, walking.

"Liara. I—" Nagarath's hesitation forced Liara's gaze upon him. He smiled wanly. "How are you feeling?"

She shrugged. *Empty. Helpless. Stupid.*

"Liara, I— We— I am hoping you'll forgive me my having not been forthcoming with you as to our destination."

"Your ever-mysterious place of safety. You mean your home." Liara smirked, enjoying the wizard's puzzlement. "You told me you're from England."

"Did I?"

The night you sang to me and played the cindra, and I first wondered if I loved you. Liara blushed, substituting her thought with the words, "Yeah. Once. A long time back."

"Oh. Well, then!" Nagarath's nonplussed reaction stole from him whatever speech he'd planned on making to her. Instead he stood upon the path, mussing his hair and gazing over the countryside. He seemed rather nervous. "I was beginning to be rather unsure if the— If the efforts of keeping your magick under control had done anything to make you forget such inconsequential details."

Liara raised her eyebrows to Nagarath's "inconsequential details" and managed a reassuring smile. She realized that her mage was not nervous so much as tense. It brought to mind her own home of Dvigrad and her tumultuous time within its walls. Nothing there had been trivial. Not while she had lived there. And certainly not after having brought doom upon its citizens. Home. Liara couldn't conceive of a home that didn't come tainted by pain and misery. It certainly didn't conjure concepts of a "place of safety."

Still, the path became further delineated from the wilds by small stone guides built along either edge. Though not a well-trod path, the effect was charming. The trees grew thicker here, allowing Liara to feel as though she'd finally gotten herself away from prying eyes. The hike continued forward along the gently curving path, Liara's pulse quickening to match her wizard's steps. Ahead, a low wall, heavily overgrown on the further side, put out its own air of "don't you dare."

Nagarath dared. Well, at least he did after trying the gate and finding it rusted fast. Liara raised her eyebrows at the mage's funny little smile as he hopped over the stone fence.

Misgivings growing, she allowed herself to be helped over.

"A rather unorthodox way to cross into your property, don't you think?" she ventured, finding her question met with that same curious smile.

"Come." He gestured she follow, again starting off along the path with his overly rapid pace. He seemed to her an odd mix of someone both wholly at ease and incredibly apprehensive. In a moment, Liara saw why.

Through the trees she could see the building that graced the grounds. Topped by a square-toothed crown of battlements and marked with countless arched windows and doors, the imposing edifice seemed to bring the surrounding into haughty subjugation. It was very unlike Nagarath in almost every way possible. Liara almost felt she ought to bow to the building, silly as the instinct seemed. Long high walls, gardens, a pond, and even a cottage completed the picture. Coming closer, she could see the main path off to the right, the grand entrance to the home yet out of view.

She slowed, her eyes on the rows of dark windows. Nagarath noticed her lagging steps and returned to Liara's side. He held out a hand, reassuring her with yet another smile.

A shot rang out, and both Liara and Nagarath ducked, the wizard springing between her and the threat without hesitation.

From the woods stepped a portly man of advancing age. In his arms he held a smoking rifle, his hands making rapid adjustments so as to reload, though he did not take his eyes from the two trespassers. He called out, "Not a step more. The archmage is not at home, you understand? How many times do we need to tell you folk that we—"

Liara could feel Nagarath's caution dissolve. He, in fact, looked as though he were about to burst into a fit of laughter as he threw his arms wide in greeting. "It's me!"

"Master Na— Mary. Mary, get out here!" Face flushing a deep red, the stranger moved as if to run forward. Quickly changing his mind, he glanced to the weapon in his hand and flushing deeper—if that were even possible!—laid it aside. He cried out again, "Mary!"

Before Liara could get so much as a glance in that direction, a scream erupted from the cottage, and the door flew open. Jumping at the sound, she turned to see that Nagarath had broken out into a loping run towards a short, round little woman who'd emerged from the cozy building. Squealing her delight, the woman embraced the gangly mage, laughing and scolding all at once.

"Oh, sir. I thought it might be you comin' back. All these big trunks bein' dropped at the manor door. An' nobody reads like you do. Ben didn' believe me, the old skeptic. But I says, 'Must be 'im, I bet.' Who else would it be? Buying up half that nation's lit'rature. Lord love ya, whatever happened to your face, dear?" Mary leaned back from her hug and forcibly turned Nagarath's chin to and fro, peering at the long-healed damage and tut-tutting.

"I tell you, that calling of your'n. Dangerous. You ought to settle down in peace and quiet— Oh!" Mary interrupted her own scolding, having at last caught a glimpse of Liara standing gape-mouthed on the path. "An' who's this one?"

She gestured wildly for Liara to approach, fat arms wagging with the exertion.

Liara curtsied awkwardly, shooting Nagarath daggers in one quick glance. "Liara, mum."

"Mrs. Hertford, dear. Though you can call me Mary." The woman, Mrs. Hertford, didn't wait for invitation. She delivered Liara a crushing hug before dragging her into the cottage alongside Nagarath.

The diminutive door to the quaint little cottage was such that the wizard had to duck as he entered. Mr. Hertford followed behind, huffing his florid apologies.

Within moments Liara found herself seated with a mug of hot tea and a buttered scone, not entirely sure how it all came about. Nagarath managed the forcible hospitality better and stood by the hearth with cup and plate. His eyes twinkled at Liara's bewilderment while Mary fussed over the state of his hair, his clothes, and his thinness.

Mr. Hertford stumped about in the background, his presence made secondary under the glow of his wife's bright cordiality. But Liara could tell he was pleased at Nagarath's presence from the grin which had spread itself across his swarthy features and stayed.

Liara's own nerves were quieting as if by magick, and she briefly wondered if Mary was a hedgewitch, glancing about the homey cottage to look for the proper signs. Her thoughts were interrupted by further apologies and explanations from Mr. Hertford for his alarming greeting. "They've been coming up on us more and more, stirred up by these papers. I thought you one of them, what with the hooded cloaks and all. Merlin's Prophecies. Bah."

"Archmage." Nagarath's rumination came with his typical pensive chin rub. His eyes regained their focus long enough to cast their reproof. "Nice touch, that. If a bit of an overreach. You know that I don't—"

"Bah," Ben repeated his rough dismissal and waved a careless hand at the wizard. He did not elaborate upon his un-asked-for exaggeration. Liara decided that she quite liked him and smiled quiet agreement.

"And how did you end up blowing about the country with our dear old Nathaniel, love?" Mary turned her bright disposition onto her other guest.

Liara nearly choked on her tea. *Nathaniel?*

Nagarath stepped forward, quiet rescue that Liara strained to hear but couldn't quite. Likely as he intended. A knowing look passed between the Hertfords. Liara's face heated in a blush. But whatever the mage said seemed to effect the change he'd desired. Mary fluttered past to collect plate and cup with an expert sweep of her arm. "Oh, you dears. I'm chattering away and keeping you from rest and quiet."

Liara again almost suspected magick of the woman save that, in her experience, Mrs. Mary Hertford was as un-magely a being as she had ever encountered. Wholly likable in spite of being everything that Liara abhorred. Sparing a glance to look around the cozy cottage, she felt a lump form in the back of her throat. Jealousy of a new and unexpected sort.

Liara found her gaze settling back on Nagarath. Brave if stupid, as it prompted yet another pointed glance between the Hertfords, she found she couldn't look away from him. He seemed so real and relaxed. Turned outward rather than inward. Fully familiar and himself, yet possessing a joy she had rarely, if ever, seen from him. Where Liara had a knot tightening in her chest, an outsider there but by the mage's good graces and at his endorsement, something had conversely loosed in the wizard. His shoulders, wrists, and jaw—he held himself with a different bearing. Even his laugh was different. Warmer. Freer.

But the sparkle in his eyes—same as it had always been. Noting Liara's thoughtful scrutiny, he fixed his warm gaze upon hers, then shifted to come stand close by. Liara practically melted in her chair when he gave her shoulder a gentle squeeze. She half-suspected he passed a spell onto her, save for the fact that the thrill which shook her soul felt nothing like magick.

"Beggin' your pardon, Master Nathan, but even with the comings and goin's up at the house, it's been so long since your last visit that things might not be aired as they ought. A year and a half, love. Too long away. Too long. We'd begun to worry." Mary's scolding carried an unmistakable note of sadness. Liara's heart went out to her even as she puzzled through the words. *A year and a half? Had Nagarath been sneaking visits here on the sly?*

The thought—tinged with that same new brand of jealousy—surprised Liara.

Since when had I any real claim on the wizard? Granted, Liara'd mostly had him all to herself since the day he had taken her to Parentino. She had come to rely upon it. The knife of her unanswered affections twisted deeper in her chest, and she cast her eyes downward.

As such, Liara hardly noted Nagarath's gentle guiding her to her feet and from the cozy cottage, nor the misty-eyed wishings of good night from the Hertfords. She needed to get out of there. The air was simply too thick with emotion for her to breathe properly.

Leaning on Nagarath's arm, Liara sucked the damp evening air, trying to center her thoughts. So many questions jostled for attention. She found herself fairly dizzy with the effort to keep them sorted.

All she knew was that she'd been brought into something joyful, something dear. And she hadn't a place in it, Nagarath or no.

Nagarath.

Another shock. And one that needed addressing. Liara met Nagarath's gaze and blurted, " 'Nathaniel.' Why does she call you that?"

A wave of guilt passed through the mage's face. Guilt tempered by a smattering of surprise. He looked at her, his mouth twitching with the same good humor that sparked in his dear gray eyes. He said simply, "That's my name, Liara."

CHAPTER ELEVEN

"I'm not English," Nagarath continued, as soon as they'd gained the path leading to the manor house. With the woods grown tight around them, they had some semblance of privacy for their discussion. He clarified, "I mean, I was born abroad and rarely came home—here. And you already know that the better part of my childhood was spent in the south of France under Master Cromen."

Liara nodded numbly, her gaze removed from his and set pointedly upon the grand home ahead. The wizard's country house was a well-seated stately building full of life and character. She wasn't mad at it or him or anything else. Yet something about it all added up to an uncomfortable hurt somewhere near her heart. She quickened her steps to escape the pain.

"But my name really is Nathaniel."

Again Liara nodded, dutifully acknowledging that she had heard him.

"Liara, stop." The mage halted on the path, gently

catching Liara by the shoulder so as to turn her face to his.

"More secrets? I thought we were past that," Liara accused, fighting foolish tears. "I thought I knew you. Look where we've been, what we've done together and yet you still—"

"Hid my own shameful past?"

"Shameful! That!" Liara pointed through the trees to the wizard's home.

"Yes," Nagarath whispered the word and turned from her. "Or near enough. I've run from everything. Everything save the consequences of Anisthe's actions in Limska Draga. And even that took me a good decade to face."

He took a shuddering breath, steadying himself before turning back to her, a sheepish smile on his face. "I just became so used to not talking about my life before . . . A bad habit for which I am sorry. And when I realized what a perfect hiding spot Little Larkhill would make, I remembered you knew next to nothing of who I was before I became Nagarath of Parentino. So, I thought I would surprise you."

He gestured feebly to the grand house, "Um . . . Surprise!"

Liara had to admit that if she were someone else and he were someone else, it would make for a wonderful surprise.

Except he really is someone else. She sat down on a nearby stump, head in her hands.

"You know I hate surprises," she scolded halfheartedly, knowing he'd been hoping for a better reaction than this awkward disappointment. "You know I need some sort of explanat—"

"And before this point had I any opportunity? What with dear Mrs. Hertford and your own classically open mind blocking me at every turn?" Nagarath raised an eyebrow, challenging her.

"Point taken. I'm sorry." And Liara was surprised to discover that, in fact, she was. Chin on her hands, she leaned forward. "Well? Tell me. Who is Master Nathaniel, and why haven't I ever heard of him?"

"To the house first. Refreshment and comfort awaits, and if there are any curious onlookers about, I would rather not discuss my affairs in public. Remember, I'm proper now." He held out his hand.

"Proper again," Liara corrected and took the offered arm with a small smile.

Put at ease, if but temporarily, Liara approached the home's entrance with something akin to excitement. At least, that was how she chose to read the quickening of her pulse and trembling of her fingers when Nagarath's hand closed gently over her own. Ignoring her distracted flush, she tried to concentrate on the mage's home—or Little Larkhill, as he had called it. The name was quaint but oddly fitting, even with the imposing facade of the building.

Massive and built of some sort of brownish stone, the manor stood proud and strong, despite being worn rough by time and the elements. Liara swept an appraising eye over the grounds and entrance, noting layout and masonry—France had educated her in so many startling ways—but knew the time to explore would come later. She allowed herself to be led to the kitchens.

Tapping her foot impatiently, Liara waited as Nagarath secured the makings of tea. At length he turned to the fireplace, swiping a finger across the hearth. "Swept clean and well-laid. Bravo, Mary." With one smooth motion, he lit the fire and secreted his wand, turning back to Liara. "All right. Where do I start?"

"How about 'I actually am Nathaniel.' " Liara raised an eyebrow at the mage.

Nagarath took a deep breath. "Yes. Well, then. You know that I studied the Magickal Arts under Cromen in France alongside Anisthe. Well, the archmage died, Liara. A few years before my apprenticeship was to be completed. Mere months before Anisthe's anticipated completion, though, by then, we were all of us not under his tutorage." He sighed, looking off into the past.

"Died? But how?"

"He was old. And he died. It happens." Nagarath frowned, eyes still focused inwards. "But it left our education incomplete. Anisthe who, as you know, was more martial in his interests, went on to become a war mage. He wielded his power alongside barons, then dukes, even princes eventually. He always wanted to have the ear of a king but never had that pleasure, as far as I can tell. His attacks on your valley were under the service of Francesco Erizzo, Doge of Venizia."

"I thought he was advisor for the Habsburg monarchy."

"Funny thing, Anisthe's loyalty. You'll get a different answer from him every day of the week." Nagarath grew bitter with the words. "Meanwhile, I came here, convinced I would never be a mage. Which was fine, really. I had educated myself. I had means, was coming home to the family seat in Britain and was considered well-off. Except the house was empty. My family—never big to begin with—was . . . gone. It is assumed that my father died on a trip to Venice. My mother, gone of a broken heart soon after.

"The dear Hertfords had stayed on to care for the place, knowing I had but a few years left of schooling. For reasons unknown, their letter detailing my family's situation never got to me. When I returned, they were surprised to learn that I was unaware of my parents' demise, assuming the timing of my return had something to do with it. I never corrected them, letting them assume I had purposefully abandoned my studies. While England may have a proud magickal lineage, magecraft was not exactly welcomed." He smiled. "As you can see they, uh, figured it out anyhow."

Nagarath leaned back in his chair, long arms stretched over his head. "So I rattled around hither and yon, always returning here before I discovered Anisthe's little mess in Limska Draga and came to the rescue."

Liara nodded, trying to picture scholarly Nagarath as a young rake traveling the known world. "And why Nathaniel?"

"That's my name, Liara." He blinked in surprise. "You didn't think my family named me 'Nagarath' did you? No more than Anisthe's parents named him 'Anisthe.' "

Fingering his jaw, he mused quietly, "Come to think

of it, I cannot recall his real name . . . We wizards like our sense of the dramatic."

"I'd have never guessed."

"And so choose fantastical, unique names to differentiate ourselves from the everyday artless." He smacked his palm to his head. "Silly me! I suppose you will need a name of power."

"Me? I've done nothing special."

"You defeated a powerful warlock. Rendered him incantate in his own home, if I recall."

"And then he got his power back. And, besides, I had help."

"Haven't we all," Nagarath winked. "Well?"

"Just Liara. Thanks."

"Mmm . . . Jusliara. Could strike fear into the hearts of thousands." Nagarath closed his eyes in mock rapture.

Liara laughed. "There's no living with you, you know."

"Then I suppose you'll not stay here long enough to need a tour?" He glanced at her slyly.

She smiled back.

Idiot. Of course she wanted a tour.

Not that she needed to tell him that.

Nagarath leapt to his feet, and Liara put aside her empty teacup. Dining; great hall; parlor. Liara's head spun by the time she had seen all three. Each with massive fireplaces and wood-paneled walls that rendered the rooms cozy in spite of their size, she needed the wizard to take her by the hand and lead her onward lest she simply ensconce in one of the windows that begged to be sat beside. The whole of it was homespun, grand,

and infinitely comfortable. All at once. How could Nagarath have ever left such a place on purpose?

Oh. That's how. Re-entering the main hallway Liara noticed, for the first time, the portraits frowning down from the walls. Though herself orphaned at a small age, she knew well what the glare of kindly-meant familial responsibility looked like. Still, Liara peered at the paintings, trying to determine whether she could see any resemblance to her wizard.

Nagarath urged her onward and upward. Liara's free hand trailed over the grand stairway's sturdy banister of carved wood, her other not daring to lessen her hold on Nagarath's hand. More rooms. Sitting. Music. Bedroom. Each were filled with the sort of things that she had come to associate with Nagarath—Nathaniel—only in much better shape than any found in Parentino. Bookshelves. Deep, wing-backed chairs. Oddities that she was only given half a glance at before being rushed into the next room and the room after that. And the room after that.

Distantly, Liara wondered at the library. Mrs. Hertford had mentioned books. In fact, based on the layout of the first floor—

Nagarath spoke, drawing her attention as he swept an arm in illustration. Liara found she stood in a room dominated by a stately canopied bed and matching furniture. "Mary, of course, readied this room in anticipation. But any of the others are easily made up."

Grinning, he dropped her hand to cross the room. Opening a door—hardly noticeable within the surrounding paneling—he beckoned. "I thought you might prefer this one for the other luxury it offers."

Taking her hands and drawing her forward, Nagarath presented to Liara a small tower with a hidden stairwell. Liara's pulse raced, for yes, he had saved the best for last: Little Larkhill's library.

Choked with the various deliveries that Mary had mentioned—*ah, there's the familiar disarray!*—it was still very obviously a fine collection.

'The key is hid away. In a book, if you must know.' Nagarath's words returned to haunt Liara. She shivered and thrust the memory aside.

The library had, of course, another massive fireplace flanked by some more comfy chairs à la Nagarath—Nathaniel. Ugh, would she ever get it right? But the truly magickal appearance lent the space came not from warmth or coziness or the quality of its collection, but from the windows that stretched over one entire wall. Dropping her mage's hand, Liara approached the massive casings, marveling at the intricate designs and smiling wholeheartedly at the strange rainbows they cast upon the carpeted floor.

She brought her gaze back upward, jumping as a sliding, shifting, shivery motion caught her gaze and held it. Liara watched, dumbfounded, as the picture formed by the many-hued panes rippled and changed, the figures therein seeming to move, if slowly.

It was, of course, magick. But an utterly frivolous use of the Art. Something in which she was unused to seeing Nagarath indulge. Loathe to take her eyes from the marvel, Liara flitted her attention sideways but for a moment.

"Stained glass. Well, the sort a wizard would have

were the wizard young and foolish and wasteful with his powers once upon a time. Every mage is allowed his one harmless frivolity. Do you like it?" Nagarath kept his explanation curt and so his question took Liara by surprise. He gently recalled her attention back on him with a touch to her elbow. Eyes sparkling, he regarded her intently.

Liara hardly dared breathe under the fervent assessment. As for answering him intelligently? Impossible with him looking at her so. Liara almost escaped back into the colorful windows. But then her mage spoke again.

"Whatever you want, magpie. Ask and you'll have it of me. Truly. No more secrets. Merlin? I will see to it that we find him. Anisthe's book? The Rishon Kesem? I'll—"

The shadow at the back of Liara's mind shifted, and she swayed dizzily. Nagarath steadied her. "We'll fix everything. We will."

"You know full well why you shouldn't tell me all. It's too much, Nagarath." Liara's protest felt weak and sounded as much. With it, the wizard closed himself off to her, turning so that he could drag a chair over for her use. "Even your real name. Not with him listening."

Khariton. Liara mouthed the word. She teared up in spite of her best efforts to the contrary. As if in her silence she could hide from the archmage. Kerri'tarre lived beside her heart, a shadow cast across her soul. There was no hiding anything from him.

Nagarath's eyes burned into her. Fear, worry, hope . . . all of it wrapped up in his never-ending compassion.

"You are my—" Nagarath choked and looked away.

"You are my apprentice. It is my responsibility to see you safe. And if it is within my power to do so, this is where it will happen. In this room. With these books and these hands."

"It is not your responsibility," Liara corrected gently. "This is now mine. I did it. I didn't know what I did, sure. But . . . but I did it all the same. I bargained with Kerri'-tarre. I listened to his words. Even with you and Anisthe and even Amsalla having warned me. I'm sorry."

Liara glanced around the library, feeling her magick rising within her and knowing she would again have to drain herself of her Art before much longer, wishing she could avoid bringing further sadness to such a lovely home.

'In magick, you can never have friends. Only rivals.'
Kerri'tarre's words.

Hardening her heart, Liara vowed to fight him. She would live to see the praecantator fail. She would die to do it, if that's what it took.

CHAPTER TWELVE

I n the end, Nagarath assigned Liara the master suite,
claiming that he didn't need the easy library access.
He would likely be hanging about the library at all
hours anyhow. Left in the cozy, if over-large room, Liara
struggled to refresh and make herself presentable.

Not that she wasn't, per se. They had been on the road
for days and had managed, at last, to procure some
replacements for the basic necessities they had lost when
leaving France. But to her, a careworn inn and crisply
drawn carriage over a dusty road demanded different
niceties than . . . Little Larkhill.

Goodness, just thinking of where she stood made
Liara's knees all wobbly. Nagarath's home. His inheri-
tance, really. A place where he went by a different name,
walked with a different bearing. She sank onto the edge
of the bed, the act itself a strange sort of indulgence. For
the bed was his. His and his. All of it.

She moved to rise, then stopped, concluding it a

stupid thing to be weird about. Liara had lived in Nagarath's home of Parentino for the better part of a year. Together they had travelled through all manner of places under all manner of unorthodox arrangements. Why should this place, of all places, set her head to spinning?

"Because how I feel for him has changed," Liara breathed the quiet confession. It had changed, and she couldn't undo it. Her fingers knotted the bed's blanket as she thought out loud, "What do I do now?"

Move forward, of course.

Beginning by not giving in to stupid hopes. After all, Liara had bigger concerns. Bigger fears and dangers. Both she and Nagarath did.

She still needed to burn off her magick, to start. For some indeterminate reason, she found that she didn't want to do it in the bedroom. Smoothing her skirts, Liara prodded the wall for the secret panel that led to the concealed stairwell.

Breath hitching, Liara returned to the main floor of the manor, intent on passing straight through the library and heading out to explore the grounds and bleed her magick there. But really, she just wanted to check on her wizard.

Nagarath was busy with his books—not putting them away, of course. Rather, he sat on the floor amongst the crates, sampling the texts at random. Liara hid her smile as she passed him.

'Find the book.' The ghost of Anisthe's charge chased her from the library.

Shaking, Liara drew a steadying breath in the quiet

hallway. How dare she. How dare she bring that unearned trust with her here to Little Larkhill, the enmity between the two men being what it was.

"And what of yours, Liara? Where is your hatred of the man?" Nagarath's accusation at Versailles, rephrased and given from Liara's own lips. Her mage had seen it. He had seen the—might she admit it?—the attachment rebuilding between herself and her progenaurae while at the king's party. Certainly the Laws tied her life to his for almost two years more. But, really, was her fascination mere magick? Or simply weakness of character?

It was instinct. Anisthe had changed. Well, near enough. Humiliation had softened his hard edges, stolen the bite from his bitter need for revenge. He cared what happened to Liara. He did. And not simply to serve his own selfish ends. True, Anisthe would never be humble, would never be good. True also that Nagarath forever would step between her and Anisthe. And quite right too.

Brothers-in-magick become enemies. What Liara had against Anisthe, Nagarath had suffered for far longer.

To trust Anisthe, to follow his word was to stand against Nagarath. Whom Liara loved.

She could never do that.

'Find the book.'

"Find it yourself!"

Again the line of family portraits caught her eye. Liara slowed and craned her neck upward at the paintings, peering at age-dimmed eyes, long-outmoded stylings of dress and hair. They were not a friendly bunch, Nagarath's ancestors. It took her at least three—

she guessed—generations to find a gentleman reminiscent of her wizard. Gaunter. Paler. But possessing kind eyes and a mouth that proclaimed half-concealed humor. She wondered if there were other mages in Nagarath's family line. His parents had made sure that he had the proper tutelage under Cromen. Turning back to the open library door, she half started back. But, no, she had spellwork to do first.

An uneasy tightness had developed in her chest, the ghost of remembrance triggered by something nearby. Liara looked around for the source of her unease. It was not the paintings, no. Nor was it some strange and exotic maybe-magick curiosity. Rather, the source of her troubles took an unexpected form.

A vaseful of dusty blossoms.

Lavender.

Memories rose thick and fast and scented the air sickly sweet. For a longing had again risen within Liara, one she could not quell nor for which she had answer. And the little purple blooms would not let her be, smelling of guilt and loss. Of an enchanted forest in Spain and secret spellwork. Of a home only barely hers and completely his. Everything so far out of reach as . . . as the sparkling moon itself. And with it came a tight pain in her limbs that made her magick sluggish and hot. Stifling.

Her fingers recalled the sorting of spell components on a dark winter's night, a fire burning in the room's hearth and glinting off the fragrant herbs. Striking, the similarities between Parentino and Little Larkhill. The wizard probably hadn't even realized how he had re-patterned his new life after his old. Would Liara wreck this too? Would she, in the end, again take what Nagarath gladly gave of himself and burn it to the ground?

No. Never.

Whispering a protective ward over the vase, Liara did what she could to ally herself with the mage. The spell was a gesture more than anything practical, though she had power enough for it at present. The guilt which pressed upon her chest did not ease. It occurred to her, at long last, that it was possible that the instinct which had her trusting her progenaurae came from the enemy within. Kerri'tarre, whom Anisthe had been looking to help in the first place, knew well how a heart worked and how to exploit its weakness.

Her conscience fully embattled, Liara made for the safety of the breathy outdoors. She flung open the front door to espy a sky that promised rain. Dark clouds and the distant flash of lightning further warned her of the folly in leaving the manor just then. Turning back, Liara took her restless frustrations into the various rooms and hallways Nagarath had shown to her but a short time before, in turns avoiding the wizard and burning off the power that threatened to consume her soul.

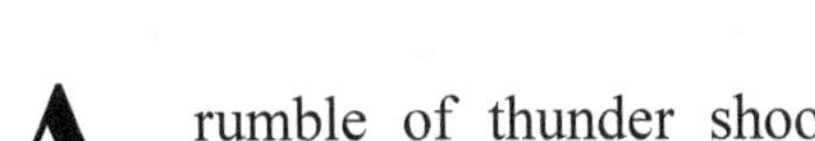

A rumble of thunder shook Nagarath from his reading. With the movement came a list of complaints from the rest of him, extraneous details that had slid from his consciousness. Back and knees reminded him kindly that he ought to sit in his chair to read, rather than on the rug. His eyes informed him that the light had grown inferior, and his stomach accused him of missing the midday meal.

"Topsy-turvy household, Nathaniel." He laughed. His real name sounded funny even when he said it. No wonder it had thrown Liara so out of sorts. "Speaking of which."

His index finger strayed to the pendant at his neck. Where had his magpie gone off to?

The spark of the charm connected with his Art, and Nagarath knew Liara to be on the southward lawn. Rising, he glanced to the windows and frowned. Rain wasn't on the way. It had arrived. He could see it streaming down the outside of the colored panes. With it, the figures depicted appeared to weep. Again he brushed the pendant and felt a sliver of fear bolt through him.

Nagarath was out the door with the next rumble of thunder. He turned south onto the path that skirted the building, hastening to a swift jog. Through the connected charms he could tell that Liara hadn't moved. Why?

Cresting the small rise that allowed commanding views of the surrounding fields and forests, Nagarath spotted her. A fair ways off down the slope, Liara was simply standing, her back to the manor and to him.

"Liara."

The woman did not turn at the sound of her name.

"Liara!" Nagarath tried again, more urgently this time. Something in her stance, her head thrown back to the sky, shoulders and arms strangely locked into an awkward outstretched position. A qualm shook his magickal senses as he approached, fear that he might again have to defend himself, worry that he could well have interrupted a casting had she responded to his call.

Still Liara did not move—not even to blink though, with the rain streaming down, Nagarath could not understand how she had not. Save for if she were bewitched. He hurried his steps, catching her arm with a hand. "Liara."

A vibration shook her, the magick loosening its grip. Now she did blink, swinging her gaze to meet his. "Oh. It's you."

An answering tremor shook Nagarath's limbs. Liara's tone, blank and lifeless, sounded a memory within his own soul. A half-remembered nightmare from months back. He was barely conscious of his hand tightening on her arm. With it came the familiar flash in Liara's eyes. Her streak of independence returned. This followed by scorn and a shying away.

Ashamed—by his worries as much as by his action—Nagarath let go and stumbled through his explanations, "When you did not move at my calling, I—"

"I was reading the stars." Liara's answer came muted by distance. Her attention was back on the overcast sky.

"But, Liara, it's raining." Nagarath tried to affect mirth. Tried and failed.

"The stars. They are still there." This time, it was Liara making the arresting motion. Her fingers found Nagarath's forearm and pinched in their ferocity. "See?"

The hissed word and spark of magick drew Nagarath's gaze upward. Waving her free hand, Liara's spell wiped the sky clear. Black and glittering with stars, the heavens dried their tears for the two wizards. An impossibility. An abomination.

Terror pricked Nagarath's skin, burned the edges of his Art.

And then Liara slumped against him, losing her grip on both magick and the wizard's arm. The clouds resumed their reign. Liara's eyes refocused and lost their silvery sheen.

"I'm cold." Liara's quiet complaint was as slight as the woman herself.

Gods. She would catch her death, soaked through as she was. Not brooking any arguments, Nagarath hoisted Liara into his arms. Half her weight had to be in her saturated robes alone.

Concerns for her health crowded out his questions about her spellwork. Leastways until, halfway to the house, Liara shifted in his arms and murmured, "Whatever are we doing outside, Nagarath?"

A tremor shook Nagarath's heart. He whispered, "Hush. No questions. Caught ourselves in a downpour is all. You will be warm by the fire soon enough."

Though Nagarath's glowing hearth dried Liara quickly, a chill took hold of her sometime late in the afternoon and refused to let go. A smattering of rain against the manor house continued through the hours, helped by a gusting and uneasy wind. A gloomy day all around. She couldn't recall why she had been outside or even how she had gotten there. All she knew was it was bad. In the recesses of her mind, Kerri'-tarre laughed his triumph.

In the other chair, Nagarath read. Which helped some. Though he had long adopted the habit of not exclaiming his victories or murmuring his defeats out of deference to his companion, the wizard proved an animated reader. Liara liked to watch his eyes squinting darkly as they crossed and re-crossed the page, his intelligent face filing the knowledge away or coming to some conclusion. She found it equally delicious when he got stuck along the way, often letting the book close in his lap, his attention then drawn to the flickering fire and his finger straying to lips and nose to begin their gentle exploration as he thought. A nose pinch meant disaster and often heralded the abandonment of his pursuit altogether.

Watching her friend, Liara found herself carried along on the gentle rise and fall of his absorption of the text. And then she had to look away, an unexpected heat rising into her face, a quickening of her pulse as a memory stirred within her. That of a quiet and clandestine meeting in Julien Jeffers' house, her silly fears and the wizard's kind allaying of such in the form of a music box chiming out a stately dance and impromptu lessons. At the time it had merely seemed comically improper. She herself had not yet been aware of the stirrings of affection or what said feelings might mean. Since that time, such senti-ments had come to haunt her over and over.

Liara had once called the mage slovenly. Such an epithet was unfair. Slovenly implied a lack of care. It occurred to her then that Nagarath read like he danced, like he did all things. Quiet conviction mixed with thoughtful intelligence. What she had once read as careless was really just an intense attention to very particular details. Nothing with that man was forgot, nothing marginalized or dismissed until it had been put through rigorous analysis.

It made Liara dizzy to think of it, how intimidating the man truly was, how overreaching her affection for him must be.

And then a sliding, crunching thump and mild curse from the mage. He'd dropped his book while reaching for another he had left just out of reach. His subsequent sheepish apology to Liara had her sighing in relief.

A moment later her tension was right back as Nagarath rose to his feet and came over to her chair. "Would you be fine by yourself for a moment if I go make something in the kitchens, Liara?"

Half afraid she would start to shiver and give away how terrible she really felt, Liara nodded. Nagarath didn't buy it. Bending close, he gently clasped her shoulder and gave it a reassuring squeeze. Impulsively, Liara covered his hand with her own still-cold fingers and refused to let go. For one long moment, neither of them moved, and Liara drowned anew in the mage's gray eyes.

"Sorry. Yes. I'm fine, thanks." Liara looked away first, fearful for the first time that something, rather than nothing, might come of it. She kept her gaze on the blazing fire as the wizard quietly left the room.

The minutes ticked past, leaving Liara to her warm thoughts. The pinched whistle of wind brought her attention on the windows. There the blurred silhouettes of trees whipped back and forth while rain painted a layer of frenetic energy onto the slowly shifting patterns.

Smiling to herself as she recalled the story of said windows, Liara rested her chin on her hands and tried to picture a young Nagarath frowning over the panes of glass on his workbench all those years ago. The story went that, upon returning to his family's estate after leaving Cromen's tutelage, the mage had immediately set about making improvements to the place—one of those being the addition of three large stained-glass windows in the library, such as he had seen in his travels abroad.

Determined to have a certain degree of magnificence gracing his walls, Nagarath had taken it upon himself to design and implement the construction of the windows all by himself. After tinkering in his "study" for months, he'd been able to produce three large, incredibly detailed, and glittering works of art. They depicted the Archangels Michael, Gabriel, and Raphael. Liara found the mage's chosen motif rather amusing. She wondered what Father Phenlick would have thought, as one of the three figures seemed to turn and fix her a watery glare even as she watched and contemplated.

Thinking back on Dvigrad, she considered Nagarath's having driven himself to dangerous magickal depletion on more than one occasion. He had even borrowed from his own life force at one point, much to his great peril. Had the windows ceased their restless movement during those moments when the mage lay incapacitated? She shuddered to think and certainly dare not ask.

Nagarath returned with a laden tray to find Liara at her introspection. Jumping at the sound, she threw off her blanket and hurried to help him. She strove with her motions to put color back in her cheeks and summon a smile to her face. Anything for the mage to feel reassured. Anything to keep him at bay.

Awkward silence thickened the air.

At length both she and Nagarath settled back into their fireside chairs. Each sipped at his or her tea. The wizard had yet to break the uncomfortable quiet while Liara's heart hammered in her chest, and she still did not know what to say.

Kerri'tarre had come to her weak. Liara was strong. His frustration had become a warm glow deep in the heart of her magick. Its presence reminded her that she was winning.

Most of the time.

And the rest? She still could not recall the events leading up to finding herself in Nagarath's arms, rain pouring down and with her soaked to the bone. *'Liara.'* An echo of a memory rather than true knowledge. The mage had called her name, had come running outside to find her. But his face as he had carried her inside Little Larkhill? That she would not easily forget.

That memory warmed Liara more than the fire, more than the tea, ever could.

"I'm going to use the stone again, Liara."

Nagarath's pronouncement dragged Liara mercilessly back into the present.

He rose to his feet voicing a deep sigh, accompanied by Liara's own protestations. "Are you joking? We don't even know what Kerri'tarre meant by dragging me out into the rain. Anything could happen, Nagarath."

"Enough, Liara." Closing his eyes to her argument, Nagarath grasped the cinnabar staff and called its magick. He spoke over its resulting roar, "I'm using it. Not you. For the magick that I need to attempt I will need both its strength and the safety it offers."

The wizard's spell hit Liara, and everything went white.

CHAPTER THIRTEEN

Nagarath told himself that his spell shouldn't hurt Liara. At least not physically. Betrayal, the unasked-for incursion, was another matter that he would have to later deal with. The goal right then was to trick Kerri'tarre into the mistake of contentment and thus gain the advantage of surprise.

Slumped in the chair with her eyes closed, his Liara looked such that Nagarath felt a shiver of fear regardless of his assurances to himself. He played a dangerous game with the young woman's soul. Nevertheless he reached out and gently touched his index finger to her forehead. He whispered the words of the incantation, and the cinnabar stone flared to life.

The magick dissolved the room into a hot reddish black.

Stepping through the mists of Liara's einatus, Nagarath advanced upon the figure who lived at its heart. He spoke, hearing his words echo in the whirling brightness that surrounded them, "Archmagus Kerri'tarre. I demand audience."

The praecantator had become a shimmering skeletal husk of his former humanity. More ghost than man. Clad in an ancient style of wizard's robes, invisible hands lowered his hood to reveal a mage of indeterminate race and indeterminate age. His eyes blazed as coals, his visage stayed veiled within the mists of time and sparked with pure magick. But Khariton's voice rang strong and true. "Master Nathaniel. Our resident lawful lawbreaker. The pretender who didn't want me now comes calling without so much a please and thank you to his dear, dear ward and apprentice. And he wants a chat."

The unexpected accusation roused Nagarath's temper. It caught him and held firm, guiding his next words. "Your memory must be clouded by time, old one. I've broken no laws. You, on the other hand, are currently possessing the einatus of a young woman incapable of making the bargain that freed you. Liara is only just eighteen, two years shy of autonomy from the mage who made her and therefore subject to the Laws Creatio. Your agreement with her is null and void; tantamount to zielsor."

"Who is the rightful owner of the cinnabar stone?"

In an eyeblink, Khariton had leapt close. His burning, claw-like fingers dug painfully into Nagarath's forearms. The screaming of the archmage's magick—the pitched and unceasing wail of a thousand stolen souls—filled Nagarath's ears. "Who? Not you. This I can tell with every beat of your sorry heart. Guilt, it cries. Guilt. Guilt. Tell me, how is it you didn't die at Parentino? How have you survived this long and travelled this far? You have stolen power same as me via that pretty little stone. Think before you accuse, magus. Think."

Nagarath stumbled back, freeing himself from the clinging fog of Khariton's aura.

Guilt. Yes. He felt it. Daily. Dizzily, he shook his head, crying out, "I had to use the power—!"

"So have I!" Kerri'tarre's anger sparked. Basest of emotions, with it he gained almost a semblance of humanity. "One thousand years of captivity, borne only by my having made certain I could survive. Those auras you see? Willingly given. Proudly. By witches and wizards eager to serve the cause. I preserved their souls and made sure they saw another day."

"Cause." Nagarath hadn't meant his rejoinder to sound weak. Gods, he was losing the argument. Trapped within Kerri'tarre's lies by his own curiosity.

Khariton only smiled.

"Have you forgotten your history?" The archmage paused, cocking his head as though listening. "Yes. Yes, I see that you have. I can see what Liara has learned, first as your librarian and then as your apprentice. Smart thing. Strong, yes. And hurting. Craving. Ambitious. A pity her academics have been so skewed by the writers of books. They have forgotten. Cabal. Avanei. Draper. Rundeweld. Loothemere. I know she knows of Merlin and has read of me. But what we did, what we achieved and why . . . Forgotten. All of it lost."

With each tallied realization, Kerri'tarre sank deeper into a sort of shocked horror. Gone was his indulgent arrogance. Gone, too, was his anger. He continued, half to himself, "We were dying. No, not the simple stuffs of bone and flesh. Or even of magick. People. Mages and artless alike. Our world was falling to the fae. The fae that even you, Nagarath of Parentino, were taught to call myth but a thousand years later. By the gods . . . magick's children have forgotten our lore. The Laws, they worked both too well and not well enough. Whole wars and countless souls forgotten under an easy and tame magick."

"As you say, your time was a thousand years ago." Nagarath refused to fall to the archmage's glamor, intrigued as he was. "And we, the mages of the modern age, thank you. But Liara. She is one soul. She is but one way for you to enter this world again. Why her? Why my—?"

"She chose me," Kerri'tarre snapped.

The annoyance in the archmage's tone rang hollow. Complaint rather than protest guided the hasty retort. Nagarath blinked in sudden surprise. "You made a mistake. With Liara."

The archmage made no response save to turn away from Nagarath and shroud himself in his hood once more.

"You did not realize her age and situation until it was too late. An aurenaurae. Half-magick and too strong even for you. You . . . She's able to fight back."

"For the time being." Kerri'tarre turned blazing eyes back on Nagarath. "But I have the luxury of patience. Your own mistake is my advantage—"

"My mistake!"

"That of love. You care for her too much to let her go; to do what would need to be done to defeat me. But I, too, have things I am deeply fond of. Living, not least. Give me the stone from your staff and a replacement body, and I shall rescind my claim upon the girl's life."

The futility of Nagarath's position stung him. A body, a soul—that he would gladly give to save Liara. But the cinnabar stone? He answered, "You can take me in exchange for her. But as you yourself have said, the stone is borrowed power. It was never mine to claim and therefore not my bargain to make."

"Oh, I agree," Kerri'tarre sneered. "But the offer stands. Remember that when it's too late. Remember that I gave you a choice when I didn't have to." The archmage waved his hand, turning his back on Nagarath.

The spell hit, and Nagarath found himself falling, falling, falling . . .

$\sim$

With a gasp, Liara woke in her chair. She had dreamed that she was drowning in light while Nagarath argued with Khariton. But, as in the case with most dreams, she found she could not recall the details of their exchange.

Quickly she turned and saw that Nagarath was there in the library with her. He lay asleep in the companion chair to hers. The hearth fire roared, newly rebuilt via the mage's magick. Too exhausted to move, Liara merely closed her eyes and endeavored to return to sleep.

But haunted, half-remembered images of her wizard confronting Kerri'tarre refused to leave Liara be. And so she was as unable to return to slumber as she was to rid herself of such bleak thoughts. When she again opened her eyes, night had fallen. She rose and left the mage to his quiet fireside repose.

A quick whisper rebuilt the fire anew. Another lit the lamps. The rest of her power—diminished as of yet—she kept for herself. She would require its aid for her next task.

'Find the book.'

If Anisthe had meant Liara to understand his charge, he'd done a poor job of it. Find the book. This to the woman who had destroyed the world's foremost collection of spell books in a fit of pique.

What, then, had he meant? Which book? That book of Merlin and Kerri'tarre's? What was it called . . . the Rishon Kesem?

How that name had come to Liara's attention still gave her the shivers. It was as though her remembrance was faulty on that account. Try as she might, she could not recall having run across any mention of the ancient book in all of her studies. It felt . . . it felt like a stolen memory, something Liara had gained from Khariton's einatus blending with her own.

And if that were the case, then Anisthe's words were most certainly not to be trusted. Particularly with the ambitions to which that man was bound. Myth. Lost like Merlin, Nagarath had said.

But she did trust Anisthe. In that one matter, at least.

Liara found that she had unconsciously raised her fingers to brush her cheek, recalling Anisthe's fevered charge, his bright, strange gaze boring into her.

No, the book must be something reasonable. Something real. Something Liara could discover from so cryptic a suggestion.

Perhaps Anisthe meant for Liara to find another edition of the codex which she had taken for him from Parentino the night she'd fled the castle for good. That little volume had set them all onto the search for Kerri'tarre's Mirror. And the book's size and heft, its burgundy binding and woodcut of Snow White's stepmother's arrest . . . those details had been burned indelibly into Liara's memory. Perhaps Nagarath's library of Little Larkhill had a reference to it. Perhaps she might find that the old story contained a hint at how to defeat the mirror's master.

Ridiculous. And to think she had once thought she might understand her progenaurae after all.

Khariton chuckled. The girl was right. The message had not been meant for Liara at all.

Nagarath's words rose in Liara's mind: *'You've felt the power of the cinnabar stone. A force. Raw and nigh unfathomable magick. And you are but peering at its true nature through a keyhole. The other half is hidden. In a book . . .'*

His war could wait. Kerri'tarre wanted the stone. Wanted it whole and within his control. He reached outward, marveling with Liara's eyes at the young woman's pale fingers. So young. So full of potential. So unlike his prison for the past millennium. "Thank you, Anisthe. I suppose I will owe you something, after all, you sly wizard."

He rifled through Liara's memories in an attempt to gauge the cataloging scheme of Nagarath's other library.

The one at Parentino. Perhaps it would offer clues for searching the one in which Khariton currently stood.

Useless. Prior to Liara organizing Parentino's library, it had become mere storage. Embarrassment for the mage and therefore something he'd sought to avoid, Nagarath had simply begun piling books into the room as they lost their usefulness to him. The only thing left of those memories was pain. Kerri'tarre abandoned that tack, sidestepping Liara's last thoughts of the ruined collection.

Whispering a spell of one of the languages long forgotten by man—belonging to one of the Faerie realms itself—Khariton doused the lights and waited. The fire crackled and danced shadows across the midnight-darkened shelves. And then, a swirling mist of faintest blue. Dust motes enlivened by sorcery shifted and made visible the air currents of the room. Watching their dance, Kerri'tarre drew Liara to where the airborne river flowed swiftest.

He watched the convergence of magick through foreign, hungry eyes. There lay the undisturbed volumes. There the things that Little Larkhill's master had counted on having been forgot.

"As safe as Nagarath could render it." Khariton smirked and raised a hand to pull down a sampling.

A silent warning, a twinge of disquiet in the back of Nagarath's mind woke the mage from his slumber. A pale shaft of early morning sunlight streamed over his robes in a jagged line. His gaze shifted to the empty chair beside him. *Liara!*

On his feet in instant, Nagarath looked about the library for his apprentice. He found that he stood on the shore of a sea of codices. Liara sat adrift in the center, her eyes clinging to an open page as if to a bit of driftwood meant to keep her afloat. Her lips moved in silent mimicry of the words she read. Head bobbing, she looked about to fall asleep mid-sentence. Yes, even as Nagarath watched, a wide yawn crossed her face, and her eyes seemed to swirl and flash. Silver, like a mirror reflecting sunshine.

Her hand dropped the book. She jumped to her feet. With a flutter, Liara's eyes cleared. Nagarath released his readiness for the defensive spell he had called to mind and breathed a sigh of relief.

"Oh gods. Whatever did I do?" Liara looked about the mess in dismay. She seemed on the verge of tears.

"Read like one possessed, it would seem." Blanching, for the words hit too near the truth of the matter, Nagarath stepped forward into the chaos to drown alongside her. "How are you feeling?"

Eyes still on the wash of books which papered the floor, Liara shook her head. "He kept me this time. Or, I suppose, I kept him from pushing me down. That or he didn't care what I saw. Maybe he even wanted to use me —use my knowledge—against me."

She shuddered and hugged her elbows tight.

Nagarath bent to examine the books. "This looks like intent . . ."

Bright colors of illumination—rarities in spell books, as the inks themselves had power that could warp a working if not done properly—they snagged at Nagarath's eyes as he studied the chaos at his feet. It had a pattern to it. Red. Lots of red. Vermilion.

Nagarath's jaw tightened in grim satisfaction. His ruse had worked, clearly. Oh, he had spoken truth when telling his apprentice about the cinnabar stone's purposeful imperfection. But the ancient archmage's eye was no longer cast toward the Rishon Kesem. Or Merlin, for that matter.

"What was Khariton seeking?" Nagarath didn't look up. He already knew the answer. He gripped his staff a little tighter, his free hand drifting towards his wand. When Liara made no response, he darted his eyes to her. She, too, was looking down. Not at the books but at her hands. She stumbled backwards, saying nothing.

"The spell, Liara. Remove yourself from the magick." *Oh, come back to me, magpie. Please.*

"Find the book." She again met his gaze. Her eyes swirled; control over her magick balanced on a knife's edge.

Her hesitation forced Nagarath's hand. *"Kšr mće'dš' h'einatus."*

Tears cleared Liara's eyes. She swayed and grew pale. Stepping forward, Nagarath caught her.

She shook him off, angrily wiping away her tears. "How dare you!"

"How dare me?" Incensed, Nagarath's ire clashed with hers, lighting the room as surely as his curse had a moment before. "Of all the foolish, irresponsible, perilous tricks. Draining yourself of magick allows the archmage easy footing when your power returns. Far different from blocking yourself off from your magick. I taught you that curse for a reason, Liara."

"How did you know that I was only—?"

"Because I'm not an idiot!" Drawing a steadying breath, Nagarath continued, quieter. "What do you think it is that spell was meant to do, Liara? The one I used on you just now. I could see your aura. That and little else. Your actions . . . they tell the rest."

"But the other solution hurts and, too, breaks down in the end." Liara's complaint came out a near whisper. "If both options will eventually fail, why can't I at least try the one that causes less pain?"

Nagarath had no answer for that. His apology was to direct his gaze back to the mess of books at Liara's feet. "I'll have Praecantator Khariton know that the key to the cinnabar stone, the vermilion spell—the book itself —is not in codex form. It is not lying about to be picked up by a casual user of the library. It's safer than that."

He darted a warning look to Liara, reading her face, her aura. He continued, unable to resist the lecture and baring of pride, "As I said, Cromen considered the danger the whole and unblemished stone would pose and I . . . I furthered his protections."

Catching his apprentice's interest as expected,

Nagarath gave a small smile. "You've seen the attraction its power poses to those of our ilk, myself included?"

"Sure."

"I suggested to the archmage that the key be inaccessible to anyone of the Art. A bit of a test of purity of heart, so to speak. Or so I thought. Only an artless can read the spell that unites the stone."

" 'The words, not the speaker, possess the magick . . .' " Liara recalled his lesson from another time, in another place.

"Precisely. And also another reason to have been worried over Anisthe becoming incantate. Had he known I possessed the stone, he might have chosen a different aim than that of Kerri'tarre's Mirror."

" 'Find the book,' " Liara repeated. "And you're certain he doesn't know?"

"I can't see how. You're the only one I told." Nagarath stopped his rising anger, lest he heap more accusations upon the scene. He continued, sitting down on the window seat and contemplating options through a gentle exploration of the bridge of his nose. "Cromen, perhaps . . . ? No, that's silly. Not that wizard. Not that man. Amsalla, maybe. She, too, was the archmage's confidante from time to time."

"If this is such a danger, why keep it at all? Why not simply destroy it? Why go through all that effort with a keyspell hidden in a book? Why not ensure the safety of us all by locking away that power? Why does every solution with magick prove but temporary?" Liara stepped close once more as she made her gentle but pointed argument.

Even under the remonstrance, Nagarath smiled. *Ah, there's my Liara. Cold logic and antagonistic attitude all mixed up together.* He baited, "Because destruction is never the answer. And because, Liara, a clock always winds down in the end. The fatewreaker always comes to collect. It is wise to not be empty-handed when she does."

"Destiny, Nagarath?"

"If you like. I see it more as the universe preserving itself through its very interconnectivity—magick being the through line with which I am most familiar. Anisthe's grave mistake could prove to have a purpose, might need to be used or freed for some as yet unforeseen and unfathomable reason."

Liara bent to begin cleaning up the mess, her motions inexact and dizzy.

"Anisthe again." She frowned. "Nothing good ever came out of anything he's done."

"Hush, go rest yourself. I will handle this." Nagarath waved his wand and books rose into the air around them. If Liara planned to argue with him that he wouldn't put them back in the proper order—he wouldn't—the words stuck in her throat unsaid. Instead, flashing him a small smile, her eyes still on the codices whirling thickly through the library air, she left without further dispute.

Her silent departure left Nagarath staring at the empty doorway. Still, he had more in him. One last point to make. "Without Anisthe, I wouldn't have you, Liara."

CHAPTER FOURTEEN

Nagarath kept his eyes trained on the summer-green canopy above his head and breathed deep the mid-morning richness of soil and loam. The day had kept its clear-eyed promise and already grown hot while he had visited with the Hertfords.

He doubly regretted having worn his wizard's cloak down the hillside to the cottage. One, it marked him as magick—something Nagarath had always striven to minimize around the practical Benjamin and Mary. Two, sweat beaded at the back of his neck and made the hood itch. For the life of him, he couldn't fathom what had made him don it in the first place that morning.

Then again, without the cinnabar staff in his possession, perhaps he felt he needed some mark of the Power about him. He was beginning to feel more and more like Nathaniel and less like Nagarath with each passing day.

He had needed to check up on the cinnabar stave. Disguised, of course, and left with the Hertfords five days prior while Liara was sleeping off yet another forced expenditure and blockage of her magick. Even Mary and Ben did not know what had been left in their care, only knowing that it was important that they keep the thing hidden and to call upon Nathaniel's aid if needed.

Mary had tried in vain to refuse the silver charm Nagarath had devised for such an occasion. Poor woman. He hated himself for putting her out thus. Dear that she was, she had not held out in protestation for long. But her efforts had provided him more than enough guilt that he felt it his duty to come calling every day thereafter. That and her cooking was far better than his. Had the situation with Liara not grown so perilous, he would gladly have welcomed Mary and Ben back as proper caretakers of the manor.

Dire as circumstances had become, Nagarath had to chuckle, thinking of how one of the great magickal artifacts of the age had been reduced to something so mundane as a cooking ladle and hidden amongst the spices of an English country cottage kitchen. Still, as it had when becoming a walking stick, the honey-colored wood had retained its distinctive twist, and the red stone still clung to its home in the bulbous handle. Not an inconspicuous disguise, but serviceable.

Thankfully, Liara had noted but not asked about the missing article. She, in fact, appeared rather relieved at his choice of action. His apprentice seemed to be improving overall, actually. Color in her cheeks. Higher spirits. She had continued with draining herself of her power both morning and night, walling herself off from her magick for the rest. A compromise. Nagarath believed it worked, having tried to test it with a careful—and asked for—application of his own magick.

The archmage was sealed. For how long? Unknown. But they needed the rest. And the ease of heart. Nagarath needed to scry Anisthe without worry. He had also needed time to look further into the Merlin Prophecies and see if there was any answer to be had there.

Nagarath had harbored a brief hope—and fear—that, perhaps, his warning had been heeded and the postings were a message for him. The fear he could overcome. If his enchantment upon Krešimir had been successful, if Merlin were alive to receive the sending, then Nagarath would have to answer for the transgression of having employed such unsanctioned magicks. Used to having the moral high ground in his dealings with the likes of Anisthe and Amsalla, it was jarring to think that he, for once, stood as the lesser mage, no matter his good intentions. And there was the cinnabar stone to consider.

As it was, nobody knew who was posting the texts, and so died both hope and fear. Some folks claimed a fairy sprite did the ancient mage's bidding. It was as Nagarath had proclaimed to Liara: the prophecies were mere nonsense to rouse the rabble and nothing more. A prank.

They were on their own, he and Liara.

Unless Nagarath were to fly back to France and liberate Anisthe—hateful idea—or somehow convince Amsalla to join their cause. She was a smart, resourceful wizard. Perhaps she might see the wisdom in seeking Merlin out, now that Kerri'tarre no longer had cause to see her as his liberator. That was, if the woman could look past her own jealousies of Liara.

Liara, who he could not leave behind, alone in her peril. As for the possibility of taking her with? Out of the question considering the magicks involved.

Plus, we'd look silly clinging to a cooking ladle as we traversed time and space. Nagarath smiled grimly, willing the dark humor to catch hold.

Motion ahead caught Nagarath's eye. Liara. And heading his way with haste. He quickened his steps to meet her, self-conscious of his secret enterprise, even having come back to the house in a roundabout manner.

"Liara." Waving his greeting, Nagarath felt a genuine smile take hold.

She stopped not thirty paces back. Eyes glinting like blank, still pools, she uttered one word. One word in a language of magick long forgotten and most certainly not learned of him. And in a voice certainly not her own.

Bracing, Nagarath crossed his arms in front of him, allowing his magick to make the shield under the direction of his will, his heart. Liara's curse collided harmlessly off it. "Liara. Hold—"

Another hex followed the first. Another.

Each time, Nagarath affected a passive defense. He tried again, "Liara—"

"Help." As she spoke, Liara looked at him . . . then through him. Her eyes grew silver once more. Another curse; another blast of power. And that time, she managed to break through Nagarath's defenses.

Spun sideways by the icy breath of Liara's spell, Nagarath stumbled. And with it, he found his resolve.

Nothing in their master/apprentice arrangement demanded he stand by and take a beating he hadn't earned. And clumsy and uncontrolled as her attack might be, the power Liara was putting out was such that she truly might kill him.

Whirling backwards, his aura trailing behind him to draw his opponent's spells, Nagarath called lightning into his fingers. Liara, seeing his intent, adjusted her own attack, meeting like with like.

But this, too, was a feint. Shifting his spells again, Nagarath instead emptied his power into the air behind his apprentice. Blue-gray fog, it pressed forward at his call. Unwilling to make herself turn from her attacker to face the cloud, it rolled over Liara in a matter of seconds, slowing her movements, stealing the energy from her hexes. Forced to address this new problem and thus caught with divided attention, Liara was made vulnerable without her realizing it. A beginner's mistake.

But a mistake that did not render her power any less great. Nagarath still must defeat her. And it hurt. Oh, how it hurt him to do so. Daggers of light shot from his free hand, the points lancing through the air, quick as thought. The new attack again hit at Liara's weakest point, her ill-guarded back. Nagarath's curse found its mark. Liara's magick ended, and she crumpled to the ground.

"Liara!" Nagarath ran to her. "Oh, no no. No no no no no . . ."

A shudder; a shift. And Liara's otherworldly gaze met his, darkness swirling from her wand and wrapping itself about the wizard's knees and ankles. It melted away as swiftly as it had come, allowing Nagarath time to draw a shaky breath as the woman regained her feet. She stepped away, her wand held at the ready. She seemed taller than normal. And she was . . . smiling. "Very good, Master Mage."

"Liara, I—" Nagarath tried to take another step towards his apprentice and found he could not. Looking down in alarm, he saw that the ground held his feet firm. Or, more accurately, it held him fast, for the rich soil had given way to a treacherous morass.

Permeated with black magicks, the hungry ground sucked eagerly at its victim. Patterned much as his fog spell had been but a moment before, Nagarath felt its intrusion into his counter-spells, slowing his attempts to free himself. The thick mud had reached his knees, clawed at his robes. Every spell he cast at Liara she turned aside with ease, the bite going out of Nagarath's castings with the black bog devouring them.

Wincing, Nagarath let Liara's next whirlwind of fire lick at his defenses. First things first. He directed his next spell downward. His casting was simply: ice.

The hex fed itself, growing his intended effect instead of negating it as the ground ate the magick. Screaming aloud as pain enveloped his shins and feet, Nagarath felt the soil freeze and grow solid once more. The weakness in his casting ceased, and with a quick gesture, he freed himself, stumbling backwards on legs that had gone near useless with cold.

Liara advanced, still shooting fire and rage. Nagarath retreated, counter-casting and shielding in turns. And retreated further. A flake of snow drifted past. Then another. His spell that had frozen the ground followed him, followed his magick. Liara advanced further, summoning a shield rather than attack in the next exchange, her eyes widening as she saw where their duel had taken them.

Nagarath nodded, smiling grimly as he knelt to the ice upon which they stood. He had frozen the pond on his family's grounds. And with his touch to the water's surface . . . he shattered it.

Liara disappeared with a scream and a splash.

CHAPTER FIFTEEN

It was but the work of a gesture and thought for Nagarath to bring her back up.

Coughing and shaking on the shoreline, Liara did not attempt to cast even a spell to aid herself.

Nagarath ran to her, testing her aura as he did so. The warmth of his magick nearly set Liara to tears. Her mage. Her clever, clever wizard. The shock of the icy waters had stunned Liara's magickal inclination as he had, likely, intended. They were safe . . . for the moment.

"Nagarath." Liara retched and looked away. "Wait."

The wizard had his wand trained on her in an instant.

"Don't come any closer." She locked her gaze to his, pleading. "I can't control it. I can't."

"I know, magpie." Nagarath knelt at her side. "That said, the tactic of surprise . . ."

" '—Will forever be better than magick.' Magus Loothemere," Liara quoted dutifully, then smiled in spite of herself.

"How do you feel?"

"You can see my aura?"

"Yes."

"Then you'd best stand back, Nagarath. For I still have some strength, even with the shock you provided," Liara warned, placing her palms to the ground and covering her wand. "Don't worry, this time I won't wreck the ground."

The tremor was small as Liara expended the last of her available magick. It served to set to rights the weather she and Nagarath had so carelessly ruined. But it left her effectively disarmed of her Art. For the time being.

"Be careful, magpie. Do not go so far that you cannot call the magick back," Nagarath warned.

"Maybe I should. Incantate would be safer for us all. But Kerri'tarre . . . he won't allow that to happen. I should know. I've been trying it on the sly for days." Liara closed her eyes to the truth of it, afraid that she might yet cry atop everything else.

She felt Nagarath sit down by her side. His sensitive fingers sought hers, and Liara clung fast, thinking again of how she could well have killed her mage while under Khariton's influence. She held tight, even as she turned from him to have her silent tears at last.

"I try and I try, but . . ." Liara gulped. "But I really think that he'll win in the end. Khariton is growing stronger. Eventually he will be stronger than me. Stronger than how I feel for— I couldn't face it if I were to . . ."

She trailed off, unable to say the words. Unable to make either claim, though the words burned in her throat for having been left unsaid. *I love you, Nagarath. Do not let my rogue magicks take you from this earth.*

No. Far better the sentiment be left unsaid. Perhaps, then, there was a chance of his doing what needed doing.

Instead, Nagarath chose to ruin her hopes with some of his own. He said, "We will solve this. I promise you that, my— Liara."

A ripple of emotion stirred within her, some sort of signal, a returning to themselves. A stepping down from the harrowing moment when they had been adversaries, if through no fault of their own. Still, even if some things must remain unsaid, Liara could say something. After all, she had employed some rather injurious hexes on the man.

"Nagarath, I don't think there is apology enough in the world for—" Liara found herself speaking into a pressing kiss. Startled, she pulled away. And discovered that she stared into equally stunned gray eyes. Stunned and embarrassed. Nagarath didn't say a word, seeming to hunt for an apology of his own.

Her cheeks sparking a heated blush, Liara took a short, quick breath and kissed him back.

Kissing. Nagarath. It was . . . it was as nonsensical an act as her having attacked her mage with magick she could no longer control. It was ridiculous.

It was wonderful. It was every hope made real.

Another tear snuck out, escaping the corner of Liara's eye and following the path of its predecessors down her cheek. Nagarath's thumb stopped it, his hand coming to rest itself along the side of her face. A tender gesture. And wholly at odds with the wizardly combat that had preceded it minutes before.

Liara leaned into the mage's palm, her breath hitching

as his other hand came up to stroke—oh, so tenderly—her fevered temple. Her own hands, they too decided they had a role to play. Her fingers moved along the folds of Nagarath's hood, grasping and releasing bits of the soft well-travelled, much-abused material and drawing him closer.

He shuddered, removing his hands from their cautious caress to again place Liara at arm's length. Nagarath's voice broke, "No."

"No," Liara's complaint argued against his discretion, attempted to pull him back to her.

It was too late for all that. Didn't he see? They'd stepped out of the circle of their protection.

"Time enough . . ." Nagarath's protest shattered him, and he stopped to draw a shaky breath. "Liara, we need to first—"

"No. Not first one thing or another. Now." Liara's reply came harsher than she intended, and she lowered her voice, casting her eyes downward. Her fingers still picked fitfully at Nagarath's robe. "There is no time left. If this happens again—"

"Stop."

"If—when—Kerri'tarre comes at you with the intent to kill, our time will be up. And when that happens I need you to defend yourself. Properly."

"Liara!"

Angrily she met his gaze. "Who will you allow Khariton to hurt? You? The Hertfords? Little Larkhill? How far? Nagarath, you cannot stop this magick. I cannot contain it. He wants that stupid stone, and I can't stop him. Can you?"

"I—"

"Listen!"

"Liara, I—"

"Shut up for one second, won't you?"

"I love you."

He—what? Again. Tears. And the exquisite agony of joy. Within it, Liara completely forgot what it was she had intended to say. Whatever scold she'd wanted to give him was buried within her need to bring him close again. He loved her. An impossibility.

A glorious impossibility. And yet the evidence had been stamped on her lips and burned onto Liara's heart. She almost laughed aloud, feeling, somehow, the mage's desire to apologize for his sentiment. She caught his eye, daring him to say it.

Instead he repeated, "I love you, my magpie."

"I love you, too, Nagarath." The confession freed Liara in ways she hadn't even considered. The words tasted sweeter than the kiss. Yet, she felt called to compare the two anew. She leaned into him, finding his lips with her own as though they dare not separate for long now that they'd found a way one to the other.

Her frustrations—her fears—broke through Liara's joyful relief. They found voice. "So that's it, then. You won't hurt me, and I can hurt you. And Kerri'tarre knows it and will use it all against us. Can't you just— I mean, I wish— What are we to do, Nagarath?"

"You know, Liara, I do believe you are the only person on this earth who could take love and turn it into an argument."

Liara glared at the mage and then leaned into him,

resigned to her fate. A fate intertwined with his. Theirs a messy, ill-formed, stranger-than-magick companionship that she wouldn't trade for all the world. Not for ease of heart. Not for the illusion of safety nor the tranquillity of mind. He loved her. Surely that was enough. Surely the solution to Khariton's threat lay somewhere within that mutual regard.

BASTILLE SAINT-ANTOINE:

Anisthe had long given up any consideration of escape. He had stopped counting the hours, the days, of his imprisonment. Not that he languished long. A week, maybe two, maybe three. It was hard to tell in the perpetual twilight of his dungeon dwelling. Never a change. Never a reprieve. He had even become used to the rank odor of the place.

Amsalla had called on him twice more since their initial meeting days after his capture. But for all her tears and handwringing, she certainly had not bothered to reinstate him to better accommodations. Anisthe could only guess at her game. But what he could guess at had him worried.

Two doors. Eight locks. Fourteen inches of cold iron. And Domagoj's magick had been thwarted by but a taste of such methods when Anisthe had been captured back in Almazar.

Perhaps Amsalla really could not work his release through the correct channels, and her own greedy theft of the half-fey's magick had prevented her from freeing Anisthe herself.

If only he could scry the outside world, see what Liara, what Nagarath, were up to. Had they followed his advice? Had it led them to Merlin? And, considering what Anisthe had learned of Amsalla's relationship with England's archmage, had this inadvertently put them in danger?

How strong was an aurenaurae's magick, and did its strength thwart Kerri'tarre or doom them all?

Were Anisthe's own ambitions yet to be realized?

"Ambitions." Anisthe snorted and looked about his dim hole of a dungeon. King of slime. Counsellor to toads and newts, spiders and rats. "So, not much change, then, magus."

He stretched out on the scant straw that had been strewn over the wooden planks of his bed.

"If I die, Liara dies." He had lost track of how often he repeated the phrase. Like a novice wizard learning his first spells, Anisthe held tight to the rules that governed Magick.

Merlin and Kerri'tarre's perfect Laws.

The irony of the situation was not lost on him. Anisthe smiled. "The Laws of Magick Creatio. Law The First: Magickal power mimics the Magickal signature of the originating or altering power. Law The Second: Once the age of twenty has been reached, a subservient power gains autonomy, and its signature is fixed. Law The Third: The destruction of an originating power subsequently destroys the magickal properties of its surrogate.

If I die, Liara dies. If Liara dies, you die, Archmagus Khariton."

If Amsalla DeBouverelle truly wished the praecantator alive and well, she would find a way to free her prisoner. And if that happened, she most certainly had Anisthe's loyalty.

But only so far as would bring him back to Liara, whose trust he had earned through his sacrifice. And assuming his aurenaurae worked at Anisthe's problem from the other end. Even cut off from magick by his cage of iron, Anisthe could feel the scales beginning to tip.

Freedom and power. Soon he would have both. Soon.

CHAPTER SIXTEEN

Liara and Nagarath repaired to the house, hand in hand, heart clinging to tired heart. She shivered in spite of the summer's heat, and Nagarath let go her hand to put his arm around her. Looking up at him, she asked, "What do we do now?"

"Do, magpie?" Nagarath seemed alarmed by her simple query.

Not about that. Leaning in, Liara tried to lose herself to contentment. If Nagarath wasn't ready to address her having outright engaged him in a wizard's duel, she would allow herself the moment of bliss.

Liara spotted the quick smile that flitted over her mage's face. He knew his own joke then. He, too, wished to dwell on things other than Kerri'tarre's treachery. Together they crunched along the gravel path, lost to their separate thoughts. The front of the house loomed above them as they approached, frowning as if to say "I know what you were about out there." Liara half expected she should not be given entrance. She remembered well the protections the mage had laid upon Parentino. The ruined castle in faraway Istria had supported charms meant to sort out allegiances. She had long been subject to the mage's defenses, the testing of heart and of magick.

But therein lay the problem. Were not Liara's heart and magick at odds on the issue of Nagarath?

Yes and no.

Perhaps, had Liara's sorcery not gotten away from her in so dramatic a fashion, neither of their confessions might have ever found utterance. Both had grown so reliant upon their elaborate defenses, it had taken the clashing of their magicks for truth to find its way into the light. *He loves me. Me. How is that even possible? What does that even mean for the likes of him and me?*

Nagarath led Liara into his library and, with a muttered spell, sparked a drying fire within the hearth. Another wave of his wand had his robes lifting up off his shoulders and swirling around Liara's. Thus enveloped in warmth and regard, her cheeks heated in a blush.

"I suppose . . ." she tested. "I suppose I could say it again. Properly, this time."

Her pronouncement was met with a quirked eyebrow.

"I do love you, Nath—"

His arms encircled her, his lips crushing hers anew, before Liara could finish her declaration. Stumbling giddily, they found the window seat and half-sat, half-fell, still entangled one in the other. A clumsy passion and all the more honest for it, Nagarath pulled back, chiding her huskily, "Nagarath. Please, Liara."

Nodding, and slightly confused at the correction, Liara remedied the proclamation, "I love you, Nagarath."

"And I, you, Liara. Since Spain at the least. When our hodgepodge collection of traveling companions kept nosing in between you and me. Did you know it, how I felt and how, foolishly, I thought it was helping to keep my burdensome regard from you?"

She nodded again, not trusting herself to the words. She had known. It had driven her jealousy of Amsalla. It had fueled her angry words to the wizard in France. It had forged forgiveness. Could it yet provide salvation?

Breath catching, Liara had to break the moment and address her most pressing fear. "So what are we to do now?"

Silence. And a growing distance, one made real when the wizard rose and strode across the library. In the flickering light, Liara could see Nagarath's jaw clench and unclench. She tried again. "Are we going to talk about it at least?"

"My duel with Khariton?" Nagarath spoke without facing her. Leaning on the mantle, he seemed caught up in his thoughts.

Liara considered his phrasing, how he had removed her from the equation. She waited, her heart pounding.

"No." Turning, he regarded Liara again with that strange, calm demeanor. "No, we will not talk about what that archmage does with your magick."

"But why not?"

"Because, in all honesty, it makes me sick to think on it. Because the only outcome I can even face imagining is one where I am clever enough to find a way to have everything. And I just do not think I am that wizard, my magpie. Not were I to have all the books in all the world."

"I'm sorry."

He flinched. "And because it makes me mad, Liara. And when I am angry, I make mistakes. And, right now, after what Kerri'tarre did out there—pitching my Art against yours, forcing me to almost have to . . ."

Nagarath approached, and sitting by her side on the window seat, he let his hand fall atop Liara's. "Right now we cannot afford any mistakes. Especially in light of, well, in light of knowing what we each now know."

"I trust you. Because you are that wizard, Nagarath."

Nagarath's answer: a gentle squeeze of Liara's fingers and a weak smile. "And, I suppose, because I do have all the books in all the world."

She leaned into her mage, sensing in Nagarath his silent war against himself. Several minutes passed. Long enough that Liara judged she had been given her opening. She said, "Regardless, I need your assurance that you'll do what needs to be done. If—when—Khariton again pits my magick against yours."

" 'What needs to be done.' " There was no mistaking the bitterness in Nagarath's echoing back of her words. "You are strong, Liara. This situation is not a case of you losing control, throwing a spell at me, and my simply defeating you with a word and a curse. An aurenaurae's magick; it is what has kept Kerri'tarre as contained as he has been. Anyone else would have been lost to him long before now. Myself included."

"We need more time. That strength of my magick? He will turn it, and it will be used against you. Against us."

Under her distress, Nagarath had pulled away from her. Together they sat side by side, bathed in the broken multi-hued light of the window at their backs.

"We need more time, yes." Nagarath broke the silence.

Liara trembled and checked her magick before speaking. She was spent and so could summon no further delay in voicing the idea she held. Her heart closed itself to the ruining of the moment she had shared with Nagarath. Her regard for—fear for—Nagarath's safety was far greater than the needs of her own love-thirsty soul. She ventured, "Can Khariton survive in the heart of an incantate mage?"

"He—" Nagarath shot Liara a warning glance.

"Kiih'ed einatae," Liara whispered, gritting her teeth against the hollow ache within the ravaged heart of her magick.

His hand again sought hers. Liara moved to rise, almost certain that Nagarath might prevent her from making her point. He let her go. He didn't want to, but he let her go. Liara turned and hurried to where she had accumulated a small collection of books days before. Just another pile amongst all the others. The library's master hadn't disturbed it.

Liara handed Nagarath a few of the items and then moved off to her usual fireside chair. She craved the self-punishment of distance. Staring into the dying coals—for she hadn't even art enough to restart it—she waited, listening to the quiet turning of pages.

Flinching, she heard Nagarath approach. Shock and anger radiated from him like heat from a fire.

"What the— What the hell is this?" Incensed,

Nagarath gripped the book in his hand as if he might crush it and the spells inside.

Liara shook her head minutely, eyes widening.

"Yes. Yes, I know what you mean by this. Yes, I don't even care whether or not Kerri'tarre IS listening. This! This is out of the question!"

"But would it work?"

"No." Nagarath's reply came harsh and broken. Defeated.

Disheartened by her angst, her own breaking heart, Liara half-rose to comfort him.

Nagarath waved her off, skimming through the rest of the books, dropping them one after the other. Ire and pain built in his face with each passing page. The wizard paged through the last book, and he stopped to read. Long moments ticked past and then, "This. This would."

Liara's heart went out to him. She followed, gently lifting his face from the book to meet her own.

His hand grasped hers, and he held it to his cheek. A claim and promise. His eyes blazed. "But I won't—! I will not do that."

She wasn't certain what expression must have flitted over her face, but it prompted such compassion in her wizard's. He moved to reassure her. The book thumped to the floor, abandoned so that Nagarath might cradle Liara's face in his free hand. "No, magpie. I would not love you any less were you no longer a mage. But you are asking me to hurt you. These curses, they are nothing like the black magicks used to temporarily separate you from your aura. The spells that render a magus incantate, they are agony."

In her mind's eye, Liara envisioned a room wrapped in mage-born lightning. Herself at the center, she held a cracked amulet in her hand. Power whistled through it, draining the war mage who stood not twenty paces away.

Liara pictured an embattled Nagarath. She saw herself cutting him down under the curse of Kerri'tarre, murdering him with her magick. What agony could compare?

Liara regained her focus on the present. Nagarath had subdued his anguish, though the light in his eyes had dulled. He said, "Yes. Yes, I can do as you ask. But only if pressed. Only if I must will I enact such sorcery as would strip your own. But that is all we'll say on this lest we warn your interlocutor. I will make the arrangements, magpie."

"Thank you." Really, she meant '*I love you.*'

She knew that he knew.

CHAPTER SEVENTEEN

The morning fields of Little Larkhill teemed with life. Five days. And this the first to produce the clinging mist which dampened the air and rendered the wizard's grounds near unrecognizable.

Liara's skirts were soaked through before she'd gone ten feet from the gravel path. She made a mental note to save some of her powers to make herself presentable before entering the house.

The air bathed the fevered brow, and the ear rejoiced in the endless bold chorus of birds. There was no disentangling one call from the rest. Each strove to out-shout the other, like women haggling in a marketplace. Advertisement and complaint. Joy.

Liara believed it came from the frank openness of the space. Here the sound rolled across hill and plain, unmuted by tree trunks and undergrowth. It rose up to mingle with the clouds, breaking up what cover there was and sending shafts of sunlight streaming through, a competition of sound and sight. The hard and soft of life.

With it came the desire to breathe deep. To absorb the wet, the wild, the pungent, and the pure. Manure. Peat. The meaty, cloth-like thickness of fallen leaves. The slippery silver of grass and sharp tang of wildflowers whose names Liara did not know. All lay against the tongue, a feast.

Liara stared at the surrounding and tried to imagine Nagarath as a child there, knowing full well that he did not actually grow up in England. She indulged all the same, picturing a lanky dark-haired child tumbling through the brush and bramble, eyes as wild as the skies.

Liara sucked in a cool lungful of the blanketing whiteness and tried to tell herself that she was cleansed by such. Fog chasing fog through her mind and magick. But the chilly dampness failed to do for her what an immersion in ice water had but days before.

Following the edge of the pond, Liara eyed the mirror-like surface of the waters, imagining it frozen. In place of the memory sprang another. Warmer. And equally as shocking.

The kiss. The confession. Both had awakened in her a permanent ache. Far from settling the question that had long hung over Liara's heart with regards to her mage, the realized feelings had thrown her into a different sort of fog than that which she walked through. She couldn't think; couldn't reason. Thankfully, neither were required of her at present to fight Khariton. The archmage hadn't bothered her in the days following her duel with Nagarath. Perhaps he feared he had overplayed his hand in his attempt. With some hope, Liara was inclined to believe that her daily efforts and near constant vigilance were working.

Entering the tree line, Liara looked up into the fog-dimmed branches and wondered if her signal would be visible from the house that day. The cottage, perhaps. She laughed, picturing Mary and Ben looking anxiously out their window to espy the strange effect the morning sun seemed to have on their woods of late.

"*Atsmi'i shinah ata yal'ad,*" Liara whispered the words of her spell and felt the magick take. Gasping as the last of her power bled from her, she closed her eyes to the sign in the leaves above her head. She'd seen it more than enough. Nagarath seemed to find amusement in it though. Which helped somewhat.

She opened her eyes to a clearing fog. Sunlight streamed warm upon Liara's skin, burning off the mist and glinting through the transformed leaves above her head. Crystalline and bright, the foliage fractured the light into rainbows such that she had to throw a shielding hand to her brow to look upward. Almost as if on cue, a leaf floated down, trembling in the fragrant and living air. Reaching out, she caught it in her hand. Despite its magicked condition, said leaf was healthy and whole.

And pink as a winter sunset.

"Kiih'ed einatae." The second spell had no effect. Liara's magick was gone. She could safely return to the house.

Entering Little Larkhill, Liara went straight for the library. There she found Nagarath sitting on the floor, surrounded by books and frustration.

Her heart leapt in her chest just to see him. Irresistibly

drawn, Liara gingerly stepped over the mess just to come sit close at his side. Looking up in acknowledgment but for a moment, Nagarath patted her hand and returned to his reading.

"How are you feeling?" he asked.

In answer, Liara tried to dim the library lights. *"Hit 'k'."*

Failing that, she smiled tiredly and leaned into Nagarath's arm. Setting aside the book, he shifted so that he could draw her closer. He murmured into her hair, "Good work, Liara."

"And I feel . . ." Liara finished her answer by turning her face to his. Thrilling at the warm kiss exchanged with her wizard, she ventured, "Do you think there's a chance that something changed with my magick? That Kerri'-tarre can't take and make it his own after our fight and everything that followed?"

"Are you asking if, truly, *'vincit omnia amor'*?" A smile flickered over Nagarath's face, then vanished into soft sadness. "No. It does not."

Liara's cheek rubbed the mage's homespun robes as she nodded her assent. She hadn't harbored such hopes. Not really. But the past several days had been so . . . easeful, so wonderful. Okay, so she'd had some hope.

Having returned to his book, Nagarath adjusted to Liara's incursion on his space. Closing her eyes, she could feel when he turned the page and reveled in the deep rumble of his voice when he exclaimed one way or other over what he read. Minutes, hours, days, passed while she sat thus. Time stopped. Magick of a new order.

At length she sat up and separated from her wizard.

He appeared to hardly notice, again shifting to accommodate. Liara rose and found that her fingers had entwined in Nagarath's. A joyful, awkward disentangling ensued, separation sweetened by the conviction that he loved her, that she would never have to leave his side nor he hers.

And then Liara was on her own to explore the library.

She had read the page of Nagarath's book with disinterested eyes and felt her restless legs beg movement. But as she eyed the shelves, she discovered that all books, in fact, filled her with a strange disquiet. Her answers were not within those pages.

Liara needed to get back outside. Into the sunshine. Into the warmth of a summer sky. Far from worrying her, the restlessness invigorated. It drew her outward, calling her name. She obeyed.

The trees were still their same translucent pink. The sky the same brilliant blue. Heart pounding, Liara broke into a loping run. Her blood raced in her veins. Her mind drew back to Nagarath. Her mage, well and truly.

Thin gray smoke danced upon the breeze. It caught at Liara's senses and drew her forward towards the Hertfords' cottage. She would visit with Mary awhile. Such an encounter would be sure to exhaust her aching soul. And besides, it promised scones.

Upon Liara's leaving, Nagarath waited through a count of five. Her footsteps receded and then bled into the sound of a quiet door opening somewhere. Its closing echoed back at him, and he jumped to his feet, dropping his book. Long strides carried him over to the windows where he peered out. Bobbing his head so as to match the slow shifting in the pattern, Nagarath looked out into a world colored in the hazy blue of time-warped glass.

Yes, she had gone. Drawing a shaky breath, he sprang into motion, picking through the untidy pile of books on the window seat until he found the one he sought. Cold to the touch, the deep violet leather of the cover burned Nagarath's hand, and so he simply laid it open on the low bench. His eyes paced the pages, reading and confirming that, yes, he had what he needed, while his ears burned with the knowledge that Liara had not returned to save him from himself. He waited in the silence, willing something to change. Anything.

When nothing did, Nagarath fished in a hidden pocket for the one component that the spell required. And again waited. Thinking of Liara, of his magpie who had learned sorcery of him, to whom he had given Cromen's wand as well as his own heart, Nagarath's fingers strayed to his collar wherein normally rode his magicked pendant. But he had removed the charm. His apprentice could not know the magick he worked lest Khariton feel himself in peril and interfere.

Unmoving, Nagarath stared at the strand of hair he held in his hand. Long and black. He had found it clinging to his robes the day before. Liara's. With the solitary strand, he could affect the hex that she had asked of him. With it, he would enact the dark magicks that would take Liara's magick from her.

In order to even contemplate such sorcery, he had set

his thoughts against the change between himself and his apprentice. But he could not separate his heart—and, thereby, his magick—from thoughts of her. The newly realized love sang within his veins. It beat frantically against his present efforts, a futile plea for mercy.

Nagarath recalled having once told Liara that a wizard ought to be versed in all magick, including those of the darker Arts. He found himself wishing he were not so well informed. *But then I would not be able to help Liara.*

"Is this helping? Truly?" Angrily, Nagarath looked at the long dark strand of hair that lay across his open palm. And in that moment he hated magick. All of it.

Enough to take Liara's from her?

To cause her nigh unbearable agony? Agony he could not heal, help, or hinder?

Enough. Reaching up, he plucked a hair from his own head. With a twist, Nagarath joined the two strands, hastily snatching his heart out of the reach of his conscience.

"Atsmi'i."

I, Magus.

Nagarath choked on his own declaration. His words faltered. The magick died.

It should be him. It ought to be Nagarath facing the reality of a life without magick. For, unlike Anisthe— unlike Anisthe's daughter—he could live quite happily without the Art. In the early years following the creation of the cinnabar stone, he had sworn off sorcery. Or near enough. Small workings. Tentative magick. Nagarath had taken Anisthe's lesson and made it his own. Fear had frozen his hand and stilled his lips. With time he had found refuge in his books. Far safer to read and learn than to act.

Until possession of such knowledge and desperate need for its application called all that Nagarath valued into question.

In the end he had learned there was no place of safety. Nagarath had no right path to tread. No answers. Not in magick. Not in anything.

The books were empty. Cold and heartless academia.

"Curse all!" he cried. "I, Magus. Astmi'i!"

The thread in Nagarath's hand flared to brightness. Invisibly, he felt its pull on his einatus, and he gasped.

"Shaav ich'r hitiyr einatae. Kšr mće'dš; astmi'i."

Nagarath moved to make the appropriate sign in the air. Wincing under the spell's bite, he half-finished the rune and stopped.

No.

He could not, dare not, finish.

I, Magus.

"And what kind of mage?" The curse whined and strained under the constraint of Nagarath's incantation. He still had mastery of the spell, if barely.

With a snap, the magick broke free. Nagarath watched the thin strand make its lazy, softly-swirling dance on the still library air as the hair fell to the floor. The gentle, silent moment stood in eerie contrast to the sharp violence of the magick which had bound it.

Relief broke over Nagarath, an angry storm punctuated by the lightning flash of regret and guilt. Spent and shaken, he leaned heavily against the window sill and told himself they would yet find a solution to Kerri'tarre's assault upon Liara's soul. Solace in lies. A broken hope consisting of cowardly falsehood. Again.

~

Liara's greeting was not immediately answered. A clamoring on the other side of the Hertfords' cottage door prompted her to wait in uneasy silence under the bright glare of the sun. And then she was subject to the full force of Mary's enthusiasm.

"Oh, my dear, come in!" Mary ushered her guest in with the same unbridled exuberance as on their last meeting.

Liara fought the urge to grit her teeth and reminded herself she had come there of her own accord. Her quick eyes assessed the space, and she asked, "Is Benjamin out?"

"Just us women, dear." Mary fixed Liara a pointed, questioning look.

"Ah." Liara blushed, not knowing what else to say. She sat at Mary's bidding and again found her eyes wandering the cozy cottage.

"Has Nathaniel learned what he was looking for with regards to Merlin, dear?"

Liara gawked, and a buzzing sounded within her ears. She had dismissed all word of the purported "Merlinic Prophecies" as a hoax. She had thought Nagarath in agreement on that point.

But if her mage was asking over Merlin without Liara's knowledge, then he likely meant to keep it a secret from Khariton. Perhaps he harbored a plan to aid Liara in her struggle with the archmage.

And there she was, learning of it.

It made a certain sense. After all, Merlin and Kerri'-tarre had been confederates—or so legend claimed. They had been contemporaries if nothing else. But surely Merlin had died under his apprentice's curse. Khariton's having survived a thousand years was a quirk enough of fate.

Perhaps Nagarath meant something else by his inquiries. Mayhap Anisthe's veiled words to Liara at their parting had sounded some memory in her teacher's extensive knowledge. He had recoiled from her asking over the Rishon Kesem. Could that, too, have been part of the ruse? Nagarath and Anisthe had seemed to have found some sense of conciliation in Versailles.

'Find the book.' Deception or deliverance? Could Liara trust her own mind?

"—lad had a foreign look about him. That's to say, he was certainly not from around these misty fields. Printer said he'd come 'round again with "the usual," as he called it. Nothing usual about asking about Nathaniel by his wizard's name if you ask me."

Mary tut-tutted through her news, and Liara ground her teeth, silently cursing herself for having let her attention drift away from the woman's chatter. She quickly tried to attune and realized she could hardly hear above the pounding of her pulse. The air felt thick. Smoky. And yet the chimney appeared to be in working order. She tried her voice, "Nathaniel mentioned coming down later."

The words came out thick and syrupy.

Oh, no. Not now. Not in front of Mary. Liara fought the rising magick. The sparking sourness was not to be deterred, however. Khariton had returned. And with fire and force.

Help.

Mary seemed to sense Liara's distress, for she had armed herself. Carefully. So as not to alarm her guest. But Liara knew the fire iron in her hand for what it was. A quick defense.

"You have it. The staff." The words were not Liara's own, though it was her voice that gave them utterance.

"I d-do not." Stammering, Mary shrank from her, falling towards the wall and brandishing her weapon before her. "The master warned me—"

"Lies." Liara set the chair to tumbling in her wake. She could feel her hair standing on end. The room seemed to glow with unearthly light. Had it been midnight, she believed she could have seen her surroundings as easily. The power, it burned her blood and danced along her fingertips.

And yet, Kerri'tarre did not banish Liara. He, mayhap, wanted her to see. Wanted her to feel fully his strength and give in to despair at last, a battle already lost.

Use it. Use what he gives you, then. Liara thought fast, trying to see without seeing, to think and to plan without inadvertently arming the archmage against poor Mary Hertford.

Mary Hertford. Alone in her house and helpless in the face of magick. Surely Nagarath would have seen to giving her some sort of defense if he entrusted his staff to her. Even if she had refused such, he would have put in place some semblance of spellwork.

Which meant that Liara had to find some way to trigger the protections. *Think like your mage, Liara. What would Nagarath have done? What would he guard against?*

Liara worked to slow her steps. She held her arms tight to her sides, forced her eyes closed, and tried to bleed out whatever of her magick had renewed itself in the space of the morning.

Khariton had waited on Liara doing exactly that. In an eye blink, she lost all control and could only watch, helplessly, as the poker became a weapon for him. He held it at his victim's throat. "The staff. The wizard's staff. Where is it?"

Mary made no reply, only whimpered helplessly in Liara's arms.

"I will not ask again. Where is the red stone?"

"P-please. Mercy." Mary made to clasp her hands.

And Liara saw her chance in the quick flash of metal. A silver charm worn 'round the wrist. Delicately wrought. Nagarath's work.

Liara stumbled backwards, bringing the poker down hard as she caught Kerri'tarre off guard. He had expected her to try to reclaim her magick, not merely her mobility. The heavy iron bar clattered to the floor while Mary screamed and clutched her bleeding wrist to her chest.

The broken chain of the magick charm lay in a shining heap on the floor.

The door burst open.

"I heard a shout." Benjamin Hertford. And with his rifle in hand.

"Mary!" He leveled the gun at Liara, and she raised her wand, back under Kerri'tarre's control. Save for the tears that gathered in her eyes. Those were fully hers.

"Let 'er go. I'm warning ya."

I can't. Liara felt her einatus stir under Khariton's call. She steeled herself for the curse, certain now that she had misunderstood the purpose of Nathaniel's charm of protection lent to Mary.

And then a whirlwind, Nagarath himself, appeared in their midst.

Hands outstretched, his black robes swirling with sorcery, the wizard took quick stock of the situation. His eyes flashed darkly as they met Liara's. "Let her go."

"Hardly," Kerri'tarre sneered. But the wand in his hand trembled and stayed mute.

Past Nagarath's shoulder, Liara could see Ben raise the gun.

Mary screamed, and Liara felt Nagarath's silent curse rip the wand from Khariton's hand. A second jinx turned Ben's rifle aside. The wizard leapt forward to catch Mary as she slumped in a faint while Liara felt her own legs abandon her.

Nagarath's third spell bound Liara's hands and gummed her mouth.

"Burn it off. All of it." Nagarath's command was spoken in a reasonable tone but, to Liara's ears, it sounded as though he screamed the words.

Incapacitated as she was, Liara did not think it likely she could obey. Nagarath knelt swiftly at her side and, placing his open palm on her forehead, pulled at her Art. Magick bled from her and danced sparkles into the corner of the Hertfords' home. Wood rippled and metal warped. Liara felt her eyes roll in her head under the strain. And then a blessed, empty silence.

Incantate. Or near enough. With Kerri'tarre's mocking laughter the last to die to silence. The hex around Liara's hands and face lifted, and she breathed deep, trying to ward off the faint that threatened with her total expenditure of magick.

"I'm sorry. I really am." With that woefully inadequate apology, Nagarath grabbed Liara's shoulder and brought them both back to Little Larkhill's library.

There the force of his spell separated them. But only for a moment.

Nagarath's hands were back on Liara's shoulders, his face peering into hers. Such anguish from so close threatened to bring her to tears.

"Are you there? Liara?"

"Yes. Yes, I'm me," Liara choked out and tumbled into him.

His hands pressed gently into her back and against her hair, soothing. "You called me to Mary. You used her charm. You won against the archmage this time."

Liara shook her head. "No. He merely let me see. I paid attention and was lucky, that's all."

"I'm glad for it, magpie. So, so glad. If anything had . . . No. No." Liara could feel Nagarath shaking. "Ben, he—"

"It's okay, Nagarath."

"In one more second he would have sh— He would have—" Nagarath could not continue.

Liara held tight to her wizard. She recalled the touch of Nagarath's hand on her forehead. She remembered the burn of his magick. "What was it you did to bleed out my power?"

"Something I hope never to have to do again." Nagarath's face darkened, and he tried to turn away from her.

Liara allowed him his moment of shame. Her wizard had rules beyond what the Laws bound his magick. Nagarath lived under a strict morality as to the use of the Art. As did most mages, good or evil. Even Anisthe had professed to having something akin to honor.

Whatever hex Nagarath had performed on her, it violated every tenet of proper magecraft; his aiding Liara eroded his dignity towards the Art, spell by spell.

Oh, Nagarath. Don't lose yourself while trying to save me.

Slipping her hand into Nagarath's once more, Liara wept.

CHAPTER EIGHTEEN

At length Nagarath left Little Larkhill to go see to Mary and Benjamin. Which gave Liara ample time to worry and ruminate on her own. Alone, she fretted her distress by restlessly pacing her room. Not that the wizard could have brought her with him on his visit down to the cottage. Liara wouldn't have allowed it, even were the option proposed.

Her fate was to wait. She had again begged Nagarath to make her incantate. In response, he had told her of his aborted sorcery in the library. He had said the words, made the sign. But his heart had faltered. Love barred the way of his curse.

The threat to Mary and Ben, though—it had changed everything. This time Nagarath would do as Liara asked. He would try his spell again. And he would use it on her when least suspected.

But could he do it? Could he really? Had Nagarath within him the capacity to take Liara's magick from her?

Even with Liara's permission, even with her having asked for it for their own sake?

What were the alternatives?

Danger and ruin.

She feared Nagarath would never—could never—hurt her. He would believe to the end that they might yet find a way around the problem rather than attack it at its source.

Khariton would have the cinnabar stone for himself.

And then he would find Merlin, take his immortality, take Anisthe's Rishon Kesem, and control the Laws of Magick for himself.

And Nagarath wouldn't stop him out of love for Liara.

Liara's instinct was to shout at him, sit him down and explain how damning his hope was. She had, of course, not done so. But she had accepted Kerri'tarre. She'd loosed the archmage upon the world. Why could Nagarath not see that and use the threat of it to fuel his anger? Why did that not outweigh his love for her?

Because, when he looked at her he saw Liara, not Kerri'tarre. Saw a chance and a hope and clung to it.

"Which makes him a great fool." Liara's words came punctuated by a harsh, short laugh. The unkind reproof stung her heart.

For love? Love is never foolish.

"Well, it is. Of course it is," Liara countered, thinking back on her own tangle of stupid words with the wizard when Amsalla had threatened to take him from her. "Love is inconvenient. Frustrating. Inconsistently illogical."

Much like Nagarath himself, Liara observed, her cheeks warming with the thought.

"Love is annoying. And wholly unstoppable," she concluded, miserable.

One might as well demand the sun not rise. Liara laughed again, thinking of the magick that would employ, the consequences that would entertain.

"The magick that it would take to stop love . . ."

A chill struck Liara. It shivered through her veins and breathed frost into her soul. She knew where to find such spells. Nagarath had given her the room with a shortcut to such. And he had given her his real name.

Surely her heart would die. Or turn to stone. Better that than destroy what remained of Nagarath's home, his people. Or Nagarath himself. And a spell like that? He would never know of its having been enacted. She could arm him—save him—without his even knowing it.

"Oh, but I couldn't." Hands to her mouth, Liara tried to un-think her horrid thought. But an idea once pondered is an idea birthed. She couldn't stop herself from striding to the writing desk across the room. Her hands uncapped ink while her eyes inspected the nib of the pen. A scrap of paper sufficed.

She wrote his name.

Nathaniel Clemson.

Liara knew enough of the mechanics of love spells to have her beginning. Little Larkhill's library would supply the rest. She went downstairs via the hidden stairwell. All was quiet. The fire on the hearth had died to cold ash. The wizard was not present.

Thickness in Liara's throat rendered it hard to breathe.

Not the archmage's incursion that time, no. Kerri'tarre, it would seem, had no desire to interfere with her misery. That or . . . Liara called her magick into her fingers. *Still there. Not incantate, then. Stop me, Nagarath, you cowardly wizard.*

Liara pleaded through silent tears, "Take my magick, and render me incapable of doing this. Please."

Having made a relatively thorough inspection of Little Larkhill's library in past explorations, Liara knew exactly where to find the spells she sought. She remembered the codex; remembered what shelf.

Standing tip-toe next to one of the window casings, Liara squinted through the slanted multi-colored sunlight and considered Nagarath's situation. His visit with the Hertfords had grown long. Perhaps he hadn't had time yet to enact the curse that would erase Liara's magickal inclination. But then she thought of Mary, of her frightened face. *'Mercy.'*

Before leaving, Nagarath had mentioned that the Hertfords had known something of the curse Liara was under. It was why they had never ventured to the house proper since the arrival of the wizard and his apprentice. They had been warned away.

Hands shaking, her knees growing weak, Liara quickly retrieved the book she sought and then sat on the window seat, soundly cursing Khariton. "You made me watch, you unforgivable evil."

Her terror and hatred helped make her decision for her.

As did her tears.

Shaking, weakness overtook her for one searing

moment. But her misery could not stop Liara from thumbing through to the proper spell. It did not veil her eyes such that she might not read the text, though drops of sorrow fell to dot the page. No matter. For this curse, the power was not in the book itself, but rather in the scrap of paper with her beloved's name and in the words that would guide the fire to consume it.

Through it all, Liara pleaded and hoped. Let her mage find a way to take the magick away. Gods, how it would hurt to have the Art ripped from her. But she was ready for it. Again anxiety prickled the back of Liara's neck. Anticipation for attack that would nigh on kill her or at least kill the wizard inside. Mourning for the gift she must lose. Stop Khariton. Stop her.

"Which of us is worse? Me or the archmage?"

We are the same.

Kerri'tarre's thought or hers? Not that it mattered.

In the silent library, Liara waited with the book open on her lap for her magick to return to her, heart breaking further with each second that passed. For a return of her power meant that Nagarath loved her too much to hurt her. And in doing so, he doomed his own regard for Liara. Her consolation? The only one to suffer from her curse would be Liara herself. If her magick returned and she did as intended with the book in her hands, Nagarath would never know what his decision had wrought.

At length Liara gave up on her vigil and sparked a fire in the hearth. The day had grown cloudy, and she again looked to the stained glass windows, her hands straying to the pendant at her neck. But, no. Nagarath would come when called. He'd combat her actions not with spells, but with logic and caring and love. She'd lose her nerve under his endearing academia.

"You've won," she challenged through gritted teeth. Let Khariton think as much. Anything so that he would leave Nagarath alone. With the spell cast, Liara would have scant power for the archmage to use. Time enough to see if it had worked and then make her way from Little Larkhill. For after such heartache, she dare not stay. Not if she really meant to keep her wizard safe.

For all that she had agonized over it, the casting of the spell of disregard was simple enough. The paper smoked and curled. The magick sparked and danced. Liara's einatus extinguished with the expenditure of power, and she settled in to wait for the mage's return, unable even to rebuild the fire save for the roundabout way of poker and bellows. But setting sparks up into the chimney only proved a temporary distraction.

Liara browsed and found the biggest book in Nagarath's library. Tucked into a deep wing-backed chair, one well-worn into a misshapen, threadbare lump, she imagined she could feel the imprint of where Nagarath had long sat. Ridiculous, considering his on-again, off-again history with the manor. But it comforted her, held her as she waited to see what her magick had wrought.

Legs tucked up under her, Liara had endeavored to make herself as small as possible—as small as she felt—behind the cover of the large codex.

It hadn't worked. Couldn't have. Even with her magick gone.

Why had she done it? Would Nagarath be angry with her for it? Would he even know?

She shrank further still, eyes on the page in front of her and seeing nothing. Her breath had reduced to shallow exhalations. A vain attempt at stopping time lest hope wriggle from her grasp.

Footsteps in the hall brought a blazing heat to Liara's cheeks. Her heart hammered within her chest so loudly as to call the mage to her. His heart, really. Did he still want it?

Liara strained to hear his approach, not daring to look past the book in her hands. Inwardly she cursed the thick and cozy rug that carpeted the floor. Her fingers shook as she turned a page. The cowardly attempt at drawing the wizard's attention bore fruit.

"*The Varying Flight Patterns of The Familiar versus The Wild*. Bird-watching, Liara? I suppose it's a neutral enough pursuit." Nagarath's voice sounded nearer than Liara expected. She jumped. Her heart ceased its frenetic pounding to sing its sweet relief and joy. Her casting hadn't worked. Her folly would stay unrealized, thank the powers above.

She dared a glance over the top of the book.

With a fleeting smile and apologetic raise of his hands, Nagarath backed out of his having interrupted.

Liara lowered the book. "It's all right. I'm not really reading it, Nagarath."

Did she imagine the slight tightening of his jaw at the words? Paranoia and guilt warred for dominance. The mage did not respond. He, instead, bent to browse one of the lower shelves.

Liara debated pushing further. The words stuck in her throat.

Had it worked, then? Her magick?

She needed to know.

"Nagarath, I—"

"Master Nagarath, Liara."

The slap of his murmured correction sparked tears in Liara's eyes. But Nagarath, of course, remained oblivious to her distress. Because it had worked. Her magick, her horrible, horrible spell had worked.

A broken sob escaped her before she could call it back. The ugly sound echoed in the quiet space and brought Nagarath's attention back on Liara. The book was quickly raised back into place with hands that trembled. The shaking grew to reach her arms, her legs. It set her teeth rattling in her head—ill-concealed hysterics that threatened to take her over. A strange brightness seeped into her vision. She thought she might faint, welcomed it, even. For then she could hide from those dispassionate eyes that bore into her from across the room. She looked at him and found that she faced, not unkindness from the mage, but mere distance. It was as if he did not know her. Or she him. And yet, obviously, he did know her. He hadn't come ranting and spell-casting into the library to chase her from his home. He knew her name, knew her to have a place within the armchair by the fire. The only thing gone was the love.

CHAPTER NINETEEN

"They're fine, Liara. The Hertfords. Had a good scare though. I dressed the scratch on Mary's arm and explained things as best I could." Nagarath held Liara's tear-filled gaze for one long moment.

The massive book did not move back to hide his apprentice's face, and Nagarath was the first to look away. He worried through the reigning silence, picking through the library shelf at hand but not really seeing the books. He frowned, adding, "And now we have to leave."

"We?" Startled to her feet, Liara laid aside her reading material. She trembled. Nagarath could see that even from a distance of ten paces.

Still, Nagarath could not keep his frown from deepening. "Yes. We. Is something amiss?"

"I guess I thought that I—we—would . . . part ways. After what happened." Liara seemed to sway under the weight of her ineptly-hidden agitation. Nagarath could not remember her so contrite, so apologetic, so unable to give a convincing lie. It spooked him to see her thus. She was acting very unlike herself—Khariton's influence included. Liara seemed hollowed out.

"Nonsense. You are my apprentice. My responsibility. And as such I cannot have you off wandering about doing gods know what." Smiling in an attempt to brush past the growing unease in the back of his mind, Nagarath continued, "We still need to fix you. And, well, in light of today's events, I am unable to leave you here alone while I—"

Liara's hopeful if blank face stopped him short. Nagarath felt himself grow flustered under the young woman's bright earnestness. He explained, "Ah, I am sorry. Mary had news from town. It would appear that Merlin's messenger is one of flesh and blood. And knows me, apparently."

Opening her mouth, Liara made as if to speak. But no sound came out, and instead, she bent to collect the massive book she had laid aside. Her self-control returned with the placement of the book upon its shelf. She turned back to regard him thoughtfully.

"When do we leave?" And then, after a moment's pause, an afterthought, "Master Nagarath?"

It was Nagarath's turn to hesitate. "I promised the Hertfords we would be gone by sundown."

Liara received the news with the same grave quiet. "I'll ready a few things."

"Fine, yes." Nagarath waved her off, eager to be out from under her discomfiting mood. "Front hall. Five minutes."

Left to his own concerns amongst his books, Nagarath

gave a casual flick of his wand and then pocketed the item. Somewhere upstairs a bag began packing itself for him. With a pang, he realized all the things he might have taught Liara and simply had not. Practical magicks. Perhaps such mental fortitude might have armed her against Kerri'tarre's tricks. But the time for that had passed.

Nagarath put his mind back on the issue of Merlin.

Such timing for Mary's news. Merlin's messenger, a definite live link to the archmage and help for Liara. Possibly; hopefully. Nagarath presumed it Krešimir, of course. That would make Liara happy. He smiled at the thought, concluding that he ought not have corrected her so flatly. The Hertfords' scare was nothing compared to his apprentice's, he was sure. All muddy in his mind, Nagarath could only remember the danger Kerri'tarre had posed, how close he had been to getting at the hidden cinnabar stone and the immense power it proclaimed.

Nagarath would have to find a way to get Liara's wand from her. Without arousing suspicion from either her or Khariton. And soon. Why he had not done so already was yet another mystery. *Getting soft, magus. Taking shortcuts—you and her. All under the excuse of the peril the praecantator poses.*

Shortcuts. For all that Merlin might help them, Nagarath dreaded having to confront England's archmage. He had crossed many lines to send word of Anisthe's designs, the warning that Kerri'tarre might soon be freed to wreak his revenge. Darkest sorceries. And on an Artless like Krešimir.

Never mind that they had failed.

If it were me and Anisthe, if he came to me having done the same, telling a similar story . . . Nagarath would be merciless. He would adhere to the principles imposed upon all wizards, that of upholding the Art even unto death.

And he hadn't a fraction of the power Merlin was reported to have. The archmage might even be well and truly immortal, a formidable enemy to make. But, too, an incredible ally to have, particularly in light of having failed to contain Kerri'tarre.

And therein lay Nagarath's certainty of soul. He had done the wrong thing for the right reasons. He could defend that. And with Khariton threatening the einatus of an aurenaurae, they had no other choice. The future of magick was at stake.

Yes, they must find Merlin straight away.

Hope, at last, gained solid footing in Nagarath's heart. With it, he no longer felt so emptied, no longer himself so strangely spent and adrift.

~

L iara and Nagarath set out from Little Larkhill under skies that had grown disgruntled. Another summer storm rumbled in from over the distant rolling hills. As such, it was still a fair ways off. But it would be wet before nightfall.

Concentrating on the cauliflower clouds that hung low above their heads, Liara tried her best to quell the nervous flutterings of her heart. She told herself that she had played this role before, at the court of the king of

France, as far back as Ragusa. The coolness she felt from her wizard? She could emulate that. For his sake. Or . . . or maybe she no longer had to. After all, they were going to find Merlin. With the thought, bright anticipation rose to hum alongside her anxiety. England's archmage, Kerri'tarre's confederate, would give her her life back. And until then? For Nagarath's sake, Liara could pretend a little while longer. She had learned all too well the dangers of complacency.

"As hope grows, so doth danger. Though I have no doubt he will take to you, what with you being of his type and all." Nagarath's attention shifted to Liara, testing. Sure enough, a smile played about his lips. His steps had gotten their old spring back.

Liara forged ahead, determined to keep her wizard at arm's length. But not coldly so. She offered a tentative smile. Not quite teasing him back, neither did she discourage his good humor. "Left-handed?"

The wizard's short laugh echoed off the nearby trees. "Aurenaurae."

Liara slowed, utterly shocked and suspecting a trick in the answer.

"I thought you would have known that, having read— or skimmed—through every one of my books at Parentino. 'Tis a bit of a well-known fact. A true wizard in that what we only half-know about Merlin is what we best remember."

Liara hid the hot blush of her ignorance from Nagarath with a shake of the head. She ventured, "You removed from the library all the books that made mention of aurenauraes, if you'll recall, Master Nagarath."

"That I did, didn't I." Nagarath thumbed his chin thoughtfully. "Well, in my defense, you were not destined to be my apprentice at that point. But, in any event, the story goes thus:

"Merlin Sylvestris was born in the late fifth century. Now, this was at a point in magickal history when even wizards believed in the existence of creatures and powers outside our ken. I speak, of course, of your dragons, Liara, amongst other things. Magecraft . . . Well, you would not recognize it for how much it has changed.

"Magick became a serious study under Merlin's guidance. It was through him that we began to call sorcery a formal Art. Due to his great and natural talent and his relatively humble origins, his mysterious parentage was called into question. Various stories sprang up. Some claimed Merlin the son of an incubus, some a changeling. Others called him a gift from the old gods to man. In any event, his mother was known to be his—and confirmed by Merlin himself—while his father remained an unknown magickal benefactor.

"His powers were beyond what modern mages have ever been able to recreate. Even the story of his entrapment for all this time—filled with superstitions of fey sorcery and secrets known only to himself and his apprentice."

"Vivien." Liara hadn't meant to slow her steps nor lower her gaze. Guilt weighed heavily upon her soul. Guilt and fear.

Nagarath seemed to feel it, too. "Even with such incredible strength of Gift, his regard for her was his downfall in the end."

The wizard had slowed to meet Liara's pace. Nagarath coming alongside so gently, with words that wounded without his having meant—having known— forced Liara to close her eyes for one long moment. She wanted to promise her mage safety, promise him love. She could do neither.

"You contacted Merlin." Liara sought escape from the sorrow that pressed upon her heart. "You said that you sent him a message. Via magick?"

Nagarath's jaw clenched, and his eyes grew hard. With a curt nod, he turned and strode quickly down the path that would lead them into town. Liara hurried to follow, unsure why such a simple question would have provoked such a response.

At length he gave his reasons, "You saw the books of dark magick in my tower in Parentino. You questioned their purpose as well as my intent. For most of my life, I have enjoyed the luxury of believing myself above the sort of morally suspect sorcery that your progenaurae has employed throughout his ignoble career.

"In Sardinia, I stumbled on my path. I cursed your Krešimir. I spellbound his will to my bidding and sent him through the corridors of magick with the aim to warn Merlin, should we fail in our quest to stop Anisthe. At the time, defeat seemed likely. I was angry and worried. I thought—I hoped—that my methods would be forgiven in light of our situation. I later feared that I might simply have botched the spell."

Swaying, Liara caught herself on the rough wood of a split-rail fence. Krešimir. Nagarath could have killed him using such magicks. That he would have kept such a secret to himself for so many months, that he would have had Liara believing he had merely left Dvigrad's woodsman at a roadside inn somewhere, brought a bit of her own anger rushing to her cheeks.

And on its heels, the cool bite of compassion. Knowing Nagarath as she did, Liara recognized the shame that had held him silent. She forgave him. Of course she must if she trusted him, trusted his magicks, at all. But would Merlin? What were the Laws on such?

Thankfully, Nagarath did not even try to voice his apologies to Liara.

Those he must save for the archmage.

Lifting her gaze to find that Nagarath waited patiently by, the edge of town not a hundred yards off, Liara strove to catch him up. As she did so, the first drops of rain began to fall. Together they hurried towards the nearest inn.

CHAPTER TWENTY

Two rooms in quiet and comfortable lodgings. The inn itself was kept by the most pleasant little man who had the sense to keep his questions to himself, though Liara could not help but notice his bulge-eyed curiosity as he looked the two wizards over. For there was no denying she and Nagarath were wizards.

But. Two rooms. Her silent suffering on that account had been enough to rouse Liara from her worries. For everything else had gone beige for her from the moment they had stepped inside. Her pack in her room. Nagarath's bag in his. And then down to the common room to take a meal and make their inquiries over the printer in town and the man whom the Hertfords claimed had been asking about Nagarath.

From the food on their plates to the attitude of the folk her wizard questioned to the half-curious stares Liara drew: all of it bland and unexciting.

Liara supposed she ought to be grateful, and in some

ways, she was. She just couldn't adjust to it, and she squirmed under the quiet, disinterested normalcy. Her eyes had forgotten where to look when not glancing over one's shoulder, her ears to not strain at the contents of every conversation within reach. The smell of the rain through the open door and windows, the fresh damp ushered in on strangers' cloaks and hats. Liara wanted to arm herself against it, to guard against its soporific effects lest she fall to error in front of the mage. Unprovoked anxiety rose in her chest, and she whispered the words of Nagarath's counter-curse to her magick, "Kiih'ed einatae."

Nothing. At present, Liara had no power to call.

"Liara?"

She looked up and into stern gray eyes. Liara's breath caught before she could master herself, and she felt the blood drain from her cheeks in a cold trickle. She whispered, "I was just checking."

Nagarath searched her face. Liara fought the instinct to duck, to hide. Tears pricked the corners of her eyes, and she blinked them away.

"Good. Thank you," he concluded at last, then averted his eyes to examine their surroundings.

Liara lowered her gaze to stare at the table. The anxiety steepened and grew noisy. She needed escape. She needed a chance, a moment free from having to not pretend so many things at once.

At the edge of her vision she saw Nagarath place his hand on the table. The movement drew her attention and chased her despondency. The wizard's query came again, "Liara?"

"I've a headache," she blurted. A serviceable lie. With it, Liara could escape to the privacy of her room. Her room—not theirs. The subtle stabbing in her soul ached anew at the thought. A practical inner voice shouted over it. Alone was safer. For the fact of the matter was that she didn't know how to act around Nagarath. Well, really, she did. Of course she did. And she hated it. Yes, a headache and solitude sounded quite pleasant in contrast.

Nagarath saw her off at the door to her room with a silent, grave smile. Neither had words for the other. It seemed to Liara that her tension had infected her companion, and her heart flipped in her chest oddly as he walked off down the short hallway to his room. Liara shut the door and stared at the wood of it for about two breaths and then reconsidered her cowardice. Frustrated—and, really, looking for any excuse to just . . . to just bring Nagarath back—Liara opened her door to ask after him.

She discovered that she confronted an empty hallway.

Liara shut her door, disappointed and inwardly scolding herself for her moment of weakness. It was better for all, their current arrangement. And she had only just made her mind up on the matter when, a moment later, Nagarath appeared in the corner of her room.

"Are you decent?" The wizard rather pointedly had his hand up over his eyes.

Eased in spite of all, Liara laughed. He just looked so silly. Ever so much the man she had come to fiercely love. She said, "You left me at the door not even a minute ago."

Her response was not particularly an answer. The hand lowered slowly, and Nagarath stood where his spell had deposited him looking awkward and out of place. Liara reined her laughter in before it had her lapsing over into hysterics. By then he, too, had caught a case of the giggles. Easeful. Hopeful. Relaxed. If only a touch.

He furthered the familiarity by claiming the chair by the fire. Liara tensed and backed out of the moment as best she could. The hex she had affected at Little Larkhill was such a small spell, really. A thin illusion. Just as magick had no true way of creating love, the opposite— the killing off of regard—rang equally false and therefore tenuous. Watching Nagarath's face relax in good humor, she found herself afraid all the more of her own feelings for him and how it might spark his anew.

Nagarath's regard remained somewhere beneath the curse, a lamp hidden under a basket. Liara clung to that knowledge as she moved away from the mage to lean against the window. The rain-washed glass cooled and soothed her rioting nerves.

"How are you feeling?" he asked, not looking up.

"Kiih—"

"Your headache, Liara." He set his eyes to hers, and Liara went dizzy with hope.

"Fine." She swallowed drily. "What is it you want?"

At her directness, he appeared nonplussed. "You thought I dare leave you alone at this juncture? With Kerri'tarre pressing and so close to what it is that he desires?"

Again, Liara whispered the spell to quell her magick. The words sounded a whimper within her signature and nothing more.

Nagarath grunted approval. "Kerri'tarre wants more

than the little trinket that I have carried. Kerri'tarre wants power. An audience and a following. He wants magick back and roaming free and respected within the world. Wants to force Merlin's hand, dare that confrontation . . ."

The mage's eyes unfocused, and his fingers came up to pinch the bridge of his nose. Unable to bear the quiet, Liara continued, "And we've been asking over the man who can lead him to Merlin. Openly."

Nagarath's attention returned to the present. He nodded and said, "Which means, Liara, you're under my . . . protection. For the time being."

At this Liara felt a shock go through her. She looked to her hands, feeling the tingle pulse over her fingertips, the ghost of an itch. The touch of Nagarath's spellwork had been so light she had not felt it. Or had she simply been that distracted?

"What was that?" *Master Nagarath.* Liara gritted her teeth against the accidental omission.

He smiled enigmatically, lost in his academics. "Never you mind what. It is similar to that which allowed you access to the secrets of Parentino. And only works so long as you have drained your power as you have. I thank you for that foresight and caution, my apprentice."

"Why now? Why not before when we were so—?" Liara bit her lip lest she say the wrong thing and lead them down a conversation they must avoid.

The caution was unwarranted. Nagarath had shifted to stare into the fire. Stirring it to brightness with a gesture, he murmured, "Time. Besides magick, she is our greatest enemy."

Liara waited for him to elaborate further. He did not.

Left to their own separate thoughts, they sat in ruined silence. Meanwhile the summer storm outside passed overhead, and the sky turned to night.

Both kept their vigil—Nagarath out of duty and the need to keep up his spellwork, Liara for the feeling that it might well really be the ending of her time with him. Her quiet foreboding prevented her from sleep in spite of the mage's repeated gentle encouragement. In the end, the bed remained un-slept-in, and neither wizard nor apprentice moved from their respective choice of perch.

Morning came, and she and Nagarath took leave of their lodgings. The day had dawned heavy and promised both heat and further storms. Liara waited anxiously by the wizard's side. They stood within the shadows of the building across the street from the printer's shop. Seeming to sense her agitation, Nagarath gave her hand a gentle squeeze. Surprised hope tangled with sickening rationality. Liara's heart thrummed in her chest. Luckily, her eyes lit on something compelling enough to tear her thoughts from the mage's kindly meant gesture.

Krešimir, mysterious publisher of the Merlinic Prophecies.

Had she not gripped Nagarath's hand tight in her distress, Liara might well have slipped unconscious onto the ground, leaving the wizard to meet Dvigrad's only other survivor.

Quickly recovering, Liara stepped forward. Nagarath's gentle restraint, his own unreadable expression, stopped her. A distant tingling in her aura informed her that her mage affected a silent and invisible spell.

"Come." With a nod, Nagarath signaled the all-clear

and, giving Liara's hand another reassuring squeeze, drew forward into the street.

Krešimir strode towards the woods having delivered his charge, wholly unaware of his pursuers. Same sandy straw hair glinting in the sunlight. Same jaunty step and strong shoulders. He stopped, whipping around suddenly to face the two mages who had followed him to the edge of town. In his hand he held a small willow wand. But his face . . . Liara found that she had to lower her eyes to avoid the force of his gaze. When Nagarath shifted beside her to draw forth his own wand, Liara realized she had shrunk into the wizard, and she hated herself for it.

She darted her gaze back to Krešimir and saw that he had lowered his wand.

'*Teach me some magick, Liara. Don't make me beg.*' Words from a time and a world away. How far they both had come. Liara's thoughts ran deep into the forest of the Limska Draga Valley. A gurgling stream and sunlight glinting through pink foliage, wished-for promises not made . . . She needed no spell to relive that memory.

The hand holding hers gently slipped free and returned Liara to the present. Both men looked at her expectantly. Liara didn't know what to do. So she chose to sink into the warmth of sweet relief. Krešimir alive and well and there with them in England. Merlin's messenger. It made a mad sort of sense after everything they had been through. How dare she be anything but happy?

And if Krešimir loves me—well and truly loves me— then at the very least it might aid in my not accidentally breaking the curse that I put on Nagarath. The thought brought a hot blush to Liara's cheeks. She needed to affect a careful neutrality. No causing false hopes and wronging Krešimir as once he had wronged her.

But had he wronged her? Liara considered his journey, his own dark path and the steadfast heart that had walked it. Surely such actions spoke over the silence of his non-offer of help back in Dvigrad. And even then, his helping Phenlick—really a poor, misguided attempt at helping her and Nagarath—had meant a lot. If nothing else, it had saved his life.

Krešimir was not her Nagarath. But neither did Krešimir mean nothing to her. Liara's shocked substitute for a smile was replaced by the real thing. But Krešimir's attention was directed elsewhere. He focused entirely on the mage. Some combination of compassion and respect, Liara could not fully read his expression. For a brief and terrifying moment, Liara thought: he knows!

Such was, of course, utterly impossible. Nagarath had not yet loved her the last time they had all met. Liara recalled the rock-strewn beach of Sardinia, and the ghost of pain rose within her einatus—

Liara swayed again under the force of the memory, amazed to think that both men could have come to a shaky peace after everything they had been through.

Or, perhaps, that was too much to hope for.

Nagarath eyed the wand in Krešimir's hand, then secreted his own. "Not here."

Krešimir inclined his head in a nod. He turned to lead them from town. With his gaze averted, Liara could move again. And yet . . . That he had still not spoken sounded a tremor in Liara's heart. The air snapped with tension and filled her head with waves of unease. Somewhere deep within the heart of her magick, Kerri'tarre waited for any opportunity to arise.

The trio left the path behind and entered a quiet, tall-treed wood. Liara looked to Nagarath and saw he weathered the short journey with stone-faced calm. Like a man being led to the gallows—she could feel his apprehension but resisted the urge to comfort him. It never occurred to her to be fearful herself.

Least not until Krešimir's willow wand again made appearance.

Nagarath raised one eyebrow, his lips puckering with mirth as he asked, "What has he taught you, then?"

"Enough for me to find you." The wand wavered but did not lower. "Enough for Merlin to see what has been going on in the world. Enough to know that you failed Liara. And that we're all in danger now."

"I—"

"You cursed me! Flung me into darkness and halfway across the world into Merlin's prison!"

"If you understand the repercussions of our failure in Versailles, then you understand the need for my message to Merlin back in Sardinia when it seemed Anisthe would win."

"And now it is you who've . . . won."

Nagarath remained impassive under Krešimir's veiled accusation, though Liara could see his jaw tighten almost imperceptibly. It chilled her heart to see him so careful, so disconnected from easy anger.

Liara stepped forward between the men, tears stinging her eyes. *Stop.*

"Go. I will take her to Merlin. You, wizard—you

are not needed for this leg of the journey. Nor do I believe that I've been granted the strength of spell to get you both to the archmage." The words left Liara cold.

Again Nagarath had wisdom enough not to rise to Krešimir's provocation. Even so, from the corner of her eye Liara could see that her mage again held his wand at the ready. "If one hair of her is harmed—"

"I know what spells you are capable of, yes. Merlin and I both." Krešimir's lip curled his disdain. "I should think you would be relieved that he has no desire to see you after the magecraft you've employed of late. Come, Liara."

"Fly, magpie." Nagarath's voice at her back already came colored by distance.

She hesitated, wanting—needing—her goodbye to Nagarath in spite of all; in spite of the danger her regard for him might yet pose. Backing away and swallowing her tears, Liara took leave of her mage at wand point. "Will I— Can I see you again at Little Larkhill? Nagarath?"

Blanching, he did not correct her impulsive disrespect. Rather, his face softened, and he lowered his wand. "A visit from you, Liara, will always be welcome."

A visit.

Krešimir's hand grasped hers. Liara's anguish found its voice.

Hand and hand with Krešimir. She had wanted that for so long. And now all it could do was make her cry. Her vision blurred behind the veil of her sorrow, partly obscuring Nagarath's lifting of his free hand in a silent wave. His other wove the spell that took him back to his home in a shattering of sparkles.

At her side, Krešimir's face lost its fierce strength. Tenderness grayed his eyes, and his hand left Liara's to enfold her in a gentle embrace. Her lower lip trembled, and her cheeks flushed hot, then cold. Liara could feel her control over her magick weakening with her efforts to stop crying, and she hurried to master herself.

Why must she feel that way? She had hope. If Merlin could help her, then she could return to Nagarath.

Krešimir stepped back and began a halting incantation in mostly well-formed words of magick. Liara's expert ear cringed, and her tongue twitched with the desire to correct his deficiencies in pronunciation. Serviceable sorcery, the magick of the world responded to the woodsman's imperfect call. The scene around them melted into a silent black warmth.

And, just as quickly, it faded, leaving Liara and Krešimir standing on the edge of a lonely moor. Liara blinked her surprise at the gentle magick.

Wordlessly Krešimir led them onward, his hand clinging tight with Liara's. A claim of ownership. Liara could not—dare not—make the correction. They made their way in silence towards a distant hovel that sat astride a low hill. The only witness to their steady progress, a lone raven flew high in the gray skies above and screamed its warning.

Walking in silence, Liara determined that her Krešimir had changed. He had grown cold. Hardened. When she had last seen Dvigrad's woodsman, his anger had been sharp but his devotion to Liara tangible. Now she felt neither. Even in spite of his being momentarily close and having taken her by the hand.

What Liara had affected for her wizard seemed to have occurred in Krešimir through other means.

By time? By Nagarath's magick? Guilt shuddered through Liara, a suspicion that she was partially to blame.

Her worries were interrupted by their arrival at the little house. An old man huddled by the door, a long pipe clamped in his teeth. From it, a thin curl of smoke rose to dance 'round his head. He did not move. But Liara could see, even from a distance, that Merlin's eyes stayed on his visitors as they approached.

A second black bird sat at the wizard's feet, picking and tearing at something on the ground. Liara spotted a thin brown tail and averted her eyes, not wishing to better see the small creature which had met its death. Memories savaged her heart, as though Merlin's raven had turned its beak on Liara herself. Her hiding away on her first day in Nagarath's company to read about book repair. Feeding a mouse in an upper hallway only to have the wizard jest that it was his former apprentice.

Face warming under her blush, Liara approached the archmage with her hand still clasped within Krešimir's. Their presence startled the wizard's raven, and it flapped heavily up onto Merlin's waiting shoulder.

"Ah, Krešimir. You've found her." The wizard's voice rang strong in spite of his incredibly worn aspect. Resonant and warm, had a mountain chosen to speak, Liara believed it would sound much the same. She liked the archmage instantly.

The raven cawed and cackled and turned its bright

beady eye to Merlin. He listened with an air of attentiveness and then nodded sagely, rising on joints that creaked and cracked. He himself voiced no complaint but merely turned and bid his guests follow. "Come, it's best if we went inside."

"Why? What did she say?" Krešimir half-drew his wand in alarm, and Liara turned fearful eyes to the empty fields around them.

"Bah. Much as these old bones would love to lie about in the sun, our presence is ruining Hrafn's hunt." Merlin turned his gimlet eye to graze the skies, then back to Krešimir. He raised his eyebrows. "Why? Did the bird tell you something else?"

Krešimir opened his mouth to address empty air. Merlin hadn't waited for a response and gone inside. It was surprising how fast the man could move.

Liara ducked to enter the sagging doorway and found that she stood alone in a sunlit field. Two black birds wheeled in the sky far above her head. It seemed to Liara that their raucous cackling had turned to laughter. Merlin's house, Krešimir, even the archmage himself—all gone.

CHAPTER TWENTY-ONE

Alone. Spent of her magicks save for those that might put her at Kerri'tarre's mercy. Liara hugged her arms tight about her, despairing. She stumbled backwards, the first steps of retracing her path—never mind that magick had taken her and Krešimir most of the way.

"—you knew that the curse on her was too strong!"

Krešimir's voice.

Liara choked on the swift hope that rose within her, and she groped about blindly for the bounds of the illusion.

"How would I know any such thing? Guessed, perhaps. But— Ah! There we are."

Merlin's home wavered back into being. The archmage and Krešimir stood arguing at its threshold.

"Liara!" Krešimir rushed back to her side. He faced the archmage. "More tricks, Merlin? Even now. After everything I told you."

"Oh, stop the dramatics. You know I'll help her. If I

can." Merlin stomped forward and peered up into Liara's face. She fought the desire to shrink back under the scrutiny. She concluded she must have flinched, for he beckoned, saying, "I would say you've a pace more before you walk straight through my prison again. I'm at my limit where I stand."

Liara's neck prickled, and her hair stood on end. His limit?

Krešimir explained, "Vivien's curse. See the wood of his house?"

Liara noted then the smooth bark and knotty thorns that comprised the walls of Merlin's home. The roof was thatched by thick, lobed, summer-green leaves. Nagarath was right. Merlin was still entombed beneath the hawthorn tree. Liara shuddered.

"It's not so terrible as that." Merlin's eyes twinkled. "I've managed to gain three paces outside in every direction. Not bad for a millennium of captivity in faerie."

"Faerie?" Liara gawked.

"Krešimir, fetch me my chair. And one for our guest. Faerie, yes. An old spell. And quite a good one, I must admit." He cackled. Madness shone within Merlin's smile. Madness and magick. The archmage's burning gaze stayed focused on Liara, and she realized that he was seeing not her, but he who lived within her magick. His next words confirmed it as Merlin addressed, not Liara, but Khariton himself. "Yes. I have what you want, and you cannot take it from me. Much as I cannot get out, you know that you cannot get in, old friend."

"But . . . but you'll help me. Right?" Tears momentarily blinded Liara. In addressing Khariton, it told her that Merlin had already given up on her. If he could not see her, and see her distress, then he could not help her.

Grunting, Merlin sat on the chair Krešimir had brought forward for him. His gaze upon Liara again became distinctly direct. He smiled. "Have a seat, girl, and I'll see what I can do."

Liara blinked her foolishness away and looked to Krešimir who smiled gentle reassurance at her. In his hands he held a stool. Simple and solid. She knew the craftsmanship, and this time when her heart leapt in her chest, she knew it to be out of true regard for the man at her side. Dvigrad's woodsman. She had missed him without hardly knowing it. A wave of homesickness swept through her. She sat, thinking of everything she had lost, wondering if she would ever again not be heartbroken.

Krešimir sat down at her side and offered his silent support. Merlin had unearthed his pipe and engaged in the process of lighting it. It would not take.

Liara opened her mouth to again make her plea.

"Oh, dragons take me!" Merlin growled and flicked a spark of magefire into brightness along his fingers. The stubborn pipe lit at last, and he shook his hand to rid himself of the lingering magick. His eyes flicked to the woodsman, but his words were to Liara. "I will not entertain requests while you are yet armed. Barrier or no barrier."

Liara could feel Krešimir's alarm. She strove to hide her embarrassment and told herself that, while insulting, Merlin's request was prudent.

"It's fine." Liara produced her wand, meaning to hand

it to Krešimir for surrender to the archmage. But when her eyes lit on the familiar honey-colored wood, she stopped. Cromen's wand. And Master Lumin before him. And Cabal. And Ryn'ne. And so many others.

And Nagarath's . . . He'd never have forced its surrender, would never have asked that of her.

Krešimir gently accepted the wand. He gave Liara a small smile before returning his attentions to the wand itself. He let his gaze run over its golden-toned length, appraising with his woodworker's eye.

"I'll take good care of it," he promised.

Rising, Krešimir turned to step back through the magick which separated Liara from Merlin, separated Merlin from the rest of the known world. The archmage leaned forward, stopping him with a look. "All of it, Liara."

Baffled, Liara tried to think what the archmage could possibly mean.

He prompted, "You've one more artifact of power upon your person. Inert. Small. But that's how the enemy gains on us. Through the smallest of openings, the most simplistic of opportunities. The overlooked weaknesses of anger and pride."

With a twist of the wrist, Merlin invisibly jerked at the chain 'round Liara's neck. Her hands came up, a quick gesture that proved useless. For, with a snap, the chain's silver pendant broke free and flew to the archmage's waiting palm.

How dare he! Bitter tears filled Liara's eyes. Her last tangible connection to Nagarath.

"There. No more tricks. Now we may speak like civilized mages." Merlin narrowed his gaze, poking one bony finger into the air and speaking a spell in a language that Liara did not know.

But Kerri'tarre did.

Gasping, Liara pitched backward under the praecantator's control. Foreign words poured from her mouth, drawing magick from her soul. *"Baa aru ni guli. Ni erimĝal kunu. Ab-bur! Siil!"*

The light of Liara's resulting spell rolled over the cottage, over the space surrounding the ancient mage and his messenger. Combative yet harmless.

Merlin shouted once more, *"Kaar."*

And then again.

"Kaar. Kaar!"

On the third time, the cottage wavered and passed from sight without Liara having moved towards it. The last of her spent magick burnt itself out, silencing Kerri'tarre's voice and returning control to Liara. Falling to her knees, she cried atop the empty hill. Head bowed, she groped for the stool that had tumbled to the ground. Her fingers connected with Krešimir's solid workmanship, and her heart clenched. He was nearby. *Kunu.* Close, as Kerri'tarre had said in his ancient language of magick.

Only he had been talking of his enemy.

To his enemy. Liara made the silent correction.

Anger's quick bite warmed her cheeks and dried her tears. She reveled in it, stoking it carefully and holding fast. For this anger belonged to her and not he who had profaned the heart of her magick.

There was more strength to be found within stubbornness than in sorrow. And Liara? She was well-versed in obstinacy. She had made an art of it long before. She would do so again. She would . . . she would wait. She would dry her tears, and she would wait.

Merlin could not hide forever. Not trapped as he was. Not with Krešimir who had loved her, who had crossed the wide world for her and, Liara was sure, would fight for her. And so she sat and vowed to wait, her anger—her indomitability—and Kerri'tarre's being very much the same in that moment.

~

"**A**rchmage!" Krešimir had watched, helpless, as Liara disappeared behind the wall of Merlin's magick. Following the wizard into this home, he demanded explanation.

Merlin was not to be hurried, however. He sat heavily and waved the door shut behind them. "Did you see her eyes?"

"Her eyes?"

"Yes. Her eyes." The wizard rolled over Krešimir's ill-tempered insolence with a calm quiet. But the hands that relit his pipe trembled. "Silver. Bright as a shilling in a river. And as lost."

Krešimir sputtered, "Then help her!"

"I cannot! The power that has taken Liara's magick has grown too strong. Kerri'tarre is of equal match to me. Equal. Not inferior, as Nagarath had once hoped when he sent you to me. Before those two let Khariton free of his own prison in the mirror."

Krešimir pleaded, "Listen to her tears! Listen to her! I'm not having it. You're wrong. You have to be."

Turning back to the door, Krešimir found his way barred by more of Merlin's magick. He rounded on the mage, raising Liara's wand. With a flick of the archmage's finger, the wand snapped out of Krešimir's hands. It flew into a dark corner, made darker beneath Merlin's shadow as the archmage rose to his feet. The magick in that small, wizened man filled the room, pushing outward as though it might finally traverse the bounds of his faerie prison.

"I will do what I can." Menacing. Powerful. Convincing.

Krešimir believed the claim. Or at least believed that Merlin believed his words.

The wizard cast a glowering eye at Krešimir. "You were to have brought both of them to me. Not merely the woman who you are so taken by."

Krešimir froze, adopting a hasty defense as he said, "He would not come. And, besides, I doubt that Nagarath would have given—"

"Hush, lad. Hush!" Merlin moved close, clamping a hand over Krešimir's mouth. "Liara's ears are Khariton's."

He stepped back and continued in a low voice, "I do not want Khariton to win. And saving Liara is tied to the action of my defeating my old rival. Understood? The praecantator, he still knows the old language. He can perform workings that you can scarce imagine. He can tear down the barrier that keeps myself and my secrets—

all of magick itself!—safe. All he needs is time. And power. And rage."

"What will we do?"

Turning, Merlin made no answer. He lost himself to thumbing through old spell components and other arcane oddities that had long since found their way into his home. They filled the walls of the little hut, lining crevices in the living wood that served as shelving. Many of the items were in poor repair. Indeed, some crumbled to dust as he touched them.

"And Liara?" Krešimir was unable to keep anxiety from cracking his voice.

"I'll get to her as I can. My promise to help you holds. But right now the aim is to avoid death at Kerri'-tarre's hands. I've not spent a thousand years trapped in this way only to lose my immortality to some jealous thief."

"Now. After a thousand years, you're motivated."

"Yes."

"So you could, potentially, have left any time."

"No. And yes, perhaps maybe. It's complicated."

"Uncomplicate it. You've been gone for centuries. Our world has—"

"Your world."

Krešimir blinked his surprise and gave no rejoinder.

"There. Did that uncomplicate it enough for you?"

Krešimir's stunned silence continued.

"How is the state of magick in your world, Krešimir? Wonders abound? Wizards everywhere, well-loved and respected? No? There you go. Not my world, then."

Krešimir swallowed. "You were working to change that."

"And you were willing to help . . . for Liara's sake. Dirtying your hands as much as you dared. You who had once feared magick. Or hated yourself for not possessing what Liara so clearly desired."

"Fine. And me?"

"You want magick, boy. We're to walk into the heart of it. Perhaps someone, somewhere, has been listening to my pleas."

Sullen but having little choice in the matter, Krešimir sat to the side, waiting for the moment when Merlin would either break them from his prison or see to it that Krešimir, at the least, went free. Liara's brokenhearted sobbing had long ceased. But within the windowless hovel, he liked to imagine she still stood firm outside the door.

At length Merlin fell to dozing in his chair before the fire, a half a dozen failed attempts at his spellwork lying scattered in his wake, his spell book forgotten on his lap. To Krešimir it seemed the archmage had gone further into faerie, for sparks of magick bubbled from his lips as he murmured in his sleep, rendering the wizard a cousin to the fabled dragons of a long-forgotten age.

With a start, Krešimir found that he, too, had begun to nod off. Not that it mattered all that much, what with him trapped within Merlin's house by hexes he could never hope to combat. But he had something he'd wanted to do while the archmage slept.

Slipping forward, Krešimir crossed over to the far

corner of the room and bent to retrieve the forgotten object there.

Liara's wand. And the most beautiful one Krešimir had ever seen. Not that he had seen many, of course. But unlike the barely whittled stick that Merlin had provided for his use, or even the archmage's own rustic and rough baton, the weapon they had taken from Liara had been crafted with an eye attuned to proportion and artistry. The balance: superb. The lines oh so elegant. Solid and dependable maple, Krešimir could tell the item was old, had seen many hands.

And yet . . .

He peered close, feeling a shiver pull at his eyes and set his spine to trembling. Something was decidedly wrong about Liara's wand. Unnatural. Not pronounced, no.

The grain of the wood. It was all wrong. Off. As if some person—some mage—had changed the wood through magick and then done their best to clean up the mess. It was the sort of thing only one such as Krešimir himself might note and that a wizard, apparently, never would.

Merlin stirred. Discomfited without exactly knowing why, Krešimir quickly hid the wand away. His skin prickled where he had touched the arcane item. Guilt. Or revulsion.

No, no; Krešimir did not want magick for himself.

He looked up to find Merlin's eyes on him.

"I could not have left at any time, no. Nor have I given up on the world that once was mine." The arch-mage's words came mild, wistful. As though he wanted to apologize but, instead, opted to substitute other thoughts and excuses. " *'Baa aru ni guli. Ni erim-ĝal kunu.'* Open to my friend. My enemy is close. That's quite the greeting, is it not?"

Leaning forward, Merlin seemed to lose himself as he gazed into the fire. Krešimir couldn't say from his vantage point across the room, but it looked as though the archmage's cheeks were wet with tears. The ancient wizard continued, mostly to himself, "Friend. Enemy. Always both. Do you know that magick is dying, Khariton? Do you fear what we have wrought? Perhaps I— No, no, as you said, Krešimir, Nagarath would not come. And I could never surrender the . . . For I would have to give you—and him—all my trust, my hopes, alongside it."

He turned back to Krešimir, who saw that the wizard was not, in fact, crying at all. Rather, his face had darkened in rage. Bitterness twisted his mouth and dulled his eyes. A trick of the light? Mere illusion? He spoke, "Khariton will kill us. And then move to take the rest of the world and all the magick that is left."

"Do you really think Liara would—?"

"Any morality in magick and how it is wielded amongst us mages? All is owed to Kerri'tarre Uticae. Not because he is good, no. But rather because each and every limit, the totality of wizardly etiquette, rises directly from his having violated all bounds of common decency with his magecraft. We had been friends. Together we brought magick from the darkness of wild chaos into order and safety. We made magick useful—he and I. And then he lost his way. He became that which we so diligently fought. And all under the new order we had imposed. I made my mistakes, sure, but . . . this was different."

"He is evil."

"He is lost. And Liara with him."

A rumble seemed to shake the wizard's house. It struck alongside Merlin's words, adding confirmation and agreement. A dark finality lit by a piercing flash of light from without the hut, Krešimir jumped in alarm. Merlin did not move.

Instead, the mage continued his moody smoke, eventually knocking dottle from his pipe into the fitful fire. The flames had begun to hiss and spit from the rain falling down the faulty chimney. No ancient mage using Liara's magick came raging through the worn front door, just an ill-tempered wind.

It set to ruffling Krešimir's ire anew. The very idea of Liara waiting out in the dark and in such weather. He shifted in his chair, restless, helpless, and unable to offer anything else in the face of Merlin's damning edict. Why, oh, why was Krešimir himself not a wizard? It would have saved them so many times over.

The mage was mumbling to himself, his fingers idly drawing themselves over the cover of the spell book that lay in his lap. "Whose patience is greater? Whose strength? Like me . . . so very like me."

"Let her in. Talk to her. Reason with him. Nobody is completely evil."

Krešimir's answer was a look from Merlin, a long unreadable pause. The wizard rose. He stumped across the room. But the wood pile was his short journey's end. The mage returned to his seat to silently rebuild the fire.

Another spark of magick and Merlin's pipe was relit. Wreathed smoke surrounded his sly, curious smile. He asked, "What were you looking at there, Krešimir, my boy?"

Krešimir clenched his hand around the concealed length of wood and almost didn't answer. In the end, honesty won out. "I was looking at Liara's wand. I didn't think it right to leave it where it fell."

Merlin grunted.

The mage's non-interest proved more disarming than curiosity would have been. Krešimir found he had to ask, "Do folks . . . do wizards have a habit of keeping things inside their wands?"

"No. That would be unusual and obscenely difficult to do without wrecking the intents of such a delicate tool." Merlin barely flicked an eyelid. "If you are still worried, her wand poses no danger, we on the one side, her on the other. Sleep, Krešimir. I am inclined to believe, at this point, that she will leave of her own volition, finding that what keeps me in is as effective at keeping the undesired elements out."

Sleep. Bah. Krešimir fought Merlin's edict as long as he could. In the dim flickering of the dying firelight, his mind invented scenarios wherein he might intervene and save Liara yet. But, soon, his eyelids grew heavy of their own accord. He would have suspected witchery were he not too tired to puzzle it out. In his hand he still held Liara's wand, and dreaming, he felt its secret magicks working on his heart.

CHAPTER TWENTY-TWO

Nagarath's spell dropped him just outside Little Larkhill's library door. Annoyed, for he had meant to land amongst his books, he strode forward into the room. The rug muffled his steps. The library lay quiet, its hearth cold. Emptiness overtook him for one startling moment. Taken aback, Nagarath attempted to master his despondency, addressing the silent books with a simple: "Well. That is that."

He considered his decision to rescind his claim on Liara. It made sense to give her over to Krešimir. The paths to the archmage were few, and Dvigrad's woodsman knew the way and had his trust. And, besides, the solution had presented itself neatly, so conveniently, what with Nagarath not altogether eager to meet Merlin. Liara should be with her fellow countryman. That, as Nagarath had already concluded, was that.

But Nagarath felt . . .

He felt like a dulled knife. Both more and less terrible than he expected to after the parting of the ways. It had a blank simplicity to it. A wound already healed, if imperfectly. Mayhap it was the tension of the situation that gnawed at him still. For unless he scried Liara, Nagarath had no way of knowing how Merlin would fix her curse.

Who cared! Drat it all. He was done. He was free. Nagarath could do . . . He could do whatever he wanted. Having been forced from Parentino by Liara, by Anisthe, he had finally found purpose. Even if it had been in service to someone else.

Purpose. Had he purpose of his own? Of course he did. Of course he did.

Nagarath ground his teeth, finding himself a bit too insistent on that last point. He stalked over to the fireplace and set a hex there. A swish of his wand called a book to his hand. He would follow in Cromen's footsteps. That's what he would do. He would take on another apprentice or two.

"Never mind that it all fell to pieces with Liara in the end and that we had skirted disaster every step along the way."

She was Anisthe's. Patterned after her progenaurae, what else could Nagarath have expected of her?

Nagarath blanched and let the book slip from his fingers unread. Bitterness was making him unfair and unkind to Liara. As penance he forced himself to remember the sweet moments; recollect how they had become close, caring, in spite of her being Anisthe's and in spite of the guilt with which Nagarath had approached his guardianship of the young woman.

Again the silence of the house pressed upon Nagarath's heart. At last, he had to admit defeat. He was lonely. He missed her. Five minutes gone and all manner of chaos and danger sidestepped and—and all he could do is miss her disorder in his life.

Disorder. Ha! Nagarath looked around the library. *Ironic, that.*

He dropped the book and whisked another to his waiting hands. The dark barbs of the runes on the page snagged at his eyes. Nagarath found he could not read the words. Not for any lack of magick. Aimless passion had misled his mind. Baffled it.

He threw the book down in a fit of pique. Moodily, Nagarath's fingers strayed to the bridge of his nose. Staring into the fire, he recalled Amsalla's scrying variant, a technique that did not use one's own magick. Rather, the seeing spell relied upon the energy present within the flames, the power in the world itself. "Volatile," Nagarath had called it. Well? Everything they did was dangerous, was it not?

Guilt swept through Nagarath anew. He ought have taught Liara the trick. He ought have taught her so many things. Maybe then she would not have fallen to Kerri'tarre's influence. "It's too late for that, you fool, fool wizard," he growled at himself.

Merlin had her now. The greatest wizard who had ever lived, Merlin would undo the mess Liara had brought upon herself. Not Nagarath. Not Cromen's cowardly bookworm.

A figure in the flames arrested his attention. In that moment, Amsalla's cleverness served Nagarath well. Not limited to mere sight and sound, her scrying method allowed the viewer to sense the unseen, to feel the nature of the spellwork being scried.

And so he could feel the power radiating off his apprentice. He could tell the magnitude of the curses Liara hurled at her invisible enemy much as he knew that her target was Merlin himself.

"No!" Nagarath pitched forward, bracing himself on the mantle as he screamed into the flames. As if his apprentice could hear him. As if, under Kerri'tarre's control, she would ever pay him any heed. Tears blurred his vision in the flames, and he scrambled backward in search of his staff.

But that he had left in Ben and Mary's care.

Mary and Ben! Panicked, Nagarath drew his wand and simply appeared in the Hertfords' cottage. For once luck was on his side. Nobody saw his startling entrance or witnessed his frantic plundering of the kitchen for the disguised cinnabar stave. Finding it, he turned and waved a hand over the table. "Forgive me, Mary."

Black marks drew themselves onto the worn wood. The message read:

I have it. –N

He dare not say more, though Nagarath wished with all his heart to apologize to the lovely woman for having ruined her table. He vowed to make amends in person. Later. There would be time. At present, the need was to stop Liara—Kerri'tarre—from getting everything. Every tie must be severed, and he must run, run before Khariton gave up his battering on Merlin's impenetrable defenses and turn his eye back towards the cinnabar stone.

"She has Cromen's wand. You gave Liara the key to

all, you fool, fool wizard." Nagarath shuddered under the horror of his realization. His oversight. His mistake. So eager to be gone, so wrapped up in his own guilt and fearful of facing Merlin, Nagarath had forgotten to take back the one thing that could be most dangerous in Kerri'tarre's hands—outside the cinnabar stone itself.

Nagarath glanced back to the kitchen table and debated adding a second message to the first. *Leave. Now!*

A shadow fell across the window, and Nagarath ducked, readying his magick. A quick rattle and the door opened to Mary Hertford.

"Oh, you startled me so." Her hand flew to her throat, and she let out a breathy, self-conscious laugh. Mary's eyes, however, remained tense and searching. She looked to the wand in Nagarath's hand and the heavy-handled ladle in the other. "And Liara?"

"Gone." Nagarath hadn't meant the word to come out broken as it did. But there it was. His emptiness returned, rendering him vulnerable. He swayed unsteadily against the wall. "I am sorry about your table. I can fix it."

Mary blinked, completely nonplussed even as she bustled over to the table and ran her fingers along the marks. "Magick, magick. Is there anything it touches that it doesn't wreck?"

She paused and, not looking up, added, "Are we in danger?"

"Yes."

Two terrified eyes swung up to meet his. Nagarath moved to reassure Mary Hertford, the idea forming even as he spoke, "But I can stop her. Liara. The curse, it needs her. And her life is tied to another's."

Anisthe. He'd kill Anisthe.

Nagarath affected his next spell with a mere thought directed toward the ladle in his hand. The magick around it broke. The artifact became a staff once more. He turned back to Mary. "I can move you to someplace safer, should my apprentice return looking for me. I will not be here but . . ."

Wordlessly, Mary nodded. Then, "What are you going to do?"

He did not answer.

Nagarath moved to the window and peered out. "Where's Ben?"

"Nathaniel Clemson, son of Michael at Little Larkhill, you will stop for one second and answer me."

"I am going to stop Liara." Nagarath turned to his housekeeper, the woman who had been a substitute mother for him and who was practically the only family he had. He looked her in the eye and lied. "I am going to stop Kerri'tarre. With the help of an old friend. It is going to be all right, Mary. But I do need to remove you and Ben to somewhere unconnected to me. As a precaution. Until this is all over."

Nagarath closed his eyes, considering the spellwork. He had means and magick. He could set Ben and Mary up somewhere warmer and sunnier. It would not be among the rolling hills and wide skies that they loved, but they would be safe and comfortable.

Footsteps on the path drew Nagarath's attention. Benjamin Hertford, thank the gods. Steeling himself against the push of his conscience, Nagarath locked his gaze to Mary and called upon the power of the cinnabar staff.

Both the Hertfords disappeared in the blink of an eye. Deep magicks. The only sign of the power's expenditure: a thinning red smoke on the air and a buzzing within Nagarath's einatus. The guilt he would feel later. At present he had greater things to attend to.

Liara—therefore, Kerri'tarre—had the key to the cinnabar stone in her grasp, whether she knew it or not. Its discovery was only a matter of time. So Nagarath would hurry.

With a wave of his wand, he materialized back in Little Larkhill's library. Not pausing, he took the steps of the hidden stairwell three at a time, fishing in his shirt collar as he did so for the amulet that connected him to his apprentice. His thumb looped under the chain, and Nagarath clenched his fist, tensing.

He stopped and let his fingers slide down to where the pendant lay cold and inert. He had no need to sever the spell. The magick was already dead on Liara's end, final confirmation of her having fallen to Khariton at long last. What secret part of Nagarath had had him daring to believe still? Why had he, in the face of so much evidence, held on to foolish faith?

Gaining his rooms, Nagarath realized that he had no actual plan, merely half-formed ideas and hopes. All of which had failed. Fear pressed into his spirit, smothering Nagarath, robbing him of light, of air. He sat down, unmoving and unable to call his magick, to even think.

The cinnabar stone in his staff winked its brightness

as a shaft of sunlight fell across the arcane item. The sole window in the room brightened and dimmed with a quickly passing cloud. A sign?

A hope?

Nagarath considered.

Yes. That would be something that Khariton could not have expected him to dare. Gripping his wand, Nagarath felt for the stone's key with his mind. It was still safe. Well, still undiscovered. That would simply have to be enough. For what other choice did they have with Merlin refusing to come forth and face his enemy?

With such weak reassurances, Nagarath sighed and steeled himself for the magick.

Closing his eyes, Nagarath reached for the soul of his power and connected it to the hungry cinnabar stone. *"Ha Olam goral kala iy'ha ann'f m'ha mot shl' schresch aatz iy'ha dam m'ha nahhar. Atsmi'i shinah h n'tiyah. Atsmi'i ma'ab ha adam. Atsmi'i shiin ha goral."*

No sooner than the words were ripped out of him, Nagarath felt the change. Magick, thickly raining down upon his einatus. It beat him backwards, torrential and unrelenting.

—powers of the world—

"No." Thrusting the staff from him, Nagarath sought to hide himself from its blood-tinged light. Still it came, glowing brighter, a star, a sun. It burned, eternal mistake and damnation.

—trees whose roots bathe in the blood of the rivers—

"No!" Memories. A book, tearing itself asunder under Nagarath's outstretched palm, its spells checked only by the power of the cinnabar stone . . . Liara, holding the power of another's amber-bound essence within her fingers, bespelled by the wonder of grim destruction. A young Anisthe—nigh on two decades in the past—dared into recklessness by his peer in the Art. Another mistake; in another time.

I, Magus, change that course.

I flood the land. I make the fates.

"Nathaniel, you careless mage."

Desperate and reckless. Like Anisthe, and therefore doomed to die.

Crying out, his magick swallowed by the stone's hunger, its unquenchable, searing anger, the world went dark around Nagarath, leaving naught but the echo of the words in his ears:

Wrought with fire, I am the phoenix, eternally rising; I am the dragon, forever timeless.

CHAPTER TWENTY-THREE

Nagarath came to and found that he lay upon his back on the floor of the master suite in Little Larkhill. He had been out for, perhaps, mere moments. Making to rise, he cried out in pain as the cinnabar staff rolled just out of reach of his fingers. One, maybe two inches and the slight shift had tugged at his magick.

An einatus enslaved to the power of the cinnabar stone, a new and terrible reality. It felt . . . It was as if a part of his heart was missing.

Still, it was the only way to ensure that Khariton could not take the stone from him by force. The whisper of the staff had quieted at long last. After years as its keeper, Nagarath had lost the battle for his own independence. The stone had gotten what it wanted.

Shaking off the sensation and concentrating, rather, on the surging of his strength, Nagarath gripped the staff tight and got to his feet.

Yes, the feeling was temporary. The raging seas of his

einatus were already finding their song. Through it Nagarath could practically hear the incantations required of him to find and stop his rogue apprentice. With the stone's power linked to his own—*made my own*—he could defeat even Khariton.

"No. No overreach. Binding my mage's soul to that of the stone's may prevent its being taken from my hand, but the bridging brings with it other perils," Nagarath cautioned himself, lest pride overtake even his magick. The stone could be tricksy. The path to mastering the new arrangement had pitfalls yet to be discovered. One already simply being the agony of finding that his heart now had a home outside of his body. After a fashion.

But Nagarath, he too was clever. Again, the thought he had held while in the Hertfords' home rose within his mind.

Anisthe rotted in a French jail.

Anisthe was Liara's progenaurae.

And Liara was not yet twenty.

Horror shook him. "No. No, Nagarath. Never go there with your magick. Never."

And yet it was no longer his magick, was it?

History was littered with the victims of mages who had gone wrong. Countless stories had been writ of wizards who had had to stop wayward apprentices. Such was the duty of any who took on that responsibility.

"Left-handed. Sinistral tendencies." The fault was Nagarath's own. The blood that would be on his hands with such a cold and unfair murder? He had earned it by apprenticing Liara in the first place.

But Anisthe? Could he really kill an imprisoned and near helpless man?

"You have fought with him for the better part of your life, magus. And apologized for the rest."

He'd kill him. He would.

"He would kill me." But Nagarath knew such reasoning made little sense. He was not Anisthe; had, in fact, prided himself on precisely their differences. "High-minded twattle, Nagarath. You pretend to distinction. When all you really are is a coward, and all you can claim is guilt."

But then, guilt had been the gulf between them, had it not? Knowing Anisthe's arrogance, his dangerous single-minded ambition, Nagarath could see, too, the war mage's lack of apology for his actions and for the conse-quences they gave rise to. And so Nagarath had worn the guilt for both, having, through his own actions, earned the culpability.

Suffering a guilty conscience was not penance. It was, in many ways, a compounding of one's error. Nagarath had never moved on. He had never made—or even attempted to make—amends. Not with Anisthe. Not even with Cromen. Certainly he had not with Amsalla.

Instead he had hidden himself away in Limska Draga, telling himself that, if he could keep an eye on the fallout of Anisthe's actions, he was doing right. Keep safe the cinnabar stone and be free of his own accountability in its creation. Protect Dvigrad, protect Liara, and he was blameless for all that had come before.

Liara. The gods only knew why Nagarath had allowed

her to get under his skin. A thief and a liar. Anisthe's threats given breath, given life. A mistake.

A mistake for which Nagarath had to atone, having done nothing—worse than nothing—for nigh on twenty years.

"And let everyone be blamed but yourself."

Yes, the blood was already on his hands. It was high time he faced it.

"And with Liara holding the key to the cinnabar stone? Unbeknownst to her or not . . ."

Yes, he must act. He must. This last realization cleared his conscience for action.

A flick of Nagarath's wrist and a whispered word of sorcery hurled him into whirling darkness.

～

Light tore at Anisthe's eyes. Magick burned and writhed within his grip.

He was dreaming, as he did so often, of a moment long past. And, as in most dreams, the details were altered. He was not changing the Laws this time. No. He was saving them. Anisthe dreamed he held the power of the world, of magick itself, in his hands. And the globe was cracked. Fractured, like an amber pendant, bleeding internally like a dying half-fey, dark-haired blue-eyed man . . .

And nobody saw it but Anisthe. Not a mage amongst them had the insight, the ambition, to fix what had been broken. None save for himself.

Figures flickered at the edges of the light, looming

shadows thrown against a greater darkness. And through the screaming whistle of pain and power, Anisthe heard the scratch of an incantation. Words he did not know, in a language he could not understand, his heart knew it as sorcery. He looked to the speaker and found that he could not see their face for the mage's cloak and hood.

Thunder shook the stones of his cell. Anisthe lay awake on his narrow bench before he knew what he was about. Another peal grounded him and stole the last of his dream from him. The unhelpful drip of dirty water on his forehead furthered his wakefulness. He shifted, peevish both from the insult of yet another misery and the haunting echo of his dream. Another thrumming roll of thunder rattled the door and set Anisthe to gritting his teeth.

The rattling persisted. Sitting upright, Anisthe watched as the door grunted open. Rescue? A midnight execution? His heart raced such that it practically drowned out the next clap of thunder.

Magelight sprang into brightness in the hand of a hooded figure. The wizard strode quickly into the room, his eyes darting about, observing, as he threw back his cloak and put a finger to his lips.

Anisthe gaped. "Nagarath!"

"Shh."

Nagarath brandished a key and made quick work of Anisthe's manacles.

"Thank you." Anisthe rubbed his sore, weakened wrists, stunned at the sudden freedom.

Wordlessly, Nagarath nodded, and Anisthe felt his breath catch. The man looked awful. His face drawn and dark with tension, Nagarath waved a hand to send his magelight hovering up near the low-pressing ceiling.

Why was he alone?

Something clenched within Anisthe's chest, and he asked, "Liara. Where is she?"

Nagarath's whispered answer arced through the air of the dungeon. Accursed fire leapt from his wand. Rolling forward, Anisthe moved without thought or plan. He landed in an ungainly heap on the floor and thrust upward with both hands. It wasn't much, but the flash of his oriaurant magick was enough to throw his assailant from his feet.

"Nagarath!" Anisthe wheezed, rising to his feet. Another hex sparked through the air, and he dove to the side, hands still outstretched. "Mercy. I'm unarmed!"

"You are never unarmed, magus," Nagarath growled, leveling his wand and enacting another curse as he, too, found his feet once more.

Anisthe's shield rebuffed the next assault. And the next. He thought fast: Nagarath had freed him before attacking. Magick's incompatibility with cold iron aside, the act spoke to his opponent's honor. Nagarath would not slay a helpless, imprisoned man.

And yet, murder lived in those eyes. Those dead, dead eyes. What had happened? Spun sideways by the force of Nagarath's renewed assault, Anisthe tried again, "Please! Where is Liara? What—"

Nagarath's answer came in two slashing strokes of his wand. Strange power. Unfamiliar magick. Anisthe could see that Amsalla had spoken truth, as his attentions fell on his opponent's staff. Nagarath clearly had not yet fully mastered the cinnabar stone.

Whereas Anisthe had an oriaurant's magick and many long hours to learn its use. He smiled and let loose a hex of his own.

Caught off guard, forced to enact his own shielding spells, Nagarath's onslaught faltered.

Another attack followed without pause or pity. Anisthe sneered as his opponent again was forced to defend himself from the lightning which arced through the room. "That is a pretty toy, Nagarath. Strange that you did not bring it with you to Vrsar. I should have thought that you would keep such a treasure with you at all times, leave Amsalla to her fate under Merlin's unjust accusations."

"Merlin!" Under the flickering light of the warring magicks, Nagarath's unnerving impassivity appeared to crack. Yet, even under the recrimination, he did not break.

Still firing spells and counter-spells, Anisthe took a step backwards. Nagarath, alone without Liara. Why? What had happened? Why couldn't Anisthe get through to him? This man was not the same wizard he had known, the enemy he had long hated. This was something wild and fierce. Something cold. Something grim and heartless.

Nagarath leveled his mage's staff at Anisthe. He spoke no words, uttered no curse. Yet the blow from its magick threw Anisthe back against the wall. The world around him exploded in flame, and Anisthe was forced to put every bit of his magick into his wavering shield. Everything. He had but moments. Nagarath's hex or Anisthe's own defense would be the end of him. He locked eyes with Nagarath and tried one last time, "Liara—"

A shadow seemed to pass through Nagarath's face.

Anisthe pressed, "If you kill me—"

"Then Kerri'tarre is defeated through your aurenaurae's death." Whatever humanity he had briefly regained fled Nagarath's eyes. The wizard's wrath twisted itself into a dark, uncaring smile. Unloving.

That was when Anisthe saw the truth of it. Saw what Liara must have done to the mage.

The only thing left of Nagarath was his anger, his magick, and his honor. Hard, cold, and unyielding.

Bracing himself, trusting that he understood even the stilted heart of his enemy, Anisthe looked into his eyes and said, "So go on, then, and do it. Kill me to kill Kerri'tarre. You've proven yourself an apt replacement for him, considering what you've allowed Amsalla to go through by taking that stone and leaving her to hang for it."

Anisthe let his shield drop.

CHAPTER TWENTY-FOUR

Anisthe's magick died, and he flinched, anticipating the snuffing of his life under Nagarath's sorcery.

Nothing happened.

"Well?" he rasped, impatient. Still nothing. He opened his eyes to see Nagarath lower his staff and take an unsteady step backwards. Anisthe smirked to see the broken uncertainty flood his enemy's face. Coward.

Nagarath's magelight still flickered overhead, and the rolling echo of the dying storm outside warned both men that their business had better conclude soon lest their actions be noted by the guard.

Still Anisthe did not move as he considered the small miracle of his life having been spared, the searing incredulity of his having been right about Nagarath, even considering the circumstances.

Something in Anisthe's chest quivered. Some strange and distant response to Nagarath's anguish which called forth the need to speak words of comfort, of understanding. Again he thought of Liara and the terrible spell she had wrought and wondered if he couldn't use it to his advantage. "Nagarath, I—"

"Don't." Nagarath's eyes regained their spark, and he leveled his wand back against Anisthe's throat.

Anisthe froze. He might be alive still, but that could change very quickly. Only Nagarath's deep-rooted incorruptibility stood in argument against cold murder.

"I am nowhere near the same kind of wizard as Khariton. Amsalla? She . . . You have to believe that I did not know. She never told me. Hinted, yes. But I did not know."

Anisthe shrugged, the gesture lessened by his perilous position. "And you never stopped to ask yourself—really ask yourself—what possible motives she could have had for digging up Kerri'tarre's Mirror."

"I sent Liara to Merlin in hopes of his being able to help her. After you as much as set her and me to looking for him, knowing full well that I had Cromen's stone."

"I am not working with Amsalla, if that is what you're after."

"What I am after is a way out of this mess that you— yes, you—started."

"I gave you a way just now. You did not take it." Anisthe smiled.

"You would think that way, yes. As I said, I am not that kind of wizard. I am not an executioner," Nagarath growled, then lowered his weapon. "I will not add your crimes to my own reckoning with Merlin."

Freed, Anisthe raised a hand to his throat, and he considered their differences. He would have done it. Slain his enemy, that is. And with far less noble aims. He might yet, but for the fact that he needed his help.

"Please know that, while my preference in this is to save my wayward apprentice, I will not hesitate to finish you off should you give me reason to do so," Nagarath muttered, looking about the dark space.

"Yes, yes, we know. You're the honorable one. And I'm the dangerous, corrupt one." Anisthe buried deep any emotional qualms he might have had. The mask was back in place. His manacles were off and the door to the dungeon open. He felt safe, in control, once more. "However, if this means that you would rather rescue than murder me, I should think our window for that is closing rather fast."

As if cued by Anisthe's words, distant shouts echoed off the stone walls. He thrust his head out the double door to his cell, eyeing their only route of escape. "Can you get us out?"

"Well," Nagarath began, thumbing his chin in thoughtful consideration. "The staff will need another minute before I can be truly useful again. What have you in the way of sorcery?"

"None at present. You managed to use up what I had by forcing me to defend myself. I take it you didn't actually hurt any of the guards."

"When liberating the keys? Of course not."

"Why am I not surprised," Anisthe sneered. "At least I have the stomach for it. Come on."

Nagarath had no choice but to follow.

The shouts grew louder, and footsteps sounded in the stairwell. Nagarath doused his magelight, leaving both men in darkness. He whispered, "No killing. We do this my way, or I will rip you out of this dungeon with little care as to your health and wholeness. I only need you alive, friend. Not well."

"Noted. Friend," Anisthe breathed his own vexation back.

They waited.

"Here." Nagarath passed his wand to Anisthe.

"Cromen's?"

"No."

"Then how do you expect me to use the thing without having any connection to it."

"Fine. Give it back."

"No."

Six men entered the dungeons. Two held lanterns, the rest: muskets.

Nagarath's magelight flashed into brightness as he and Anisthe leapt forward. Cinnabar stone and wand sent their hexes after the guards. Easy marks, all six of the king's men fell within moments.

Anisthe froze seeing next what he and Nagarath hadn't accounted for in their hasty plan.

Spellpiercers.

Stepping over the brave men-at-arms who had insisted on going first, the three anti-mages snuffed the life out of the cinnabar staff with their mere presence. Nagarath's magelight flickered and dimmed, and he reached out to draw Anisthe back.

Anisthe shook him off. He muttered, "I feel them. Remember that their dampening of my magick is somewhat different."

A flick of his wrist and two of the fallen guards shifted. Each of their muskets lifted into the air, aided by some invisible force. With a smile, Anisthe called them to himself, clubbing one of the spellpiercers across the back with one of the guns as they passed. The musket was in his hands and fired at the second of the three men before Nagarath could react.

Catching the other gun, Nagarath lifted it to aim, only to have Anisthe snatch it from his hands. "Thank you."

The words were lost in his firing of the second weapon. The third spellpiercer fell. Anisthe tossed aside the spent musket in favor of his borrowed wand. A sparkling curse further immobilized the man he had first downed.

"Come on," Anisthe beckoned and bent to liberate one of the remaining guards' weapons as he ran towards the stairwell. Nagarath followed. But not without setting his eyes on the two men Anisthe had shot.

Anisthe noted the look. "I did not think your edict applied to their sort. Also, I did not use your wand to kill them. Did you still want it back?"

Nagarath voiced no argument as he ran up the stairs behind Anisthe.

They passed swiftly through the empty guards' room and out into the courtyard. There Anisthe gasped and stared skyward, transfixed.

Overcast, with the silver gleam of the moon darting through here and there, the skies were mainly cloaked in a sooty black. And yet, to Anisthe it might have been the most beautiful thing he had ever seen.

"Sorry." Anisthe sniffed and blinked away discomforting tears. He quickly distanced himself from the unexpected show of emotion with a roll of his shoulders and then brandished his wand once more.

Reaching forward, Nagarath clasped Anisthe's arm, and the cinnabar stone winked into brilliance. Still spent from both his battle with Anisthe and their brief encounter with the king's spellpiercers, the magick of the staff sparked and burned unevenly. He raised it skyward, straining to control the flickering forks of lightning. He shouted above the din, "There are more spellpiercers. I can feel them through my connection to the stone. Can you—?"

Anisthe nodded.

The guards' musket was good for but one shot. It flew wide. Scowling, Anisthe dropped the gun and opted for the weapon with which he was most comfortable. Three spellpiercers fell under a quick hex. His mage's fire revealed more of their adversaries closing in.

He and Nagarath were surrounded.

"Come on!" Nagarath cried his challenge to the skies. But the magick faltered and refused to come.

The spellpiercers drew closer, and Anisthe felt his own einatus shudder under the strain of the anti-magick. Desperation gripped Anisthe, and he turned and reached for, not Nagarath's arm, but the cinnabar staff itself.

Nagarath's eyes widened in surprise. "Don't you dare—!"

The world dissolved into the roar and rush of Anisthe's spell.

CHAPTER TWENTY-FIVE

Kerri'tarre's curse had released Liara long hours prior, the spark of her magick finally dying alongside the swiftly passing thunderstorm. As the rain had sluiced down from the heavens, she had distantly wondered if she might simply drown while waiting on Merlin's mercy. But then, the evil wizard who held her soul captive would likely not allow it. And so she lay where Merlin and Krešimir had left her, huddled half-asleep and miserable under her cloak. Liara kept her eyes on Merlin's cottage while she clung fast to her side of the battle of wills. Kerri'tarre might win in the end, but she would delay that victory as long as she had any strength at all.

Somewhere ahead in the darkness a whispering sound beckoned. Liara's eyes refocused on the small motion. Krešimir. Eyes on the doorway behind him, she fumbled in search of her wand, instinct overriding memory.

Seeing her gesture, Krešimir raised his hands. The reaction sparked new anger. Liara scowled, preferring that he saw that over her helpless tears. He who had chosen to serve the enemy.

Krešimir hushed her and looked behind him anxiously. "We must hurry."

"Why? Is the great Merlin not as trapped as he says?"

Krešimir's jaw tightened. His angry silence cut the air. It was then that Liara saw the wand in his hand. Her wand.

"I've had enough of wizards' curses and arrogant arguments." Again Krešimir turned to peer back. "I don't agree with Merlin, and he has decided the issue closed. I'd rather we leave without explanation."

Liara's eyes were still on her wand. The pendant, that she missed. But a wand? She could not be trusted with a wand. At present she was free and reveled in that temporary freedom.

Liara did not move to reclaim the item.

Krešimir waited through her hesitation, not questioning, not correcting. At length he nodded and, having put away the wand, held out his hand to her. A moment later saw them running off together under the cover of a black, moonless sky.

They ran until Liara's legs burned, and her lungs felt ready to burst. She gave no protest, finding solace in exhaustion. Nagarath had once proposed such a solution to the Kerri'tarre problem: rest returned a wizard's magick to him. Fatigue delayed.

They needed the delay.

Krešimir, woodsman of the Limska Draga valley in faraway Istria. Liara of Dvigrad, unwanted aurenaurae-turned-vessel for the dangerous praecantator Kerri'tarre.

Together they fled from the one mage who could help them. And Liara had cursed into disregard the one wizard who might try.

Why? Why must the fates be so cruel?

They needed a plan, she and Krešimir. Stumbling on her tired feet, Liara tried to catch her breath. Running was foolish. They carried their troubles with them.

Surely Merlin was the answer and her only hope.

Gasping, Liara buried her pride. She would run no more. "We need to go back. Without Merlin's help . . ."

"The world went a thousand years without his help. And his treatment of you? Unacceptable. We've our own magick, you and I. We'll find our own solution."

Liara smiled at Krešimir's hopeful naïveté. "Krešimir. That's—that's ridiculous."

"Shut up! Just, stop. Don't you see? You've found your way back. To me. And I to you. Don't tell me you don't see the power in that, what it might mean."

"Krešimir." Liara choked on the name. "Life . . . life and magick took us apart. And now I've changed—"

"And I'll change you back!" Krešimir would not hear it. "We will. Look at where we stand. Look at me. There's nobody else."

"But, Krešimir . . ."

"Tell me you don't feel it, what magick took from us. Look me in the eye, and tell me you can't feel the weight of every lost soul from Dvigrad. Tell me that we don't owe them something."

"We can't change the past."

"No. But it made us. It gave us responsibilities, we who should have been dead with the rest. Fate gave us debts to be repaid. While you've chased after the mage who killed our friends, our family. Anisthe, who—"

"He's my progenaurae. My life is tied to his."

"My life is tied to yours!"

"You don't understand magick, Krešimir."

"And you don't understand love."

Liara recoiled as if slapped. She recovered quickly. "I don't think you understand me."

"Let me." Krešimir's hands found the sides of Liara's face. His eyes gazed into hers. Mere inches separated them, and she could feel his breath on her cheeks and lips. "Please. Let me love you. Let me save you."

"Don't. Krešimir, please." Liara closed her eyes to unexpected tears.

He dropped his hands, prompting a gush of relief from Liara. She'd half feared he might kiss her. Having never expected to see her Krešimir again after Sardinia, her confused heart did not know what to do with his love.

"Why not?" A challenge from Krešimir. Not given as a pure question, but as admonishment. An accusation. He knew full well why not. But he wanted Liara to own to it. Cruelly, he did not wait for her response. "Don't tell me. Don't you tell me that you love him. That wizard."

"Krešimir, I'm sor—"

"Don't! Don't." It was Krešimir's turn for tears. "Why? Is it the magick? What, Liara? Is it because he's a great wizard, and I'm just some woodsman from a forgotten hamlet? Because from what I could see, he was perfectly content to abandon you to me. He doesn't love you."

"He did." Liara gulped air, sitting hurriedly lest she

faint. Even so, the threat remained, and she had to focus her attention on the ground. "He did love me. And I put a stop to it. To keep him safe."

"Is that it, then? Are you pushing me away as well? For my protection?" Krešimir spat the word.

Liara flinched. "I'm being honest."

"Thank you for that." Krešimir's anger roared over her. "I feel so much better for your honesty."

"Go, then." Liara's words came out small. A weak protest, but she needed him gone. She needed him not standing over her and yelling at her about something she could not control. She had loved him once upon a time. And he had squandered it. It was unfair of him to expect that she had never changed in the intervening year and a half, a time when first she thought him disinterested, a time she had thought him dead. A time during which she had come to love another.

"I can't." Krešimir's strangled grief pulled at Liara's heart. "I can't walk away now. Even if . . . I need to know you'll be all right."

Liara smiled grimly. "We just now ran from my last option."

"Then we return to Nagarath."

Liara could see how it cost Krešimir to make such an offer. She shook her head. "His hopes were in Merlin as well. Had he not brought me to you, one or the other of us would end up dead. As with Merlin, Nagarath has something that Kerri'tarre covets."

Together they sat in sullen silence, each lost in their lonely misery.

At length Krešimir spoke. "What is it that Kerri'tarre wants?"

"Power. Immortality. The world worshiping magick, with him in control of all the Art. Revenge." Liara took a shuddering breath. "I can read his heart. At night, we share each other's dreams. Soon I fear I won't know which is me and which is him. Nor will you or anyone else, save by my—his—actions. He . . . he uses my own magick against me. My magick and his knowledge. My power and his demands."

"Your eyes glow," Krešimir said. "All silvery and pale. When Kerri'tarre uses your Art, we can tell. At least for the moment. I don't know what will happen when he eventually . . ."

He trailed off, unable to say what would happen when Kerri'tarre triumphed over Liara's will. More silence reigned between them. In the sky above their heads, stars had begun to wink out from behind the fast-fleeing clouds. A heavy wetness rose from the ground, steamy aftermath of the earlier storm.

"We need to ward the camp." Liara rose, brushing wet clumps of grass from her skirt. "Burn off my magick before it returns and gain us a few hours of rest."

Krešimir stood as well. This time when he captured her hands within his own, his eyes held a sharp earnestness. Liara found herself transfixed by his compassion. He said, "What went wrong? With Nagarath, I mean."

Stepping back, Liara turned and walked a circle of protection around their camp. Stumbling with exhaustion, she was glad the wards were easy and came to mind without much prompting. In pacing, she considered her answer to Krešimir's question. When she finished her spellwork and left her einatus emptied and aching, she returned to where Dvigrad's woodsman had sparked a small fire.

Staring into the new flames, Liara began her story, starting with Vrsar. She told of Anisthe, her hopes and subsequent dark discoveries. Of the aftermath of the wizards' duel. Of the perils she and Nagarath faced prior to having encountered Krešimir on the ship to Messina and of their travels after the parting of ways. She told him of Sophie. Domagoj. Amsalla. She described the king's court but omitted the heartache found within.

Through it all, Krešimir listened patiently, only inter-jecting to ask for clarification here or explanation there as Liara recounted her confrontation with Kerri'tarre's Mirror. Fleeing spellpiercers. Anisthe's apparent surrender.

Lastly, Liara owned to the events of Little Larkhill. Her discovery that Nagarath felt for her as she felt for him. Khariton's actions towards the Hertfords, doubling back in her tale to explain the cinnabar stone and Nagarath's precautions for it. Her ransacking the mage's collection for a spell writ in bright vermilion on a scroll, in a codex, in a sheaf of paper.

The hardest thing to recount: Liara's cursing of her wizard with the spell of disregard, lest his love for her blind him to the danger Kerri'tarre posed.

At last, spent of words and emotions, Liara could only lean weakly against Krešimir's offered shoulder and stare into the fire. To his credit, he said nothing more, and under their companionable silence, Liara drifted off to sleep.

❧

Krešimir gently guided Liara's sleeping form down onto the ground, resting her head on one of their packs. Magick wards or no, he would stand guard until the morning. He couldn't sleep anyhow. Not with the fear surging in his veins.

To be useless, to be helpless. He hated it. Hated it nearly as much as he'd hated having to stand by and comfort Liara while she spoke of loving another. The difference was that losing her love hurt only Krešimir, while Kerri'tarre's threat could hurt not just Liara, but so many others besides.

It would be Dvigrad all over again. Perhaps such had been destined from the start. Painful as the admission was, Krešimir had to consider that Liara's ties to Vrsar's war mage might have left her with a predilection for ruin.

Liara loved Nagarath. Why? Why must she love a man who, with such power as he reportedly had at his call, could have given them back Dvigrad and had, instead, chosen not to?

Loyalty to his own, Krešimir supposed. Just as Merlin would hide from Kerri'tarre rather than confront him; would call him both friend and enemy.

"Were I to have such power, I would bring them back. Phenlick. Tomislav. Piotr. Every last one. The wizardry against them was a crime. And while I cannot punish the man responsible without putting Liara in harm's way, I could certainly see to it that his legacy of death and hatred was undone." Krešimir cast dark eyes over the dwindling fire. He could let it die. The night had yet to cool. But he wanted the light. The darkness pressed too close to his soul for him to want to see naught but the distant stars of the wider world.

The cinnabar stone and its key. Something in Liara's story snagged at Krešimir's mind. The secretive nature of that damnable wizard of hers. Puzzles and careful lies.

Krešimir began breathing heavily under the advance of a new thought. His hands strayed into his pack for the wand that Merlin had taken from Liara. The fire rebuilt within moments, he crouched near its renewed blaze and considered anew the strangeness he had espied within the maple artifact. The imperfect imitation of a proper wood grain glared back at him. A dare. A lock set over a secret.

No. Not a lock. A key.

Gnashing his teeth, for he had no magick himself, Krešimir considered waking Liara. But it was pride, rather than unease, that stopped him. He had been the one to notice the wrongness in the wood. It was his secret to discover.

Krešimir cast his mind over his memories of spell work. Words Liara had spoken within his presence, the hexes cast by both Merlin and Kerri'tarre. Perhaps one of those curses contained the word for "open" in the language of magick. He would be no worse off if it didn't work.

"Kunu ba yel. Atsmi'i?" Krešimir directed his garbled hopes at the wand in his hand and waited. Feeling both

foolish and guilty, he moved to set the item back in his pack.

It was then that he saw the small crack in the wood. One he was absolutely certain had not been there before. In the space of a breath, the gap widened. Krešimir held the wand to the firelight to better see. He could not be sure, but it seemed to him that a small roll of paper was visible in the new crevice. Grabbing his knife, he probed the crack, careful not to mar the wood or the object hidden within. The secret yielded to his touch, and he recoiled, lest he damage the paper and the spell that had been laid upon it.

Quickly hiding the wand back in his pack, Krešimir sat with shaking hands and considered his position. Had he just been gifted with the one thing that might help Liara? More to the point: how was it the wand had opened to him? And did that mean Krešimir himself had magick after all?

CHAPTER TWENTY-SIX

"Don't you EVER touch that staff again!" Nagarath yanked the cinnabar stave from Anisthe's hands. "Where are we?"

The dark trunks of trees pressed close. They glimmered wetly in the light from the cinnabar stone. Nagarath wondered if the same storm which had battered the Bastille had rained down upon where Anisthe had landed them. As if in answer, the flash of distant lightning illuminated the forest. The growl of thunder followed belatedly.

"About thirty miles northwest of where we were." Anisthe made a show of looking about and then turned back to Nagarath. He sneered, "You have quite a bit of power at your behest with that stone."

Nagarath fixed Anisthe with a long, silent look.

The war mage seemed taken aback. "I'm— We should go. I have spent too many days in the cold and damp dark. I would rather we not wait on the whim of the clouds above our head. Amsalla, I believe, still resides at court these days, even if her power is more in title than actual."

"Versailles?"

"Where else?" Anisthe gritted his teeth and touched the hem of Nagarath's sleeve. With a word he affected invisibility on them both.

Nagarath exchanged forest for manicured gardens in an instant. Stumbling on one of the Palais de Versailles' many graveled paths, they shook off the lingering effects of the cinnabar stone's magick.

"That was a rough go. You should use your own magick for this sort of thing," Anisthe complained.

Nagarath let the cinnabar staff die to darkness, feeling the pang of it in his heart. If Anisthe could not tell what Nagarath had done with the stone's power, he was not about to tell him. The two of them ducked back behind the cover of a dense hedge. Invisibility only went so far, even worked by an oriaurant's magick. Quickly, they moved forward into the shadow of the palace. As expected, men milled about—idle guards set with a boring task.

"Spellpiercers," Anisthe whispered. "I can feel their skill brushing up against my own Art. So long as we perform no other workings than what keeps us hidden, I believe we can gain entrance to the palace itself."

"And then?"

"It would make sense for Louis to keep his pet close. He's not fool enough to be truly ignorant of her magely powers. Amsalla is as much a prisoner as I have been. Though in a far superior jail. One of privilege and destructive ambition." Anisthe paused and considered. He said, "We'll wait until the king's party disperses for the evening and pray that she's alone."

Nodding, Nagarath considered yet another challenge that lay within their path. "How do you propose we open the door without anyone noticing?"

Ansithe followed Nagarath's gaze with impassive calm. He beckoned and moved back 'round, staying out of the light and creeping forward towards the gardens. "I hadn't expected we should use the door, my friend. We've our own entrance still."

A blemish on the bright perfection of the king's palace, the site of their escape from the Hall of Mirrors short weeks prior had been but hastily boarded and left. Louis, it would seem, did not like to highlight his failures by posting guards there.

Gaining entry, Nagarath looked about the familiar ruined room and stumbled. His gaze caught and held on an alcove of shattered mirrors. Bullet holes had left their mark in the stone and glass, a furthering of Liara's destruction with the cinnabar walking stick. He greatly wanted to approach. He needed to see, by his own touch upon the fractured mirror, Kerri'tarre's prison. Nagarath had to feel for himself the ghost of the freed magicks and know at last how exactly the archmage had tricked his apprentice. But he could not move. It was as though he himself were spellbound and by little more than the sharp shards of memory.

"I'm sorry. Believe me, I am sorry."

"It's our fault." Nagarath ignored Anisthe's apology. But the spell of his own anxiety was broken, and he could move again. Mastering himself, he raised the cinnabar staff that he dare not use and asked, "Which way?"

"Considering the hour and my need to conserve my spell-strength, we had best not move from this room yet."

Then I will wait outside. Nagarath almost gave voice to the complaint, then stopped.

Anisthe regarded him curiously. He, too, seemed to have something on his mind. But then he turned away and concentrated his attentions on the dark gardens outside the windows.

Long minutes ticked past in silence. Nagarath considered their situation anew. Kerri'tarre's shattered mirror at his right. Anisthe at his left. And his own ruined purpose, centered in his mind.

He shuddered, thinking how close he had come to utter destruction. Nagarath would have traded every decent part of himself for a chance at an easy victory. He would have gladly killed Anisthe to remove Kerri'tarre from the world.

"We must be careful." Anisthe turned back from the window to pace the long room. "To publicly rip Amsalla from her position could ruin her and make us a powerful enemy in the long run. Never mind the difficulty such an abduction would pose."

Nagarath gritted his teeth against Anisthe's unspoken question and the insinuation therein. "Yes. Yes, I know which rooms are hers. But you're to take care of any attendant she might have with her. Nicely." He added the last as an afterthought, images of the slain prison spellpiercers flitting through his head.

Anisthe's measured footsteps stopped. The pause

forced Nagarath's attention onto his companion's unreadable back. The war mage straightened and turned, his face as carefully blank as his body language. "As it would dull her magickal sensibilities, Amsalla is unlikely to have any anti-mages posted near her own rooms."

"Not of her own choosing anyhow."

"Granted. But I am inclined to believe she is still very much in control of her own situation, limited though it may be with concern to the Bastille's residents."

"Your point, Anisthe?"

"I have no intentions of killing a non-threat but will do what needs doing," Anisthe's answer came soft and deadly. "The danger is Amsalla. Not in any Artless she'll have within her employ."

Nagarath nodded his assent and waited.

This time, Anisthe's hesitation shone within his eyes. He lowered his voice further. "I had hopes that we would rely upon your magick with regards to Amsalla. She still labors under the belief that I am yet incantate."

"And your reasoning for such concealment?" Annoyance sharpened Nagarath's question in spite of his best efforts.

"Let us just say, insurance."

"I don't trust her either, if you are concerned on that account." Nagarath frowned. "But I agree that could be a useful card to be holding, yes. Come. My magick is ready, and I would like us to be hidden within her rooms long before anyone approaches. One hiding spot is as good as another at this point."

Nagarath's magick deposited them in Amsalla's quarters, sure enough. He found himself as discomforted as in their first hiding place within the palace but for different reasons. Anisthe's insinuations about the nature of the relationship between Nagarath and Mlle DeBouverelle had landed too near his heart.

Time passed in the dark room, marked only by one tense point along the way when a door in the adjacent rooms opened, ushering in a servant who readied Amsalla's room, lighting a few lamps and then dispersing quickly as they had come. In that instance, Anisthe had been forced to use his magick. Invisibility around the two mages was swiftly taken up and dropped just as fast.

At length footsteps and muted conversation could be heard in the hallway. Nagarath was given the gift of seeing his companion's face go near purple with silent, ill-concealed rage in the instant before the war mage hid himself behind the wardrobe. No betrayal as of yet, then, from Liara's progenaurae. Nagarath remained composed, choosing to take up a seat just inside the door and out of direct sight.

Amsalla entered alone.

The door closed behind her, and Nagarath rose to his feet. Starting, Amsalla whirled on her unexpected visitor, quickly mastering herself.

"Well now. Is every man going to throw himself at me?" Amsalla stepped close, her eyes soft and her voice falling into a throaty intimacy. "You do realize, Nagarath, that I was but waiting for exactly this opportunity. I love a good duel. A—lover's quarrel, if you will."

One shapely arm came up to rest on Nagarath's arm, fine fingers tripping up his shoulder to play along his shirt collar. The other hand slipped down into the folds of her skirt.

Nagarath captured the wizard's wrist before she could do little more than get her fingers around her wand and half draw the weapon. Reveling in the angry flash of her eyes, he directed Amsalla's game against her. His free hand he allowed to brush along her hair, his fingers caressing the woman's intricate curls. She sighed, leaning into his touch.

"And what of your apprentice?"

"I'm sure, by now, you are aware of her falling to Kerri'tarre's influence. After all, you've made sure that Anisthe was kept alive and within your power."

The fire returned to Amsalla's eyes. "Nagarath, I—"

Nagarath smiled and leaned close to whisper, "Hush, now. We're not alone, you see."

He directed his gaze to where Anisthe had stepped out from his hiding spot.

"And this is not the ending of a quarrel. It's surrender." A spark of magick arced through Nagarath's soft touch to stun Amsalla's magical inclination. Powerless, she could only stumble backwards from him. He held firm to her wrist. "No, no, my dear. You are how we meet Merlin."

Another touch, this time a stroke of his hand upon on her temple and cheek, allowed Nagarath into her mind. She gasped.

As did Anisthe. "Black magicks."

"Yes." Nagarth hardened to the accusation. "But there is little I could say or do to convince her to otherwise give us the information."

Tears sprang into the corner of Amsalla's eyes under the assault on her memories. "Please. Don't. Merlin— He'll kill me. With my having unearthed Kerri'tarre's Mirror and Liara having—"

"Stop it." Nagarath withdrew the invasive touch of his magick. "When I say surrender, I meant me."

Hurt puzzlement cleared the tears from Amsalla's eyes.

"Kerri'tarre is not why you fear Merlin," Nagarath explained for the benefit of Anisthe. "You have been under Merlin's thrall for years. He accused you of taking what he saw as rightfully his, yes? Cromen's bequeathal in the form of one smallish nondescript red stone. Cinnabar. Pure magick wrought from the mistake of two young mages. And you denied it. You had to, as it was the truth. Because it was I who had it. Cromen had already given it to me."

Amsalla said nothing, her eyes drawn to that self-same stone.

"Deny it with your silence. I have now seen the truth." Nagarath laid his index finger on the center of Amsalla's brow. He dropped his hands, freeing his hostage. "Why didn't you tell me? Why not trust me, Amsalla? I would have helped you without question."

Amsalla averted her gaze but not before Nagarath could see that large tears threatened to drown her eyes. Her perfect lips quivered.

Nagarath frowned. "Unless, of course, help was something you never wanted."

Still Amsalla refused to speak, prompting Nagarath to fear that he had crossed more lines than was forgivable by even such a woman as her. He cleared his throat, fully self-conscious. "Nevertheless, we are going to England's archmage. My having what Merlin accused you of taking clears you of the charge. Khariton? Well, that is your own explanation to give. You are a clever enough wizard to come up with a reasonable explanation. Perhaps you might even try the truth for a change."

He turned to Anisthe. "The magick will be difficult and the going rough. Merlin is not in this world, exactly. Nor is he in any Other. He is between. Still trapped by Vivien's curse."

"Well then, I—"

"I am not extending an invitation. Merely giving warning." Nagarath's spell came silent and tinged blood-red by the stone that gave the sorcery its strength.

In an eye blink the three wizards found themselves standing at the doorway to a tiny hut in the middle of a lonely moor. The fitful clumps of tall grasses gave no utterance of insect or beast. No bird wheeled within the pre-morning skies, themselves a piercing, pale blue.

"I thought you said he was not in this world," Anisthe's protest cut through the breathy silence of the windswept plain.

"He's not," Amsalla answered, her voice small. "This is the window that connects him, open to few."

"Chosen mages, such as Amsalla. As well as a messenger of my own, whom I had never intended to walk this path." Nagarath dropped off his explanation as the door opened to them.

CHAPTER TWENTY-SEVEN

Crabbed with age and stooped to the point where his long, scraggly beard dragged upon the ground, the owner of the small house shuffled forward to greet his visitors.

Nagarath gaped at the ancient archmage, disbelieving. Amsalla was afraid of that, that relic? He could sense no power on the man. "Are you . . . Merlin?"

"I used to be. Who's asking? You?" Rheumy eyes glared their distrust at Nagarath, Anisthe, and Amsalla.

Nagarath opened his mouth to answer, but Merlin's wrinkled and tremoring hand beckoned them in all the same. "Never you mind. Come. We'll have our chat inside."

Though he and his companions had to duck to enter Merlin's house, Nagarath found the inside far more comfortable than was promised by the humble exterior. Larger, too, though not by any extravagant measures. Open shelves held crockery and neatly folded linens. A few books. Table, stool, and bed—simple wooden furnishings—occupied the corners. A broom stood next to the hearth, bristles down and therefore not anything powerful. A cloak lay in a soft heap on the floor. The great magick held by the archmage remained hidden.

Nagarath cleared his throat, self-conscious. "We—the three of us—we are former pupils of the late Archmage Cromen of Tours de Merle. We beg your assistance. My apprentice and I had sought to prevent the return of Prae-cantator Kerri'tarre to the world and—"

"I received your message, wizard. You failed."

"Yes, well—"

"I expected as much, though I'm not certain as to what you thought I could do about it now."

"Yes, well—"

"And cease that silly spellwork in my household, magus. I'll not have it here."

With a start, Nagarath felt his hold on Amsalla fall away under the casual flick of Merlin's finger. England's archmage turned back to him, his age-fogged eyes searching for focus before arresting Nagarath with grave purpose. "Why me? Why would you send warning to me when you must use such dark magicks to do so? Why when you, clearly, are still in close contact with the wizard I've chosen as my intermediary to the outside world and friends with the one you were warning me of?"

"At the time of my sending Krešimir to you, I had no idea of Magus DeBouverelle's servitude to you, and Anisthe was proving a worthy adversary, even while incantate. You are the most powerful wizard to have—"

"Bah. You didn't know I was even alive. I shouldn't be. You're saying you trust to rumor and superstition on something so important as Kerri'tarre's freedom, then? It's enough to make one question your true loyalties. Perhaps you only meant it a test. A way to open the door to me and my secrets, should I prove to be alive after all."

"Not true!" Nagarath betrayed his anger before he mastered himself. He continued, more gently, "Not true, Archmage. You have named my contemporaries, my"—he flinched—"enemies. There is nobody else."

"Nobody else?" Cocking his head, Merlin allowed a slow smile to spread across his face. "And where are the other wizards?"

Nagarath found himself bereft of speech. The man had a point. Where were the other wizards? The rarity of the Gift, that he granted. Persecution of the craft? He knew all too well how prevalent that had become. But such excuses only went so far. Even if their numbers were being strangled by hatred and distrust, the blood of warlocks growing thinner with each generation, the world was still missing thousands—tens of thousands—of mages. If not more.

Nagarath shot a glance to Amsalla and Anisthe and found that they, too, seemed discomforted by Merlin's question. A question they had not thought to ask, being so wrapped up in their drama, so lost within their own secretive dealings.

Merlin smirked at Nagarath's lack of rejoinder and crossed the small room. Settling at last, the venerable mage sat stock still, pipe clamped firmly between his pinched lips, a slow curl of wispy, fragrant smoke the only movement in the room save for the crackling of the fire. In that moment of heavy silence, Nagarath would have thought the archmage dead but for the fact that the man could not die.

"Archmage—"

"Cromen had much to say about you."

"About me?"

"About all of you," Merlin growled, his eyes gaining a spark of vitality at long last. "Tried to wreck magick. Put pride and petty jealousies above the Art. Nothing. Nothing is greater than the Gift!

"You seek my help? He who would tear apart the Laws that keep our kind safe, keep us in power. She who would sell her soul for a bit of sorcery. And you, who think yourself noble and principled but who is, in fact, as useful as a broken grimoire. Full of knowledge all locked away. You're a waste of magick. Each of you. And, besides, I cannot help you."

"Cannot? Or will not?" Anisthe stepped forward. "History has you on the same side as Khariton in most of the stories. Have we inadvertently done you a favor, then?"

"You would like that, wouldn't you, Anisthe of Nobody-Knows-Where. But no. We each have what the other wants, Kerri'tarre and I. Newly released from his mirror, he has freedom and no immortality. While I have immortality and no freedom."

Merlin rose and hobbled back across the room, reaching toward his shelf of books. Trembling fingers made their selection. He flipped through the aged codex, thumbing the pages carelessly. He stopped and peered close, muttering, as if to himself, "And then mayhap I have a chance."

He replaced the book and turned back. "In the meanwhile, I've a bit of other judgment to exact. Punishment for failure of a different sort. Amsalla, did I not warn you of what would happen if you returned to me empty-handed and unapologetic yet again?"

Sharp words of magick sliced through the air, and sparks erupted along Merlin's outstretched fingers.

Nagarath tensed, recognizing the language and realizing his own futility in stopping such ancient sorcery. "No, wait! It's here. The stone."

Amsalla shrank into Nagarath, pleading, "I never took it. Please, Merlin. It was him. Cromen gave it to Nagarath. Nathani—?"

The archmage finished his spell. Amsalla vanished, gone from that plane and the next.

"No!" Shaking, Nagarath leveled his staff at Merlin. The magick called itself. And he could barely hang on. The violent blast of his wordless curse shrieked, unstoppable through the space between the wizards. Ugly, impure magick, it violated every decency afforded one mage to another, ignored every tenet of a proper duel. And this against the foremost archmage of the history of magick . . . and one who had, just then, made very clear his stance on the proper use of the Art.

Nagarath didn't care. He had made his own judgment. Or rather, it had been made for him in the echo of Amsalla's fading cry. Unfair. Unfair and downright evil.

"It was me," he screamed, not caring that the confession fell dead behind the roar of his next curse. "It was me. It was me! It was me!"

Hex after hex; attack upon attack. Nagarath showed

no mercy. Amsalla's eulogy would be written in the blood of England's archmage. She deserved no less.

"It was me and you knew it." Nagarath stood over Merlin's broken body, his chest hitching with grief. Guilt and regret. But no remorse.

Anisthe still stood wild-eyed to the side. He had known to keep himself safe, thank the gods.

Merlin stirred. Nagarath blasted him again.

"Cannot—die—" Merlin wheezed.

"I don't care."

Nagarath would try. He would try and try and—

Merlin's counter-spell, spoken in the glittering shards of a language older than the Green, sliced through Nagarath's own. Nagarath threw himself against the magick, trusting in the power of the cinnabar stone and feeling reckless for it. In his head, Amsalla's name—her shattered scream—sounded over and over again.

Something gave. Nagarath felt his mistake in the quaking of his einatus as he let his next curse fly at Merlin. His oft-repeated misstep of overextension, this time there would be no escaping its consequences.

The error compounded as Merlin raised his hand, and a hex arced outward to seize Nagarath's staff and the powerful stone within. Power Nagarath had been charged to protect. Magick he had linked with his own. Sorcery that England's wizard now claimed for himself.

Merlin sneered, "And as for YOU—!"

CHAPTER TWENTY-EIGHT

Nagarath tried to hold fast to the power of the cinnabar stone. But Merlin—ancient, doddering, cruel mage that he was—had strength unbounded. The magick snapped and sparked under the archmage's call. Lightning in Nagarath's veins, his mage's soul strained under the forced separation. It was as though Merlin ripped the beating heart from his chest. Unbearable. He could feel his Gift fragmenting. Shattered rainbows of magick cut the darkness in which he swam.

Through the haze of his agony, Nagarath heard Anisthe cry out, "Stop it! You're killing him!"

"Only his magick. Of which he has proven singularly unworthy."

"Zielsor!" Anisthe's accusation nearly lost itself within the din of the archmage's sorcery.

No. Not zielsor. Not truly. Nagarath tried to speak and found only discordant syllables.

"He lost his claim over his power when he joined to the stone, to magick!" Merlin supplied the lesson for

Anisthe. "He thought it safe. Correction, it was safe. Safe from a ruined apprentice and her new master. Safe from you, Anisthe. Even Amsalla, whom I honestly thought had stolen it from me all those years ago."

"Cromen willed it to you."

"Yes. And when the stone was not amongst his effects as delivered by Magus DeBouverelle, I assumed the obvious. Given her character, given Archmage Cromen's fastidiousness—"

"He gave it to me," Nagarath managed to croak. He turned unseeing eyes to where he believed Merlin yet stood over him.

"Liar," Merlin's voice whispered in his ear. "Else the stone's magick would not come at my call. The sorcery tells. The will of the wizard survives even now."

For all that he spoke softly, Merlin's words rang strong and true. It was the voice of a younger man, a mage newly invigorated from his touch upon the stone's magick.

The power of the cinnabar stave had begun to reverse the aging of a thousand years. Soon it would free Merlin from Vivien's curse. Good. Nagarath closed his eyes, glad to have been of some use in the end, unfair as it was. Perhaps . . . perhaps there would yet be a way to help Liara once Merlin had finished with him.

Merlin crowed his triumph, "Magick belongs to me!"

No.

That last claim, that Nagarath objected to. But he hadn't the vitality to fight it. His strength was fading fast. His light was dying.

The world grew dark around him. Nagarath slipped

with ease into painless silence but not without wishing he could have done more with his magick and with his life.

~

Two refrains ran through Anisthe's head: He must help Nagarath! He mustn't intervene.

In the end, Anisthe watched from the shadows as Merlin tore at Nagarath's magick. The archmage was right in that the sorcery exposed the truth of it. If the power of the cinnabar stone could be called by Merlin, then it was as Cromen had willed it.

And yet . . . Nagarath was no liar or thief. Of this Anisthe was certain.

The small hovel rang with the deadly knell of Merlin's sorcery. Having joined his Gift to that of the stone's—*fool move!*—Nagarath's einatus was forfeit under Merlin's claim.

Anisthe's conscience barely made itself known above the din. *Save him. Save Nagarath.*

He would. He owed Liara that, if nothing else.

But first, he would collect what Anisthe had most hoped their meeting with Merlin might provide him. His heart's desire, bound in ancient and blackened leather and sitting on a shelf. An item of incalculable value—greater than the cinnabar stone itself—and foolishly pointed out by Merlin in the moments before his murder of Amsalla.

In one smooth motion, Anisthe snatched the book and turned to grab Nagarath. The spell was on his lips, swift as thought. Nagarath might not be a thief but Anisthe, Anisthe most certainly was.

"Tra'shuk."

Magick stabbed like a thousand knives. Raw and raging, it pulled at Anisthe's power, bleeding him until all he could sense and see was a searing whiteness. He panicked, wondering if he had run afoul of Merlin's attack. The Void had never appeared so to Anisthe. Still, he refused to give up and so held tight to Nagarath's arm.

Why? What do I even care?

His complaint followed the two mages into the calm silence of safety. Tumbling into the thick grass of goodness-knew-where, Anisthe felt the pain recede and his senses grow steady once more. His sigh of relief snagged on sudden anxiety. Nagarath had yet to move.

I'm too late.

Anisthe thrust his enemy away and sat up, hating himself.

Senseless sentimentality.

He forced his attention on the book held tight in his other hand. A smile spread unbidden across his face. Unexpected reward for a lifetime of hoping.

And—*damn it!*—he did need Nagarath. A quick glance at the book's contents confirmed it. Anisthe turned frustrated eyes to the still form lying next to him.

"Get up." He provided a casual kick as encouragement.

Nagarath did not stir; for all the world appeared dead. Mayhap the strain put upon his mage's soul by the cinnabar stone had proven fatal.

The two were connected. Wizard and staff. Connected and a danger to Anisthe and Nagarath still, considering that Merlin stood at the other end. The kite could flutter and snap in the breeze of the Void, but the archmage, holding its string, could follow them anywhere so long as he held on to the power.

Merlin, freed after a millennium trapped within the hawthorn tree. Anisthe felt compassion stir in his chest. He angrily moved to shove it down, desperate that he feel nothing. He stopped short.

Amsalla was dead.

A crack appeared in Anisthe's armor. A fault. It grew under the pressure of his wanting it gone.

Discomfited, Anisthe tried to hide from his own heart. But with Nagarath yet lying unmoving at his side, he could not run far from his feelings. He needed Nagarath to get up. He needed him to not be dead. And not just for the scholarship his friend possessed, knowledge of the older languages of magick that could assist him in deciphering Merlin's book.

Anisthe cast his eyes to the Rishon Kesem, pouring his energies, his animosity, there. Hatred and love. The bite, the bliss of each were very much the same. How easily they could be confused, one with the other.

It was not the first he had felt that way. Really the confusion had lived within his heart for a long time. What Anisthe had thought was emptiness, spite, jealousy, fondness for his aurenaurae . . . It was none of those things save, perhaps, mere denial.

Anisthe's loneliness of heart signaled a codependence. One upon the other. He needed Nagarath alive for the sake of their continued enmity. Or however it was he chose to call this misshapen love they had. Far better than to have to face the horrid weakness of actually caring.

Love. Such a curious burden. Its own sort of curse, really. In that, Anisthe agreed with Liara. And as such, he looked again to his friend, worry coursing through his heart.

"You can't die on me, you fool mage."

CHAPTER TWENTY-NINE

"Nagarath."

A none-too-gentle hand jostled Nagarath's shoulder. Magick still bled from him, a streak of blinding light. The raw, aching wound would finish him off before long. In his agony, he welcomed the promised peace.

"Nagarath!" Anisthe's shouted exclamation repeated close by Nagarath's ear. "For the sake of the powers above, answer me!"

No. Nagarath turned from Anisthe and found that he lay in tall damp grass. Silent stinging tears gathered in the corners of his eyes, extinguishing the white fire that pressed into his vision. With it, he identified the jagged edges of his physical pain, saw how it would not kill him —not yet, anyhow—only to have that discovery allow room for the emotional pain that tore at his heart.

Memories thickened in Nagarath's throat.

"Liara." His magpie. How could he have let her go?

Anisthe broke in on Nagarath's thoughts, violating his

private anguish with a quiet prompting, "So you remember?"

Remember! That he loved Liara? He turned back towards Anisthe, revulsion gripping Nagarath as he noted the war mage's cutting concern.

"You knew." Nagarath's accusation came out weak.

Anisthe nodded his assent. "When you came to the Bastille to kill me, I knew it then. Well, guessed at it. You weren't yourself. And having, myself, dabbled in those sorts of magicks and understanding how Liara might have felt—"

"Understanding! You! For that, you would have to understand love, Anisthe."

The war mage met Nagarath's statement with that same strange, quavering calm. No curl of the lip. No caustic retort. He simply waited, that in itself ringing a loud response.

There were few things in the world that magick could not accomplish. Death, life, and love encompassed the whole of its limitations. Whatever curse Liara had chosen to enact upon Nagarath, however she had chosen to bury his regard for her to buy him a chance at stopping Khariton, it had been temporary, and it had been noticed by Anisthe from the first.

And it had been broken through the war mage's saving of Nagarath's life at peril to himself.

"Brothers in magick" Nagarath had once claimed for them. Brothers in the Art and, consequently, with a fraternal regard in spite of all. That love stood in argument against years—decades—of jealousy and mistrust and enmity.

Nagarath's heartsick realization, that he, too, loved his enemy—that he relied on him, needed him as surely as Anisthe needed Nagarath . . . He crumpled under the weight of it. This alongside a sickening sorrow as he considered anew what dangers, through magick's curse, he had left Liara to face. Magick he might no longer have for himself—though he was pretty certain that Anisthe had saved him from becoming incantate under Merlin's attack.

Nagarath had been wrong about everything. Every. Single. Thing.

Which left nothing for him. He had failed in every conceivable way. And it had taken his enemy to tell him of it. And at a time when it was too late. A hole had been ripped wide within Nagarath's einatus. He could feel the vitality bleeding away.

"Nagarath." This time, Anisthe's plea wavered. "You have to—"

"Stop," Nagarath wheezed. "It's over."

"It's not. It is absolutely not. Look."

Nagarath sank deeper into his heartache, steadfastly ignoring whatever it was that Anisthe insisted he see. Without moving, he ran from Anisthe's concern. He could not think. He was nothing save for grief and pain and defeat.

Threads of despair wound around Nagarath, binding him. And so he lay, strangled in a tapestry of pain: The cinnabar stone. The magick. Merlin's betrayal and treachery.

Amsalla, dead.

Liara, lost.

Guilt and responsibility cut Nagarath loose from his bonds so that he fell headlong back into grief.

And, still, Anisthe would not stop talking. "We've our chance at last. If you could only—"

"Please. Stop."

"But I—we—have it. And Merlin will come looking for it."

It? The stone? Have it, Anisthe, with my compliments.

The words dragged at Nagarath's brain. But he lacked even the wherewithal to speak, never mind move. The world felt heavy. It would crush him before long.

Nagarath closed his eyes.

"Please, Nagarath. This might be our only opportunity. Your having merged your einatus with the stone's power . . . it could lead Merlin right to us. The trail of broken sorcery coupled with that kind of raw magick, whatever were you thinking, doing that with your Gift?"

What indeed?

"Kerri'tarre—" The name scarred Nagarath's throat. Unable to continue, he lay as he had. The wait for death grew long.

"Come." Anisthe tugged on Nagarath's shoulder, helping him into a seated position. With the assistance came a spark of magick. It was not much, but color and sound returned more fully to Nagarath's senses. The world ceased to ripple 'round him.

No, he would not die from Merlin's attack on his einatus. But he was weak, weaker than Nagarath could recall ever having been—itself a feat considering all he had been through. The damage this time was likely permanent.

"Save your magick, magus," Nagarath coughed.

"I've strength of spell to spare. And heavens know I am not that generous." Smiling grimly, Anisthe would not be deterred. "Damn that Merlin. Curse him and his greedy betrayal. And damn Cromen, too. I have no doubt he crossed you as well, the tricky old devil."

"That or he simply did not realize he had made conflicting promises." Nagarath roused himself, unable to simply sit by and allow their mentor's name to be disparaged. "In the end, he had become forgetful, too inattentive to even scry properly. It's how you managed to ensconce yourself with the Ottomans without my knowing. Granted, by the time I learned of it, I no longer much cared what you got up to."

"For you had what you wanted. My cinnabar stone."

Anger rose, bright and furious. It gave Nagarath strength. Just as Anisthe had hoped. One look at the man's brittle smile confirmed it. Nagarath said, "If your two methods for making me well again are limited to magick and provoking me, I think I would prefer your hexes."

"I'm sorry."

From Anisthe's tone, Nagarath knew it to be a genuine apology. It caught him up short.

Again silence stretched between them. Nagarath concluded that he did feel a touch better physically, even if he was still beaten in spirit.

Whatever were they to do now? Was there anything to do, anything left that he could do himself without Anisthe's help? A cautious calling of his magick proved to Nagarath he still had the Art. His threadbare aura had not fully unraveled under Merlin's assault. He was not incantate.

The shock of the discovery set Nagarath to shivering. It meant that Anisthe was right, and Merlin might come at any time. If he could find them. The thread of sorcery between soul and stone might function as an opening of the door to Merlin's prison, but it was not some blazing signpost directing him to his two fugitives. Perhaps he would care little about Anisthe and Nagarath and instead look for Liara. Merlin had a score to settle with Khariton, and he had new power at his behest.

With the little power he had left, could Nagarath get to Liara—find Liara—first?

And if he did not?

Surely the archmage would have realized the cinnabar stone's incompleteness, the need for a key to unlock its full potential. In Merlin's hands the artifact was a threat to Kerri'tarre, sure. But it remained a weapon without teeth. Thus Nagarath's life was not forfeit. And, yes, Anisthe was again correct but without knowing why.

Merlin would come once he had battered his way free of his prison.

But Liara, Nagarath must find Liara. He must warn her, help her as best he could.

He looked to Anisthe. The war mage, again, had lost himself to thoughtful silence.

He was going to make him ask. Nagarath pressed, "You had a plan then, yes? Some chance for Liara?"

"For Liara. For all of us. Those missing mages Merlin talked of? I might have the answer."

Even for Anisthe, it was a rather big claim. Warning

signals sounded in Nagarath's head, and he darted his eyes to the book in Anisthe's hand. A new fear prickled, and he asked, "What have you done?"

Of course Anisthe hadn't rescued Nagarath out of any sort of regard or honor. Of course he would have been acting to serve himself. *And, of course, he's expecting me to get him out of it somehow. With Merlin coming down on us. And with me spent and half dead.*

New anger mingled with Nagarath's fear. "Is that . . . ?"

"The Rishon Kesem. I think. I mean, I can't—"

" 'Get the book.' " Nagarath leapt to his feet. Stunned, enraged sputtering became words. "Was that your plan, then? All along. Keep your hands clean. Keep yourself safe and leave Liara to serve you."

"No! It was not my—as you say it—plan. I saw what happened and decided to use it instead of wringing my hands and waiting."

"And to think I regarded any of this as my fault," Nagarath muttered.

"What?"

"And to think I regarded any of this as my fault!" Nagarath found himself shouting. "Mine. When it was and is and always will be your fault! From the beginning, from your stupid, arrogant obsession with the Laws of Magick. All based on one off-handed challenge meant to rankle. That and a bit of ill-conceived, poorly-educated research amongst Cromen's library.

"That stone was yours. Sure. Your mistake made manifest. Power that ought have blown us all to bits, taking every scrap of magick with it. I stepped forward at

Archmage Cromen's request. I took it upon myself to clean up your messes. I did so in Tours de Merle. I did so in Limska Draga—"

Nagarath bit off his tirade, seeing that Anisthe had moved to speak. But his adversary merely twisted his smile into a silent snarl. No rejoinder came.

"And me. Why save me? Clearly I must fit into this plan of yours. What with you never doing anything out of the kindness of your heart. Nothing for others; nothing for what is right."

"This! This is right!" Anisthe thundered back, raising the book. The unexpected act of aggression forced Nagarath backwards. "I am right. I have been all along. This book? Merlin and Khariton's great achievement, the thing that they would kill each other to have? It controls magick. It makes the Laws. It is the Laws."

With that, Nagarath's outrage snapped. Frank disbelief gripped him, and he turned away, head in his hands, so that he would not have to look at the mad hope in Anisthe's eyes.

"Please, Nagarath."

Coolness flooded Nagarath's veins. Emptied, he had passed beyond anger. But would Anisthe even listen to reason? He tried anyhow. Tried and found himself falling back into old habits, old enmity. Nagarath said, "You can't read it, can you? A thousand years old. More than, even. That magick in that book predates the Green Language. I doubt you even know what it is you have."

"Please." Anisthe offered the book.

Nagarath made no move save to look down at the nondescript tome and then back up at Anisthe. That codex stood at the very heart of their twenty-year quarrel in too many ways to count. And here Anisthe was, still insisting, still pushing his way. Even as Nagarath lost everything—everything! Anisthe, that misguided mage, sending Liara on some vague errand when she had such little time left herself; manipulating Nagarath into positioning him to get exactly what he wanted.

Again, Anisthe's earnest need stared him down, and Nagarath almost believed.

In that moment, Nagarath was reminded of Liara. The eyes that begged forgiveness. A passionate plea for the aid of his magick. The likeness, the hurtful, hateful resemblance between Nagarath's enemy and the woman he loved proved too much.

Liara. He needed to see her. The sand had run from the hourglass. For both of them. She had seen it first, had done her best to save him from it. Nagarath searched Anisthe's eyes, making his own apology. Or, rather, his own explanation. "I thought, for a moment . . . But, no. Nothing, nothing about you has changed, Anisthe."

"Everything has."

But Nagarath had already closed his heart to his former friend. He could feel their time ending. Merlin and Kerri'tarre? Their age, their magick, was returning. If he was to see Liara, forward any plea to save her, he had no more words to waste on Anisthe.

Nagarath took what little power he had remaining to him and set off for home along the corridors of magick.

CHAPTER THIRTY

I t was only when dawn's first light began to rake its fingers across the skies that Krešimir let their campfire die. Strangely, he was not tired nor did he feel particularly anxious. Liara slept soundly at his side, however, and that was all that mattered for now. Watching her, he could pretend, just for a moment, that they had found their peace at last, their happy ending in their long and perilous story. It would all work out as it should for, after everything, he had found his way to her and she to him.

But then Krešimir would remember the wand again.

He reached for his pack for the fiftieth time and checked its contents once more. He breathed fervent thanks to the powers above that the crack in the wand appeared to have more or less sealed itself away during the few hours it had sat concealed in his bag. It was the less which had him sighing with relief that foolish hopes had not simply played tricks on his mind. But no, a sliver of a gap yet remained, marring the imperfect wood.

With luck, Liara might not notice anything had changed.

The thought had Krešimir wondering why he was so reluctant that she know. It was her wand. Atop that, it was the most likely solution to satisfying Kerri'tarre so that he might leave Liara alone.

Scowling, Krešimir closed his pack and stared into the glowing embers of the dying fire. He had agreed to return to Nagarath and ask him for his help. They had deemed Merlin's magick not an option and fled into the night. Now was not the time for lagging steps or selfish reluctance from Krešimir. Not with the dangers Liara faced.

He looked to her again. Yes. Yes, he could give her up for himself so long as Krešimir was assured of her safety and happiness. He could not more force her to love him than he could, himself, use magick. But that did not mean he would not do his part.

Krešimir closed his eyes, and his breath hitched when, a moment later, Liara felt for his hand. He saw that the sun had risen fully, driving steamy clouds of thinning dew into the air. So he had slept. Wordlessly he rose to his feet, taking Liara's uneasy frown as a cue for silence.

They each stooped to gather their belongings.

Say something to her. But Krešimir did not know what he should say. The guilty secret of Liara's wand lay heavy in his pack. His jealous anticipation of seeing Nagarath once more weighed hard against his heart.

Liara's hand again sought his.

"Tra'shuk."

The world dissolved behind Liara's whispered word

of magick. A moment later, they stood within the front hall of a quiet manor.

Dropping both their packs, Liara strode forward, her head swiveling back and forth as she looked around. She turned back a moment later, an apologetic smile on her face. " 'M sorry, I forgot. This is Little Larkhill. Family seat of Nagarath, Magus of Parentino."

With that crisp explanation, she turned away and resumed her cautious listening. To Krešimir it seemed the house was empty. But what did he know? Perhaps the wizard was invisible, employing any number of traps against the unwary.

Liara interrupted his thoughts. "I'll look upstairs, if you could check the library. He's likely to be in one or the other of those places."

Her puzzled frown told Krešimir that Liara did not much believe this claim. In any event, he followed her gaze and opened a door that stood to his right.

Wincing, Krešimir waited for a shouted exclamation and the likelihood that he'd be turned into something icky. He opened one eye and then the other to espy an empty room. No startled wizard rose from either chair beside the cold hearth. No hex reached out to arrest him.

Motion in the corner of Krešimir's vision had him throwing his hands up in surrender. But it was just an illusion. Some shadow behind the colored glass windows.

"No. Wait," Krešimir breathed in surprise and approached. The glass moved. Some sort of enchantment shifted the colored panes and made the figures depicted therein change. Shy, for he could feel the scrutiny of the translucent curious onlookers, Krešimir made a small bow with his head. "Um. Is your master, by chance, at home?"

"That's not how it works." Liara's good-natured laugh behind him had Krešimir jumping. He whirled around, trying to hide from her the scare she had given him.

"I don't think he's here."

With that, it looked as though Liara might cry. Krešimir moved to comfort her.

She backed away and whispered, mostly to herself, "I'll have to go see the Hertfords. Wait here, please."

In a blink, Liara had gone.

A moment later had her charging through the door to the library.

Again, Krešimir had to hide his surprise. Was she showing off, or had she merely forgotten he hadn't the experience with magick that Liara did?

Liara was clearly angry. Her face was red and pinched as she paced the room, shouting, "Where did everyone go? Why? Why leave me and then pick up and go yourselves?"

"Liara. I'm more than willing to wait here until—"

They both froze. A sound in the hallway! The wizard returned. Joyfully, Liara ran and threw open the door.

To Merlin.

The archmage forwent any greeting. His curse threw Liara backwards into the room.

"You!" Wrathful, Liara charged the wizard, throwing hexes of her own. "What have you done with him?"

Dodging, Merlin managed a smile. An invisible shield crackled in the air before him. It rebounded the sparks of Liara's magick. He stood unharmed. Krešimir looked hard at him. Merlin appeared to be younger and haler than Krešimir remembered. Impossible.

"You have his staff. What have you done with Nagarath?" Liara's repeated question came broken by anguish. And accompanied by yet another curse.

This second flew wildly to the side. Not deflected but a misfire. Merlin took advantage of her grief. Fire flew from his outstretched hands. Krešimir leapt into action, throwing himself between them.

"Stop it!"

Someone—he wasn't certain as to who—threw Krešimir to the side with another hex. His head cracked hard against the wood of the long window seat, and he fell heavily at its foot.

Sparks of blue and purple, gold and green, lit the room and dashed themselves against the protective defenses of both mages. Power tore at the air and flung books from shelves. Liara and Merlin in turns lost their footing, only to regain their ground.

Krešimir could not be certain, but it seemed to him that Liara's eyes flashed silver.

Kerri'tarre battled Merlin, then, rather than Liara herself.

Wordlessly, viciously, the wizards attacked one another. Now Krešimir regretted his pitiful interference and instead groveled against the wall, hoping he would be forgotten by whomever rose as the victor.

And then Liara fell. Krešimir's heart leapt into his throat, and his protest scratched for escape. But no sound came.

It would have been drowned in the roar of Merlin's

sorcery anyhow. The archmage stalked close to his downed enemy, raising the staff with its evil red stone and bringing it heavily downward in one cruel blow. The concussive blast rocked the library and shattered the windows.

Shards of glass rained down on Krešimir. He risked a look.

Liara's arm was raised. Her hand clutched Merlin's staff. And her eyes blazed a bright pale madness. Rising to her feet, still clutching the weapon between them, she grinned. "A mistake of arrogance, old one. How like you."

Merlin tugged feebly against Kerri'tarre's hold upon the staff. His eyes stood a mirror to hers. Furious. Fearful.

"Mav." The solitary syllable seemed to hang for a moment—wrath made visible—before coalescing into a whirlwind of dark smoke that enveloped Merlin. Her curse loosed, Liara stumbled backwards, still clutching the stave. She waited, unmoving, for the air to clear. The fog of her magick dissipated to reveal Merlin's body upon the library floor.

Kneeling at his side, she peered with her silvery eyes at his face while her hands searched the front hem of his heavy wizard's cloak. Stopping, her fingers disappeared into a hidden pouch within the mage's robes. She drew forth a silvery length of chain and quickly clasped it about her neck. Krešimir saw a small bright something disappear into the folds of Liara's shirt.

Then she looked straight at him . . .

And, with a whispered word, disappeared behind the red mist of the stave's magick.

With the fading light of the cinnabar stone a curse seemed to lift. Krešimir shuddered under the renewed brightness of the world. Sunlight through the broken windows slashed across the ruined library and further highlighted the damage therein. Smoke and the dying spark of angry magicks thickened the air. Merlin had yet to move.

Krešimir scrambled forward.

"Krešimir."

"Merlin!" In spite of all, tears sprang to Krešimir's eyes at the sound of the archmage's voice.

"Hush, lad." Merlin took a deep breath and then moved to sit. "I am immortal, if you remember."

"But I thought that—"

"Kerri'tarre finished me off at long last?" Merlin chuckled. "Gave me the beating of a lifetime, perhaps. But that will happen when you cannot die, and you face an enemy such as he."

"Liara's lost to him, isn't she?"

"For the moment. Yes."

For the moment? Hope rose to overtake even the pounding of Krešimir's pulse. Hope flung him back under the archmage's protection once more. Hope guided his hands and set him to looking about the scattered books for his pack.

He still had Liara's wand. She—Khariton—now had the cinnabar stone, but Krešimir had the wand containing its vital secret. He drew it forth. To Krešimir's eyes the newly-healed crack seemed to glimmer with unmatched brightness, and he was forced to look away.

"Now, you may clear your debt to me by explaining

what exactly it is that makes that girl's wand so interesting to you."

Krešimir hesitated, realizing he was caught, knowing
he had no choice but to trust in Merlin. Whatever quarrel
Liara had with the archmage, whatever Merlin had done
to Nagarath to claim the powerful magicks of the
cinnabar stave for himself . . . Krešimir's fight was
always for her. He would use whatever weapon fate had
placed in his hands, whichever wizard had the power to
aid him.

Quickly, he recounted Liara's explanation of the
cinnabar stone, its key, and the terms which Nagarath had
claimed for its discovery and use. He then explained his
own discoveries from the night before. In saying it aloud
to Merlin, Krešimir realized he was the Artless who
might read the spell on the scroll within Liara's wand. He
was the one who could make whole that dangerous
weapon.

"If we are careful, you realize that it might just be
what saves Liara." Merlin nodded towards the wand in
Krešimir's hand. That he had not moved to claim it for
himself and instead merely took out his pipe, placing it in
his mouth and lighting it, proved a comfort.

Eyes on the hidden pouch where Krešimir had only
recently seen Liara's fingers delving while the mage had
been unconscious, he blurted, "What did she take? It was
some sort of silver chain with a pendant."

Krešimir's cheeks heated at his insolence, and Merlin
smiled, this time to himself. "A mistake, Kerri'tarre?
How . . . like you."

Rising to his feet, Merlin held out his hand. "Wand please, Krešimir."

Krešimir surrendered the wand, feeling foolish for having entertained the possibility that he was at all important to the drama being played out between the magick users.

Eyeing the item, Merlin breathed smoke onto it from his still-sparking pipe. "Remarkable. Doubtless Magus Nagarath never expected a skilled woodworker should get a close look at the item, eh?"

He moved to hand it back. Krešimir received the wand with no small surprise.

"Magick enough to allow us to follow Kerri'tarre wherever he went. The key wants the stone, and the stone wants the key. Hold my sleeve, please." Merlin removed his pipe from his lips and fiddled with a small pouch of what appeared to be a lustrous bit of sand.

Krešimir never even heard the spell take hold. An instant later, he felt its effects.

Air rushed into Krešimir's lungs, a drowning in reverse. In fact, each of his senses screamed at him. And then silence and piercing brightness. He swayed, dizzy and ready to fall but for Merlin's steadying hand upon his shoulder.

"Breathe," the archmage gave his quiet command, then left him to his fate.

Krešimir's response was to double over and mentally curse out every bit of magick he had ever encountered. Devil's work. Small wonder if felt like death. The rock and stone seemed to swirl, the struggling sunlight dancing in fragments at his feet.

No, not stones. He bent further, reaching down with tremulous fingers to grasp one of the parchment-thin objects. A leaf skeleton. Strangely translucent and palest pink, the delicate oak leaf shimmered in the light breeze, refracting the glow of the sinking sun.

Merlin's hand on his shoulder again called Krešimir's attention to his surroundings. The magus had his cowl thrown back, and his watery eyes trained upward into the leafy canopy. Featherlight jewels, every leaf in every tree had been changed same as that which Krešimir held. Eerie, they fractured the fading daylight, slashing it to watery ribbons.

He knew this spell; knew its caster.

Hope. Just as Merlin had prophesied.

But it was where they had been witched that caught at Krešimir's attention.

The courtyard in which they stood belonged to a broken stone building. A castle, more like. And a horribly familiar one, in spite of its dilapidation. Recognition sent icy fingers crawling up Krešimir's spine to settle at the base of his skull. Liara had led them home. To Parentino in the Limska Draga valley.

A scream rent the blue-gray of the coming night. Black wings swooped close, and both men ducked instinctively. But the bird merely wheeled about, executing a neat turn in the air before landing in one of the trees to scold the intruders.

"One of yours?" Krešimir blurted the question without thinking.

"Yes, Krešimir. There are only two birds in all the

world, and they are both mine." Merlin's response came gruff, but his eyes twinkled.

Warmth surged in Krešimir's chest. If the wizard could joke at such a time . . .

Krešimir urged his steps forward. But Merlin's gentle restraint remained firm. A whispered word of magick revealed why.

At the archmage's rasped command, black symbols edged in fire rose from the courtyard cobbles. Skeletons of runes, they danced in the air. Even Krešimir could feel their jangling powers, the protection they offered to the ruined castle.

"What happened here?"

"Something horrible. Something . . . I don't know what. But it was massive. The power scattered about? Sundered spell books all." Merlin's brow furrowed, and he looked up at Parentino's scarred edifice. "We're walking into a trap."

The last Merlin murmured to himself, but his words caught Krešimir all the same. He choked on sudden fear. "A trap!"

Merlin ignored the interjection, again choosing to converse with himself rather than his companion. "Ah, beware the heart of she whom you so carelessly deceived, Kerri'tarre, old friend. Parentino's mage has some tricks in him yet."

In answer, Krešimir cast his eyes over the hulking wreck ahead of them.

"Come." The archmage stepped forward into the bright chaos of warring spells. They died as he neared, clearing a path that Krešimir hastened to enter lest the magick reignite in Merlin's wake. Already he could feel the last of the day fading to a fast twilight, and the formerly familiar woods seemed to hold extra menace in the deepening gloom—pale pink leaves or not.

Gaining the castle proper, Merlin sparked a ball of spell-light that he sent to hovering above their heads. Blue-green, the illumination threw looming shadows upon the crooked and cracked walls. The hexes that had choked the courtyard had entered the hallways of Parentino itself. And though they seemed to have their origins in the deeper darkness ahead, they flickered feebly.

Looking closer, Krešimir saw bits of parchment and paper ground into the cracks between the castle's stones. They set him to thinking about the tightly scrolled spell concealed within Liara's wand. He reached for it instinctively.

Merlin noted the gesture and leaned close. He whispered, "Whichever happens, do not act without thought. Kerri'tarre is tricky. Powerful as that stone is, he cannot —will not—defeat me. But it will not be easy. We must . . . tread carefully."

As if Krešimir needed a reminder of that last. Suppressing a shiver, he wondered anew what awesome power had all but destroyed the building and cast the chaotic magicks which permeated the castle.

They stopped before a torn and dingy wall-covering. It only half concealed the lighted doorway behind. Krešimir tried to peer around the archmage, only to be blocked by the wave of an arm and another spell.

At least he thought it another spell. For nothing happened.

Merlin, too, seemed surprised. He extinguished his guiding illumination and moved the tapestry aside. But even bereft of the archmage's spell, they had not been plunged into total darkness.

It was no trick of the eyes, however. A lofty and large room. Krešimir, too, could see a light within. Strange, considering it was as much a wreck as the rest of the castle.

Together, they tried their best to gain vantage without, themselves, being seen. There was plenty to hide behind. The room's contents—twisted and broken bookshelves, the remains of two balconies and their incidental stair-wells, more codices and scrolls—had been swept to the side as if by some giant hand. Or by magick.

A man in wizard's robes occupied the center of the once grand space. Hood thrown casually back, his sharp features caught in the light of a plain tallow candle, Nagarath was reading a book.

CHAPTER THIRTY-ONE

Movement in the corner of his vision forced Nagarath to look up from his reading. He had in hand one of the sole surviving specimens of the disaster that had befallen his library and had, in fact, been delighted to discover the book shortly after arriving at Parentino hours before.

But nothing—nothing—set his heart to racing more than the sight of his Liara stepping from the deeper shadows and into the silvery moonlight which marked the cracked stone floor. Nagarath rose to his feet. The precious tome fell to the ground forgotten.

He tried to speak, but his throat worked emptily around the sentiment he dared not express. His Liara. In Parentino. He had expected her arrival in the triggering of the magick in the pendant he wore. His gaze had crossed and re-crossed the pages of the book in his hand while he had waited nervously for his apprentice.

But now he saw her eyes.

Pale like moons. Empty and cold as a winter field. Liara

stared at Nagarath across the space of his broken library and said nothing. And she had his cinnabar staff in hand.

"No," he whispered, seeking for any sign of hope. Any at all.

Kerri'tarre smiled from Liara's face.

"You took her," Nagarath challenged.

"And the stone. Yes. And your pendant that she was ever so happy to have back." Kerri'tarre continued his unaffected smile. "Even so, my victory over Merlin was but temporary. He will be back, and at present, my prize is incomplete. Liara appears to be lacking some very crucial information. That or she's managed to hide it from me, amongst . . . other memories. Full of resolve, your aurenaurae apprentice. She has a head full of riddles, this sinistral sorceress with whom you are so taken."

Nagarath raised his wand. "You came at my call. You stand in my house."

Kerri'tarre cast his eyes upward to the fractured ceiling. "That's it? You're going to stand here in this dilapidated wreck and threaten me?"

Nagarath waited, impassive.

Khariton sneered, "You've nothing to bargain with."

"My life."

"That offer has expired." Raising the stave, Kerri'tarre moved to strike.

Nagarath did not so much as flinch as his opponent stepped forward.

The praecantator hesitated. He narrowed his eyes. "Your life comes with the key to the cinnabar stone."

"Information as to where it is. Yes."

"And I'm assuming your terms are that you won't otherwise say a word of it."

"Upon your leaving Liara to have your einatus reside within my mage's soul, the information you seek will become yours."

At this, Khariton paused, considering. "Why? Why would you do that?"

"Because it frees her," Nagarath cried. "Because you've won. Because in a future with either you or Merlin winning, I would rather it be you at this point. Take your pick."

"Your plan is to trick me. You'd—"

"I don't want him to win! I don't want her to lose!" He surrendered. Anxious pleading tore tears from Nagarath's eyes. They streamed down his face and blurred his vision. He blinked them away, continuing, "And I sure as hell don't want Merlin—already immortal, murdering, power-hungry Merlin—to have that stone. As I decided nearly two decades ago!"

"You sent a warning to Merlin!" Kerri'tarre countered. "You sought his help."

"And I was wrong."

"You've already told me, it's not your stone to give. In the meantime, it has become mine to take."

"Prove it. Hit me with its power. Show me that you have mastered it." Nagarath threw wide his arms. He waited and then advanced to meet his enemy. "See? Not a bad deal . . . if you're still willing to bargain."

"And if I cheat you?"

"You won't. You can't. Not with the Laws in effect.

And, besides, I know now that you have an interest in keeping things that way."

"I can change them."

"Certainly. But you could do that anyway, so long as you gain hold of the Rishon Kesem or outlast any of us or sway Merlin or any number of scenarios."

"Then what are you—?"

"I'm picking a side!"

At last the smile on Kerri'tarre's face grew genuine. "Finally."

"Too bad it's the wrong side," Merlin's voice rang out from the shadows.

Nagarath and Kerri'tarre both turned to see the archmage striding toward them, Krešimir close behind.

CHAPTER THIRTY-TWO

Merlin!

Nagarath's anger surged. He checked it just as quickly, thinking fast. He had drawn Kerri'tarre to Parentino through Liara's pendant. But how had Merlin followed?

England's archmage surveyed the room with confident, shifty eyes. Krešimir sulked behind him, harboring the attitude of a whipped dog. Nagarath risked a glance to Kerri'tarre. The praecantator stood leisurely off to the side, as if amused by the whole thing. There was such similarity between the two ancient wizards, in their stance, in their attitude, that Nagarath's ire rekindled. The two were likely allied for all he knew!

Amsalla's fading scream echoed in Nagarath's heart as he drew his wand.

"Krešimir, go. It's not safe here." Nagarath jerked his head in indication. Dvigrad's woodworker took a step backwards into the shadows. Nagarath could see Krešimir's eyes glance about around the ruined library, the man thinking hard, hesitating as his gaze swept past Liara.

Nagarath leveled his wand at Merlin. "I ought to kill you for what you did to me."

Merlin sighed and raised his own wand. "Many have tried. Including Kerri'tarre. Including you. As you can see, I am no worse for it. I, in fact, feel better than I have in centuries. Stronger, certainly."

"And yet Kerri'tarre took the stone from you."

"And how quickly you managed to call your apprentice here, Nagarath. A prearranged signal? Some secret sorcery? I believe I heard some talk of bargains when we entered your"—Merlin's mouth twitched—"library."

Nagarath set his jaw to the insult and insinuation. Yet he now had at least one answer. The pointed manner in which the archmage flicked his gaze to the ruined ceiling told him that Merlin understood what powers still held sway in the place. In the stones of the ruined fortification and scattered bones of countless broken spell books: magick enough to trap Kerri'tarre.

He flinched, readying himself for the duel that must bury them all. All save for immortal Merlin. He hoped that, if Merlin had an alternate plan in mind, he would reveal it now. Even so, Nagarath tried again to salvage what he could, repeating, "Krešimir. Go."

The man had crept forward again during the wizards' brief exchange. "But, Liara—"

"She's gone," Nagarath snapped. The words pulled Krešimir up short. With it, more cowering from the woodsman as he directed his attentions to Merlin. A check and silent inquiry.

What was their game? Didn't Merlin know how this must play out? The second that Kerri'tarre realized what had been hid within Liara's wand, as soon as he got his hands on the cinnabar stone's full power, they would be lost. Nagarath shouted, "Merlin, get that Artless out of here!"

To Nagarath's surprise, Merlin stepped to Krešimir's side. The wizard laid a gentle hand on his arm. Quiet words passed between them, and Nagarath frowned. So Krešimir was present for a reason.

Krešimir seemed frozen with indecision rather than mollified by the exchange. But he did not move. Kerri'-tarre, too, appeared interested in the hushed dialogue and was no doubt calculating his best way out of their strained impasse.

With a muttered word and wave of his wand, Merlin sent his magick into what lanterns had survived the library's destruction. Some cracked, most lying upon the ground, the globe lights flickered to life. Satisfied, the archmage nodded, and under that greater illumination, he turned to his old enemy.

Through force of will, Kerri'tarre had maintained his casual insolence. He raised the cinnabar stave, coolly admiring it as he said, "If your plan was to kill me and be done with it, you would have already done so. You value your own lives too dearly. Or is it that you secretly agree with my ambitions? Perhaps my aims, if not my methods?

"One of you three has that which completes my prize. And each of you wants something from this lustrous little stone. Give me what I want, and I will gladly hold audience."

Nervous fingers flicked the wand in Merlin's hand, half a threat and little more. His voice was soft as he asked, "Every wizard has a weakness, and her name is Magick. But what of you, Kerri'tarre? You speak of wants and ambitions. What, besides that stone which you've only just learned of—?"

"For a thousand years I have watched our world fall apart while you cowered under the branches of a tree. I had to. For a mirror never sleeps, never ceases its witness. Even long after my limited guidance was no longer heeded—even left amongst the discarded hopes of a forgotten age—I could hear the screams. I could hear magick dying. And I intend to live. Live and never die." Kerri'tarre gripped tight the mage's staff. The stone atop it flashed with its own inner light. It seemed to Nagarath that Liara's silvered pupils reflected that power for one bright moment.

"Immortality, you will find, is extraordinarily overrated." A shadow seemed to pass through Merlin's face as he said the words.

"You gave up! You, Merlin. You turned your back. Whereas I was forced to watch. See for yourself how it feels." The cinnabar stone stirred to life. "Immortality. I will have it of you."

The silent attack sent Nagarath to his knees. For all that the cinnabar stone had changed hands twice since its joining to his einatus, the connection remained strong. A searing wind seemed to whistle through the hole in his magick, sucking breath, siphoning strength. Through his agony, Nagarath barely noted that Merlin, too, had been cut down. Cromen's will with regards to the cinnabar stone yet endured, and both owners suffered for it.

Kerri'tarre lowered his weapon, ending the assault. "I thought as much. Greedy wizards all."

"Would you give us back Liara, Archmage?" Taking a sharp breath, Krešimir stepped forward, drawing all eyes upon him. "Would you let her be if you got what it was you wanted?"

"Krešimir, no!" Exhaustion robbed Nagarath's words of their power. That or he hadn't even strength enough to speak his warning aloud. In either event, Krešimir was undeterred.

Kerri'tarre made no answer.

Krešimir tried again. "If I can help you to get what it is you—"

"Yes, yes. I heard you." Kerri'tarre cocked his head and seemed to weigh the offer. Shining eyes had been drawn to the wand in Krešimir's hand. He had guessed, like Nagarath, that the woodsman had been brought for good reason.

"An Artless man who . . . loves Liara." Kerri'tarre's contemplative tone struck Nagarath's heart. None least as he had been the one to foolishly tell the archmage of Krešimir's lack of wizardry.

"You love the woman. And she— Well, she has told you quite a lot, hasn't she. Enough to make you jealous. Enough to make you curious about this stone. And Merlin thought you worth bringing. An Artless. I need one. Unless I render incantate either of these meddlers. But I don't think you know quite enough to be of use to me."

"Don't I, though?" Krešimir took one wavering step forward. "As you've said, you need an Artless per the terms of the spell that binds the power in your staff. And there's something of that secret that you can't steal from Liara's heart. For she does not know where that spell has been hidden."

"But you do." Kerri'tarre's eyes became shining slits. Distrust. But he was listening. He made a sign in the air. The globe lanterns of the library sparked an answering illumination, all the better to show the change that had come over the room in the space of a breath. The cracks that riddled the floor, the holes in walls and ceiling—all healed. Balconies and bookshelves righted. Order restored. "And the price of this bargain, Krešimir?"

"It's illusion, you fool!" Nagarath could only manage a weak protest. From the corner of his eye he could see that Merlin had not yet moved. Desperate, Nagarath reached out with the last of his Art, and Parentino returned to bleak ruin. With that one simple spell, his einatus screamed and wavered. The flame of his magick was going out.

"Illusion, yes. But I can make illusion fact," Liara's voice spoke Kerri'tarre's words. "Anything is possible with magick. Dvigrad? Would you like it restored as well? We could go home, Krešimir."

Krešimir's eyes widened.

Fighting unconsciousness, Nagarath tried to voice his protest. No words came. His heart seized as he tried to summon vitality, any power at all, from his emptied aura.

Krešimir took a slow step forward, and in his hand he held a wand. Liara's wand. "I would strike the same bargain as Nagarath. Knowledge of the keyspell. And in exchange, I want Liara, and I want Dvigrad. And I need more than your word, Kerri'tarre. I require a binding agreement."

Kerri'tarre licked his lips, his eyes bright and fixed upon the power in Krešimir's hand. "If you can give me what I ask, then I can swear on the very Laws of Magick that my einatus is bound by the promise I give you. Liara came here at Nagarath's call, but she has ceased fighting my control. Believe her if you won't hear me. She knows I speak truth when I tell you that I won't need her body nor her magick if I get what I want. She will be free. You are her hope."

Krešimir's eyes never left Liara's face. Wordlessly he held out Liara's wand and snapped it in two, revealing the tight scroll hidden at its core. "Liara had the spell all along, even if she did not know of it. She had it and gave it to me to hold on to."

"Find the book." Kerri'tarre smiled. "And you. You can read it."

"I can try. She said—"

"You fool!" At last Nagarath found his feet, his voice. But not his strength. He swayed unsteadily as the room spun 'round him. He had to stall. For he had seen Merlin stir at last. Immortal Merlin who was their only hope now that Krešimir threatened all with his weakness of heart. "That stone. You cannot unlock its power."

"I can, and why not?" Krešimir rounded on him. "You had planned to! You promised to give the key to Kerri'tarre."

"And I was lying."

"Ha! I said you would cross me!"

"Merlin. Stop him."

"I have been for several minutes now." Merlin lurched to his feet, giving Nagarath a broken smile as he did so. Puzzled, Nagarath tried to determine what the wizard meant. But before he could consider further, he saw Merlin fix his gaze towards the shattered library entryway. England's archmage peered into the dark, saying, "Thank you, Amsalla. I see you have him. But do you have it?"

Nagarath turned to see Amsalla DeBouverelle. Alive. In Parentino.

And she was not alone. Arms pinioned, eyes struggling to meet Nagarath's, Anisthe stumbled alongside his captor's footsteps. Amsalla had her wand pressed to Anisthe's throat. "I have done as we agreed, Merlin."

"Utter one word of the spell on that scroll, Krešimir, and Amsalla will ensure that Kerri'tarre never has the opportunity to use that power." Though he spoke to Dvigrad's woodsman, Merlin's gaze sought Nagarath's.

"Krešimir. Please." Nagarath surprised himself in his even being able to speak, to move. The shock was too great. They had seen her die. He and Anisthe. They had seen Merlin whisk that wizard into oblivion with the flick of a wrist. Nagarath had mourned her. He had tried, even, to avenge her. And she had all along been working with the wizard whom she claimed to live in complete terror of? Nagarath had seen into her mind and found no sign, no hint, of such a grand deception.

The depth of Amsalla's lies—of Merlin's duplicity—stole Nagarath's breath as surely as any hostile hex. The weakness in his heart and limbs was matched only by the frantic efforts of his mind to scream at him. He must do something.

Amsalla set her attention on him. Nagarath could no longer tell what a genuine apology from her might look like—perhaps he never had—but he liked to think that the regret in the woman's face had to be something akin to sincerity.

She looked past him to Kerri'tarre.

"I owe Merlin for the mercy he has shown me; for his patience when I proposed that we lay a trap for the enemies of magick by bringing into the light an ancient mirror certain to sway all who looked upon its face," Amsalla said. "I am, however, willing to pledge loyalty to another, depending on the terms of the arrangement."

"Your loyalty appears to be easily foresworn, Magus DeBouverelle," Kerri'tarre snarled.

"And you, Archmage, are soul-bound to a wizard whose magick is yet hers to claim per the Laws," Amsalla countered. Arching her eyebrows, she regarded Kerri'-tarre. "I believe we are of a similar nature. We desire the same things. And, quite frankly, I don't see how you have much choice if you want the Rishon Kesem."

Carefully keeping Anisthe within wand-point, Amsalla reached into her cloak and produced a smallish codex that, for its unremarkable appearance, Nagarath recognized.

With that, Kerri'tarre's certainty rebounded, and he sneered, "You, wizard, are not worthy to even touch that book. You're a dabbler. A hollow-hearted flirt and little more."

"Fine, then." Amsalla's face grew ugly. "Merlin? I accept your terms."

She flicked her wrist. In the dim light of the ruined library, something small, thin, metallic, and altogether wicked flashed in Amsalla's hand.

Panicked, Kerri'tarre leapt forward, shouting to Krešimir, "Do it! Enact the spell, and I'll give you anything you ask for."

Torn, Nagarath trusted to Merlin to stop Krešimir's foolish act. His quick curse turned Amsalla's blade aside. But he had misread the situation. For Merlin, too, had moved to stop Amsalla.

Which left nobody to prevent Krešimir from loosing the terrible power of the cinnabar stone. In his hands, the scroll burned with a searing whiteness. His lips moved silently as they read the words on the page.

CHAPTER THIRTY-THREE

The keyspell grew radiant in the hands of Dvigrad's woodworker.

A sparkling, violent blast arced through the library.

Surprise glimmered briefly in Krešimir's eyes, and then he slumped forward. In his hand he still clutched the parchment. It no longer blazed. Just as Krešimir no longer moved.

"I'm sorry," Amsalla gasped. Shaking, she had her wand held out in front of her. "But I had to. He would have . . . I had to."

"No!" Liara ran towards Krešimir's limp body. Her eyes had cleared of their silvery sheen. Throwing the wizard's staff from her, she held Krešimir in her arms. She whispered, "Please, no."

Liara paused, shaking her head as though confused. She looked around her with eyes that flashed blankly as they lit upon the abandoned cinnabar stone.

"Merlin!" Amsalla's outcry drew everyone's attention. Throwing Anisthe to the ground, she leveled her wand at his heart. Her curse came swift and sure.

Searing brightness tore through the library. The deadly hex then turned upon its caster. It rebounded on Amsalla and threw her backwards. All in the space of a breath, breath stolen by the brief vacuum of magick realigning itself along the edges of the aura strike.

For Anisthe stood strong. Unscathed. The only wizard in the room with any power and presence of mind, he advanced, wand out, smiling in the face of Amsalla's defeat.

"You—! You have magick. You've had magick all along." Amsalla cowered in terror and disbelief. Quivering, she turned to England's archmage, affecting rage as she shrieked, "Merlin, he—"

"I—what?" Anisthe snarled. "Didn't tell you that Domagoj had given me some of his magick long before you killed him for the rest?"

Anisthe slashed the air with his wand, calling the oriaurant's magick to him. Zielsor, but condoned by the Laws Eversio. Amsalla would soon know what it was to be incantate. Anisthe looked down upon his fallen enemy and bent to reclaim the Rishon Kesem. "This, Merlin. This is the kind of wizard she is. She's as bad as Kerri'tarre—"

"I know. We all us mages are."

A sharp flick of his wrist and Merlin slew Anisthe without one word more.

"Anisthe! No!" Nagarath screamed. He ran to Anisthe's side, falling to his knees and cradling the wizard in his arms. But it was too late. Merlin's spell had killed the man the instant it struck. Still Nagarath pleaded and hoped and tried. *Stay. Come back. If you die, then I can't save her . . .*

Nagarath's magick met a void. There was no reviving the emptied body. Anisthe was already dead.

What cruelty. What mad cunning. England's archmage had played each of them against themselves. Merlin had patiently waited for the perfect moment to sever the thread of Liara's life. He had made sure that Kerri'tarre stood alone and without mage or artifact in which to retreat.

Liara lay in a crumpled heap. The cloud of her aura was weak. It fell about Nagarath's apprentice warm and bright, like sunshine.

But he could not go to her lest any shadow of Kerri'-tarre's magick remain.

Nagarath found his feet. Let Merlin blast him for it, he would be damned if he stayed away from Liara in her last moments. Hands shaking, legs buckling beneath him, Nagarath reached Liara's side. He held her close. His magpie who love, who all the magick in the world, could not save.

And then Liara went still, and Nagarath knew her to be gone from him.

CHAPTER THIRTY-FOUR

Nagarath had lived this nightmare before. A half a world away, in the shallows of a cruel sea, he had felt the dying ripple of Liara's magick. Then he had been naive enough to hope. Then the story had ended differently.

But now? Now Nagarath found that he was too numb to even feel, too heartsick to even think. To act. To move. To hope. Oh, how had he ever dared to hope!

It all made a broken sort of sense. The heart of Merlin's cruel curse had carried in it a crooked justice for Anisthe's innumerable crimes. In upholding the Laws he and Kerri'tarre had created once upon a time, Magick had inflicted its promised penalty.

A hard whiteness flashed inside Nagarath's reeling mind. A lightning strike of inspiration, immediately rejected for its terrible impracticality, set him to shaking.

Bitter hatred veiled his eyes and burned his throat. This from Nagarath who had never known such, even with regards to Anisthe. Even with Amsalla DeBouverelle, who had wounded him in so many personal ways. With it, something inside him hardened. Something crystalized. Like magick made into a stone of power, resolve wrapped in agony and pain.

Gently laying Liara where she had fallen, Nagarath rose and returned to Anisthe's side. The Rishon Kesem sat forgotten, mere inches from his outstretched hand.

Simple and unassuming. Ancient and indifferent. The spell book looked quite the opposite of bright hope, really.

Kneeling, Nagarath opened the age-darkened cover, distantly surprised when no one questioned his incursion, no magicks leapt out at him to prevent his touching the pages. He spared a glance to note that Merlin had moved to claim the cinnabar staff. The archmage's only acknowledgment of Nagarath's actions was a narrow-eyed, piercing frown. But no challenge. Amsalla was nowhere to be found.

Nagarath no longer cared. Let Merlin stop him if he will. At present, he desired only one thing.

A quick eye cast over the first page and Nagarath understood. Understood the guilt, the greed, the arrogance, the noble intents of two wizards past, all collated and bound within the old covers. The Rishon Kesem was a spell book with but one spell. And it was a spell begun over a thousand years ago and pointedly, purposely, left incomplete. Only a handful of people in the world might be able to decipher the text of this living spell, let alone read it with the power required to finish the incantation.

Nagarath, scholar of magick in all its forms and all its

expressions, was one of those people. And finish it he would.

> *Paahre azal-ulu ilu. Isiiš. Inanna.*
> *Allal, amaru sizkurre. Namurru darie.*
> *Kain-imma kurrku šiiršiir niĝul sigil kiliib*
>   *burre.*

> Gather all into the song. Tears of joy. Tears
>   of pain.
> A river, a flood to intercede. Power in
>   eternal refrain.
> Incantation set in motion and sung until a
>   distant time stops all, frees all.

The words on the page glowed. All save for the last three. And these Nagarath now read aloud, summoning the last of his magick as he did so. "*Sigil kiliib burre.*"

A whispering wind swept through Parentino's ruins. They stirred the pages of the book in Nagarath's hand, and then all was silent and still.

"Frees all," Nagarath breathed and looked up to find Merlin's unreadable gaze upon him. He wondered at what he saw therein. Approval? Condemnation? Again, Nagarath didn't much care. The book in Nagarath's hand lay dead. He hadn't the heart to look at Liara. Time resumed its steady crawl forward through an empty world.

Merlin spoke, "Cromen's knowledge-hungry apprentice, Parentino's Mage, calmly reading from a book as the world comes to an end around him . . . You do understand what it is you've done." The ancient archmage let his questioning statement hang in the air, putting up his wand so that he might free his hands. He leaned heavily upon the cinnabar staff. In fact, it looked as though he might collapse at any moment. A coughing fit nearly took the man's legs out from under him, and Nagarath fought the instinct to go to his aid.

Instead, Nagarath looked from the book in his hand to Merlin and back to the Rishon Kesem. His mind caught on the wizard's cryptic challenge. What had he done? He hoped . . . He daren't even think what it was he hoped.

"Talented, if a bit dense. I believe that was Cromen's sobriquet for you," Merlin drew Nagarath's attention back on him. With a wave of his wrist, the archmagus made a sign in the air. *Maa'ome*. Calling light. The simplest of spells. With it, every lantern in the room flared, then died, the magick disobedient to the call. Merlin smiled at his failure, and even in the dimmed lighting, Nagarath could see that his eyes sparkled. He said, "Excellently done."

Stunned, Nagarath did not move. Searching his own heart for the power, he found that it shivered and waved like a candle in a draft, furious and untamed. It was there but resistant to the command of his mind.

Merlin nodded. "You might well have been in time, Archmage, though I'd suggest to leave her for a moment longer. Best to let these things settle."

Nagarath followed his gaze to Liara's still form. His heart broke itself anew.

She stirred.

"It's a trick of the—" A thickness in his throat

stopped Nagarath's disbelief from finding voice. The lanterns were extinguished, the magick gone. Which meant it had to be true. Oh, could it really be possible? Rushing forward, he fell to his knees in his haste, scrambling so that he was at Liara's side in less than the time it took for his own heart to again begin to beat. Liara opened her eyes and smiled.

His Liara. Smiling. Sobbing, Nagarath feared to touch her lest the miracle prove untrue. But even that hesitation went unheeded in his joy, his incredible, delirious joy. She was in his arms within moments. "Nagarath."

"Impossible," he murmured, holding her close.

"Anisthe! He—!" Liara stiffened and then looked about the shattered library. Her eyes widened as she saw Anisthe's body. "The Laws, Nagarath!"

Nagarath blanched, hiding his face even from her.

"Nagarath." Liara's gentle hand on his cheek brought him back out of his guilt. "The book. Anisthe said to find the book. He did mean the Rishon Kesem. He meant for us—you—to end that which gave magick itself to the wizards."

"I know, magpie. I know."

"But magick! You haven't that right, Nagarath!"

"It's"—Nagarath choked—"it's nothing compared to you. Isn't that right, Merlin? Did I not make the right choice?"

He turned to call his challenge to Merlin. The edge had crept back into Nagarath's words. With Liara returned to him, he could afford to feel.

But Merlin was not listening. He had gone to Krešimir's side. Nagarath's heart clenched. He had forgotten. He had even forgotten how the sight of Krešimir falling under Amsalla's hex had nearly freed Liara from Kerri'tarre's control.

Liara. Who was alive in spite of all.

"You save the people you love, Archmagus. Every time," Merlin's voice rose from where he knelt beside Dvigrad's woodsman.

"Krešimir." Liara began to quiver, and one large tear freed itself to roll unheeded down her cheek.

"Hush, my dear. I'm doing what I can," Merlin spoke through gritted teeth. Beads of sweat stood out on his forehead, and his skin had gone sickly yellow. " 'Tis my fault he was cut down. I tamed these wild magicks once. I can do it again."

Liara took a shuddering breath and looked again to her progenaurae. She seemed largely unmoved by his death, strangely silent. At length she whispered, "Good-bye, Anisthe," and then turned away from the sight of him.

Anisthe of Vrsar. Gone at long last. Remorse thickened in Nagarath's throat. Whatever was he to do without his enemy? So much of his life, his energies, had been spent hating, goading, ignoring, obsessing over that man. What happened next?

Liara buried her face in Nagarath's chest. "I cursed you."

Nagarath smiled. He had long found that a broken apology was often Liara's best apology.

"I was so afraid of what Kerri'tarre would make me do. I believed I was helping. I wanted to save you, keep you from loving me, keep you away."

"Do you believe I do not love you now?" Nagarath quirked, pulling back so that he could look into Liara's tear-smudged eyes. "I have just unraveled every bit of magick our world has ever known to save you. I, in fact, think my mess is a bit more dramatic than what you once did to Parentino here."

"A poor comparison to make," Liara sniffled. But, too, she tried to laugh. It was something. She leaned back into him, her hard angularity, her fierce vitality crushing Nagarath anew. But with love.

"Welcome back, lad." Merlin's shouted exclamation drew their attention back on him. The archmage turned to Nagarath and Liara. "He's still gravely ill, but with the right care, I believe he will pull through. Instinct tells me that this is one of the more . . . intact . . . rooms in this castle?"

Liara smiled softly and said, "We know a place."

EPILOGUE

SIX MONTHS LATER:

Liara was out in the garden when Nagarath trudged up the small footpath leading to their cottage, his arms heavy with firewood. Deep in the heart of the Limska Draga valley, the cozy dwelling had been built by an expert woodsman, their neighbor and apprentice to one Merlin Sylvestris.

The fence could wait. She hurried to help.

"Rabbits again?" Nagarath quirked, raising an eyebrow.

"Squirrels this time."

"Ah, well, a fence is not the most effective barrier to their ingenuity, Liara."

Liara frowned. "I'm not the reason we cannot debate with them like civilized mages anymore."

"Can you blame me?"

She smiled and shook her head. "Never. I think you like that nothing works as it ought."

Nagarath shrugged and moved to divest himself of his burden. Logs tumbled to the ground in an uneven heap.

Liara clicked her tongue. Her wizard still wanted magick for every little thing. Without it, the task of stacking the firewood would likely wait until they simply burned the logs for fires.

The mage proved her wrong when, a moment later, he stooped to pick through the mess. The tidying was haphazard, and she helped him with the task. She asked, "How is he?"

"Merlin? He grows weaker, and I do believe the archmage is well and truly mortal now. Your Krešimir is a great help to him, for his interest in magick . . ."

Nagarath's face grew troubled, and Liara reached for her mage. She could feel his sorrow merge with hers as he held her. Long moments passed thus, a comfortable silence punctuated only by the sounds of the slumbering winter wood. She found that she wished she could see the magick, the sparkling auras that lived at the heart of everything, living and non. With the loosing of the Rishon Kesem's hold on all of magick, a dam had burst. She guessed that, if she could but see it, the world would be rather pretty.

"Come. Let's go inside."

Liara nodded at Nagarath's invitation. He was right; the fence could wait.

"Tea, magpie?" Nagarath knelt by the hearth.

Liara made no answer, waiting until he was looking straight at her. With a flourish, she made a sign in the air. Nagarath's cloak rose from his shoulders to float to a hook on the wall. Missing her goal, it landed in a soft heap on the floor.

"Well, that is progress. Next we scry?"

Liara rolled her eyes. Every day the same thing. Books. Scrying. Wands.

Magick had become dangerous, untamed, and unpredictable since the shattering of the Laws. It seemed to her that Nagarath liked it that way. The scholar. At least it gave him something to do.

It kept him from brooding.

Liara sat and stared into the fire, half-watching Nagarath in his preparations for tea.

"Potions before scrying, Master Nagarath," she quipped.

But the mood had already taken hold of her mage. Anisthe's death and Amsalla's disappearance still affected Nagarath on a daily basis. She knew he worried over the Hertfords, too, having sent them away on his magick before he himself had left England to see to Anisthe. Mages, all. At least, that was Merlin's theory. So far in their isolated valley, they had not met another person outside themselves. They only had Krešimir's clumsy new magick by which to measure the consequences of their actions.

In the long days of recovery at Dvigrad following the events at Parentino, Nagarath had little by little told Liara of what had happened after they had parted ways. Just as she explained to him her side of things. Neither confession had come easily.

In the time it took the water to boil in the pot, Nagarath's moroseness had caught Liara. Rising, she gazed intently at the mantle whereupon sat a smallish stone. Red. And unlike any other item in the world.

For it had no magick.

Brushing her fingers against its cool surface, Liara asked, "How did you know things would work out the way they did?"

"I didn't. But I believe you may recall my once stating that the universe takes care of its own."

Liara caught Nagarath's tone and wrinkled her nose at him. "Fate."

"The universe." Nagarath rose to his feet and stood by her side. "The power that connects all things, living and non. Mother; Father; Fate; God. We give her many names. She is the same by whichever we give her and whichever creed we profess. How else could we rise to face each new day? She is kindness. We are her hands and agency. And thus we have hope."

"And love."

"Yes. Love."

APPENDICES

THE LAWS OF MAGICK

Laws of Magick Creatio

Law The First: Magickal power mimics the Magickal signature of the originating or altering power.

Law The Second: Once the age of twenty has been reached, a subservient power gains autonomy and its signature is fixed.

Law The Third: The destruction of an originating power subsequently destroys the magickal properties of its surrogate. In the case of Magicked Artifacts, the Second Law of Transferre applies.

Laws of Magick Transferre

Law The First of Magicked Artifacts: A Magicked Artifact must be sound both physically and magickally in order to function as intended.

Law The Second of Magicked Artifacts: Damage to either the physical or magickal condition of a Magicked Artifact will affect the outcome of Magicks performed through said Artifact.

Addendum: It has been found that these atypical results are often of an unpredictable, uncontrollable, and highly undesirable nature. Purposeful damage to a Magicked Artifact for experimental purposes is not recommended.

Laws of Magick Eversio

*Author's note: The following govern the spells of sundering, unmagicking. Originally taught as Laws alongside those of Creatio and Transferre, over time the Eversio Laws were shown to harbor uniquely exploitable weaknesses and therefore are not applicable as true Laws of Magick. They are, subsequently, no longer actively taught and are considered "hidden" or lost laws.

Law The First of Eversio: Magickal power given to another retains its originating signature. As this typically results in two signatures co-mingling, the larger portion of the Magick held will exert dominance.

Law The Second of Eversio: The giving of Power is not directly reversible.

Additional guidance on The Laws of Eversio:

The giving of power is only condoned so long as certain conditions are met:

Condition the First: Said Power must be given freely and not coerced.

Condition the Second: Said Power must have clear and unemcumbered provenance.

Condition the Third: The purposeful transferring of magick out of a body must be done with the aim of not physically harming said body.

amésos

/'ə ˌmeɪ soʊs/

A weapon traditionally given alongside a wizard's first wand when apprenticeship begins; a mage's last resort. Mainly symbolic, the gesture has since has fallen out of fashion.

aurenaurae

/'ɔ reɪ ˌnɑ reɪ/

The act of copulation between a human and a magickal creature; also the product of such a union when life is conceived. As most such unions are nonviable, a human aurenaurae is exceptionally rare and would be directly subject to the Laws of Magick Creatio.

einatus

/'aɪ neɪ tʌs/

A mage's Art; Wizard's word similar to the Artless word for 'soul' incantate

/ˈɪn kæn ˌteɪt/

A mage who has permanently lost his or her magick. While there are some that say that a magick user may regain their Art, these tales are generally dismissed as rumor and wishful thinking.

oriaurant

/ˈɔɪ ri ˌɑr rɛnt/

The half-fae offspring of a magickal being and that of another race—typically human. Said offspring often carries within them a purer, 'wilder' magick, not easily sensed by spellpiercers or even other mages.

Common examples in history include the product of relations between faerie/human or merfolk/human.

praecantator

/ˈpreɪ can ˌteɪt ɔr/

Archaic term for Archmage; Latin for poisoner, wizard.

progenaurae

/ˈproʊ dʒɛ ˌnɑ reɪ/

An indirect participant in the act of aurenaurae via their Art; the mage responsible for the creation and control of the magickal creature involved. When said copulation results in offspring, the power signatures of both aurenaurae and progenaurae are identical per the Laws of Magick Creatio.

spellpiercer

/ˈspel pɪrs ər/

Art-less human who can sense, and interfere with, magick.

Note: Mages cannot sense whether someone is a spellpiercer or not unless their Art is affected.

zielsor

/ˈzil sɔːr/

The crime of devouring the magick gift of others.

High crime and gross violation of the 'hidden' Eversio Laws.

ACKNOWLEDGMENTS

Once upon a time in 2004, I awoke from a dream and began writing down everything I knew about the two wizards whom I had witnessed battling it out while I slept. That one scene is found on page 397 of book 1 of the *Bookminder* trilogy. At the time I called the story *The Wizard's Librarian,* for I was working in the department of collection preservation of UW-Madison Memorial Library. Clearly work had decided to follow me home.

Somewhere along the way I finished my manuscript and, through a quirk of fate, I landed in the capable hands of the team at Xchyler Publishing. To them—and Penny, in particular—I owe eternal thanks.

I've become quite fond of torturing my editor MeriLyn with my chronic comma misplacement. (Sorry and thank you.) To Egle Zioma, fantastic artist who has made my characters appear real in a beautiful and poignant way: Many thanks.

And to the voice of these wizards, Mr. Bernard Faricy who, through the strange timing in which publishing sometimes works (e.g. the audio edition is often recorded after print is set), has never received my proper thanks in the acknowledgements: Thank you.

And to my friends . . .

To those I have met along the way in this bookish journey . . .

To my endlessly patient husband and family who suffer through the spoiling of multi-year, multi-book plot lines and who have supported me without hesitation. . .

To everyone who has seen and agreed and believed that Liara and Nagarath are real . . .

Hvala lijepa! ❤

ABOUT THE AUTHOR

M. K. Wiseman has degrees in Interarts & Technology and Library & Information Studies from the University of Wisconsin-Madison. Her office, therefore, is a curious mix of storyboards and reference materials. Both help immensely in the writing of historical novels. She currently resides in Cedarburg, Wisconsin.

The Bookminder (Book 1, Bookminder series)

The Kithseeker (Book 2, Bookminder series)

Magical Intelligence

Sherlock Holmes & the Ripper of Whitechapel

Forthcoming:

The Poison Game

Sherlock Holmes & the Singular Affair